Praise for *The First to Lie*

"Book clubs will gobble up *The First to Lie*."
—Sarah Pekkanen

"Stellar . . . Ryan could win a sixth Agatha with this one." —*Publishers Weekly* (starred review)

"A magnificent, intricately plotted thriller that will have you questioning everyone's motives until the stunning ending." —Samantha M. Bailey, bestselling author of *Woman on the Edge*

"Filled with sharp insights, *The First to Lie* is a house of mirrors, taking us on a thrilling ride of dizzying twists and shocking revelations." —Angie Kim, national bestselling author of *Miracle Creek*

"A must-read for thriller lovers—the compelling and twist-filled plot fearlessly delves into the intersections of revenge and family secrets." —Vanessa Lillie, bestselling author of *Little Voices*

"Expert pacing, richly drawn characters, and seamless storytelling are just some of the ingredients that make this novel impossible to put down. Fabulous!" —Hannah Mary McKinnon, internationally bestselling author of *Sister Dear*

Praise for *The Murder List*

"A cracker of a read—her best yet!" —B. A. Paris

"A fireworks display of a novel: exciting, explosive, relentless—and likely to leave you gasping."
—A. J. Finn

THE
FIRST
TO LIE

HANK PHILLIPPI RYAN

A TOM DOHERTY ASSOCIATES BOOK
NEW YORK

This is a work of fiction. All of the characters, organizations, and events portrayed in this novel are either products of the author's imagination or are used fictitiously.

THE FIRST TO LIE

Copyright © 2020 by Hank Phillippi Ryan

All rights reserved.

A Forge Book
Published by Tom Doherty Associates
120 Broadway
New York, NY 10271

www.tor-forge.com

Forge® is a registered trademark of Macmillan Publishing Group, LLC.

ISBN 978-1-250-25882-3

Our books may be purchased in bulk for promotional, educational, or business use. Please contact your local bookseller or the Macmillan Corporate and Premium Sales Department at 1-800-221-7945, extension 5442, or by email at MacmillanSpecialMarkets@macmillan.com.

First Edition: August 2020
First Mass Market Edition: July 2021

Printed in the United States of America

0 9 8 7 6 5 4 3 2 1

As always, for Jonathan

. . . everyone tells a story about themselves inside their own head. Always. All the time. That story makes you what you are. We build ourselves out of that story.

Patrick Rothfuss, *The Name of the Wind*

THE
FIRST
TO LIE

Without any sneaky fine print and knowing everything you know, if you could start your adult life over as someone else, would you do it?

Say you could choose the person. Where they live and what they do. You could choose what parts of your prior knowledge to retain, and what parts to "forget." Family baggage? Discard it. Friends and lovers and commitments? Erased, along with your vanished past. Obsessions? Obsessions could stay.

How you look and how you sound, your goals and motivations and deepest desires. Whatever you want, you could do it, be it, love it, lose it.

Sound good?

I fibbed. There is one bit of fine print. You. Every time you'd look in the mirror, you'd remember.

Mirrors make such false promises. They tell you: *Look here, and you'll see yourself.*

But that's the first lie. You see a face and a body, sure. But a mirror doesn't show your *true* self.

That you have to find on your own. By looking inside. And no seductive piece of silvered glass can help you.

Still. I know all it takes is a tweak here and a twist there to become someone else. So would you do it? To get what you always wanted? Sure you would.

All you have to do is lie.

CHAPTER 1

NORA

Lies have a complicated half-life. Nora—for now—tried to calculate the life span of her most recent one as she waited on the corner of Tremont and Union Park, the evening's first snowflakes beginning to accumulate on her new—to her—black cashmere coat. Boston was new to her too, with its treacherous weather and confusing streets and wary response to newcomers. They'd warned her, laughing, not to ask for directions. *You can't get there from here,* people told her.

Now, after just three weeks as a sales rep, she knew it was true, all of it. But this was the right corner, and Douglas had said he'd lived here for years, so she could rely on him for directions. Geographical, at least. The other directions—those he'd take from her. That was the plan. She could, indeed, get there from here.

Douglas would arrive soon, and he'd be happy to brush the snowflakes from her shoulders, take her someplace private and scotch-infused. She closed her eyes with the rhythm of her process. With keeping her balance. Not crossing a line.

Behind her, a horn beeped. She turned, carefully casual. Nothing. She checked for surveillance cameras: none. A seemingly oblivious passerby pinged her inner alarm, but the guy with the backpack was too focused on his phone to be a threat—someone following her, or watching her. The interior lights came on in a maybe-Volvo parked half a block down the street.

Nora eased, slowly, into the lee of the streetlight, keeping to the shadows. But it was just a mom, or nanny, extricating a baby from a car seat in the back. Nothing about Nora.

"Nora? Ms. Quinn?"

She whirled as the voice came from behind her. So much for her detective skills.

"Douglas," she said, softening her face into Nora's face, relaxing her smile into Nora's welcoming smile, opening her arms like Nora did. Establishing first names. But had she already failed? Douglas might notice her artifice. How she'd first flinched at his voice.

"Did I scare you?" He came toward her, leaned to her, his breath puffing in the early evening chill. "I couldn't wait to see you. Am I early?"

Yes, you scare me, Nora wanted to tell him. *You're a monster.* "Of course not, Doctor," she said, using his title on purpose, teasing, proving her admiration. She slid her hand through the bend of his elbow to avoid his clumsy attempt to kiss her. She was Nora, she'd be Nora, she had to stay Nora.

A turning headlight grazed his face then slipped past, leaving the memory of paisley and camel hair, of gray at the temples and Ivy League posture. Chin up, shoulders back, privilege confidently in place. Nora tried to match him stride for stride in her ridiculous but necessary suede heels, but she stumbled on a jagged shard of sidewalk.

"Oh!" she cried, suddenly precarious, grabbing his

sleeve. A reflex, not a tactic. Her heels, inappropriately but deliberately too high, would be ruined.

"Gotcha." Douglas caught her, collecting her with a paternal chuckle, preventing her from landing on the cold and gritty concrete below. "Have you already started on wine?"

"No, silly." *Gotcha?* Really? Nora ignored his patronizing tone, then pivoted to cash in on her unintentional damsel-in-distress moment. "Oh, no! Look at that!"

She extended her bare leg from under her coat, pointed her toe so daintily, and pretended to pout. Sometimes it was scary, honestly scary, that this came to her so easily. "These poor little shoes are probably the worse for wear."

"Nice leg," Douglas said.

You idiot, she thought. *Gotcha.*

They walked arm in arm toward the hip South End restaurant he'd chosen, Calabria. Nora had scouted it in advance, all dripping ferns and dark wood and sophisticated stained glass and subdued lighting, with high-backed mahogany booths for those who needed privacy, and spotlighted center tables for those who needed to be noticed. *Dr. Hawkins has selected a booth*, the obliging maître d' had informed her. Perfect.

She'd met Hawkins earlier this morning in his clinic office, where he'd been flat-out fifty-three minutes late for their appointment. She'd hung her coat on the rack, then kept track of every passing minute, using the calculation to intensify her resolve.

Doctors. So many of them thought *they* were the important ones. That the women waiting, appointment-bound, fidgeting in hypoallergenic chairs and carefully choosing glossy magazines from the glass-topped coffee table, were merely supplicants. Needy. They should be grateful for the eventual attention, for whatever medications the doctors chose.

As if the doctors could have known about these medications on their own. As if they'd chosen them without the persuasion of a salesperson like Nora. She'd patted her square black briefcase, as if to reassure herself that all her ammunition was still at the ready. Notebooks, pamphlets, dosage instructions. Samples. Those she'd taken from her personal storage unit this morning. Carefully counted, making sure, then locking the unit again. Nora wasn't the only one with a key. Her new employer, Pharminex, could have their security goons check her supplies anytime they wanted.

The other women in the doctor's waiting room, leafing through the array of magazines or glued to their phones, some even wearing sunglasses, all needed the good doctor. They'd realized, maybe, with the gasp of mortality or a push from a spouse, that their window of time for having a child of their own, a biological child, was slipping away. Now they waited, some hopeful, yearning, optimistic. Some fearing failure.

A dark-haired prospect, wearing the expensive Uggs and pill-free leggings, wrapped a cashmere shawl closer around her shoulders and flipped at her cell phone screen with a manicured finger. Her feet betrayed her, though, one toe tapping persistently on the thin-piled beige carpeting. A weary blonde, posture sagging and dark circles not hidden even by too-big sunglasses, cocooned on an ivory tweed club chair next to Nora, studying the floor. The zipper of one salt-edged brown boot was not fully closed. Not *her* first time here, Nora thought. Maybe her last.

Their eyes met in a flash of sisterhood, maybe, or sympathy. She's probably evaluating *me*, Nora thought. Good luck with that. It'd be impossible for anyone observing her to reach the correct conclusion.

Was she a possibility? Nora might point out her unzipped boot, maybe segue into the weather, and then see where the conversation went. Strange that infertility clinics like this felt like safe spaces, Nora thought, filled with instant sisters. A sorority no one wanted to be in.

The best way to start a conversation was to find common ground, go from there and see what she could find out. Trying to chat with women, strangers, in doctors' offices like these, she needed to be careful, subtle, intruding gently on their personal space. Probably easier at a pediatrician's, where squabbling children and maternal choices might engender instant camaraderie. But easy wasn't the point. She knew to wait until it felt right. Scout for a possible victim. And then take the first step.

Announced by a gentle *ping* of the door chime, a new patient arrived in the waiting room, this one bundled in black wool against the lingering March winter, revealing only red lipstick and fatigued eyes. The woman scanned the room and chose a spot on a maroon leather love seat, spaced as far away from each of the others as possible. Aloof, solitary, wary. Not a possibility, Nora decided.

Each woman here, reading, or texting, or simply staring at the soothing butterscotch walls, possessed the same hopes and the same fears.

Except for Nora.

"Could you hand me that magazine?" Nora said to the woman in the boots. "I don't want to reach over you to the table."

The woman handed her the outdated *Newsweek* with a wan smile.

"Oh, dear," Nora said, flipping the pages. "I've read this one." She chuckled softly. "Guess I've been here too often."

"Once is too often," the woman said.

"Got that right." Nora nodded, sympathetic. Commiserating. "It's so hard, but we just want, I mean, I just . . ." She let her voice trail off, wistful. "Never mind, sorry to bother."

"Oh, no, no bother." The woman shifted in her seat, turned to her, wrapped her cardigan closer. "You okay? You look sad."

"We all look sad, right?" Nora shrugged. "You can tell the ones who . . ."

"I know." The woman pressed her lips together.

"Could I ask—I mean . . ." Nora looked at the ceiling, then moved closer to her, whispering. "Were you . . . surprised? At anything? Was it like they said? Or different? I don't mean to intrude, and I know I'm kind of being inarticulate, but I only—"

"It's awful," she said. "My husband is so disappointed, and I am too, but we're hoping they can—" She closed her eyes, opened them again. "That's what I'm here to find out. Supposedly. I'm sure it'll be fine. They can fix anything. I tell myself that. I'll try anything."

"They're supposed to have a miracle drug here," Nora whispered. "Well, not a *miracle* drug, I guess. But something that really works." She paused, deciding how far to push. "Is that why you're here? Did they say they could help you get pregnant?"

She nodded.

"Did they?"

The woman's eyes welled.

"Not yet," she whispered. "And maybe not . . . ever. But I can't think about that. I won't."

When the white-coated receptionist called her

name—"Nora?"—she was so focused on the other woman's story that it took a moment before it registered, and she remembered Nora was her. The others had lifted their eyes as the receptionist stood, eager. Then they exchanged embarrassed glances, as if to say, *Oh, not yet? She's first? Oh, okay. I'm okay.* Nora had acknowledged them all with a sympathetic half smile as she picked up the brass-latched sample bag she'd tucked under her chair. *You'll be fine,* she tried to telegraph.

"I am so sorry, that's me," Nora said. She should have gotten the woman's contact information, or even just her name, but there was no time now. *Damn.* Nora reached into her jacket pocket, pulled out one of her cards. She touched the woman's arm, a split-second gesture, kept her voice low. Handed her the simple white rectangle, as she'd done several times before with other women like her. "Call me if you want to talk. I'll be thinking of you."

"You too," the woman murmured. "Thank you."

Douglas Hawkins, MD, had been almost an hour late. Craggy, experienced, congenial. White coat and stethoscope. Since he knew she was a pharmaceutical company salesperson pitching him, he didn't bother with bedside manner. Nora had been instantly forgiving of his tardiness, brushing aside his perfunctory apologies. Negotiations could be delicate, and it was best to start with sympathy on your side. *Points for politeness,* her mother had always told her.

"Thank you so much," Nora had said. "I'm brand new to this and to Boston, so I'm grateful for your time. And truly, I simply want to leave you with some materials about our company's latest—"

Hawkins didn't let her finish her sentence.

"Sure," he said. "I have fifteen minutes. I'll check my email while you prepare."

He gestured her to one of the navy-blue upholstered guest chairs across from his desk. Strange, she
thought as she took her seat, for a doctor's office to
look more like a lawyer's or banker's. Syracuse, Johns
Hopkins, Massachusetts Board of Registration in
Medicine—the framed parchment credentials were
placed precisely at a visitor's eye level. Nora set her
sample case at her feet and clicked it open. She'd expected the usual exam room, white-walled and glar-
ingly fluorescent. And was relieved she didn't have to
endure one of those again. Maybe this inner sanctum
was where he and his patients conferred, where he
presented his news, happy or sad. Where there was
room for a spouse, if there was one.

"Ready?" Hawkins glanced again at his computer
screen, then back at her. Seemed to take her in, her
now-auburn chin-length hair, pale green eyes and severe dark suit. She looked like a Nora Quinn; she'd
planned it that way.

"Fourteen minutes now." His tone had changed,
now almost amused or welcoming. She noticed his
wedding ring, a conservative gold band. "But who's
counting?"

"Thanks." She pretended to wince, drawing in her
shoulders, looking at him with apprehension in her
eyes. "Like I said, I'm new, so you probably have a
lot more experience than I do in this . . ." She kept
talking, pitching, hardly looking at her detail sheet,
careful to portray nothing but business. It fascinated
her, the way some men—not all, but some—believed
so devoutly in their authority. Forgetting how quickly
one can go from king to pawn.

Though Dr. Hawkins was already a pawn. Poor
thing. After she started talking, he hadn't looked at
his computer again. Not once. Nora was good at what
she did. That's who "Nora" was.

The glow of the restaurant now beckoned down darkening Appleton Street, coppery lights warm through the dark wood entrance. Douglas reached out to open the restaurant door for her. Nora walked through, and when she turned, she saw he was smiling.

Gotcha, she thought.

CHAPTER 2

ELLIE

Ellie Berensen stopped in the apartment hallway as the elevator doors clanked shut behind her. A woman sat cross-legged on the dark neutral carpeting in front of 3-B, two brown cardboard moving boxes stacked next to her.

Ellie was already exhausted from having battled through the day. And cold, since the snow was getting worse and her navy leather gloves were hip but worthless. Her feet were wet, too, because one of her furry boots had decided to leak. And even though the knit cap covering her hair and ears was drenched, it was warmer to keep it on. Why would anyone *choose* to live in a bleak and winter-locked place like Boston? Now, lugging her briefcase and shoe bag and longing for redemption in the form of red wine and hot tea and maybe even chocolate, she'd encountered one more barrier between her and apartment 3-A: this woman.

"Are you okay?" Ellie asked.

"Yeah, no," the woman replied. "Yeah, I'm okay. Thanks." She saluted with a red Solo cup, then got to her feet, brushing down dusty acid-washed jeans.

With her dark hair in a bouncy ponytail, she almost looked fifties-era, with shaggy bangs and sweetly pink lipstick.

Trying to look younger than she was, Ellie assessed, but she figured fortyish, older than Ellie herself. Not city. Not chic. And definitely not scary. But who really knew anyone?

"Truly, thanks," the woman went on. "Just waiting for my keys. Am I in your way?"

Ellie heard a faint Midwest-or-something accent. "Keys?" Her weary brain finally clicked the pieces into place. *Duh.* This is why she got the big investigative reporter bucks. "Oh. Are you a new tenant?"

"Yeah, no," the woman said again. "I mean, yeah, I'm the new tenant—or will be, if the person with my keys ever arrives. You live here?" She held out a hand. "I'm Meg. Meg Weest." She spelled it. "Weest, with two e's. A family thing."

Ellie put down her briefcase, slipped off a glove, shook hands. "Ellie Berensen. And I'm sorry, I'm zonked." She took a deep breath, let it out. "When's—whoever—coming to let you in?"

"Ten minutes ago." Meg took a sip from her cup, gave a weak smile. "Wine, I fear," she said. "Wine at the end of the tunnel is the only thing that's gotten me through this crazy day. Most of my stuff is already inside, thank goodness, but Jimmy just went down to . . ." She tucked a lock of escaped ponytail behind one ear, but it instantly came loose. "Wherever. To get another key. I should have gone inside before he left, but I didn't. It'll all be over soon. I'm so tired I'm not thinking straight."

"That makes two of us.'" Ellie had already unlocked her apartment door, swung it open. "Come in," she offered, gesturing toward her almost familiar living room. As she flipped on the lights, she quickly assessed whether she'd moved the laundry from the couch or left any unwashed dishes on the coffee table—not that it would matter. Housekeeping wasn't her biggest worry now, not as long as she had soggy clothes and dripping hair. Blinker padded to the door, her white tail on high alert, and entwined herself through Ellie's legs and various bags. "Have a seat. You can wait for Jimmy here. Just let me, um, take off this hat. And dump my stuff. Hope you're okay with the cat."

By the time Ellie returned, Blinker was on Meg's lap, one white-tipped paw extended to touch a tired throw pillow on the humdrum tweedy couch that came with this furnished apartment. Stupid cat barely registered Ellie's arrival. So much for feline gratitude.

"Sorry to take so long," Ellie said. "I was soaked through and through, you know? And I needed to rip out my contacts and wash my face. But I see you've made a pal." Ellie gestured at the two of them as she stood in front of the fireplace. She wished it actually worked, making her new place wood-smoky and cozy, but it was only for show. Pretending to be a fireplace. A *fauxplace*. "Blinker usually disdains newcomers. Except if they hate cats. My boyfriend is semi-allergic, so of course Blink won't let him out of her sight." She shrugged. "Cats."

"Boyfriend?" Meg stroked the cat head to tail as the fickle Blinker stretched to extend the pleasure. Then Meg craned her head to the left as if to look behind Ellie. "Is he here? I don't want to interrupt—"

"Out of town," Ellie said. Then regretted it. She hadn't meant to let that little exaggeration slip, but she was tired. In truth, he had never met Blinker, but he had told her he was allergic to cats. She glanced toward the door, though she understood it was probably rude. "You have a cell phone? Want to call to see what's up? Or maybe Jimmy-with-the-key texted you?"

Meg stood so quickly Blinker scrambled to the floor and scampered away. "I'm intruding, and it's so late." She put her fingertips against her mouth, then tilted her head, apologetic. "Fine way to meet your new neighbor."

"No, no, all good," Ellie lied. "Can I offer you more wine? I'm getting some."

When Ellie returned with two glasses of malbec, Meg was on the couch again but looking at her cell phone. "I'm so ridiculous. He went to return the U-Haul. I never drive, so he did that for me. And he thought I had a key. But it's fine, it's late, the hallway is safe—I guess, isn't it?—and I can wait out there. You've already been too kind."

The opportunistic Blinker was back at Ellie's feet now. Almost midnight, and Ellie anticipated a big day tomorrow. She was on the verge, she knew it, of a big story. And now there was a stranger in her living room. She couldn't kick Meg out, but she certainly couldn't invite her to stay over. That'd be like some story her newsroom would headline: cray-cray stranger comes to town and dupe-woman welcomes her in. *Why didn't she realize?* they'd wonder. *How clueless could anyone be?*

"It's fine," Ellie lied again. Tried not to look at her watch. Doomed. As Meg accepted her red wine, Ellie plopped into the armchair by the not-fireplace, its hearth now home to a ceramic bowl of certain-to-die ferns and ivy, a welcome to Boston gift from the station. She'd checked to see if the plants were cat-friendly. "So. Long day. Sounds like we're both pretty tapped out. Sit. Tell me about yourself. Why'd you move to Boston? Are you working?"

"Broken heart, I suppose, short answer. Family

stuff. Looking for a new opportunity." Meg took a sip of wine, saluted approval with the glass. She set it on the coffee table by her Solo cup. "How about you? What brought you here?"

Ellie stared into her own wine, the fatigue of the day hitting harder now, her eyes burning and the last shred of adrenaline sapped. Every moment of every day was a juggle, remembering who knew what, and whom to tell what, and what to do after that. Being a reporter wasn't only about digging up information. It was about balancing it. Hoarding it. Using it. About understanding what to let out and what to keep in and who'd be helped by it. And who'd be harmed. Sometimes her brain felt too full, as if there were too many puzzle pieces, some old, some brand-new, and they wouldn't all fit together. Not in a picture that made sense, anyway.

"Yours is as good an answer as any," Ellie admitted. "Broken heart. Family stuff. Anyway, now, I'm a reporter at Channel Eleven. The *all-new* Channel Eleven, I'm instructed to say. Our first day on the air is in three weeks, so until then it's all prep and promo. I was hired a couple months ago, from a smaller market where I worked for a few years, and then, like many of my fellow worker bees, started at the station three weeks ago. They'll give me full-time, they say, if the story I'm working on gets the go-ahead. I live on pizza, I'm embarrassed to reveal. Plus the occasional guilt salad. As you said, same old same old."

Meg laughed, a short little maybe rueful laugh. "We're quite the team." She swirled her wine in the stemmed goblet. "Two thirtysomething women who— that's right, isn't it? You're thirtysomething? If I'm not being pushy?"

Ellie nodded. "Thirty-one coming up in April."

"Me too! Around that, at least. April. So funny." Meg toasted her. "Here's to us, the boring sisters."

Ellie laughed along with her, then Meg looked at the screen of her phone.

"Jimmy. Finally." Meg chugged the last of her wine. "Thanks, Ellie. You're very kind. Don't have to see me out, I'll be fine. And glad to be in the neighborhood. Thanks for the welcome. My turn next time, okay? I owe you."

CHAPTER 3

NORA

Nora burrowed into her pillows, punching the white-satin-cased feathers into place and trying to settle her mind. After they'd finished their crème brûlées, she'd dispatched the boozy Douglas with a chaste hug and a silky promise. Thank goodness for the existence of a Mrs. Hawkins, the doctor's wife. The hovering specter of humiliation was always valuable, and she'd used the what-if-she-finds-out weapon with the skill of a practiced surgeon. Would they meet again? Oh, yeah. Nora had made sure of that. Of course, there were limits to how far Nora would go, but the good doctor didn't need to know that.

She'd lull herself to sleep, as she did when she was revved up like this, by replaying her roles in college theater productions.

Her mother had explained how acting was the best con of all—people paid you to be someone else, and the more you hid your true self, the more successful you'd be. "Lord Olivier always said he had forgotten who he really was, honey," her mother had instructed her only daughter. "And after all those acting years, he was simply a vessel. He'd wait for a role and whoever that was became his true self. For as long as he needed to be. That's why he was so good at it, dear. Remember that."

Her mother had performed in the theater too, in college, before she got married and played the lifetime role of mother—*played* being the operative word.

Nora's pillow would not cooperate, and though all the wine and complications of the evening should have made her brain grateful to turn off the day, it continued to churn, looping as if on instant replay.

Her first day at Pharminex, three weeks ago. She'd shown up, as requested, on the ninth floor of the mirror-walled building in Boston's financial district. Two weeks before, she'd passed the first hurdle there, a gut-churning interview that was more frightening in reality than in her imagination. She'd still aced that screening, knew she'd impressed them. Nevertheless, life being one big audition, it was a relief when they'd called her back.

"Nora Quinn? I'm Maren." The haughty chignoned receptionist, hair belligerently silver and a smile like ice, had clipped out her name, then made Nora trot behind her long strides down a carpeted hallway. Photos on the walls showed shiny porcelain laboratories with white-coated scientists hunched over microscopes and watching incomprehensible digital readouts. One extreme close-up showed a purple and pink capsule so detailed Nora could see thousands of tiny multicolored spheres of medication within.

Maren stopped at an unmarked door, knocked, waited a beat, then opened it. Nora saw a fiftysomething woman standing in front of a sleek glass desk. Delicate half-open lavender roses, arranged in a crystal vase placed on a white lacquer console behind her, looked real. So did the Bearden watercolor centered on an earth-toned grass-cloth wall. So did a discreetly silver fur coat—lynx? chinchilla?—tossed casually across the back of a wing chair in the corner.

"Ms. Fiddler?" Maren spoke it as a question, though there was no one else in the room. "This is Nora Quinn, your nine thirty."

Dettalinda Fiddler, because of course Nora had researched her, was the powerful head of human resources for Pharminex, had been climbing the ladder for ten years. In the early 2000s, and continuing its storied history of market-crushing success, the company had claimed a major market share in women's antianxiety meds. Now a new drug was their star player. *Pharminex loves women,* a gushing online article in *Pharma News* had assured its readers. And Dettalinda Fiddler, who'd come to big pharma by way of humble beginnings in St. Maarten, was the poster woman for the company's outreach and opportunity. Or so Nora had read.

"Please call me Detta," the woman said, holding out a welcoming hand. "Maren, could you stash that coat? Haven't had time to . . ." She looked at Nora, assessing. "Faux," she explained, as the receptionist whisked it away.

It wasn't. "Of course," Nora agreed. She'd remembered to sit up straight, behave like she was supposed to behave. Become a job applicant. For that morning, at least, that's what she truly was.

Detta swiveled into the chair behind her desk, crossed black-stockinged legs and jiggled a conservative black patent pump. Flipped through a manila folder, which Nora assumed held her carefully written application. "Your first pharma sales job, I see."

Nora had been ready for that, prepared herself

with a whole patter about sales experience and retail experience and the similarities of persuasion, but Detta had raised a hand.

"You're gorgeous, let's get that out of the way. And I'm told your pre-interview ticked all the other boxes. I'm sure your references and identification will continue to check out . . ." She'd looked up at Nora under long dark lashes, and Nora's heart had lurched with anxiety at that hard-fought hurdle, just a beat, until Detta went back to the file. "You understand you'll be on your own most of the time, correct? Work from your home or the car we can loan you if need be, set your appointments, check in via our sales-reporting system. You'll have to know your stuff, Ms. Quinn. One training week, and if you last through the P-X tryouts, you're in."

That was fast, Nora thought. But she wasn't about to question success. Or fret about auditions. P-X, Nora knew, was what insiders called Pharminex.

"Great. Thank you so much." Nora had been so keyed up, so ready to joust and persuade and sell herself, that she'd almost not gotten the words out. This wasn't a done deal. Just another audition. Nora was used to those.

"This is life and death, Ms. Quinn." Detta stood with the air of a commander delivering a go-to-battle speech. "I'm not talking about for *you*, although your job is on the line every day. We're here to provide groundbreaking alternatives to people's lives; it's no less than that," she said. "You are the conduit between this company and the medical profession, to convince them, inform them, reassure them, that what we're producing can change their patients' medical futures. Am I clear? Do you *care* enough to do this?"

Nora almost laughed out loud as she punched her pillow yet another way. There was one streetlight outside her apartment window, persistent and annoying, that apparently was trying to keep her awake no matter how she adjusted the thin-louvered blinds. Nora flipped over, kept her eyes closed, trying to see herself as Detta Fiddler had seen her. Young enough, smart enough, attractive enough. Eager, clueless, malleable. Four out of six correct was a pretty good score.

The training session had been a breeze. Nora had filled her brain with drug names and pharmaceutical formularies, with side effects and off-label uses, with the laws on distribution and accounting and reporting. The class spent about ten seconds, seemed like, on ethics.

After each session, she'd approached her fellow novices individually, casually, getting to know them, making sure she'd be remembered as supportive. Enthusiastic. A team player. She'd written their names and emails in her notebook as soon as they weren't looking: Gerri Munroe, Lydia Frost, Jenn Wahl, Christine O'Shea. Each one more attractive than the last. Could any of them be useful to her? No way to know until the time came. She crossed her fingers it would. It had to.

She took a deep, calming breath, settled into her pillow, stared at her ceiling and imagined a stage. The one back in her junior year, when she'd snagged the lead in *A Doll's House*. She saw herself as if in the audience: a younger Nora, the real Nora this time. She could still recite every line.

She closed her eyes, letting her brain float back in time. A younger Nora. But not a happier one.

I have been performing tricks for you, Torvald.

She heard her high-school self reciting Ibsen's line, her voice studied and self-assured. Hair in upswept curls, her waist cinched impossibly small. *That's how I've survived.*

CHAPTER 4

ELLIE

Ellie beeped her entry card through the security reader, amused, yet again, by the blue-uniformed "guard" Channel 11 had posted at the reception desk. An array of green lights silently blinked on his phone console, ignored, while the guard usually watched soap operas through half-closed eyes. Today he seemed to be asleep.

"Tough night?" Ellie asked out loud, though softly, so as not to wake the guy up. She'd had a tough night too, what with her unexpected visitor. This morning Ellie had found a cellophane-wrapped package of chocolate chip cookies outside her apartment door, tied with a curly pink ribbon. *Thank you from Meg*, also in pink, was scrawled on an attached white card, followed by three exclamation marks. Ellie winced at the enthusiastic punctuation, though she would never turn down chocolate chips. They looked homemade, but that was impossible unless Meg had stayed up all night making them. Or brought them from home. Ellie realized she hadn't asked the newcomer where home was. She'd brought the cookies with her to work, though, idly wondering what Meg expected in return. Ellie wished she had time and space for friends again. Someday, maybe.

The guard didn't budge as Ellie clicked the door open. Ellie was no threat, not unless she was targeting a bad guy for her next story. Like she was now.

Two flights of stairs down to the newsroom, where the door was open to the news director's office. She winced, walking quickly. It wasn't that she didn't want to talk to Warren Zalkind, it was simply that, yeah, she didn't want to talk to him. Not quite yet. He wanted blockbuster stories. Demanded them. And had made it clear to Ellie that her job at Channel 11 depended on getting this one. The Pharminex investigation.

At least he'd understood the need for her to have flexible hours. And that she didn't have to report her whereabouts to anyone every single minute of the day.

"We usually make reporters check in, day to day, keep me up to date," Warren had said. "But, Ellie, if you want autonomy, go for it. I'm all about out of the box. Besides, it's your potential career on the line. Not mine."

"I understand." She'd agreed, appropriately grateful. And honestly so. Her success depended on her freedom.

Now she scooted past his open door and headed upstairs for the privacy of her office cranny. No window, her one tired desk, one computer, a black metal coatrack. She swore the place had been a janitor's closet in a former life, but in TV you took what you could get. There wasn't room in this makeshift cubby for any memorabilia or family photos, but she'd kept none of those anyway. She was in it for this one story. This one life-changing story. Pharminex.

Sometimes the universe provided, Ellie believed,

and when this job opening appeared in the online listings, she'd pounced.

She'd paid for her own ticket to Boston, presented herself to the news director as a crusader. *It's all about health care,* she'd told him. What could be more important to every single human being? She'd pleaded her case, ticking off the ratings-magnet topics on her fingers: measles, vaccinations, maternal mortality, autism, allergies, the latest mutation of the flu. Opioids, marijuana. Fertility.

She'd told him personal stories, how kids in her college class had sneaked Darvon from their parents' medicine cabinets. How one of her journalism school classmates had swiped her roommate's Palladone and slugged a few down with half a bottle of tequila—then almost died from the combination.

"And all those opioids," she went on. "Sure, they did what they were designed to do. But so many people, craving relief from chronic pain, became addicted. The companies who'd made those drugs totally knew the risks, and were well aware of the side effects." She let the words sink in. "*Side effects!* Even the term is absurd, right?

"But what if we'd been able to warn people *before* their loved ones died?" Ellie hoped she was getting through to him. "No matter how much money those companies pay in settlements, it will never bring those people back."

"You're persuasive, Ms. Berensen," the news director had said. "But do viewers really care? Do they want to hear—"

"Do they care? Think about the demographics of health stories," she'd interrupted, risking it, understanding it was actually advertising dollars the station craved. "We want women, correct? Ages eighteen to forty-nine? 'They' are *me*," she said, leaning in and selling it. "I care about my health and the health of my children—when I eventually have them—and the well-being of my family. Why wouldn't we want to offer that? Why wouldn't we want to help our viewers understand that?"

She knew she'd scored when Warren described her as "wholesome and fresh-faced." She'd even managed not to burst out laughing or roll her eyes. She was a commodity, after all, and he wasn't being sexist, he was simply being honest. She *did* look wholesome. Of course she did. As if her new blond bob, new studious eyeglasses—which she didn't need—and little sheath-and-pearls weren't artfully and carefully selected.

A week later, she'd snapped up the station's offer of a temporary furnished apartment and soon after moved to Boston with two suitcases, one shipped box and a cat carrier, leaving most of her stuff behind. She'd go back and retrieve it if need be.

Years ago, during her first job as a TV reporter, the requisite smaller-market stint, an even more inexperienced interviewer had inquired about her core values. Flapping open an obviously brand-new notebook, the young woman had asked Ellie, "As a journalist, what one concept do you believe in, without question?"

Easy one. "Justice," she'd said.

Now, with a lurch of a plastic handle, she adjusted her desk chair higher—had someone lowered it overnight?—logged on to her computer and pulled up her files. The sounds of the newsroom below faded to a muffled hum: phones ringing and computer keys rattling, a random burst of applause. Nothing would deter Ellie from this. If she could bring down these bastards, make their lives as miserable as they'd made hers . . . She smiled. Considered a chocolate chip cookie.

Pharminex, she typed.

Her cell phone buzzed.

She looked down, her heart fluttering. But it was Warren.

"Hey, Warren." She picked up before the first ring had ended.

"Got a surprise for you," he said. "Can you come to my office?"

Ellie did not like surprises.

The walk to the newsroom was a quick-cut mental montage of possibilities, not one of them good. Warren had nothing she wanted or needed, nothing helpful or valuable. His phony affable tone made her even more apprehensive.

When Ellie arrived at his open door, she stopped, and was certain the bafflement showed on her face before she got it under control. Warren was not alone. A woman sat on his tweedy couch. Ellie saw a pink-sweatered back and shiny black pumps.

Warren pointed to the woman with the TV remote he held. "Ellie? Meet your new assistant."

The woman stood and turned to face Ellie with a nervous-looking smile. "I know, right?" Meg said. "Crazy surprising."

CHAPTER 5

NORA

"What are you wearing?"

Nora laughed out loud at the ridiculous question, hearing Guy's voice teasing through the Bluetooth speakers. Even sitting alone in the front seat of the Mercury sedan P-X had issued her, with a thousand miles between them, that voice sent chills through her, as if she were some breathless heroine in a romance novel.

"Don't laugh, Nora. Let me guess," Guy pleaded. "I'm in bed now too, looking out at palm trees and red rocks and blue sky. But I'd rather picture you in black satin sheets . . . wearing that pale green thing, the one that matches your eyes. I'm watching you sleep, and you don't know it. And that thin strap falls from your shoulder, and I see that perfect mole in the curve of your neck and—"

"You are so ridiculous." Nora pretended to be annoyed and knew she'd failed. But she had to interrupt, had to make him stop. She had to go to work. They'd never been in her bed or anyone's bed, not together. *Not yet.* She smiled, imagining it. He *was* silly. She didn't have black satin sheets or a "green thing." Or a mole.

"What time is it there, anyway, like six A.M.?" she asked, checking the clock on the dashboard. "You're still dreaming." It was all a juggle right now. Her life, and her responsibilities and now this relationship. But he seemed like a good guy; that's what had drawn her to him in the first place.

"Guy?" she'd repeated, after he introduced himself at a neighborhood bar called Seaboard. "Just . . . generic Guy?" She'd been wary, of course, but she couldn't work every minute of every day and night, and her staid redbrick apartment was surrounded by a selection of neighborhood restaurants. Nora had chosen a middle-of-the-spectrum place, and "Seaboard" sounded authentically Bostonian. She'd sat at a bar facing a picture window, nursed an Irish coffee and watched the snow fall onto Beacon Street.

He'd laughed at her lame joke. "Named after my father," he'd told her. "A regular guy."

She deserved it, and clinked her ceramic mug with his beer glass. "Nora."

"Like neither a borrower *nor a* lender?" he'd replied.

Testing her, apparently. But messing with the wrong girl. "To thine own self be true," she'd declaimed. She'd done *Hamlet*, even played Ophelia. And knew how she felt. She turned on a hint of a drawl. Nora would have a drawl, just a touch. "Do you follow Polonius' suggestions, Guy? To thine own self be true?"

"Well, well," he'd said. "Want to try Double Jeopardy, where the scores can really change?"

Silly bar talk, and she'd gone home alone. But he'd called. Apparently she'd passed the test. And he had too. He was all there on Google, Guy MacInnis, not too-too much detail, but enough, and all fine.

"Then tell me," he persisted now. She realized she was watching the car's metal speaker as he talked, as if he were in the car, or could see her. "I'm out here raising money for the cause of the week, and I need some . . . distraction. Or send a photo, Nora. Do. I want to see you."

"Go back to sleep, you." She checked the time on the dashboard again, happy he couldn't see her do that. It might work out well that Guy was gone so much. Sad that she had to think of it that way. "I've got to—"

"I'm sending you a photo," he insisted. "A special photo. But don't show anyone. I'm trusting you."

"Call me later." She was so into her new accent that it came out like *layta*. She wished he *would* send a photo, wished she could look at him whenever she wanted, his cheekbones and almost too long hair, the way he held his shoulders and smelled like . . . She took a deep breath as if to name it and couldn't. Something rich and warm and enticing. She wished the world were different, wished she could simply be herself for once. "I have to go."

"Good luck," he said. "Knock 'em dead."

"I will," she said. And that part was true. She heard the click from hundreds of miles away, and he was gone.

The car seemed emptier without him, and the world too. He filled a space in her life, somehow, an emptiness she wasn't ready to admit she had.

And now, showtime. Nora smoothed an eyebrow in the rearview mirror, adjusted her dark green cashmere muffler, rearranged a lock of hair. It was pale auburn, maybe risky and noticeable, but she mentally patted herself on the back for having the courage to try a new color.

She clicked open the detail bag on the front seat

beside her, the clunky Pharminex-issued block of leather and brass with a shiny oval for engraved initials. She'd left hers blank. Inside, paperwork, clipboard, a few medical journal articles printed out and stapled together. A stack of yellow stickies, imprinted with the navy-blue Pharminex logo.

If a doctor took the stickies, and maybe a pen or two, it meant he or she would take the next tiny gift. There was no big-time bribery going on, no phony conventions or lavish golf weekends or free-flowing booze. No assumption that a female pharma rep was also selling herself. No more quid pro quo. The feds and a raft of indictments had made sure of that, and all to the good. Because doctors wouldn't expect those seductive inducements, it made her life easier.

Pharminex had only one goal. To make sure doctors prescribed the drugs researched, produced and offered by Pharminex. Prescribed as many and as often as they could.

Dr. McGinty was next.

She closed the car door behind her, clicked the lock. The Boston sky above her was painfully blue, perfect and cloudlessly unreal, and the wind from the harbor fluttered her coat and swirled through her hair.

CHAPTER 6

ELLIE

At least she didn't have to work with Meg every day, Ellie thought, as she approached the front door of her apartment building. She'd spent today researching, on her own, and now imagined the slew of potential complications having a coworker as a neighbor would inevitably present.

As a roving assistant producer, Meg wouldn't be underfoot at Channel 11 all the time. But here at the apartment? The woman had seemed almost clingy the night they'd met, prying and needy, but again—Ellie grimaced as she dug for her key, trying to separate which emotions were real and which were unfair. It had been late, and they were both tired.

The outer door clicked behind her, and Ellie skipped the elevator to trudge the three flights to her apartment, taking exercise where she could. Meg-next-door meant a real incursion into her privacy, she realized, as she clicked open her own front door.

Comings and goings and visitors could hardly be concealed. And Meg seemed like the type to snoop. Always trying to help, asking questions. And who would leave *cookies*? It was almost creepy. Stalkery.

But again, maybe Ellie was being unfair. Maybe that's what neighbors did.

Blinker padded into the room, holding something in her mouth. Ellie swore the cat spent her days moving her toys from one room to another: stuffed mice with shredded tails and missing ears, a plush hedgehog with chewed feet, a frondy felt carrot that she sometimes slept with, her paws wrapped around the thin orange cone.

"Whatchagot, cat?" Ellie opened the closet door to dump her coat.

The cat placed a crocheted white dove at her feet. Ellie picked it up between thumb and forefinger, examining it. Its nubby white form fit into Ellie's palm, and it was pretty enough, with fluttery wings and a cat-enticing tail, but its cross-stitched eyes gave it a disturbingly flat expression. Like the bird was supposed to be dead.

Ellie had never seen it before. "Where'd you get the weird bird, honey cat?" she asked. But Blinker just curled through her legs and didn't answer.

The knock on the door startled her so much she dropped the thing. Blinker grabbed it and scampered away.

"Get a grip, woman," Ellie muttered. She looked through the peephole. Sighed with the recognition of a situation. Pushed her glasses higher on her nose.

"Hi, Meg," she said as she opened the door, trying to hide her reluctance.

Meg raised her right hand. "I swear, I'm not coming in," she said. She wore a Life is Good T-shirt, jeans and flip-flops. Her toes were painted pale blue, and the polish looked wet. "I'm sure you have plans. Only wanted to make sure—without Warren around—that you were okay with this. With me being the assistant producer. I know it kinda got sprung on you. But I know what I'm doing. I promise."

"Sure." Ellie kept her arm blocking the door. "Grateful for your help when you have time. The other reporters will keep you busy too. When they get here. So—"

She saw Meg try to peer over her shoulder and into her living room. The woman's very existence made everything ridiculously complicated. Meg could easily know if anyone else were in Ellie's apartment. Not to mention know when she was and wasn't home. Just what Ellie needed, a human surveillance system.

"Cool," Meg said.

They stood there, silent for a beat. The elevator rumbled behind them. Just three apartments on this floor. Three-C was empty, far as Ellie knew.

Which reminded her. "How come you didn't tell me last night? About Channel Eleven? How'd you even get hired? You acted like you didn't know I worked at the station, and you even said—I mean, I asked you. Didn't I?" She tried to remember. Sometimes her memory went iffy.

Meg laced her fingers under her chin, made a wincing face. "A family friend wrangled me the job," she said. "They know the station owner. And I'd promised not to tell, until all the t's and i's on the paperwork were crossed and dotted." She shrugged. "Human resources red tape, I guess."

So you lied, Ellie didn't say. Although, to be fair, Meg hadn't done anything last night but sit by her boxes. Ellie had invited her in, unbidden, when she could have simply said hello, gone inside and closed the door. If Ellie had already been home, they might not have met. It wasn't like Meg had orchestrated their meeting. Ellie herself had encouraged it.

"I see. Huh. How'd you wind up living here, though?" Ellie took a step into the hallway, half closing her door behind her. "Here, particularly?"

"Warren," Meg said. "He set you up here too, right?"

"Yeah, true." Channel 11 was stashing some of its new hires in the building, short-term, even had a designated super to handle all the comings and goings.

"Warren also said you were in the midst of an investigation. A good one?"

"I wouldn't say 'midst.'" How transparently nosy could anyone be? Ellie took a step back into her apartment, signaling the conversation's end. "I'd say beginning. I'm at the library a lot. Too early to talk about. Anyway, so—"

In a flash of white, Blinker raced out the open door, became a blurry streak headed into the hall. Dumb cat. There was nowhere to go. But it was her life's ambition to escape.

"Cat!" Ellie called.

"I'll grab her!" Meg scooped her up with one swift motion. "Did you get the bird, by the way?" she asked, handing Blink back.

"That was from you?" Blinker squirmed out of Ellie's arms, racing back into the apartment.

"I put it through your mail slot." Meg pointed at the door. "My goal is to be an investigative reporter, just like you. But I make animal toys, little crafty ones, in my spare time. Weird, I know, but we all need a hobby. Crafts and cookies. Wild and crazy me. And I thought Blinker might be lonely."

"Great," Ellie said. Which she guessed it was. Ellie sure didn't have any hobbies, not anymore. "Nice of you. And, oh, thanks for the chocolate chip cookies."

"No problem," Meg said. "See you around campus."

As she turned away, finally *finally*, Ellie began to close the door.

But Meg pivoted, pointing a finger at Ellie. "Hey," she said, "know what we should do?"

"What?" Ellie tried not to let her impatience show.

"Exchange keys. In case, like, you're out on some big story, and you need me to feed Blinker? Or some work situation? Or an emergency?"

"Exchange—?"

"I don't have any, you know, friends here." Meg's expression seemed lonely and longing, a solitary newcomer in an unfamiliar apartment hallway in an unfamiliar city.

Ellie felt a twinge of conscience for her own brusque and dismissive attitude. She could be self-centered, she knew that, though she preferred to think of it as determined or driven or focused. But she couldn't always be alone in the world. No matter what, she still believed that.

"And I'm honored to be working with you," Meg went on. "It's the least I can do."

"Sure," Ellie said, half agreeing and half hustling Meg out of there. "I'll get a copy made." *Maybe,* she silently added. She needed to shower off the day, get organized and see how on earth she was going to make this work.

CHAPTER 7

NORA

Impossible to say yes. Impossible to say no.

Nora stood in the vestibule of her apartment building, still wearing her coat and shawl. Errands accomplished—drugstore and dry cleaning—she'd planned to forget about the rigors of Pharminex and collapse on her couch, another glamorous Saturday. Pizza for dinner, a good book, and a sleep-late Sunday. But then Guy's call had come. She clamped her cell phone between her ear and shoulder, frozen with indecision. Finally she lowered the two shopping bags to the floor and hooked the dry cleaning hangers over the mail table.

"Well," she began, even as she spoke, not sure how she should handle this.

"Come on, Nora." Guy's voice sounded even more persuasive than usual, and she pictured him at the bar where they'd first met, thrusting and parrying with words. "I'll be back from New York in an hour or two. I'll hop into an Uber and come right to your apartment. Just tell me where it is. I've missed you, Red, and why wait any longer?"

Nora could think of about fifty reasons why. But

she could also think of about fifty more reasons
why it might be pretty darn fabulous to see him.
Red, she thought.

She was also annoyed at the longing she felt, the
longing she had to share her life. Her future. She
couldn't bear to imagine the next fifty or however
many years with only emptiness and loveless solitude
and pizza and cable TV. Sure, she could be successful, short-term, at what she did for now. Two doctors
had just put in substantial orders, so yesterday's *atta-
girl* email to Nora from Detta Fiddler had informed
her. Pharma sales was all about pretty, and she had
pretty nailed. Score.

But her mother had warned her, long ago, that
"pretty" faded overnight. And now there was no one
left, no family she cared about, no friends, no one
connected or devoted to her. Not since high school.
Then came Guy.

And what did *he* truly want? Guy and Nora hadn't
progressed to any conversation like that, never gotten past the tantalizing shallows. She needed to find
out.

"My apartment is . . ." She stopped, midsentence,
wondering what would be appropriate and believ-
able. ". . . still a bit disorganized. You know I just
moved in." She took a chance. "How about your
place in Back Bay?"

He paused. "How about meeting somewhere in the
middle? Have a drink? Maybe dinner?"

Then she grasped what had been nagging at her.
He was lying.

"Are you on a plane?" she asked. A ponytailed
woman in a puffer jacket came into the vestibule,
letting in the night's bluster as she eyed Nora up
and down. Nora remembered to smile, then panto-
mimed, *I'm just on the phone, no problem,* before

she turned her back on her. The woman clicked open the door and vanished up the stairs.

"A plane?" Guy replied.

"Yeah. You told me you were an hour or so from here," she said. "And that you'd take an Uber here. So, you aren't driving. But you can't use the phone on a plane. So—"

"I'm on the *train,* Miss Detective," he said. "If you don't want to see me," he went on, his voice hardening as he spoke, "I get it. I won't bother you again."

Nora winced, ensnared in her own suspicion, snarled in conflicting desires.

She laughed her best Nora laugh. "You are so silly," she said, trying to draw him back to her. "But, listen, you can't show up at a girl's apartment on such short notice."

"Or to a guy's, either," he said. "So—drink? How about where we first met? Unless you've already forgotten where that was." He laughed. "I bet you haven't," he whispered.

"Seaboard," she said. "No. I haven't forgotten."

She prepared for him, aware of how much care she was taking—hair, makeup, Nora clothing—and how long it took to decide what to wear. How to be. At seven, she sat across a sleek wooden table from him. She'd chosen a soft black cashmere turtleneck. So had he.

"Did I send you a clothing memo?" He reached across the table, touched her arm so briefly she might have imagined it. "Or are we so connected that we already know what the other is thinking?"

Nora stirred her amber drink, stalling, the slender red straw whirling the cubes. A faintly seductive soundtrack, not quite recognizable, floated over them. Seaboard pulsed with the buzz of connections, strangers and scavengers and people-shoppers, eyeing each other over salt-rimmed glasses, or defaulting to their cell phones or the opening front door.

When Nora looked up, Guy was staring only at her.

"What am I thinking now?" she asked.

"You're wondering why I stayed out of town so long," he said. "How I could possibly have managed to keep my hands off of you for all that time."

"You're an idiot." He was audacious, had to give him that. She couldn't help laughing, then stopped herself. "You never crossed my mind," she lied. "But okay, now that you mention it. Where out of town were you?"

"Where do you think?"

She pursed her lips, as if trying to remember. "You mentioned palm trees and red rocks. And you were in a different time zone, you said. Arizona?"

"Your detective skills are improving, Red," he said. "Yup. Flew into JFK late last night, took a morning train to Boston, and here I am. With you. Tired, but with you."

Nora swirled her ice cubes. "What were you doing there?"

"Now it's your turn to guess what *I'm* thinking," Guy said.

"You're thinking I ask too many questions?"

"Wrong. I'm thinking—we should get some food." He picked up the menu, an iPad-size blackboard with white-chalk selections. "Truffle fries?"

"What do you do, exactly, though?" Nora asked. "What was in Arizona?"

"Calamari?"

"I don't think so." Nora used her most alluring Nora voice. "I know you're a lawyer, but—"

He peered at her over the top of his menu. "Nora?

You knew I lived in Back Bay. So you looked me up. Ah *ha*."

"I did." She raised her hands in faux surrender. "You got me."

Guy smiled at her, a cat anticipating the cream. "I know I do."

CHAPTER 8

ELLIE

"Ellie Berensen, perfect timing!" Warren's jovial voice washed over her, his booted footsteps crunching on the sidewalk's nubby blue ice-melt, the stuff layered double thick to prevent nuisance lawsuits from litigious pedestrians arriving at Channel 11. Above him, construction workers in orange parkas balanced on a two-story scaffold, wooden planks laid over a rickety-looking metal grid. Their breath showing in the Monday morning cold, the men peeled off a white protective cover from a massive photo, revealing, inch by inch, the words *The New Channel 11*, then COMING SOON, and then a row of smiling and coiffed faces, carefully diverse: Sam and Darweena and Jodi and Julianne and Xavier. Channel 11, the billboard promised, would be "all the news you need."

"See? Here we go," the news director went on, pointing at the sign with a leather-gloved finger. "It's a good morning, Ellie. Seeing this news baby come to life."

"It *is* a good morning," Ellie replied. What she'd discovered the night before, in her post-midnight one-last-time search of the internet, had pushed her already high-pressure timetable into overdrive. Sometimes the universe did provide, although sometimes what it provided was complicated. "In fact—do you have time to hear about my story?"

"For that? I'll make time." Warren, bundled in a dark blue overcoat topped by a bright yellow muffler and carrying a covered cup of Starbucks, pulled open the station's heavy glass front door and gestured her inside. "In fact, how about now? Dump your coat, grab some coffee, come see me. Five minutes."

Ellie had sneaked out of her apartment this morning, taking the stairs in Meg-avoidance mode, but when she arrived at Warren's office, coffee in hand, Meg herself was waiting outside it. She'd apparently baked a Bundt cake and carried the thing, slathered with shiny white frosting, on a foil-covered plate.

"Hey, Ellie." She held up her offering. "I made carbs."

"Come in!" Warren had draped his coat on a padded hanger and was hanging it on a hook behind his door. He settled in his swivel chair, waved off the cake, opened his computer and pulled a thermos from a battered leather briefcase. Pointed them to the two ladder-backed visitor chairs. "Sit. So. Ellie. Whaddaya got? Two weeks, three max, till you're on the air. No pressure, ha ha."

Meg had taken out a spiral notebook, had a pen poised over a blank page.

"Okay." Ellie scooted her chair to face Warren. "I haven't completely nailed it down yet. But—"

"Ellie?" Warren's face had hardened into dark slate, no longer the affable Papa Bear. "What's the story? That's what I need to hear. Right now."

Meg studied her notebook, as if to indicate she hadn't noticed Warren's disapproving tone.

"Reporters," Warren said, letting some humor

back into his voice. "Don't mess with me before I've had enough coffee."

Ellie toasted him with hers. "Understood." She took a deep breath, knowing her success depended on how well she sold this story. Too much information would either confuse him or make him lose interest; too little would make him ask too many questions. She needed a headline.

"How about 'acclaimed wonder drug harms women more than helps them'? Like the opioids. Like Vioxx and Bextra and fen-phen and thalidomide and the whole list of them."

Meg's eyes widened, but Ellie couldn't read Warren.

"You know of them, right? How terrible they—"

Warren gestured *yes* at her. "Go on."

"Those drugs were FDA-approved, and aggressively pushed on patients as lifesavers. But in truth, they were deadly. So now? Monifan, it's called. It's also FDA-approved, but only to be used to decrease recovery time after surgeries. That's all good. But Pharminex, the drug company that makes it, thinks it can also—let's see how to put this—make it easier for fertility drugs to take effect."

"Easier?" Meg asked. "Because I know—"

"You know how many women want to have children," Ellie went on, "how many try hormone treatments. It's incredibly expensive and not always covered by insurance, and in the end, it doesn't always work. But like I said, Pharminex, the company that produces Monifan, believes it also makes hormone treatments more effective. And apparently doctors agree. But since it's not approved for that, it can only be used for it off-label. Meaning—"

"Not big news." Warren's voice was brusque with dismissal. "Doctors can prescribe an approved drug for whatever they want if they think it works. We did that story in San Fran, Ellie. Years ago. Like Rogaine, the heart drug, turned out to grow hair. Viagra was created to help high blood pressure. And that stuff that makes eyelashes grow—glaucoma patients noticed the beneficial side effects."

"Right," Ellie said. "That's what *makes* it a good story. Because a doctor *can* prescribe whatever they want. But. Here's the thing. A pharmaceutical company is not supposed to *push* it for that. This one *does*. I mean, who wouldn't want a pill that increases the chances for the thing you want most in the world? A child?"

"If it works," Meg said.

"Exactly." Ellie pointed to her, punctuation. "But I'm hearing that sometimes Monifan *doesn't* work for that. Even worse—it can cause women to be *unable* to have children. Ever. Because some people have bad reactions. And apparently there's no way to predict it."

Meg's mouth opened, closed again.

"You sure?" Warren put down his coffee, leaned toward her.

Ellie nodded. "Yeah."

"How often?" Warren asked. "How often does it not work? And how do you know this?"

Ellie pressed her palms together, put them to her lips as if praying. "I have proof—just between us for now, and I only found it last night—that P-X did a cost-benefit analysis. Decided they could handle the liability for individual cases, and that it was better to settle out of court with confidentiality agreements and keep the whole thing quiet. That'd be less expensive than giving up all the profits from the times it *does* work. So goes the calculus."

The room went quiet for a moment. Ellie figured Warren was realizing what that meant. That Pharminex had calculated the cost of a human life. The cost of a woman's ability to have children versus their desire to make a profit.

"It helps some people, though, doesn't it?" Warren asked. "It must, if it's on the market. How many are helped versus how many are hurt? Do we know?"

Elle nodded. "Sure. But ask yourself, for instance, if three hundred people are helped, but one can never have children again, does that make it okay?" She shook her head. "How many successes make up for a disaster? Given those odds, what would *you* do?"

"I'd want to know," Meg said. "I'd want to *choose*."

Silence again. Ellie agreed with Meg for once. People should be given the facts.

"You have real documents?" Warren finally asked. "And someone who says she was harmed by this? A victim?"

"Looking for that, of course," she said. "And as for the documents—I have a source."

"Who? How? Where?" Warren frowned. "This could be blockbuster, Ellie. This is—a company knowingly causing women to become infertile and then covering it up to protect their own bottom line. The publicity—the lawsuits and the backlash—could destroy the company."

"Yup," Ellie said.

"And destroy us, and you, if we get it wrong," Warren continued. "So?"

Ellie crossed her legs, smoothed down her black skirt, hesitating. No turning back now. She took a stalling sip of coffee, but her cup was empty. She pretended it wasn't.

"I've been doing research much of the time since I've been here."

"At the library," Meg offered.

"Sometimes. Of course." Ellie agreed, trying harder to be inclusive. "And I've talked to some lawyers who might be putting together lawsuits. But I've also been tracking the pharmacy reps. The salespeople for Pharminex."

"Don't they have an office here?" Warren asked. "Downtown?"

"Yeah. By the Custom Tower. The training office. So I followed a couple of the new sales rep trainees. I found one or two, maybe three, who might be willing to talk about what they do. What they've been told to say."

"You've talked to them?" Warren eyed her skeptically. "Wait—you *followed* them?"

Ellie needed to derail the second-guessing train. "Really. It's fine. I'm still working on it. Seeing where they go have coffee, that kind of thing."

Warren seemed mollified. "Go on."

"One of the reps, I think, might especially be a candidate." Ellie decided to risk telling a little more. "I saw her in a doctor's office, and I know her car now and it's possible that I could . . ." Ellie paused. "Here's the leverage. If she's pushing the off-label use, she's in legal jeopardy too. As being complicit. She seems like a reasonable person. I've seen her talk to women in the waiting rooms, as if she's actually concerned about them. So either she really is—or she's a darn good actress."

"What if she recognizes you?" Warren asked.

"Yeah," Meg piped up. "What if she wonders why you're in every office?"

"That's handled." Ellie wished Meg would butt out. "The first time or two I came as myself, but it felt . . . susceptible. So now I make myself look pretty different. Every time. And I bring a briefcase, so she might think I'm a competitor. I'm careful."

"So you're just gonna, what?" Warren asked. "Why would she just spill the beans to you, Ellie?"

"I don't know," she admitted. "I have to figure it out."

"I have an idea!" Meg's voice had several exclamation marks built in. She winced, touched a palm to her chest. "Sorry, I just got excited. But what if—I could go pose as, like, a patient?" She nodded, as if urging the two to agree with her plan. "Maybe you could find out where your person is going next, and then I could come in, like I had an appointment, and sit beside her, and see if I could get her to talk. Tell me stuff."

Ellie looked at her, trying to figure out how to say *not a chance in hell* and still keep it professional.

"I love how you think." Warren spoke first. "But we don't do that, Meg. No undercover, no lying, no hiding, no pretending to be someone we're not."

"Ever?" Meg tilted her head. "Not ever?"

"Nope." Warren made a dismissive gesture, apparently in case they didn't understand the word *nope*. "Because—"

"Then how can Ellie—and I'm sorry to interrupt, but I'm trying to learn," Meg went on. "How can Ellie go into doctors' offices without revealing who she is?"

"Because I didn't say anything about anything," Ellie answered before Warren could. "I'm in a public place, public enough, a doctor's office, where anyone could logically be. I look like I belong. If not a patient, then someone's friend. I don't have to say who I am, I just can't lie if anyone asks me. The ethical bright line is that I can't actively pretend to be something I'm not. Like a cop, or a doctor or even a patient. But I *can* let people assume it."

"Exactly," Warren said.

"Okay, so I won't say anything either," Meg persisted. "It could work."

"No," Warren said. "Plus, you're new, inexperienced, and not even a reporter. Let's leave it to the pros, okay?"

"Only trying to help," Meg said.

"Much appreciated," Warren said.

"Thing is, there's a snag." Ellie pulled out her cell phone and tapped to her photos, then selected a shot. "Or maybe not a snag. Maybe an opportunity."

She held up her phone, turned the screen to show Warren and Meg.

Warren leaned across his desk, squinting. "What is it?"

"It's an email announcement, including a photo of Brinn and Winton Vanderwald," Ellie said, pointing to the black-and-white picture. "Their family, the Vanderwalds, *owns* Pharminex. Has from the start, since the early eighties. Winton took over in the early nineties. He's hands-on, very insider. And the Vanderwald family—big bucks, big power, big name."

"Vanderwald," Meg repeated.

"And?" Warren made the one-finger spiral signaling *speed it up*.

Ellie stared at the screen, at the ebullient description in the email. "This is an in-house Pharminex email I got from a source. Apparently—well, let me read it to you." Ellie cleared her throat. "'Save the Date,' it starts. Then blah blah, 'pleased to announce, all invited, wanted you to know, clear your calendars,' blah blah . . ." Ellie scanned down. "Okay. Here. 'We are proud to reveal to our Pharminex family that in honor of his continuing and generous contributions to science and medicine, the Massachusetts Medical Science Association is giving our president, Winton

Trevor Vanderwald, Jr., their coveted Humanitarian of the Year award.' There's more, and—"

"Crap," Warren interrupted. "When's this happening?"

"Less than two weeks," Ellie said. "At a 'gala,' they're calling it, in the auditorium of their new medical museum."

"We could go," Meg said. "Talk to those people."

"Crap," Warren said again. He picked up a yellow pencil, and toggled it back and forth between two fingers. "My first question is—how fast can we get this one on the air? Crap. It's a shitshow. Sorry. It's a mess. We can't hurry, or we'll make a mistake."

"Doesn't sound like the kind of person you'd want to honor," Meg said. "Someone who'd push a deadly medication like that."

"Talk about a mess," Ellie answered Warren. "There's more. At this gala, the Vanderwalds will announce they're funding a megabucks scholarship for Mass Med to give every year in honor of their son."

"Son?" The yellow pencil stopped.

"Son?" Meg tilted her head, inquiring.

"Winton the third," Ellie said. "Winton Trevor Vanderwald the third. They called him Trevor. He died."

CHAPTER 9

NORA

Nora—for now—realized her daily routine was becoming second nature. Pack her detail case, quick gossip-chat with her colleagues, drive to an appointment, wait wait wait, talk, sell, assess, go. She slammed the trunk of her car shut in yet another yellow-striped parking lot, lugged her stuff across another snowy expanse of asphalt and took an elevator to another doctor's office. Sales was sales; it was all about talking a good story. And Pharminex had one glittering definition of "a good story." Monifan. The miracle drug.

Monifan. In that week of intense classes, they'd taught her the Monifan script, drilled the new sales staff word for carefully crafted word.

Back in class, teacher Allessandra Lewes had shown them a video, some wannabe boy band singing about P-X's newest products, as if the sales force needed a fight song. *Yes, you can: Sell Monifan!* kept churning through her consciousness, relentlessly infectious. Talk about indoctrination. Monifan might be a miracle, Nora knew, but only reliably for the

Pharminex coffers. Not always for the women it was supposed to help.

And now, everyone was buzzing about the glitzy Vanderwald gala. And the big Trevor Vanderwald scholarship. She contemplated the seething irony of it all as she punched the elevator button. She'd googled the Vanderwalds, daily, if she had to admit it, studying pictures of the officious know-it-all Winton, and his vacant-eyed wife and his children—the elusive Brooke and the drowned Trevor. *Humanitarian award.* How could Winton Vanderwald accept such a thing? This bullshit award would force her to work even faster. But she could do it.

The elevator doors opened and then slid shut behind her, as if propelling her toward a goal.

She scouted this newest waiting room, struck yet again by the depth of emotion in the faces of the patients, women whose hair had not yet gone gray, whose bodies were lithe and graceful, whose clothing was moneyed and meticulous, whose makeup was precise. Dressing up for the doctor's office, so needy, as if they were clinging to something about themselves they could control.

Nine thirty-three. Nora, deliberately early for her 10 A.M. to give her time to scout for patients who might talk to her, was surprised at the crowded waiting room. Women occupied almost every beige leather or tweedy upholstered seat. Women reading, leafing through magazines or focused on their phones, some in sunglasses, many with earbuds in place, the white cords dangling in front of nubby sweaters and looped mufflers like wiry plastic necklaces. A coatrack, also crowded, showed one black coat after another. Nora took the last hanger and crammed hers into place, breathing in the soft floral scent as the fabrics brushed together. She scanned the room then took the only remaining seat, half of an ivory settee, smiling apologetically at the woman on the other half.

"Sorry." Nora slid her detail bag out of the way, hiding it beside the arm of the little couch.

"No problem," the woman said. She held an e-reader and swiped a page as Nora settled into place.

Two beats of silence. A new age underscore, music coming from hidden speakers, filled the spaces in the atmosphere. Nora figured it was designed to be relaxing, but to her it seemed blatantly manipulative, bleating its everything-will-be-okay message when these women knew it might not be. They were so vulnerable, Nora thought again. In more ways than they knew. They all wanted to have children, all might have been told Monifan could help them. For some of them, that would be correct. For others, Nora knew, it would be wrong. Devastatingly wrong.

"I haven't seen you here before," the woman said. Her red hair was pulled back in a low ponytail, and her black turtleneck came up to her chin. Coral lipstick and pale nails, a person who took care of herself. Red-rimmed eyes, though, Nora cataloged, gave away her exhaustion.

Nora had regretted not striking up a conversation sooner that first time in Hawkins's waiting room, and though she'd given several women in other offices her card, none had called her. In the next clinic, she'd pushed harder, and gotten as far as a few random pleasantries before the patients shut her down. Maybe she'd have better luck this time.

"I'm new," Nora said.

"They're always late." The woman gestured at the receptionist's desk, a semicircle of tan Formica with a phone console and a printed sign encased in a plastic frame: PLEASE TAKE A SEAT. WE'LL BE RIGHT BACK. "How can they already be running late? It's only nine thirty. This office opens at nine thirty. Are we all scheduled for the same time? It's so frustrating. Disrespectful."

A woman across the room looked up from her magazine. "Completely agree," she said. She flipped a page, then another.

"Your first appointment?" The woman next to Nora hit the conversational ball back.

Nora kept her voice low. "Yeah." She needed to be careful. "You?"

"Hardly." Her seatmate unzipped her tote bag, pulled out *What to Expect When You're Expecting*. "You'll learn to bring a book."

Another woman, a delicate twentysomething in jeans and a puffy vest, extracted one earbud and looked up. "But if *we're* late, it's, like, we get the look. Like *we're* the problem." She rolled her eyes, then put her earbud back in, apparently tuning out again.

But her unbidden two cents worth meant these women would not be put off by conversation. Or even personal questions.

Nora turned to her new friend. "Thanks for the warning. But . . . why don't you go somewhere else? To a different doctor?"

"Kidding me?" The woman made a dismissive face, pushed up the sleeves of her black turtleneck. "This is Randall McGinty. I mean, how long did you have to wait to get in? Like, months, I bet. Because of . . . you know. Monifan."

"Yeah." Nora tried to look noncommittal. "You taking it? I mean—oh, how awful of me. I am so sor—"

"No biggie." The woman looked at the ceiling, then back at Nora. "But, yes. Maybe it'll work this time.

I'm here for new results." She blew out a breath. "But I don't want to get my hopes up. Or my husband's. James is worried, because it's expensive. But I can't imagine not having . . ." She touched her fingertips to her mouth, as if she'd said too much. Then gave a faraway smile. "It's all I care about, you know? All. Since I was a little girl. You?"

"Sure," Nora agreed. Anything to keep her talking. This potential connection was more important than her sales appointment.

"And, oh, geez, all my dolls." The woman spread her hands in front of her, as if revealing an array. "Not Barbies. But baby dolls, the kind with that soft plastic skin? And the eyes that open and close with the weird *click*. I loved them. I'd talk to them and dress them and cuddle them when they cried. When my little sister was born, it was like a gift. My dolls had come to life."

"So cute." Nora knew when to keep quiet. She crossed her fingers the doctor was stuck in traffic or something, to give her more time with this talkative patient.

"James wants children as much as I do. He looks at other people's babies, in the park or wherever, it feels like he's judging me. Judging *us*. Wondering if he made the wrong decision, marrying me. If I fail again, I wonder if he'll pick up and—he's being so awful, sometimes, critical, like I'm . . . damaged goods." She winced, then widened her eyes, as if replaying what she'd confided. "*Whoa*. True confessions. Sorry. Oversharing. Hormones, right? Back to the dolls, okay?"

"It's fine. And I'm so sorry," Nora said. "It must be so difficult. But dolls? I was more of a Pink Power Ranger kid. And then . . ." She shrugged. "I guess I grew out of it. Wanted to be a movie star."

The woman shook her head. "Yeah. That's what's supposed to happen. You grow out of dolls. I did too, but right into real children. I wanted to be a nurse, or a teacher, but mostly, a mom. I read Baby-Sitters Club books, did you? I really wanted to be Mallory. Because she had red hair and freckles she hated too. I decided she was me." She tucked a stray lock behind one ear. "Mine's the same color as yours, almost."

"I was *always* Mary Anne," Nora remembered, being herself for one moment. "Very organized."

"So funny." For an instant, her face looked genuinely happy. It made Nora grasp the depth of this woman's need. "We have that in common too, it seems. Besides being here. Wanting kids."

"Yeah." Nora briefly hated herself. But she had to risk one more question. "How many times have you . . . ?"

"Four. But it doesn't always work, they told me that. But it *might*. This time it might. That's why I'm here."

"Can't hurt," Nora lied.

With a click and a swish, a door behind the reception desk opened, and a woman in a flowered tunic and a webbed necklace of dangling name badges came through. The atmosphere in the office changed, recharged. The women closed their magazines and sat up straight as the receptionist flapped down the WE'LL BE RIGHT BACK sign. Every woman in the room, Nora saw, tried to make eye contact with the sentinel behind the desk, but she defiantly pretended there was no one else present.

"Kaitlyn?" the receptionist called out.

Two women stood—Nora's new friend and a woman with a blond bob and round red glasses.

"Kaitlyn, last name *A*," the receptionist clarified. "Kaitlyn, first name with a *K*."

The blond bob sat down and Kaitlyn looked at Nora, hope in her eyes. Nora took out a business card from the stack she kept in her jacket pocket, the ones that simply had her name and phone number.

"Let me know," she whispered, handing Kaitlyn the card. "Okay? Or if you want to chat? I know you said—about your husband. I mean, I know it's tough. But we're kind of in this together."

"Adore to," Kaitlyn whispered back. Her expression softened, and she put a hand on Nora's arm. "Incredibly kind of you. You're the first person who seems to understand. I—"

The receptionist came out from behind her desk and approached them, disapproving, as if to collect a misbehaving child.

"Let me know how it goes, Kaitlyn," Nora said. "Good luck."

CHAPTER 10

ELLIE

"You just missed him." The voice of the afternoon-shift guard buzzed through the louvered speaker set into the front wall of Channel 11's plexiglass-enclosed reception desk. He held up his wristwatch, judgmental. At least he was awake.

"Missed who?" Ellie tapped her entry card against the black metal reader, then clicked open the glass security door into the inner lobby.

"Some guy? Left this for you."

Ellie took the manila envelope, wondering, as his eyes focused again on the television monitor, how the guard could guard against anything. Ellie's feet were clammy from walking on the dank slushy sidewalk, and she'd treated herself to a hot chocolate with whipped cream on top. She was trying to look at the pleasant side of life instead of the grim. Now the cream oozed out between the plastic top and the paper cup and made damp blotches on her leather gloves.

She plopped onto one of the blue pseudo-leather chairs in the Channel 11 lobby, curious about the envelope. A seagull, then two, squawked outside in the afternoon gray, then the pair swirled down to the sidewalk in front of the station's plate glass window, staring at their reflections, their webbed feet awkward in the thin carpet of snow. "Dumb birds," Ellie muttered, "staying here in the cold." She hated seagulls. Stupid and noisy. Scavengers.

She flapped up the metal prongs on the envelope and drew out a sheet of white paper, folded in thirds, with a yellow stickie attached. She peered into the envelope again. Empty. A piece of paper and a yellow stickie. All there was.

The stickie had careful block letters in black felt tip: *More like this, if you are interested,* the note said. And then a phone number. It was signed *Gabe.*

Ellie frowned. *Gabe?*

One of the seagulls complained, jabbed the other with its yellow bill. Elle shifted in her chair and opened the folded paper. She'd seen it before. The Pharminex email about Winton Vanderwald, and the Winton Trevor Vanderwald III scholarship fund.

Trevor Vanderwald, she'd read on Google, had died in a boating accident. Years ago. Google said he was being groomed to take over the company, but rough seas and an unlucky gust of wind—that had been in quotes, Ellie remembered—had ended the line of male succession in the Vanderwald family. His sister Brooke had been on the boat, too, Ellie read. The *Caduceus.* When she was nine, after Ellie had devoured every volume of the Cherry Ames, Student Nurse mysteries, she'd thought the caduceus was the symbol for medicine. But when she got older she'd learned it was also the magic wand of Hermes, messenger of the gods and patron of trade. Perfect for the Vanderwalds, she thought.

She stared at the email, trying to place "Gabe." She didn't know a Gabe, not in Boston and not anywhere. Since she was new in town, the universe of people knowing who she was and that she was here must be minuscule. Or was it? She'd called more than a few lawyers' offices, inquiring specifically about Pharminex—had someone suggested her to an insider? She'd done searches on library computers— had someone examined *her* history? Warren knew she was working on Pharminex. So did Meg.

But who was Gabe? She pulled out her phone, tapped through to the Pharminex website, clicked on the employee directory. Clicked on *call us.*

"May I speak to Gabe?" Ellie pictured the Pharminex receptionist, and the lobby, all marble and glass, masses of fresh white roses. She assumed the flowers were supposed to soften the hard edges of the place, but she saw them as proof that someone was making too much money. Why not spend the rose money on research? On truly helping people? And the fragrance was suffocating.

"Last name, please?"

Which of course she didn't know. "Oh, gosh." She made her voice sound embarrassed. "I wrote it down funny, and I can't read my own writing. It's Gabe— something? Do you have many Gabriels?"

"I only have a listing by last name, ma'am." The receptionist sounded impatient. "Do you know where this person is located?"

Which of course she didn't. Well, maybe she did. "Boston?"

"No Gabes, ma'am."

Ellie couldn't resist. "Maybe last name Vanderwald?"

"Ma'am? May I ask who this is?"

"Thanks," Ellie said, hanging up. Gabe could be anyone, from anywhere, and it might not even be his real name. Total dead end.

"Stupid Ellie," she said out loud, shaking her head

for missing the obvious. She googled the phone number he'd left. But only gobbledygook came up, nothing helpful. So much for research.

She had two choices: Call him. Or don't.

She dialed.

As she heard the phone ring, somewhere, she stood and stared through the reception area's plate glass window. Channel 11 was in the city's new Seaport District, of all places. Ellie could sometimes smell the briny scent off the harbor when she went outside, a pungent whoosh of salt and mist that some people loved. She'd been a swimmer as a kid, dashing into the ocean without a second thought, coming home salt-covered and sunburned, nose peeling and sand in her scalp. Long ago. Another life.

"Hello?"

A man's voice. She'd blocked her own caller ID, so he—whoever he was—couldn't know it was her.

"You left me a note?" Ellie began.

"Ms. Berensen," the voice said. "Listen, I know this is awkward. But I've been hearing you're interested in looking into the realities of—" He stopped. "We shouldn't do this over the phone."

"You sent me this Pharminex email about Winton Vanderwald." Ellie had to be infinitely careful, walk an impossible tightrope. This could be the call of her dreams, a Pharminex insider who had sneaked her this email to prove he had access, and was willing to offer her more. Or it could be a trap—a Pharminex fixer who was out to see where she was going, and stop her. This would prove she'd rattled their cage, though. And for better or for worse, they knew she was investigating them. "Could I ask who you are? And why you sent it? Do you work there?"

"We shouldn't do this on the phone," the voice said again.

"You dropped this note off at Channel Eleven?" Ellie peered out the wide front window again. Was Gabe out there right now, watching her watch for him? "Do you want to meet here?"

Silence on the other end. A block away, past a gravel parking lot and a loop-chained fence, she could see the edges of Boston Harbor, and past that, across the water, beyond a crisscross of sailboats and ferries and the occasional oil tanker, the low buildings of Logan airport. Flying into Boston terrified her every time, the final approach so low over the water that she grasped the armrests, feeling, to her bones, the chill of the inevitable plunge into the icy waters, her head going under, her body tangled in the—

"No," the voice said. "Perhaps it's better if we don't actually—"

"I'm so pleased you sent me the email," Ellie interrupted, needing to keep him talking. He'd already made a decision to seek her out, and signal he had knowledge and intent. Question was, intent to what? "What do you think about that award?"

"It's bull." The man's voice spat the word. "Those people need to be stopped."

"From what?" Convinced he was right outside, she stood so close to the window that her nose touched the cold glass. Seagulls swirled above, taunting her.

"We could meet somewhere neutral," the voice said. "I know what you look like, so—"

"You do?"

"I saw you walk in today," the voice said. "Black coat, blond hair, red glasses? I'd recognize you."

Ellie felt a shiver up the back of her neck, a warning. Or maybe a promise. Another call beeped in to her cell phone. She checked the caller. Clicked it away.

"I don't have long." She'd risk it. Meeting in public

wouldn't be dangerous. She could gauge his intentions, and nope out if she needed to.

"There's a coffee shop by the water, the Spinnaker?" he said. "A five-minute walk for you. It has an outside upper deck, with heaters. We can sit by the water, watch the waves. And if anyone tries to eavesdrop on us, the jets into Logan and the sound of the gulls will drown them out."

"The Spinnaker," Ellie said.

"I can help you with your story, Ellie," the voice said. "You're looking for information. I have it. Up to you."

"The Spinnaker," Ellie said again, weighing it. "Okay. Ten minutes."

She got there in eight. From the sidewalk below, she looked up to a second-floor deck, a gray-washed wooden structure with a flapping green-striped canvas canopy, possibly made of a real spinnaker sail. The place looked like it had been battered by years of salt and wind, and the powerful waves that must have sloshed over it in a lifetime of Boston nor'easters. As Gabe had promised, a bank of shiny metal heaters lined the water-side of the deck, and even from below, Ellie could see the glowing orange coils providing a band of electric heat to the hardy souls who wanted to be outdoors, even—or especially—in challenging weather.

Waves crashed against the sides of the wooden pier beside the restaurant, coils of thick ropes snaked along its edges and a lone dinghy, tethered to a metal standard, bobbled in the rough seas. The snow had ended, and the waning sun struggled to send a wintry shimmer over the harbor.

One person sat on the deck, alone, facing the street. He did not move upon Ellie's arrival, didn't stand, or wave, or stride, welcoming, to the edge of the deck. Was he pretending he didn't see her? Maybe the light was wrong. Maybe the line of fake spindle-leafed areca palms lined up in terra-cotta containers shielded his view of the street. Or maybe her spot beneath him was off just enough to hide her, and give her a chance to see him without him seeing her. Brown boots, she cataloged. Jeans, a black puffer jacket and black watch cap.

The wind picked up, and with a buffeting gust, the imitation leaves on the pretend plants fluttered and shifted. The man turned his head, and she caught his profile outlined by the steely sky.

No, Ellie thought. *No.*

CHAPTER 11

NORA

Nora's work cell rang, echoing though the car's Bluetooth.

Caller ID unknown, the readout said. She pushed the phone button on the steering wheel as she stopped for the light at the intersection. Snow had started to fall, a gentle dusting this Tuesday morning, but the steely clouds looked full, graphite and forbidding. She flipped on her wipers, the slowest speed. "Nora Quinn," she said into the phone's speaker.

The light had barely turned green when the driver behind her honked impatiently and swerved his SUV around her, passing on the right, then pulling in front of her, brusque and demanding. Boston drivers, Nora thought. *Men.*

A white silence came through the open Bluetooth line as Nora blended her car into the traffic. She was headed from her morning appointment to a bustling sandwich shop in the impersonal retail chaos of the Shoppers World mall, a short-order short-term respite where she could catch up on paperwork and then phone in her morning report to P-X, another worker bee in the buzz and hustle. And the place was near her next meeting. Google Maps had shown she could see the office building from there.

"He*llo*?" she answered again. Maybe a wrong number? Or a robocall. She frowned, poised her finger to disconnect.

"It's Kaitlyn. Kaitlyn Armistead? From yesterday morning?"

"Oh, hi, Kaitlyn. Of course." Nora's brain spooled out the possibilities, almost getting ahead of itself. She reminded herself of who she was and what she wanted. "How's it going?"

Silence again. Nora kept silent too, allowing Kaitlyn her emotional space. If she had gotten good news, no doubt she'd have yelped with delight, the words pouring out. Silence meant disappointment, and it made Nora feel guilty.

Nora heard Kaitlyn sniffle, choke back a sob or a wail. "It's . . . not good."

Nora steered her car into the tangle of the shopping center, trying to concentrate on the parking place hunt without getting bashed by texting teenagers or grocery shoppers in oversized SUVs. She slid into a spot close to the highway, no one on either side of her, and left the car running. She didn't want to have this conversation and drive at the same time. But maybe she wasn't going to stay here.

"Where are you, honey?" Nora asked. Flakes of powdery snow began to dot the windshield, each a unique treasure melting in an instant. Nora stared through the thickening flurries and out onto the highway, the swish and flash of traffic and flapping windshield wipers, the changing lights muddled by the quickly intensifying white. Squalls, they called them around here, snow-in-an-instant on a previously sunny day. Nora watched the cars in front of her blur into a blurred stream of motion and counted her blessings she'd pulled into the parking lot. And that her next appointment was within walking distance.

"I—I don't know what to do. I can't stand it," Kaitlyn's voice buzzed over the car's tinny speakers, like there was sudden snow in the transmission too. "I had to go back to Dr. McGinty again today for my *final*-final results. Can you believe it? As if I wasn't just there, just yesterday, with you. And it got my hopes all up again, like maybe there had been a mistake, but *no,* it's still awful, still horrible, still the worst thing ever. And still their fault. And today it's like oh, we know we told you yesterday, but now we need to tell you the bad news *again.*"

Nora heard the tears in Kaitlyn's voice. The sorrow. "Are you driving, Kaitlyn? Where are you? Is it snowing? Maybe pull over and then we'll talk?"

"No, no, I can't stop, I have to get home." Kaitlyn drew out the word, like a wail or a plea. *Home.* "I'm only to the reservoir, by that movie theater."

"Kaitlyn. Seriously." Nora kept talking as she shifted her car into reverse, backed up, and pulled into traffic. Lunch could wait. "Pull over. I'm on my way."

"I'm so sorry to call you, and I know it's crazy, but it's not gonna work, it's never gonna work, and we don't have any more money, and I think . . ."

Nora eased onto the highway, nosing in front of a poky sedan, skating through a yellow light that turned red while she was still in the intersection. She accelerated, gauging the traffic, gauging the distance, gauging the snow, Kaitlyn's voice growing taut and insistent.

"I really think they tricked me, Nora. That doctor

knew all along this might happen! He *said* he'd warned me, but he didn't!"

"Kaitlyn? Are you sure he didn't warn you? I mean, maybe you missed it, or maybe he didn't make it seem like a big deal?"

A red light glowed ahead of her. She had to stop. She punched "Framingham Cinema" into her GPS, near where Kaitlyn must be. She could get Kaitlyn to tell her what happened, to see if doctors like McGinty—and Hawkins, and the rest—were misleading patients about what Monifan might do. Kaitlyn might be the very person she needed.

The light turned green. Kaitlyn hadn't said a word, but through the car's speakers Nora heard the sounds of horns and windshield wipers. "Kaitlyn? You okay? Pull over. We need to talk. Okay?"

"He *didn't* warn me! He didn't. And I told him so, right to his face, this morning, and I told him I was going to—"

"Focus on driving, okay?" Nora didn't like the edgy panic in Kaitlyn's voice. Or the sounds of sniffles and tears. "We'll talk when I get there."

"I am, and I'm driving fine, but I can't believe, after all this time and all his promises—"

Nora heard a little gasp, as if Kaitlyn was choking on her tears.

"I know, I know." Nora kept her voice quiet, reassuring. "We'll figure something out. Just give me time to get to you."

Four minutes away, Nora's GPS promised. If the weather weren't so treacherous, she might make it there sooner. But she had to drive carefully; she still wasn't used to Boston's winter, or its lack of road rules.

"Is there a Starbucks? Something like that?" Nora

tried to remember that area. She'd only been to movies there once, and by herself. Her windshield wipers flapped, persistent. *Two minutes,* her GPS said. "Can you see any place nearby? I really want to talk to you, and you're in no shape to drive, Kaitlyn."

"All I wanted was *children*." Another sob. "Like I told you. And I told him that, and he promised me, promised, that it would work! And now I can *never*—"

Nora pressed her lips together, concentrating on the road, concentrating on everything, feeling something beginning and something ending, and Kaitlyn was the key.

"I'm coming to get you right now," Nora said, taking a chance, swerving into the right lane, then back to the center, feeling her tires shift and slide. Her car seemed as unreliable as her emotions. "Pull over. Stop. Just wait for me."

"Nora. Nora? I am so—I can't even see straight. I—I told him, that McGinty, that *liar,* right to his face, that I'm calling the news, I'm calling every reporter I can think of, and telling them this doesn't work! It not only doesn't work, it—ah. I swear to God, Nora, he never—"

"I'm with you, I am, but it's hard to listen properly and drive at the same time." Kaitlyn had *threatened* McGinty? She wanted to spill to a journalist? Nora's stomach twisted. That could change everything. They needed to talk. And now.

"Seriously, Kaitlyn, could you do me a favor and get off the road? Is there a gas station, someplace we could meet?"

"And *James*! I just called my husband, James, and he's a mess, and now he's coming home and I have to decide how to talk to him about it in person, which will be awful, and he'll be so angry! Like it's my fault, *again,* and it's not!"

"What kind of a car do you have, Kaitlyn?" Nora interrupted, tried to keep her voice calm and soothing. GPS showed the cinema less than half a mile away on the highway. "So I can find you?"

"It's a white hatchback," she said. "A Civic."

A Civic. Hatchback. Nora pictured that. *Okay. A small white—*

"And now," Kaitlyn interrupted her thought, "I have to decide which reporter to—*damn* it!"

"Kaitlyn? Kaitlyn?"

"Hey! Watch it!" Kaitlyn's voice had changed, high-pitched, annoyed. Then frantic. "Watch it!"

"Kaitlyn? You okay?"

Brake lights appeared ahead of Nora, blinking on in unison as if they were synchronized, red and red and red, glowing though the blustery snow. She slowed, craning her neck around the chain of cars lining up in front of her, blocking her way.

"Kaitlyn?"

She heard sounds through the speakers, wrong sounds, sounds like metal and yelling and horns.

"Hey!" she yelled, and "Kaitlyn!" But no answer. A flash of white noise. Then silence.

She yanked the wheel to the right, rumbling through the narrow potholed breakdown lane, needing to get there, hoping she wouldn't see what she had heard, what she'd imagined, hoping there was another explanation, her teeth clenched and fingers grasping the steering wheel.

Horns, and more horns now, and other cars moved in her way, with their own needs and their own goals and blocking her way to whatever had happened.

She honked too. She had to get those people to

move, clear a path, give her room. She heard the blare of sirens, and saw more red lights, their intense colored beams sweeping across the snow.

A tiny graphic pinged onto her GPS, and then blocky words: CRASH AHEAD. Seek alternate route.

CHAPTER 12

ELLIE

Ellie ripped the Channel 11 envelope from the front door of her apartment. All she needed. Another damn mystery. Someone—Meg, no doubt—had used a bit of bright blue painting tape to attach the envelope to the brass 3-A above her peephole.

She sighed, heavy with frustration about the world and why people did what they did. Take Meg, now. All that woman would have to do to see if Ellie was home was check whether the envelope on the door was gone. If Meg hadn't been wanting to keep tabs on her, she could have slid the note—or whatever was inside—under the door. If she hadn't been a complete control freak, she could have texted her. Or, imagine, talked to her at the station.

"Blinker, humans are crazy," she told the cat. She stashed her coat, then stuffed the envelope in the waistband of her skirt. She needed wine before she had the stamina to read whatever Meg had sent her. Ellie was still reeling from her day, and her meeting with Gabe. Or whoever he was. "Did Ms. Meg leave us anything dead-birdy today, cat? A severed hand? A withered apple? The black spot?"

Blinker wound herself through Ellie's legs as she headed for the fridge. For the millionth time, she wondered if she was going at this Pharminex story the wrong way. But if she didn't expose those people, who would?

She stood in front of the open fridge door, a blast of cold hitting her in the chest as she pulled out the green bottle of sauvignon blanc. No need to second-guess herself. It was a juggle, but it was the only way. More people would die if she didn't.

She poured the last of the wine into a stemmed glass, took a packet of string cheese from the fridge, and grabbed a handful of crackers and a paper towel for a plate.

And the meeting with Gabe yesterday—Gabriel Hoyt, he'd said, was his full name. She'd tried to parse what he'd told her, sift the truth from the chaff. See if any truth was left. She'd googled that name as soon as he made a trip to the Spinnaker bathroom, and found "Gabriel Hoyt" was a freelance investigator, a lawyer, who worked for whatever law firm hired him. She'd sent him a test email—got an out-of-office response. Back on the Spinnaker deck he'd told her he'd heard about her inquiries from a law firm that he worked for—he wouldn't tell her which one—that was investigating Pharminex with an eye toward a massive class action lawsuit. To benefit the women Monifan had "allegedly" harmed.

"*Allegedly* harmed?" Ellie had sat with her back to the water, her black muffler up around her ears and the back of her neck. Kept her gloves on. She'd kept her hat on as well, the black knit pulled down over her forehead, the tight ribs touching the tops of her red glasses.

"More like *definitely*." Gabe had kept his knit cap

on too, as he faced into the brisk harbor wind. "You know that as well as I do. Don't you?"

"You have victims?"

"Do you?"

This was fun. "Gabe?" She'd tried out the name, aware she was saying it as if it were an alias. "Where'd you get the in-house email about the Vanderwald gala?"

"Come on, Ellie." He seemed to give her name some baggage too. "If you'd had the email and I asked you that, would you tell me?"

Ellie had looked away, caught a glimpse of steely sky and leaden water. She'd felt safe there, unless this guy picked her up and threw her into the harbor. Inside Spinnaker, the smart customers, all in down vests and jeans, congregated at a cozy-looking weathered wooden bar, a string of buoys and iridescent light bulbs casting a glow on wineglasses and beer mugs. One yell from her and someone would surely come dashing to her rescue. This guy had been so annoying, though, answering questions with questions, she'd almost wanted to throw *him* in the water. What was his true agenda?

"You say you're working for a law firm. So you must work for one I called." Ellie held her coffee mug between her gloved hands. "Interesting. Which one? Do you know of any lawsuits where Pharminex paid victims to keep quiet?"

"They'd be confidential."

"The exact settlements would, but not the existence of the suits," Ellie countered.

"Sometimes they're sealed."

"How well I know." She toasted him with her mug. "I've scoured every court record on the planet. But now that you lured me out here, *are* there any of those? Suits against Pharminex?"

Gabe tilted back in his weather-battered chair, looked out over the harbor. "You like boating? Sailing?" he asked.

"Huh? What does that have to do with—"

"Are you from here? Boston? It's my first time here." He thunked his chair back into place. "The harbor's historic."

Really? Small talk? "How fun. To see it for the first time. It's difficult to make new friends in a new place, isn't it?"

He turned his hands palms up, then palms down, *maybe yes, maybe no.*

"Yes, no?" Ellie couldn't help it. "You've met people? New friends?"

"I've met some," he said. "Hard to be sure, though. About friends."

"Got that right." Ellie'd heard the waves lapping on the pier behind her, heard the clank of metal chains against the iron fittings attached to the dock. "So. Want to cut the chitchat? You're not here to talk about sailing."

"Cards on the table." Gabe unzipped his puffer jacket, revealing a black crewneck sweater with a black T-shirt underneath. "I've seen you before."

Her eyes widened. Her heavy glasses slid down again, and she one-fingered them back into place. She put her gloved palms up to her cheeks, leaving only her ears and nose showing, the leather chilly against her face.

"Seen me where?"

"At Dr. Hawkins's office." He held out his hands, apologizing. "And at other offices too—"

"You did?" Ellie thought hard, felt her entire face squinting. A man at these women's clinics would instantly be conspicuous. She shook her head slowly. "How could you see me if I didn't see you?"

"Lab coat." He'd squared his shoulders, adjusting an invisible white jacket. "Stethoscope. You probably did see me. All us fake doctors look alike."

Ellie frowned, even more suspicious. She definitely, *definitely* would have noticed him. Wouldn't she? Maybe not. People don't always look that closely at each other. She pulled her turtleneck higher as the sun began to disappear.

"But why were you in those clinics in the first place? How come—"

"Because my law firm is working on Pharminex already," he interrupted her. "And I was there, let's say, undercover. Like you were, correct? Did you tell anyone you were a reporter? I'll assume you have no problem with our investigative method. We're working on the same thing. And that's why I'm here. To help you."

"Can you believe it, cat?" Ellie now said out loud. "He says he was there to *help* me." She brushed a few cracker crumbs from the cat's snowy fur, which Blinker took as affection and coiled her tail around herself in contentment. "Do we believe him? Do we, Blink? We don't, do we? Do we even think *Gabe* is his real name?"

Blinker mewed in protest as Ellie tried to shift position on the couch, and finally hopped down and skittered away, her tail swishing. Ellie wished she had a tail to swish. Cats allowed their feelings to show. Humans had a more difficult time. More rules. More agendas.

Her wineglass was empty now, and the pitiful string cheese and crackers only a memory. This Gabe had promised to call her again. Insisted his offer of assistance was authentic and without ulterior motive.

Ellie didn't buy it.

Still. If he had real inside information, as he promised, then why not see what he could provide? She could handle it, either way.

Something poked her in the side as she stood. The Channel 11 envelope, the one Meg had taped to the door. Ellie pulled it from her waistband. On the front, her name was written in determined block letters in black marker.

She tucked a fingernail under the flap and ripped open the envelope. Pulled out a white piece of paper, the kind Channel 11 used in its copiers. The typed note was signed *M*.

Hey El. For our P-X story? After you left this morning, I may have found a victim of what you're talking about.

Ellie rolled her eyes. *El. Our* story. As if. But if Meg had found a victim? She read on.

I don't want to put the deets in email or text, you know how discoverable that is, and I really want to stay out of this. Super-confidential, my person says. But Abigail says she'll talk to you, only you, on the phone. I have to be with her, though. Want me to set it up?

CHAPTER 13

NORA

Nora didn't welcome any memories from high school, but this morning the row of pale neutral metal lockers—each with a built-in combination lock—in the high-security ninth-floor storage area of the Pharminex building reminded her of exactly that. High school hadn't been her happiest time, Nora thought, and beeped her laminated ID through the metal card reader that opened the entry door.

In fact, if she had to pick a happiest time in her life—she pushed open the heavy door into the storage section and found her locker—she might not be able to. Such a time might never have existed. Happiness that *lasted*, at least. She'd hoped this job would be her path to that.

Footsteps behind her made her drop the combination lock midturn. She whirled to confront whoever it was.

"Oh, sorry to freak you out!" The woman laughed. Blond waves, curvy black jacket, bright blue suede heels, little black cross-body bag. Gold and maybe-diamond earrings. And a sample case just like Nora's. "It's just me, Lydia. Another worker bee."

Lydia Frost, Nora remembered, even though she no longer wore her newbie name tag. One of her colleagues from training class. She'd seemed smart. Confident. And maybe not a zealous rule-follower.

"More like an early bird than a bee," Nora said. "It's only seven thirty. But how're you doing?"

"Sell sell sell." Lydia spun a forefinger. "I've gotta say, I'm not lovin' this. So far those doctors either come on to me like all-hands maniacs, or else they act like I'm the scourge, there to take up their oh so valuable time."

"You got that right." Nora clicked open her locker, then lifted the latch on the louvered door. Every day she removed the number of samples she'd need, then logged that number on the grid. Pharminex security also had access. At any time, they could open her locker to confirm that her supplies matched her inventory numbers. To prevent under-the-table drug dealing or use or bribing doctors with extra samples, any discrepancies were grounds for instant dismissal.

Lydia had her locker open too. "And you know what else?" she said. "I hate sitting in those doctors' waiting rooms. The women are all sad, and so needy and incredibly desperate. Sometimes I see the same people in different offices. You know? How much can that cost?"

Nora's eyes filled with tears, and for a moment she couldn't remember why. "Yeah," she finally said. "The other day? I talked to one of the women I met at a clinic, I don't know, a random thing. She seemed so unhappy. And—"

"You did?" Lydia kept one hand on the door of her locker and looked at Nora, eyebrows raised in disbelief. "You talked to a patient? We're not supposed to, you know, chitchat or elicit information. Privacy laws, like they said in class."

"She didn't know why I was there." Nora shook her head. "We were two women in a doctor's office. What was I supposed to do, ignore her? She wanted to talk, and I was there, and she seemed so despondent. We talked about our red hair and playing with dolls. Hardly consorting with the enemy."

Lydia pursed her lips. "It's your future, Nora. Be careful. You never know who's out there. Who's reporting on us, even. Who knows?"

"Then the next day, she was in a bad car accident."

"*What?*"

"Yeah." Nora now regretted bringing this up, knew she shouldn't have, but the memory of the crash was still raw. She would never know what had happened to that poor woman. "Never mind."

"No, really, what happened?"

"Let's drop it. Okay?" Nora tried to stay pleasant, pretended to count her boxes of samples, hating that Lydia seemed fascinated by the accident. "Three, four, five . . ."

Guy had called her last night, effusive and affectionate as ever. From wherever he was. And she'd simply listened, oh so supportive and enthusiastic. She hadn't mentioned Kaitlyn, even when he'd asked her what was new. Now she needed to change the subject here too, before Lydia tried to push her any further.

"Wait," Nora said. "You saw the same patients in different offices?"

Lydia's face changed. "I *know*. That's why I'm worried someone from P-X is spying on us. On *me,* especially. Maybe I'm wrong. Still. Why would the same women be in different offices?"

"Maybe they're doctor shopping?" Nora said. "Right? Having consults?"

Lydia smoothed an eyebrow, examining herself in a circular mirror she'd hung inside her locker. She turned back to Nora.

"Okay, maybe. Yeah. But I do know, for sure, once I saw a *guy* in a white lab coat hanging around a doctor's waiting room. Then I saw the same guy in *another* waiting room. He walked in and kind of stood there, pretending to be all busy on his phone, but I know he was really looking at the patients. Like, checking them out. Or checking *me* out."

"Why is that strange? Maybe he was, you know, a doctor."

"Maybe." Lydia shook her head. "Doubtful. But I noticed him because he was . . ." She batted her eyelashes, confessing. "Pretty hot. And frankly, I'm on the hunt. I know it's only been a week or so, but the moment I snag a marriage possibility, I'm so out of this place. We all deserve to be happy, don't we? With families? And now, it's like—we're in an ideal dating pool. The only people we meet are doctors and women who can't have kids."

"That's harsh." But Nora remembered to laugh, showing she wasn't being critical. "But kinda true. But this guy—did you talk to him?"

"Eight, nine, ten," Lydia was counting out loud, stacking samples into her case.

"Lydia?" Nora persisted.

Lydia closed her locker door and spun the combination lock. They both turned as more footsteps padded down the carpeted hall. Chic suit, perfect heels, earrings. Jenn Wahl, Nora remembered her name too. Another classmate, one she'd considered a potential ally.

"Hey, Jenn," Nora said. "We're just discussing a mysterious cute doctor Lydia's curious about."

"He *wasn't* a doctor." Lydia told Jenn the whole

story—handsome, white coat, several offices. "And his hands were clean, but not doctor-clean. And he kept fiddling with his stethoscope, as if he wasn't used to it. I don't know. I might be nuts."

"Think he's like . . ." Jenn tilted her head, and a lock of highlighted hair fell over one eye. As she tucked it away, she looked at the ceiling, then scanned the room as if searching for surveillance. "A spy?" she whispered.

"That's what I wondered too. Seriously. Like—watching us?" Lydia's voice lowered to a whisper. "Seeing if we say or do anything wrong. Or talk to patients. I know companies do that. It's SOP."

Nora decided to whisper too. "Wavy dark hair, tortoiseshell glasses?" She pushed back imaginary hair, used two forefingers to pantomime glasses. "Because now that you mention it, I think I've seen a person like that too."

"Yes," Lydia said. "Glasses."

"Uh-huh," Jenn agreed, nodding. "Glasses."

The three of them exchanged speculative glances, silent in the otherwise empty hallway.

Then Nora burst out laughing. "Come on, you guys," she said, using her regular voice. "There are no spies."

Jenn shook her head. "You never know."

"Yeah, you do." Nora picked up her case. Her agenda would have to wait for another day. "Let's get out there, ladies. I've got three appointments before lunch." She tried to look elaborately conspiratorial. "But listen. If any of us sees the spy, let's text each other. Let's keep on this. Together. Maybe we can expose him."

"Perfect. Make him buy us jewelry." Lydia snapped her sample case closed, then pursed her lips, scheming. "Or we'll reveal his true identity."

"Or maybe." Jenn held up a forefinger. "We'll demand Hermès bags for everyone. Or *else*."

"You two are terrible." Nora played along, as she pictured this "totally hot" guy and his stethoscope. "Maybe we'll make him take us out to dinner. And then we'll convince him to tell us the truth. But for now? I've gotta go."

Nora slammed her car door shut and slid on her sunglasses against the afternoon glare. The cops had told her on the phone they were talking to everyone on Kaitlyn's contact list, she reminded herself. She clicked her car locked, the sound echoing through the half-full parking lot of state police headquarters. At least she wouldn't be the only one called here.

She wondered if Kaitlyn's overbearing and judgmental husband would be inside, the one who'd made his wife so miserable. The one she'd worried would dump her if she failed again in her attempts to have a child. Because of him, his poor wife had been disconsolate, even considered herself a failure as a woman. Wonder how he felt now. Nora's heart had broken when they'd talked in the doctor's office, broken at Kaitlyn's melancholy and defeat. She'd confided in Nora, sobbing to a stranger. And now she was dead.

Nora could not get that final picture out of her head. After an unbearable eternity of stopped traffic, and the taunting sirens wailing in the distance, she'd managed to inch forward, closer. And closer. And then she saw it. A small white car. A telephone pole. The wash of blue police lights on the snow, the spinning red lights as the ambulance screamed away. The police officer who'd ordered her to leave, no matter what she said.

She stood now, silently, leaning against her car door feeling the frigid metal through her winter coat. Wondered if she'd ever forget the sounds she'd heard over her phone: the wrong sounds, the twisted sounds, a *whoosh*, a gasp.

You warned her. You told her to pull over, Nora tried to reassure herself yet again as she second-guessed and replayed and wondered *if*—if she'd just driven faster, or known a shortcut, or been more persuasive. *You got there as fast as you could. There was nothing more you could have done.*

That's how it was with memories, devastating ones like this, of the disaster you did not create and could not prevent, no matter what you did, and images of darkness and the sound of sirens. There you were, in the middle of it forever.

She closed her eyes for a beat, in memory, thinking of loss, and all that Kaitlyn had wanted, and all she'd lost.

Hey! Watch it! Kaitlyn's last words on this earth.

The snow had vanished now, Mother Nature practicing her magic act. Nora picked her way through slush puddles in the state police headquarters parking lot, a patch of asphalt beside the boxy redbrick structure that looked more like an insurance company than where state troopers interrogated suspects and administered Breathalyzers and stored ever-growing amounts of illegal drugs and seized weapons. She'd been told to ask for Detective Lieutenant Monteiro, assigned to accident reconstruction.

As she made her way through the white-linteled double doors, Nora remembered she'd tried to convince the officer on the phone that she couldn't help reconstruct anything. But he'd corrected her. Kaitlyn Armistead had spun out on the snow-slick street, he'd said, and smashed her car into a telephone pole.

Nora's number was the last Kaitlyn had called. So you're a possible earwitness, he'd told her, to a fatal crash.

"Earwitness." She tried the weird word out loud as she entered the bleak redbrick lobby.

Did the police know Nora had been at the scene? Her shoulders sagged with the weight of the memory. Would Dr. McGinty feel guilty about poor Kaitlyn? Would Pharminex?

By the time Nora was signed in, wanded, buzzed through, handed a paper cup of murky coffee and seated in a mustard-brown conference room, she'd figured out what to say to the trooper who'd escorted her in. *Detective Lieutenant Rafael Monteiro,* he'd introduced himself, holding out a hand and looking her square in the eyes. "Lieutenant's fine."

Maybe they sent the handsome ones to deal with women, she figured, trying to look back at Monteiro without him noticing. Maybe they thought she'd be smitten with his square shoulders, the crinkles around his dark eyes. His perfectly battered leather jacket. His pressed jeans. But she wasn't smitten. She was suspicious.

He'd unflapped a brown metal folding chair like the one she now sat in, and with one hand opened it and spun it to face her. He sat, almost close enough so they were knee to knee. Behind him, a pitted wooden desk piled with manila folders. Framed photos—if they were photos—were turned so Nora could only see their black felt backs.

Fifteen minutes later, Rafael Monteiro—those dark eyes gauging her secrets—was apparently not satisfied. He stood, snapped his chair closed and, with a clatter, slapped it back against its two mates leaning against a scarred wall. He crossed his arms in front of his leather jacket, narrowed his eyes at her.

"Ms. Quinn? One more time. You just met Ms. Armistead Monday morning?"

Nora felt him evaluating her, judging, as if he was trying to catch her in some deception or make her feel guilty.

Because Nora-the-Pharminex-rep was not supposed to be chatting up patients in doctors' waiting rooms. Definitely forbidden. Let alone hand out business cards, even generic ones. Had they found hers in Kaitlyn's wallet? And she was definitely not allowed to encourage continued communications. Nora could not afford for Pharminex to discover this indiscretion. And as far as the accident was concerned, it was a trivial omission. It wouldn't help the police uncover what happened to Kaitlyn.

It might, her conscience taunted her. But she had to ignore it.

"Yes, Lieutenant. We'd struck up a brief conversation in a doctor's office. We . . ." She tried to decide how to explain it in a benign way. "Just a woman thing, I suppose."

"A woman thing," Monteiro said. "You had a doctor's appointment too?"

"Yes." Nora put her cup of lukewarm coffee on the floor, then picked it up again. "I was—well, she was upset with some test results and it seemed she wanted someone to talk to. Then I was called in to the doctor, and when I came out, she was gone."

"And then what?"

"Well, nothing. But the next day, she called me."

"What did she want to talk to you about, Ms. Quinn?" Behind him, a rackety heater clicked on, giving off more noise than heat. He sat on the edge of the desk, his movement toppling two photos to the desktop. "On that last phone call?"

"Like I said. She was disappointed that some

medical tests had—I mean, I don't know if it's true." She realized this as she said it. "Wouldn't it be better to ask her doctor? Or her family?" Nora nodded, agreeing with herself about privacy, but wanting to help, if she could. "It was a chance encounter in a doctor's office, you know? She was . . . on medication."

Monteiro nodded, pulled out a notebook from a jacket pocket.

"Was she happy with her medication?"

"No. She said she wasn't."

"And was she happy at home?"

"Um. . . ." Nora stalled. This felt wrong, but Kaitlyn was dead, and *something* had caused her death. Monteiro was simply trying to find out what. Doing his job. "I don't think so. She told me her husband—James?—was frustrated they couldn't have children."

"James," he said. "Yes, we've contacted him. But *you're* the one she called, right before her accident. Was she angry with you? For some reason?"

"Me? No. What would she be angry with me about?"

"Just doing my job, Ms. Quinn."

"No, she wasn't angry. I mean, we'd hardly—I didn't expect her to call me."

Monteiro leaned forward. "But you gave her your phone number, didn't you? Why do that if you didn't expect her to call? *Want* her to call? And in fact, you *were* with her, weren't you? When she crashed?"

"On the *phone*!" Nora saw the seam of the coffee cup turn brown, worried the whole thing was about to collapse into her lap, murky coffee and curdling milk. She put it on the floor again. "Lieutenant? Do you think something happened?"

"Like what?"

"Like she was so despondent and depressed, she did it on purpose?"

"Did she tell you that?" Monteiro straightened.
"You *might* have mentioned that, Ms. Quinn, prefer-
ably around moment one."

"No, no." Nora put up her hands, *stop*. "Not at
all. I'm just—thinking. But it was miserable out, the
roads were terrible, she was talking on her cell and
maybe not focused on the road. It was snowing and
she probably hit a slick spot."

"You in accident recon now, Ms. Quinn?" Lieutenant Monteiro raised a skeptical eyebrow. "Know
all about collision analysis and vehicle dynamics?
Wanna give me more of the benefit of your exper-
tise?"

Nora couldn't decide whether to be suspicious or
terrified of his change in demeanor. But she had no
reason to be defensive. Cops did that to you, part
of their tactics, she knew that. She tried to shift the
power.

"Are you trying to find the car that hit her?" she
asked.

"What do you think?"

"You said you were calling other people. Maybe
they know more than I do."

"Maybe? Know?" Monteiro again looked like he'd
caught her in a lie. He sat back down, motionless,
watching her. "More than you do about what?"

"She was sad, Lieutenant." Nora let out a sigh.
"Disappointed. And I think she and her husband
were having money problems. And—" She stopped
herself, feeling as if she'd said too much, and taking
what Kaitlyn had said at face value. "But that's only
what she said to a stranger who sat next to her in a
doctor's office. I have no idea what's true."

"And yet you were on the phone with her when
she died."

Nora nodded, not trusting her voice.

"Anything more you want to tell me?"

Nora shook her head. "I keep thinking there was something I should have done," she finally said. "I kept telling her to pull over, because I was worried. That the conditions were treacherous, but she insisted—"

"How long before you got there? Arrived at the scene of the accident?"

She looked at him.

"I know you were there." Monteiro raised an eyebrow. "And wondered why you hadn't mentioned that."

"I guess . . . because it didn't matter. Lieutenant, I'm sorry. I just keep wishing it had been sooner, soon enough to prevent it. But the traffic was stopping in front of me, and all the brake lights coming on, and—"

She closed her eyes. Remembered it. Opened her eyes so the picture would go away.

"Had you ever seen her car before?"

She shook her head.

"How did you know it was Ms. Armistead's?"

"She'd described it."

Monteiro smoothed the legs of his dark jeans.

"I'm sorry I didn't tell you I'd been at the scene," she finally said. "But I might as well have been a million miles away, for all the good it did."

Monteiro nodded. "Okay."

She sighed, weary and confused, her contacts stinging like they always did after she'd worn them too long. Poor Kaitlyn, she thought, before she could stop herself. All she'd wanted was a baby. And as if her longing wasn't heartbreaking enough, her disappointment wasn't tragic enough, as if the people she'd trusted hadn't betrayed her enough, now it had all made her a victim. A victim of her own sorrow.

Nora felt her expression change before she could stop it.

"What?" Monteiro leaned forward, one hand on each denim knee, his face intent. "What did you just think of?"

"Nothing," Nora whispered. "I was only remembering how much Kaitlyn wanted a child."

BEFORE

CHAPTER 14

BROOKE

If Brooke heard her mother's voice one more time—literally, one more time—she'd use her new super-shiny lipstick to write the nastiest things she could imagine all over the hallway walls. Maybe in the living room. Her mother would Never. Freaking. Let *up*.

She didn't yell back, or slam her bedroom door, even though she really *really* wanted to. But she shut the door quietly, closing her mother out, and then leaned against the cool white wood, her bare feet deep in the plush ice-blue carpeting.

Brooke didn't want to be a bitch about everything, so cliché, but this was even more horrible than she'd possibly imagined. She stared at her stripey pale blue wallpaper, and at her bulletin board displaying her souvenir theater tickets and beach schedule and a now-wilting daisy from Liam tucked through criss-crossed lacy French blue ribbons. Summer was supposed to be fun.

She slid the daisy from behind the ribbon. Held it with two fingers over the white wicker wastebasket. Silly to keep a dead thing. She took a deep breath, sighed it out. Tucked Liam's daisy into her ponytail.

If she handled everything right—meaning, if she could be the person her parents thought she should be—maybe it would work. She just had to get past this . . . situation.

She flopped down on her bed, staring at the ceiling. Thing was, and she could not admit this to anyone, and almost not to herself, she wanted the baby. More than anything she'd ever wanted, she wanted her. A girl, Brooke knew it. Maybe she'd name her Phoebe, or Rachel, and she'd lavish her with love and never criticize her and always trust her. And notice her and talk to her and just . . . be. With her. And the baby would totally love her, Courtney, maybe, or Olivia? And they'd be happy, like in books.

She wrinkled her nose, realizing the problem with that fantasy. Nine months' worth of problem. But it was about what was right and fair. And finally Brooke could do something that wasn't only about her. She put a hand on her tummy, wondering.

It surprised her: the idea that someone—a new little person, from her own body—could be more important than herself.

"*Brooke!*" Her mother's voice grated up at her from downstairs. "*Brooke Hadley Vanderwald!*"

And Mom was calling her by her ridiculous full name, which the minute she got out of here she would never ever *ever* use again. She'd take little Olivia or Courtney and be totally someone else with a totally new name.

"*I am serious!*"

Well, Brooke was serious too. She stood, and frowned at her full-length mirror, considering. She didn't look any different than yesterday or two days before. But she was caught like a bug in a spiderweb, and someone else's life depended on hers now, and what was she supposed to do about that?

Mom didn't know. No one knew, not even Liam, and she would never tell him. He'd go crazy, and who knows what he'd do after that? He was all about Princeton or wherever the school of the week was, and he'd dump her like a rock if she ever—oh, *crap*. Wouldn't he? She loved him so so much, she totally totally adored him, but what was she supposed to do? What if she decided wrong?

She wanted to call someone, but her friends were unreliable or worse. And summer friends, like the ones she had here . . . they weren't *real* friends. She stared at the floor, at her pink-polished toes and tanned legs. Trying to think.

She was at the shore, but just for the summer, like Liam, and they'd all go back to Annapolis in the fall, but anything was possible. But how would she look in a month? Or even in a week?

She had to plan. She yanked at her Destiny's Child T-shirt so it was looser, then rolled her eyes. Pitiful. Destiny's Child, what, was like, the universe laughing at her? It wasn't her fault, it wasn't her darling Liam's fault, there was nothing about fault, except maybe his, a little, but it had all seemed so magical and now it wasn't.

"I'm leaving now, missy!" Her mom's voice again. Brooke closed her eyes, trying trying *trying* to think.

She jammed on her flip-flops and flapped into the hall. As she leaned over the banister of their summer house, she saw the top of her mom's head, blonder than ever, down by the vase of hydrangeas someone had placed in the entryway.

"Have fun, Mom." Brooke tried to act natural, like this was just another August at the shore, like they'd all done for however long she could remember, and even back when she couldn't. The sunbaked gray house with seagrass and tended blue hydrangeas and fragrant lavender meant summer to her as much as the lightning bugs and stars and ice cream at Krazie's. She almost put a hand on her stomach again, then pretended she needed to adjust her T-shirt. "See you after? I'm just gonna read."

"That's lovely, dear." Her mom looked up, and for a moment her face seemed to soften. "But I do wish you'd come to the club with me. You could read there too, couldn't you? It won't be long now before I can't show you off."

Brooke's eyes widened. What did her mom know? But Mom was looking at herself in the front hall mirror, not at Brooke.

"You'll be off to Vassar or Yale, I know you can do it." She tucked her hair under a faded red ball cap with *BJV* monogrammed on the front. Adjusted it, so her eyes showed and a few tendrils of blond casually trailed to her shoulders. She turned and looked up again. "You're so beautiful to me, Brookie, all that gorgeous hair and your wonderful eyes," she said. "And you're still so happy."

That was her Mom look, Brooke recognized it, the somehow memory of tenderness and even happiness. Brooke used to see it all the time. And now it was heartbreaking, even, how seldom that expression appeared.

"You are too, Mom." Brooke couldn't help it. For all her mom's terribleness and griping and nudging and pushing and ridiculously shallow friends and not even caring what her dad was doing half the time, she was kind of okay. But not okay enough to talk to. Brooke had to figure out what they'd do if they knew. They'd probably ship her off somewhere, if people still did that.

"Bye, honey." Her mom, thank goodness, was headed for the front door. "There's food. And Sarah made chocolate chip cookies. Don't eat more than two. It's bad for your face."

The front door clicked closed behind her, and Brooke was alone. Standing on the balcony, on the precipice, on the edge.

And alone.

She touched her belly again. Sort of alone.

BEFORE

CHAPTER 15

LACEY

Lacey Grisham paused at the top of the curved stairway of the Tri-Delt sorority house, full now of the girls—her sorority sisters—who'd stayed here in Charlottesville for this 2004 summer semester. Lacey's future stood at the bottom, one flight down, in the front hall entryway. Trevor Vanderwald, scion of the Vanderwald family, their only son and rightful heir. Well, except for that little sister, who didn't matter. Lacey assessed her beau, making use of this private moment of unbridled scrutiny.

Reasonably smart, reasonably attentive, not an athlete but reasonably fit and more than reasonably well off. All that Vanderwald money, and all his father's companies. She planned to research every single thing they owned. Every single company she'd—someday—inherit. She almost couldn't believe her luck, or maybe it had truly been her destiny because, cross her heart, this was all she'd ever wanted. Trevor, or someone like him, and for once a comfortable worry-free life and a family. *Please, for all that is good and right, a family.*

Plus, she had to admit, he was truly into her. He'd

followed her out of psychology class the first day of
the fall semester, acting like it was all so casual. She'd
noticed his turquoise polo shirt, the perfect one, the
collar just right, and his boat shoes, just right, and
no socks. The next morning, he'd waited for her at
the classroom door, and later they'd gone for a walk
on the common, the still-green maple trees fluttering their leaves above them, their steps matching and
hands almost touching. He'd held doors for her, listened to her ideas, laughed when she made a joke. He
hadn't pushed her when she'd changed the subject
away from her own family. Hadn't bragged about his
own. But by that time, she'd done her research.

For someone who'd always gotten what he wanted,
she'd realized, Trevor Vanderwald had little patience
for something unattainable. So that's what she'd made
herself. Unattainable. Which had made him want her
all the more. She wanted him too, now. Funny how
that worked.

Trevor hadn't noticed her up here yet—he had
some new cell phone that seemed like the only thing
he might love more than he loved her. She sometimes
teased him about it, told him he'd name his first child
Nokia, which he didn't think was all that funny. But
no matter. He couldn't marry that cell phone. But he
would marry her.

Lacey was sure of it.

In a flutter of pink pashminas and flirty little skirts,
a pack of Lacey's sorority summer-sisters bustled
into the entryway, their laughter floating up toward
her, surrounding Trevor with giggles and silly teasing. One of them, Priss, snatched Trevor's sunglasses
from the placket of his shirt and put them on top of
her head, posing and primping. He flipped out one
hand, palm up, demanding that she give them back.

Priss, honey, Lacey thought. Give *up*. Some sister

she was. One of them opened the front door, letting in the summer afternoon, and the group—including the insipid Priss, who tossed the sunglasses back to Trev—chattered off to wherever they all were going.

They'd all come from some planning meeting in the living room, Lacey knew, but she'd left that triviality behind her: the pledging, the hazing, the obligatory bags of candy, the bestowing of initiation nicknames that had christened her Lacey, all the nonsensical demands of sorority life. She'd been devoted to it at first, especially since she'd never had real sisters, but she was a woman now and had set her sights higher. Into the future, a future she'd imagined since she was a child in Montgomery, dressing Barbie in bridal gowns, then taping cotton balls onto Barbie's tummy to make her look pregnant.

After that she'd had a baby doll too, a boy, with ice-blue eyes, eyes that really opened, and a perfect little mouth. She'd practiced with her precious baby, swaddled him, sang to him. Loved him. Soon that all would be real.

With a deep breath and a wish on an invisible star, Lacey trotted down the carpeted stairway, head high. She felt her newly curled hair bouncing on her shoulders, and the flip of her own flirty skirt, not quite too short, against her bare legs. Her sisters had worked so hard to tan over the summer, but Lacey kept her face pale, unable to forget her mother's admonitions about wrinkles and spots. Her debut at the Vanderwalds' was set for Labor Day weekend, according to Trevor, at the family's annual goodbye-to-summer picnic. Her empty suitcase had been on the vacant twin bed in her room since July, reminding her it needed to be filled with clothes for her future.

From this summer on, that's where she'd be, with

Trevor. And soon, very soon, as Lacey Vanderwald—what a perfectly perfect name—with Maryland in the winter and the islands in the summer, with beach parties and butterfly floaties and the fragrance of sunscreen and rum, and helping her daughters be just like her, happy and pretty and like those F. Scott Fitzgerald heroines she wasn't supposed to admire but somehow still did. Other girls could go off and have jobs and careers, and she wished them all happiness, following their dreams. But what was wrong with wanting pretty things and a family? Family kept you safe and happy and secure. Mama had taught her that, because no one else was at home left to say it, and besides, she knew it in her *soul* that—well, what was a woman without a family?

She patted her flat stomach, knowing that soon, so soon, she'd be like cotton-ball Barbie and her future would be secure. Like Trev, she was class of 2005, but maybe that degree in psychology wasn't necessary. One day at a time.

"Lacey Vanderwald," she whispered to herself, just to practice. She'd never say that out loud, not yet, it was too soon. "Mrs. Winton Trevor Vanderwald. And their beloved son, Trevor the fourth."

Trevor had put his sunglasses back in place, dangling from the collar of his shirt, and was fiddling with his phone again. He glanced up at her finally, smiling, signaling hello. To Trevor, she supposed, this might only be a moment in time, a summery fling, a weekend. And she was well aware other girls had gone with him to see his parents, even other Tri-Delts, gone and come back disappointed. But Lacey had no fear of failure.

"Hey, Trevor," she said as she reached the bottom of the stairs. It came out *Trevah,* and she knew he thought it was adorable. The August sunshine sent golden light through the still-open front door, and when he looked up, appraising her, he couldn't keep the admiration from his face. And the lust. Precisely what she'd hoped for.

"Sorry to keep you waiting." She tilted her head, teasing. "Calling anyone in particular?"

"Nah, just stuff." He stashed his phone, thank goodness, and looked her up and down. She'd have been annoyed if it were anyone else, but she loved his eyes on her. "Hey, babe. What took you so long?"

She tucked her arm through the crook of his elbow and settled herself against him, close enough that he could smell the honey gardenia fragrance she'd misted through her hair, close enough that she could smell the beer already on his breath. And not even three o'clock. But that was not for her to criticize. She would never disparage this linchpin of her future. Mama had done that to Daddy, she nagged him to certain death, and look what happened. She'd married again, for whatever *that* loser was worth.

Lacey knew better. She had not let Trevor touch her down there, no matter how he tried to convince her, and once he got angry, and once he got her *so* ridiculously drunk, but it didn't work. She had big big plans, and this was her power. *Sex*. That word, harsh as it was, that was her power. The others, her sisters, that's not how they dealt with men, but Trevor wasn't just anyone. He was the one. In so many ways, she had saved herself for him. She felt like a beautiful spider, spinning a gossamer but inescapable web around her prey. It was so intoxicating she had to stop herself from smiling. She touched wood at the front door to make sure.

"Trev?" she asked as they left the house and walked down the geranium-lined front walkway. A yellow convertible squealed around the corner, top down, its radio blaring "Soak Up the Sun" and the back seat overflowing with students singing along. "Do you think your parents will like me? It matters so much that they do."

"I know they will, Lace," he said. "You're perfect."

Lacey almost burst out laughing.

BEFORE

CHAPTER 16

BROOKE

"Really? Peanut butter?"

Her mom's voice came through the kitchen door, all judgey before Brooke could even see her.

"That's what you're eating, Brooke?" Her mom went on as she strode in from the backyard, the screen door clacking shut behind her, her arms full of pink and lavender hydrangeas. "And I can't believe you're up this early."

Brooke closed her eyes in a brief instant of reluctant inevitability, then looked up from her spot at the island in the center of their kitchen, a sleek spackled marble monster with copper pots dangling overhead from cast-iron hooks. Like the sword of Damocles in the story. Metaphor, she thought. This is what they meant: dangerous stuff hanging over you. And now Mom was being critical?

"Protein, okay?" Brooke answered, trying to be polite about the peanut butter. She knew her mom meant well and was probably just surprised since Brooke hadn't eaten PB since she was a little kid. But it had sounded so good this morning. Her stomach demanded it, needed it, and she had to eat it. She was, like, always starving. And she had to decide what to do. She took another bite of it slathered on a thick slice of whole wheat, savoring the gooey smoothness on her teeth and tongue, the comforting sweetness as she swallowed it.

"It's fine, honey." Her mom dumped the flowers on the counter by the sink, took a green glass vase from a cabinet, and turned on the tap in the kitchen sink. "Whatever you want."

She looked at Brooke over her shoulder as the vase filled with water. "You okay, sweetie?"

She stashed the flowers into the vase, but instead of arranging them like she always did, she pulled a raffia stool up to the island, its cast-iron legs grating on the terra-cotta floor. She put her elbows on the marble and leaned toward Brooke. Her tanned shoulders were bare under the ties of her navy eyelet sundress, and tortoiseshell sunglasses held her streaky blond hair back from her face. She narrowed her eyes, inquiring.

"Brookie?"

Brooke swallowed and shifted her weight, unsticking her thighs from the woven seat. "Sure. I'm fine. How come?" she asked, truly curious. "Aren't you?"

Something might be up. Seriously up. Brooke had heard her parents arguing last night, and she'd even sneaked out of her bedroom and tiptoed to the balcony edge, straining to untangle the jumbled voices coming from the family room below.

But all she could hear was a murmury rumble, her dad's voice lower pitched and her mom's higher. Incredibly frustrating. They were fighting again, though, that was for sure, and Brooke wished she knew what it was about. Not her big brother, of course, since he was perfect and older and never did anything wrong. And he wasn't even arriving until next week with the girlfriend du jour, not that Brooke cared.

But recently her parents had been arguing more and more, and Brooke couldn't figure it out. It wasn't like they were drinking or anything, she would have noticed that. At least not more than the usual summer country club G-and-Ts, not like her friends' parents, *so* ridiculous. Could it be about money? There was plenty of money.

So didn't it *have* to be about her? Or maybe that was paranoid. The whole world wasn't about her. Just ask Liam, who now was ignoring her like crazy, the jerk. The creep. Loser. Brooke was better off without him. She really was.

She hadn't planned to tell him. That had been her first decision. But then the sand was warm, and she'd skooched it between her toes as she'd flapped out the blue-and-white-striped beach towel. The swish of the waves was always so peaceful, and the seagulls had squawked overhead, swooping and diving and floating above them all. And Liam had come up to her, as they'd planned, as they always did—*always* meaning this summer—in that faded red bathing suit with the dumb pockets, and a white towel around his neck, and that smile.

"Hey, Boo," he'd said. "Why're you covering up that killer bod?"

"Jerk," she teased. "Killer *bod*? What, are you, like, in an old movie?"

"Truth," he said. "And it's mine all mine."

"Good luck with *that,* loser." She stuck out her tongue as she said it, secretly pleased to feel so possessed. But freaked at the same time. Still, she had to stay normal, she did, as long as she could. Whatever normal was. Or would turn out to be. "I can wear whatever I want, right?"

"Do my back?" He'd flopped down on the towel, not answering her question. "With fifty?"

Everyone else was in the water, but Brooke was still on shore, wearing a big T-shirt, the one her parents had given her brother when he got into college. It wasn't cool to wear your own school's T-shirt, everyone but her parents knew that, so Trevor had given it to her. She felt safe in it now, safe in how big it was. She missed Trev so much. Sometimes it seemed, even though he was four years older, her brother was the only one who cared about her. She wished she could ask him about Liam, about what to do. Trev was a guy, and he knew stuff, and even when he teased her, or called her Smidge like he knew she hated, she still trusted him.

But now, Liam. He'd asked her to do his back with fifty, because he knew she knew that meant SPF 50 sunscreen, like he knew she *had* that, like they were totally together. And they were, she guessed, even more than he knew.

She sighed, her knees on the terry towel, leaning over him, feeling the warmth of his skin, the muscles of his shoulders, the rise and fall of his chest under her lotioned hands. His face was turned toward her, resting on the back of one hand, his eyes closed, eyelashes impossibly long against his tanned cheek. He'd bleached out his hair for the summer, all the cool guys had, and it was silvery-pink-blond like the inside of a clamshell. How could someone so gorgeous, so perfect, so smart and cool, how could he love *her*? But he'd said he did, he'd told her so, and she had to believe it, wanted to believe it.

"Nice," he muttered, and the seagulls swooped so low she could almost see their expressions. August at the beach, and this day stretching out in front of them, and then the week, then the summer and then life.

Could she be with him forever? She was only fifteen,

but almost sixteen, like he was, and she wanted happiness, she could envision it, but what did happiness mean? To her, it meant *Liam*. She even loved his name. Liam. Liam Endicott. And maybe he'd be happy too?

"Lee?" she said into his back.

"Mmm?"

"Seriously, Lee?"

He turned his head the other way, looking in her direction now. Opened one eye. "Seriously, Lee, what-ly?"

"Brooke? Where'd you go?" Her mom's voice brought her back to the kitchen. To now. Forty-nine hours later, and nothing from him, freaking *nothing*, and she refused to call him. He used to call her, like, every day. Twice even, sometimes. But now, he'd completely blown her off. Her eyes hurt from crying, like there were no more tears inside her.

"Whoa, spaced out, I guess." Brooke tried to laugh it off. "Peanut butter carb high, maybe." She took another bite. What was Liam doing right now? Thinking of her? Could he avoid her for the whole rest of the summer?

"Brooke. I'm talking to you, sweetheart." Her mom had made coffee and now fiddled with her white ceramic coffee mug, shifting the handle from one side to the other and back.

The swishy grating of mug on marble was making Brooke's teeth hurt. And she could smell the coffee, like the earth, acid and brown. The skin behind her ears was getting all tight, and it was like her eyes were buzzing. She looked over her mom's bare shoulder into their backyard, where the high seagrass rustled in the morning breeze, and a squawking seagull landed, with a *caw* and a rattle, behind their slatted wooden fence. Birds were bad luck.

"Brooke. Look at me." Her mother bit her lower lip, white teeth on coral lipstick. "I asked if you were okay. You look tired. Your eyes look tired."

Her mom was freaking her out again, all interest and concern. This was not how she usually acted.

"No, I'm fine, honestly," Brooke said, and then figured she should make some excuse for all of it. Make it kind of true. "My stomach is a little weird, I guess." She gestured with her PB. "Thought carbs and protein might help."

Her mom narrowed her eyes again, gave her a look, like when she knew Brooke was lying.

"Really? There's nothing else?"

"Really, Mom, whatever." Brooke ate the last of her sandwich, thought about having another one. Thought about, like, cheese. Maybe a hamburger. Or maybe that would be gross. She couldn't decide. "Aren't you going to the club?"

"I love you, honey," her mom said. "You know that."

"Love you too," she replied, though she wasn't really thinking about it. It was what they always said, ever since she could remember. Like a ritual, a thing you say. A thing *she'd* said. And Liam had too. She kept remembering that. *I love you more than the sky,* he'd said. *More than the wind. More than the stars and constellations.* She remembered, again, that June night at the beach, after the thing at the club. Maybe *I love you* never counted. People just said it, said it to get what they wanted, and then it didn't matter.

Her mother swiveled off the chair. *Cool.* Maybe she hadn't noticed. When her mom's back was turned, Brooke brushed away her tears, so ridiculous, and picked up her plate to take to the sink. Mom would leave any minute now, and Brooke could go figure stuff out.

"Here's something for your tummy." Her mom had opened her tote bag, dug around inside, then taken something out. Now she held out a flat palm, a white pill centered in the middle. "Maybe this'll help."

"What is it?" Brooke left the pill in her mother's hand. "You're always giving me stuff. Is it like a Tums?"

"Kind of," her mom said. "I know how you feel, sweetheart. That queasiness. It happens sometimes. That's what medicine is for. Just take this."

Brooke accepted the pill, examined it between her thumb and forefinger. Smelled it. It had no writing on it, a plain smooth disk.

"It's not a Tums," Brooke said.

"Brookie? I just want you to feel better, honey," her mom said. "Lucky we have these things to help us. If we lived in the old days, you'd have to—"

"O-*kay*." Brooke had to interrupt, or she'd have to kill herself. When her mom went off on her *miracle of modern medicine* speeches, she'd never let it go. Listening to her was giving Brooke even more of a stomachache. "Yeesh."

"Good." Mom handed her the rest of her water with a *drink it* expression. "One gulp. It'll help. I promise."

CHAPTER 17

ELLIE

Ellie stared at the console of the landline on her desk at Channel 11, gazing at the speaker mesh as if she could see through its layer of tiny holes and to the face beyond.

"Can you hear me?" she asked.

Her uneaten lunch sat on a crinkly piece of waxed paper on her blotter. The guy downstairs in the newsroom caf had given her a tuna sandwich instead of the turkey she'd ordered. She hated tuna. On the other end of this call, in an apartment somewhere in Massachusetts, Meg sat with the woman who was about to reveal her devastating medical outcome. In the hideous equation of journalism, this woman's tragedy could seal Ellie's success.

"We can hear you." Meg's voice, scratchy and muffled, came over the speaker. "I'm here with Abigail, as we discussed, and she's fine. You're fine, aren't you, Abigail?"

Someone said something in the background, and though Ellie strained to hear, she couldn't. She stood, closed the door to her office, sat back down. An anonymous interview was not the preferred way to get a story, but at this point, she'd take what she could get. And if it didn't pan out, so what? One step at a time, until the story was ready.

After Ellie found the note on her door the night before, she'd been forced to admit that Meg might be an asset. Being annoying didn't mean she was incompetent, and Ellie could not pull off this story alone. She'd knocked on Meg's door—and Meg had slipped out into the hallway, clicking the door closed behind her.

"My place is a mess," Meg had explained. She pushed up the sleeves of her pink sweatshirt, worn inside out over fraying jeans. "Everything's still in boxes. So embarrassing. I guess you got my note?"

"Great work," Ellie told her. She wasn't eager to invite Meg into her place again, didn't want to set a precedent. So the two women stayed in the hall, the elevator rumbling from time to time, and fake candles in sconces flickering on the walls behind them. "Listen, how'd you find this person? And you think she'll talk?"

Meg nodded. "I do. She's . . ." She scratched under her chin, seemed to be searching for a word. "I don't know how to describe it. Damaged. She's decided her life was ruined by this medicine. By Pharminex. When I told her what you said, about the company calculating how much a human life is worth, she about lost it. I almost regret that she knows it. As if her psyche wasn't damaged enough—not to mention her future—now she feels like it was on purpose. Premeditated. That they knew what might happen and didn't do anything about it. She's really out to get them."

"I completely understand." Ellie thought about that. "Well, I can imagine, I mean, how that might feel."

"Maybe."

Ellie wondered what she meant by that skeptical-sounding *maybe*, but it didn't matter. "How'd you find her?"

"Don't tell, okay? Social media private group. I pretended I was a victim too."

"Pretended?"

"Well, I had to. I couldn't say—*hey, just curious, anyone get their childbearing capability ruined by a dangerous drug? Wanna chat?* So I looked up an infertility support group, and, you know, told them I'd been given—well, the whole thing. And they let me in."

Ellie leaned back against the wallpaper, a strip of mahogany-painted molding pressing into her back. She hadn't lost her moral compass, even though she sometimes ignored it. Pretending to be a victim? Another in the sometimes necessary deceptions of the job. It always seemed like particularly bad karma, pretending to share a tragedy, faking empathy and a shared devastation. Almost like daring it to happen in real life. But, said the journalist's trusty rationalization for deceit, it was all for the greater good.

"Meg? You only learned about this project this week, and you already convinced a person to talk to a reporter? Usually that kind of negotiating and persuasion takes much longer."

Meg smiled, modest. "What can I say? Just doing my job. Sometimes things work."

"We'll have to figure out how to broach this with Warren, though," Ellie had told her. "He specifically instructed us, no pretending. So we need to come up with an acceptable explanation of how you found her."

"You and me, sister," Meg had said. "We're in this together now."

That late-night partnership agreement hadn't made Ellie exactly comfortable, but simply interviewing someone didn't mean she'd have to put the results on the air.

Now Abigail was ready to talk. Meg had said she'd set up a second cell phone, mounted on a little tripod, to record their interview. As they'd discussed, she'd position Abigail in front of a window, so their subject appeared only in silhouette.

"Ready?" Ellie asked.

By the time the interview was over, Ellie sat at her desk, spent and hollow, head in her hands, cheeks wet with tears. Television was about storytelling, information, changing the world. But hearing a personal story like Abigail's—the sorrow in her voice, and the unfiltered longing—reminded Ellie that each of her stories were about real human beings, with tender hopes and fears and desires, with bitter disappointments and unfulfilled dreams. And sometimes, with the festering damage that accrued from loss. The pain that could sharpen into a weapon.

"I hate those people." Abigail's voice had hardened after relating her pivotal consultation in the doctor's office, the moment her doctor had divulged the truth about her "adverse reaction" to the drug, the reality it meant, the emotional paralysis that followed. "I felt betrayed," Abigail said. "They'd promised me a child, a miracle, my future, my happiness. Now when I even *see* a child . . ."

Abigail had stopped, leaving silence in the space between them. Then Ellie heard soft sobs through the speakers. She imagined Meg comforting the woman. Wondered if she'd turned off the recording while she did so.

"I'm so sorry." Ellie felt guilty, guilty she had lured the woman into this agony of memory. "I know it's difficult. Do you want to take a break?"

"No, no, I want to say this. I want to. They—he—they—it made me feel as if . . ." Abigail went silent, leaving only the brown hum of the transmission. "As if I had killed my children. As if they had tricked me into murdering my own children."

"Oh, no, Abigail." She needed to reassure this woman, though that wasn't her role, but how could anyone not be sympathetic? "Please don't think that!"

"It *is* what she thinks." Meg's voice bit through the speakers. "Don't belittle that."

"I was only trying to . . ." Ellie, off balance, tried to maintain her composure. She needed to prevent Abigail from hanging up. "Forgive me, Abigail."

"It's okay." Abigail's voice came out a whisper.

"Hold on a minute," Meg said. "I'm gonna turn off the video. I'll leave the sound so you can stay connected."

For this moment at least, Ellie was relieved they weren't face-to-face. The smell of the tuna sandwich now turned her stomach. With three quick motions, she rewrapped it in the waxed paper, put it in the wastebasket and stuffed the morning newspaper on top of it. On the other end of the line, Ellie heard someone sneeze, then footsteps, a hiss, maybe the pull tab of a can of soda.

"Ellie? We're back. Abigail's fine."

"You sure?" Ellie had to ask.

More unintelligible conversation on the other end. Ellie covered her face for a beat, frustrated. But an interview like this was only one step on the journey. It was only what it would turn out to be, not what it seemed right now.

"Abigail wants to ask *you* something." Meg's voice came though clearly. "She wants to know if you've ever had children."

Ellie flinched, startled by the personal question. Realizing the irony, she almost laughed. This conversation was already as personal as it could get. Easier to be the one asking questions than the one answering. The double standard of journalism.

"Um, no, no kids," Ellie said.

"Any siblings? And any who had kids?" Meg went on, seemed to be forwarding Abigail's questions.

"Well, no, in fact." Why'd she want to know this? But maybe Abigail was testing whether Ellie could give as good as she took. Ellie wondered if she offered something deeply personal, it would reassure Abigail that her motives were pure. An emotional exchange. An agreement to be honest. "I'm not close with my family."

"Oh my gosh, since when?" Meg's voice had changed, the pitch now higher, no longer the neutral interviewer.

Ellie frowned, changed her tone to shut Meg down. It wasn't Meg she was trying to win over. "Some years ago," she said. She usually tried to avoid going to that empty black spot in the universe.

"So, unless you have a child, your immediate family dies out?" Meg asked. "Abigail is asking."

Abigail is kind of a crazy person, Ellie thought. "I suppose," she said out loud.

"Your parents are still alive? She wants to know."

You've gone too far, Abigail, Ellie thought. "They are. So now—"

"And it would make them happy, Abigail's saying, if you had a child? Since there's still time for you, Ellie, right?"

And we're done here. Ellie's sympathy—honest sympathy—had curdled into wary irritation. "I suppose," she said. "So Meg, is Abigail ready? Are we okay to continue the interview?" She tried to paper over the transition. "I know this must be difficult for you."

Silence on the other end.

"Are we still connected?" Ellie half regretted her brusque response and hoped she hadn't blown it. "Everything okay?"

She heard someone clear her throat. Then more murmurs.

"Okay," Meg said. "Just checking the recording. I'm flipping on my video again. Okay. Go ahead."

"Here's a different kind of question." Ellie was relieved they were back on topic. "How do you deal, now, with what happened?"

It was a key part of the story, the physical—and psychological—backlash from such a devastating loss. A loss not only of a child, but of trust.

After a few beats of silence, Meg answered. "Abigail says she's done talking. She told you what happened. That's all you need to know."

"It's just that—"

But all she heard was a dial tone.

CHAPTER 18

NORA

Nora couldn't decide which tactic was more ominous: that she'd been yanked off her afternoon appointments, or that Allessandra Lewes and Detta Fiddler had not offered her the elegant visitor's chair that now sat conspicuously empty in front of the Pharminex executive's desk. Today Fiddler's opulently pristine office smelled of gardenias. A pale green ceramic container held a lavish arrangement of the waxy white flower, each delicate bloom nestled among glossy green leaves. Gorgeous but aggressive, the fragrance replaced all the oxygen in the room.

"Ms. Quinn." Allessandra spoke first, her voice settling over Nora like a late spring frost. "I call you Ms. Quinn merely because it's the only name we have for you. At this point."

Nora noted the hesitation, the fidget of a careful eyebrow.

"Care to enlighten us?" Lewes asked. "On who you are?"

"I'm sorry." Nora crossed her arms over her chest, lifted her chin. Almost apologetic. "What're you saying?"

Lewes and Fiddler exchanged glances. Fiddler pursed her lips, appraising. Cocked her head at her subordinate. *Go on.*

"Your résumé, Ms. Quinn." Lewes perched on the edge of Fiddler's desk and mirrored Nora, crossing her arms over her moss-green leather jacket, then smiled oh-so-cordially. "It's a load of crap."

"There is no Nora Quinn, as you are well aware." Dettalinda Fiddler stood, her voice smoldering fire to Lewes's ice. "No thirty-three-year-old Nora Quinn from Charleston, South Carolina, with a BA in Economics from USC, two deceased parents and the valedictorian of her high school class. No Nora Quinn with the previous addresses you so helpfully provided, or the previous employers you listed—companies which had conveniently gone out of business—and no Nora Quinn with that social security number you used."

Nora listened with her best poker face, waiting for Fiddler's ire to diminish.

"So what shall we do with you, whoever you are?" Fiddler touched a manicured forefinger to her lips, glossy deep red. Nora knew the woman was only pretending to consider her next steps. Nora would have to stay nimble.

"And do tell us the purpose for this deception," Fiddler went on. "Corporate spying? Are you with the feds? Are you a reporter? Are you wired even now? Why?"

Nora heard a buzz, and Lewes pulled a cell phone from her jacket pocket. Looked at the screen. Slid the cell back in.

"You should know, *Ms. Quinn,*" Fiddler said, acknowledging the pretense, "that we have security officers outside this office door. And they are prepared, at our direction, to escort you to the authorities."

"What authorities?" Their strategies to make her feel awkward were working, though Nora would never show it. They were pros, but she was too. And they could never uncover her motives—only she knew what they were. She lowered her shoulders, found her center.

Lewes ignored her question. "Several more things we need to discuss, *Nora*. One, we have your fingerprints from your job application. And we ran them against a government database."

Nora didn't answer but mentally raised an eyebrow. The AFIS database was not open to the public. Was this a bluff?

"There were no matches, sadly, Nora," Lewes went on. "But we're still looking. I was disappointed that you didn't have TSA Global Entry. That would have made our lives so much easier."

"Why would my fingerprints be on file?" Nora pushed them, couldn't hurt. "I've never committed a crime. Never been in the armed forces or worked for the government, let alone as some kind of spy. As you could see from my résumé."

Dettalinda Fiddler's laugh reached the ceiling, surprisingly lilting from such a formidable source. "We can see *nothing* from your résumé, Nora. And I'm sure spies, governmental, corporate or otherwise, would hardly indicate that on their curriculum vitae. But suffice it to say we will continue to check every word of your submissions. As will the authorities, if we give them the green light. And your prints will remain on file. Eventually they will prove who you are. And why you attempted to mislead us."

"I'll resign," Nora said. Maybe capitulation without explanation would succeed. "I've done nothing but properly carry out the job I was hired to do. My performance is stellar, my record is unblemished."

The laugh again. But Nora continued, "I've met my sales goals every day. And more. I've never divulged a word of what was taught in class or what I've learned on the job. What does it matter what my name is? I'll resign, I'll vanish—"

"As I'm sure you're adept at doing," Lewes cut in.

"And we can put all this behind us. You'll never hear from Nora Quinn again."

"You think we'll agree to that?" Detta Fiddler leaned back in her chair and crossed her legs, resting her head against the brocade upholstery.

"I do," Nora said. She had to decide on tactics. Should she try to intimidate them? "And I have to think the public would be skeptical of your quality control procedures if you can't even quality control the hiring of your own employees. Embarrassing, no?"

"An oversight. We can tolerate a bad apple," Lewes said.

"Perhaps. But the company doesn't need negative headlines right now, correct? Especially with Winton Vanderwald about to be lauded as good guy of the century."

"Oh, please." Lewes rolled her eyes. "Mr. Vanderwald is completely—"

Detta picked up the phone on her desk.

"But I've done nothing wrong, Allessandra." Nora kept talking. "And Detta? I've been a model employee. You fire me, with any attendant hoopla, and the 'load of crap'—as you say, Allessandra—will hit the fan. Right before the Vanderwald gala."

Detta put down the phone and opened a manila folder on her desk. "Ms. Quinn? Are you familiar with Dr. Douglas Hawkins?"

"You know I am," Nora said.

"In our training sessions you must have heard the

company's absolute prohibition against personal relationships with our clients?"

Nora gestured, acquiescing. Stalling. It would be Hawkins's word against hers, she calculated. If he'd ratted her out, he'd ratted out himself as well, so she had to wonder what deal he'd made with these two to keep his part of the situation confidential. To keep his wife from getting wind of his infidelity. Not that they'd done anything physical. Not intimately physical. "And your point is?"

"You said you'd done nothing, yet you attempted to seduce Dr. Hawkins. Why? To sell more product? To increase your bonuses? It's a matter of supreme indifference to me. All that matters is that you did it. So now, Nora, what do you propose we do?"

"It was *his* idea to go to dinner, not mine. And I did not step over any line. I was professional each and every second. He's simply trying to protect himself from the wrath of his wife. And—"

Fiddler's laugh was even more derisive, and Lewes's mirth accompanied it.

"What?" Nora, frowning now, couldn't decode their reactions.

"There is no wife," Fiddler said. "But Dr. Hawkins? He's also in our . . . employ. In a general sense. Without compensation, of course. We've asked him to test our newbies. See how far they'll go. And he's happy to do so."

"Test?"

Fiddler leaned toward Nora, almost smirking. "Think about where you talked to him—was it in an exam room? No, indeed, it was in a private office. Where no patient ever goes." She shook her head, pretend-disappointed. "That conversation's on tape, my dear."

"You can't do that!" Nora couldn't hold back her

yelped protest. She knew it was illegal in Massachusetts to secretly tape someone's voice.

"You planning to take us to court over it?" Fiddler asked. "Call the police?"

"Do what you will, Nora. But Dr. Hawkins was bait." Lewes stood, pulled out her cell phone again. "And you, Nora, or whoever you are, you took it."

CHAPTER 19

ELLIE

"Hey, Ellie. Perfect timing."

Ellie, coat half unbuttoned, stood in the open door-way of her office, carrying a risky late-afternoon latte, trying to comprehend how she could be seeing what she was seeing: Meg with a phone receiver in her hand, the cord attached to the landline on Ellie's desk. Meg was using her phone? The woman had her hand clamped over the mouthpiece, as if she didn't want the person on the other end to hear.

"Perfect timing for what?" Ellie stepped into her office, reaching out her hand for the phone. "Is that for me?"

Meg made an embarrassed face, kept her hand over the mouthpiece and her voice low. "I'm so sorry, El, I—well, I came in to talk with you, and your phone was ringing, and I don't know, secretarial reflex or whatever, I picked it up. When I realized what I'd done, it was too late. So I said I was your assistant, and could I take a message. And he said—"

"He?"

"Yes, it's . . ." Meg raised her eyes to the ceiling as if trying to remember. "Gabe? From . . ." She grimaced, apologetic. "Some law office, I think. I couldn't really understand the name."

Gabe. As they'd left Spinnaker, he'd said he'd contact her when he had information. Ellie didn't trust him, of course, but that didn't mean she wouldn't listen to him. Ellie reached for the phone again, but Meg held it just out of reach.

"Want me to take his number?" Meg whispered. "It's never good when a lawyer calls. Is something wrong?" She didn't wait for Ellie to answer. "Besides, I can't wait to hash over our Abigail interview. Wasn't it amazing? I thought about it all night—but I didn't want to bother you."

Ellie put down her latte as she took the last two steps toward the phone, almost grabbing the receiver. "It's fine. Could you close the door on your way out?"

"Oh, El, I'm so sorry."

"It's *fine*." Ellie smiled forgiveness, trying to look convincing. She pointed to the phone. "He's waiting, right?"

After the door clicked closed, Ellie put the phone to her ear. "Gabe," she said. "Hey. Some confusion on this end, sorry. What's up?"

Ellie listened, her heart beating faster with every word.

"Nora Quinn?" she repeated. She checked that the door was completely closed and mentally crossed her fingers that Meg wasn't lurking on the other side with her ear plastered against it. She punched the phone to speaker, unbuttoning her coat as she talked. "Who's Nora Quinn?"

"A newish recruit at Pharminex. The most recent class. Have you seen her on your rounds? You must have. I've seen *you* in the same places, you know. She's a knockout redhead, the whole package."

Ellie was glad he couldn't see her expression.

"My take on Ms. Quinn is that she's a potential candidate to blow the whistle on the company," Gabe went on. "Here's why. I think her family has connections to Pharminex. To the Vanderwalds themselves."

"Connections?"

"I think she's related to them."

"That's why she works there?"

"The opposite. I think—just a theory—she's scheming to rat them out. Reveal what the company's doing. How it's harming women. Same as we're doing."

"Why would you think that?"

"Have you ever met her?"

"Have you?"

"Yup," Gabe said.

"Talked to her?"

"Yup. And I think I might be right. She's got ulterior motives. She's not what she seems to be."

Ellie lowered herself into her desk chair. Gabe thought this pharma rep was a Vanderwald with ulterior motives. Ellie shrugged her coat off her left shoulder, switched the phone to the other hand, shrugged off the right, draped the coat over the back of her chair.

Ellie knew, like everyone else who knew about the pharmaceutical business did, that Brinn and her soon-to-be-lauded husband Winton Vanderwald had a daughter.

"You don't think Nora Quinn is *Brooke* Vanderwald, do you? The daughter?" Brooke Hadley Vanderwald, who'd be thirtysomething now, had disappeared from news coverage years ago. Ellie had googled her relentlessly, but no matter what she tried, no recent information about Brooke ever showed up on a search. Some sites theorized she was hiding, others thought she might be dead. Might Gabe suspect she had created a new identity as a pharma rep? Nora Quinn?

"And you think she's back in the family fold? It might be cool to find her. I guess," Ellie went on. "She was in that sailing accident that killed her brother, right? Do you know if she fully recovered? She was in rehab, according to the internet. Then, like, nothing. The internet kind of wondered if she was dead."

"You think my Nora Quinn is *Brooke*?" Gabe sounded skeptical. "Huh. That'd be interesting. Think it's possible?"

"I told you. The internet thinks she might be dead."

"Right, yeah. But it was only the brother who died. Five years ago. Maybe more?"

"You were saying," Ellie said. "This pharma rep. Whoever she is or isn't—is doing what?"

More silence.

"Gabe?"

"Trying to bring down the family," Gabe said. "My theory, and who knows why, but my money's on money, is that Nora's using her insider status in the company sales force to seek out patients, women who have been harmed by their drugs. By the Pharminex drugs. And then use that knowledge to ruin the company. Or possibly blackmail it."

Ellie had no answer to that. Her mind was going too fast, a computer about to overload.

"I wonder if you've seen her." Gabe didn't wait for her response. "In doctors' offices. You'd notice her, I bet, always in black or dark colors, but wearing clothing my mother would have disapproved of." He laughed. "Looks fine to me, I gotta say."

"Nora—"

"Quinn. Yup. It's the red hair you'd see first. Which, I must say, based on my years as an investigator—"

"Her hair?"

"I'd say it's dyed. *Have* you seen her?"

"Maybe." Ellie, thinking, drew out the word.

"She has kind of a Southern accent," Gabe went on. "Also one hundred percent phony, if you ask me. Hang on," he said. "Two seconds."

Ellie held the phone to her ear but heard only white noise. How had Gabe latched on to pharma salesperson Nora Quinn and what she might—or might not—be doing? She stared at her closed office door, thinking.

Women's lives were at stake, and she had taken on the task to stop that. Stop Pharminex from pushing its deadly poisons on unsuspecting women. It was horrifying and high-stakes, and Ellie would do whatever was necessary to end it. Apparently Gabe and his law firm had embraced the same quest. Ellie had to make this work.

"I'm back. Ellie. We should talk in person." Gabe's voice had softened. "Compare notes. About Nora. Maybe over a glass of wine?"

"I'm at work."

"I meant later. There are things we shouldn't discuss over the phone."

"Like what?" Ellie's cell phone pinged with a text, then another. Meg, wondering whether Ellie wanted a cookie. Warren, who wanted them both in his office. She almost threw her cell against the wall. "I just got a text. My boss wants to see me. I have to go. But you have to tell me. Like, quickly. What can't we discuss on the phone?"

"It's possible Nora might have—wait. Do you know the name Kaitlyn Armistead?"

Ellie covered her face with her hand and closed her eyes for a second, listening to Gabe's voice through the speaker. She *had* to get out of here. But no, Ellie did not know a Kaitlyn Armistead.

She cleared her throat. "Why?"

"She was a patient of Dr. Randall McGinty's—you

must have heard of him, big Monifan advocate. Anyway. Kaitlyn Armistead was killed in a car accident right after leaving his office the other day. It's in the police report."

"That's so sad."

"It is. But we'd been wondering if Monifan might lead to suicidal thoughts or actions. So after the crash, I put doctor and patient together, and theorized Kaitlyn might have been a victim of that lethal side effect. Which, from our perspective—I know, lawyers, disgusting scum—might mean a potential lucrative settlement for her estate. Not to mention for the lawsuits we're researching."

"She killed herself? Because of the drug? Huh. I read that, in the Pharminex FDA submissions. They're fighting about whether to put it on the label. *Jerks*." Ellie realized, tragic as it was, if Kaitlyn Armistead was a victim of her medication, that could be a key part of Ellie's investigation. It could provide evidence that Monifan was dangerous, and that Pharminex had known that fact and sold it anyway. Her mind accelerated, planning. "I see what you mean. I know it's horrible, and I guess reporters are scum too. That's precisely what I'm looking for, too, and—"

"Maybe," Gabe interrupted her. "But here's the thing. My sources are saying the police aren't sure her death was an accident."

"Not an accident?"

"Listen. They know from the staff at Dr. McGinty's office that Kaitlyn and Nora Quinn sat together, and were talking the morning Kaitlyn died. Apparently, they knew each other. And, or so I'm told, Kaitlyn was upset. Crying. There's clearly way more to Nora Quinn than we know."

Ellie sat at her battered wooden desk in her tiny makeshift office, the one she'd been assigned only a few weeks ago when she'd been buoyed by determination and infinite drive to change the world, and wondered if that world was about to fall apart. She thought, as quickly as thoughts can pass through a human consciousness, of how long she'd worked on this investigation, and how much it meant to her.

"So you think—" Ellie began.

"It's not what *I* think, Ellie. It's what the police think."

"That Nora Quinn . . ." She had to say it. "That this pharma rep—or whatever Vanderwald relative she is—*caused* Kaitlyn to crash her car, and now she's going to blame it on the medicine? And Pharminex? To ruin them?"

Silence on the other end of the line.

"That would be . . ." Ellie searched for words, trying to fathom the twisted imagination of someone who would consider such a thing.

"No," she said. "I don't believe that. She'd kill some stranger to make a point?"

"You don't know her, Ellie. You don't really know anything about Nora Quinn. Do you?"

"Well—"

"She's an amateur, if you ask me." Gabe's voice was dismissive. "Hair, accent, all that. Phony as a—"

A knock at Ellie's door made her jump. It opened. Meg.

"Sorry to bother, but ready to talk to Warren about our story? I told him about our Abigail interview—that's okay, I hope." Meg had a yellow pencil tucked through her ponytail. "Oh, you're still on the phone? Is everything okay?"

CHAPTER 20

NORA

She'd waited until darkest of dark to lug the box of evidence upstairs to her apartment, so late on this too-cold March evening that every window in her building was a black rectangle, with not one light glowing through slotted blinds or filmy curtains or bare glass. Nora heard her own booted footsteps on the sidewalk, crunching through remnants of the blue snowmelt that she'd been warned would blanket every pedestrian surface in Boston until April.

Her goal was to haul this box inside from where the cab had dropped her without being seen. She feared the clack and clatter of the front door, when she finally got there, would be loud as fireworks in the building's stillness.

Nora shivered, the wind biting at her, but she couldn't delay. She had to get this stuff inside. This had been a difficult day, a revealing day, an unsettling day.

Her Saturday evening with Guy—five days ago now—had been unsettling as well. It ended so late they'd closed down the restaurant. Then they'd gone their separate ways, with Nora none the wiser, no matter what techniques she tried, about Guy's true motives. Which made her even more suspicious. The next day, Sunday, he'd texted her. Hearing the *ping*, she'd tried to prepare for his next move—but he'd only typed "great night" and that he was "headed out of town again." She shook her head. Did he think she was stupid? "Safe travels," she'd typed back. Two could play this game.

She trudged up the sidewalk, counting new worries with every step. *Dr. Hawkins was a spy for Pharminex.* What a jerk, trapping her like that. She recognized that the situation had its own irony, but Nora had thought she had been so careful. Now she wondered how many other spies the company had. Who they were. What they might be doing.

Almost to her apartment. Half a block to go. She adjusted the heavy box in her arms.

Then the confrontation in Detta Fiddler's office. *That* had surprised her. Shifted her focus. Forced her to improvise again.

To Nora's relief, the security people Fiddler had summoned this afternoon had not been cops but rent-a-guards. She instantly nicknamed them Tug and Boat, each one with a shiny shaved head, a charcoal shirt with a Pharminex logo on the front and SECURITY across their broad backs. With Tug on her left and Boat on her right, they escorted her toward the warren of lockers on the ninth floor. As the elevator carried them up, the two stared straight ahead.

The doors slid open. At five thirty in the afternoon they were alone, since the genuine pharmaceutical salespeople all left at five. Lydia and Jenn and Christine and Gerri, the ones who seemed to honestly believe the Monifan they pitched was a miracle.

As Nora marched to her locker, feeling the heat from the guards' bodies close to her, she channeled her newest role: an embarrassed victim. Turned out, to extricate herself from this, she'd had to play yet another persona.

She'd explained to Detta and Allessandra—tears in her eyes—that she changed her identity because she was an abused woman on the run, hiding from a dangerous husband. Sure, it was a nasty sort of lie, but Nora was out to help women in a different horrific situation. People like poor Kaitlyn Armistead, who had put her trust and her soul into the desperate need to have a child. Whose family was probably now planning her funeral.

"Golly," she'd said to her two inquisitors back in Detta Fidler's office, "I thought Dr. Hawkins was genuinely interested in *me*, the person." She'd played it wide-eyed, shocked, feeling her way into the new role. "I guess I'm still vulnerable. Damaged. Still looking for a man to protect me. So stupid." Channeling shame and humiliation, she concentrated on the plush carpeting for a moment, giving her tears time to form. Looked up at the two women, mortified. "He's quite a good actor. But I suppose you know that."

Fiddler and Lewes seemed almost sympathetic—enough to help Nora engineer a swift but unexplained exit from the company and a confidentiality agreement about the circumstances.

"We cannot have the slightest suspicion of unprofessional behavior, Nora." Fiddler had shaken her head, as if reluctant to pronounce this unemployment sentence on such a pitiful creature. "But we won't reveal why you changed your name. I wish you had told us, but I understand why you couldn't. Still.

Dr. Hawkins. That's a transgression no matter who you really are. We'll just say you had another opportunity."

"Thank you." Nora had been acquiescent. Cutting her losses.

Later she pointed her two security guards down corridor five. "This is mine, locker seventeen," she said. She looked up under her eyelashes at Tug, the guard who'd seemed more susceptible, trying for sympathy. "*Was* mine, I suppose."

"Three minutes, ma'am," Tug said.

She spun her lock and clacked open the metal locker, then stopped; first surprised, and then calculating. The institutional tan cabinet contained only a cello-wrapped tin of mints, a can of hair spray and the mirror she'd attached to the door. Everything else was gone. The binders of pharmaceutical specifications and drug interaction information, the Pharminex pads and pens and company swag. And no blue and white sample boxes of Monifan were stacked square in the corner of the top shelf. Not one. Her locked leather detail bag was gone too. She turned to Tug.

"Where's all my stuff?" Were they trying to trick her again? Accuse her of stealing? But they would have played that card by now.

"Not your property, ma'am," Tug said. "Your supplies were removed earlier this morning. Lucky for you, your sample count was correct."

"Seen what happens when it isn't," Boat said.

"Mighta gone different," Tug said.

But no matter. All she'd needed were three or four sample packs a day, and those had been easy enough to swipe and hide in a safe place, a few at a time. She was sorry, or maybe a little sorry, that someday, possibly, an inventory of her customers' supply cabinets might come out the tiniest bit wrong. And doctors may not have found as many samples in their gold plastic P-X goody bags as they'd expected. But it was all for a good cause.

And Nora had copied her detail book, page by necessary page, sneaking a few at a time in the office copier. After each meeting, she'd used a copy place to duplicate every single order from every single doctor. She had a stack of pads, boxes of pens, cello-wrapped stickies and, most damning, a stash of preprinted prescription pads, already filled out for Monifan and waiting for a doctor's signature. When the legal guns moved in, they'd surely subpoena that evidence from the company.

But to do her job, Nora needed her own proof of original packaging, as well as internal documents like class instructions and the damning sales pitch materials Allessandra Lewes had confidently distributed to her new recruits. All that was now in this box she'd retrieved from where she'd stashed it, and it would soon be safely hidden in her apartment.

The streetlights glowed orange-white in front of her, every parking place taken, every car dark inside, no interior lights revealing watchful eyes. She crossed the street, narrowing her shoulders, drawing her arms closer, carrying the brown cardboard box like a shield between her and the dark. No headlights in either direction.

The moment she got inside, she'd get her new show on the road.

"Mighta gone different." She whispered Tug's final words now. "But it didn't, Tug. It went precisely the way I wanted."

Balancing her box of legal ammunition on one hip,

she dug into the pocket of her handbag for the front door key.

"Thanks so much, Nora," she whispered, as she clicked open the door to her apartment building. "It's been nice being you."

BEFORE

CHAPTER 21

LACEY

"You'll make a beautiful bride, dear. No matter what dress you choose."

Lacey saw Brinn Vanderwald's smile reflected in the mirror behind her. Lacey's future mother-in-law, wearing winter-white wool trousers and a blouse set off with strappy bronze sandals and an elaborately buckled belt, had draped one arm over the back of the gold damask chaise where she sat, lush and languid. Glittering, like everything else in the opulent ivory dressing room, off-limits to all but the privileged. The massive rococo mirror mounted on the elegantly papered wall at Sonnenfield's was the store's iconic gilt-flowered symbol of access and power. Those lucky brides who were framed in the gold, the store's legend had it, were the fairest of them all, and destined to live a perfect happily ever-after. Brinn—more and more Lacey's best friend forever—had whispered to her that she believed in the promise.

Happy endings were for fairy tales, Lacey knew that. But out loud, as she and Brinn whispered like teenage confidantes as they'd set up the place cards for last year's Vanderwald Thanksgiving table, Lacey had said she believed it too.

Shiny white clamps, like glorified clothespins, now held the sample-size gown of snow-white lace taut to Lacey's waist. Fluttering beside her, arranging hemlines and fiddling with the fit, were Colomba and Artemis—so read the name tags on the sales clerks' sleek pink sheath dresses, just uniform enough to be uniforms. Together they'd lifted the gossamer train, then let it float to the carpeted floor, gasping at the beauty of it.

"You're making me blush, you two. It's *so* difficult to choose," Lacey, smiling, said into the mirror. Her entire life had been difficult, and when things worked, it was because she had made them work. Willed them to work. When things didn't work, it wasn't her fault. But then she'd simply try again. There was always another way.

"I'm so disappointed your mother can't be here to share this." Brinn crossed her slim legs, took a delicate sip of the pink drink shimmering in her tall glass. "It's a once-in-a-lifetime event. My only son, my darling son, marrying the girl of his dreams. You're both so lucky. And young enough to give me many, *many* grandchildren."

Lacey smoothed the lace at her waist and caressed the fabric over her hips. "You're so generous, Brinn," she said. "I'll tell Mother all about it, of course. Every single wonderful thing. And how lovely y'all have been." *Y'all.* Now and then Lacey wondered if she was laying it on too thick.

Her own mother, back in Montgomery with Lacey's stepfather, was "sadly unavailable." That's how Lacey had explained it to the disappointed Vanderwald family as they celebrated her engagement to Trevor in a private room of the country club, each place setting with a flute of chilled champagne and an array of silverware. They wouldn't know what disappointment was unless they met her mother. Lacey was determined that would never happen.

She adjusted the puff of illusion veil, straightened the Alençon lace that draped from her bare shoulders, and in the mirror, saw her own future too. In tennis whites and jodhpurs, in cocktail satin and belle-of-the-ball brocade, she'd be—in five months and two weeks—Lacey Grisham *Vanderwald*. She'd keep the college nickname—why not? She'd be Mrs. Trevor Vanderwald, the beloved wife of the scion of Vanderwald industries and all they controlled.

Did she love Trevor? Of course she did.

"I do adore this one, Brinn." Lacey tweaked her natural drawl to what she hoped was a more genteel and well-bred inflection, one befitting her soon-to-be stature. She turned from the mirror, smiling. "Don't you, honey?"

"Honey" was directed toward that pill, Brooke Vanderwald. Sullen as always, she had insisted on sitting on the floor. Now the sixteen-year-old had the back of her grubby jean jacket plastered against the flowered wallpaper and her garish red Chucks planted on the taupe carpeting. And always with a book. Brinn had insisted on Brooke's accompanying them, though from the girl's hostility she might have been suggesting she stop breathing. Maybe the poor girl was jealous. Or thought Lacey was stealing away her beloved big brother. So silly. The girl was getting a big sister.

Brooke would feel better once she got those braces off, and when her zits cleared up. She had a pretty enough face and incredibly long legs. Lacey almost laughed out loud, remembering what people had said to her in her awkward days. Thinking they were being reassuring. Brooke had to learn to deal with reality.

"Whatever," Brooke deigned to say.

"And you'll be a lovely bridesmaid, won't you, sweetheart?" Brinn stood, not taking her eyes off Lacey, positioning herself next to her in the mirror, the glass reflecting the two women, both in shades of white, both envisioning a future. "We'll have Christmas, and New Year's, and before we know it, a wedding. And you two will be sisters! And babies. Brooke, you'll be an auntie!"

"Whatever," Brooke repeated. "I had no idea you cared about grandchildren, Mother. How *fascinating*."

In the mirror, Lacey caught the girl's exaggerated eye roll. And Brinn's worried frown.

Lacey smiled at the gilt-edged reflection, making herself their ray of sunshine.

CHAPTER 22

BROOKE

None of this mattered, the money, and the stuff, and everything her mom and this Lacey seemed to care about. Brooke sat on the floor of the stupid wedding place's dressing room. She'd only come because her mother had forced her to. *Sisters,* her mother had gushed. She'd rather die.

She was sixteen now, just, and wanted with all her heart to walk out the store's front door and never see any of them, not ever again. She turned another page in her book to make it look like she was really reading. But there was no way to leave. She didn't have money. She didn't have anything.

She kept track, every day in her little secret diary, of how many words she said to her father, and how many to her mother. She could not go over one hundred. She had to live with the two of them because she needed food and shelter, and because she wasn't stupid. But she wasn't a pawn. They had actively tricked her, actively deceived her, and then, like, thought she'd just accept their murder of her child—because that's what it was, wasn't it? The murder of her very child? And their *grandchild*! Like it was nothing? She could feel herself getting angrier, but that's not who she would be. She would not waste her energy on parents who thought she was invisible. She would use her power for something else.

She sighed, staring at the capped white toes of her red shoes. She'd loved Liam, though. And now her heart was too heavy to carry in her body. He'd ignored her. Erased her. *I love you more than the moon and stars,* he'd said. Something like that. But she guessed he had lied to her too. Everybody lied. Liam would never miss her, no matter how much she missed him. She turned a page in her book like she was turning a page in her life. She'd tear the Liam page *out,* if she could.

But. She thought about, really thought about, what her brother Trevor would do if she vanished. Her parents would get over it, pretend to be sad and then go on with their selfish dumb lies and lives. But not Trevor.

When she was seven and Trevor was twelve, they'd made wishes under their backyard oak tree. Even now she could remember the warmth of the grass and the bumpy tree roots and the sun on her bare arms as they'd sat outside on a strangely warm March day, trying to find four-leaf clovers.

"Found one!" she crowed. "And I wish—"

"Don't say it out loud!" Trevor stood, looking down at her, with his too-long hair and his dopey *Star Wars* T-shirt. "You can't say your wish out loud, midget."

"Can too," she insisted. "And I'm *not* a midget. I wish we could stay here forever, just you and me. Be like, you know, in Narnia. And you could protect me, be my big brother forever."

"You're so weird," he said. "Okay, then, you're a smidgen. That's *smaller* than a midget. And there's no Narnia. That's a dumb wish."

"Is not!" She'd jumped to her feet, standing her ground. "I swear on this clover we—"

"You can't swear on a stupid clover, smidgen."

She pouted, almost cried, because you *could,* and then Trevor had found a clover too.

"Found one!" he said, holding it up. Then he'd shaken his head in what she now recognized as affection. "I'm your big brother *anyway,* Smidge, you don't have to *wish* that."

He'd teased her forever, after that, and did all the dumb stuff like short-sheeting her bed, and pretending he didn't like her in front of his cool friends, which drove her crazy, and even telling her she was adopted since she came so late, which was not true, totally not, and her parents had reassured her that it was just a brother thing and to ignore it. And she did, because Trev loved her, he truly did, and she was his Smidge, and now he was getting married to Lacey, who was so full of herself Brooke wondered why she didn't spill out over the edges.

But somehow Trevor loved her, whatever that meant, and he personally had asked Brooke to be a bridesmaid.

Not Lacey. Who she tried to stay away from as much as humanly possible. Easy enough because it seemed like all Lacey did was put on makeup and fuss with her hair and change clothes. At least Brooke wouldn't really have to deal with her much. She and Trevor were moving to Washington, D.C., right after the wedding. He'd told her *that* too.

She slid the envelope out from between the pages of *The Lovely Bones,* the book's cover bent and battered from its travels in her backpack, and looked at the letter from Trevor again. She knew the letter by heart, but seeing his words, all misspelled because he was probably typing so fast, made her hear his voice, talking to her.

Smidgen, it said. She heard him saying that, especially. *You are such a rock star, and I know you think I'm nuts for getting married, but someday you'll understand what love feels like. Lacey is great, and you two will be great together, and you know I'm not much for words, but you're terrific. Even for a kid. Even for a dumb sister. Kidding! Ha ha.*

So anyway, I'm not leaving you, even though we have to move to D.C. Don't tell Lacey, but I'd rather stay home with you all, but marriage is compromise. I learned that, too. And we'll see you, I know we will, and now, Smidgeroo, one big favor.

And then he'd asked her to *be a bridesmaid and do whatever they do, I know, it's girl stuff, and you're not much for that, but I promise it'll be great.*

She was doing this for Trevor, and Trevor only. And she would save this letter forever.

Lacey was preening in front of the big mirror now, acting all happy and bridey. Brooke knew, or maybe she just wanted to know, that Lacey was a bitch. She tucked the letter away. But maybe it was simply that Lacey had everything, like her brother and a future. And Brooke had only sadness. And hopelessness.

No. She had plans. She closed her book, staring at the cover, a book about a girl who died, and then watched how her family dealt with it. Now Brooke had to deal.

She'd have to live at home until college. No way out of that. Then she'd go to school somewhere far away, and untangle herself from her hideous murdering lying parents as soon as she could.

She'd seen on TV, from an old *Star Trek* from

before she was born, where Spock told Captain Kirk a Klingon proverb that said "Revenge is a dish best served cold." She'd asked her dad what it meant, and he'd told her to look it up. Now she understood. It meant she didn't have to hurry. In fact, it was better if she didn't hurry.

She watched the performance in front of her: silly Lacey, all googly and puffy in that ridiculous dress. Her mother having another pink drink and pretending it wasn't vodka.

Brooke was sad, a little, that her brother had chosen this life. To live like their parents lived, and to be like they'd wanted *her* to be too. But she would never be that. Not for real.

When she was a little girl, she'd trusted them. Even the times when she didn't want to do what they told her, she secretly believed they were right. They had cared for her and were trying to do what was best for her. But this time, what they'd done wasn't best. What they'd done was *worst*. She thought about what happened after her own mother gave her those disgusting horrible murder pills. Horribly horribly worst.

But they'd also done this to themselves. And they'd be sorry.

As soon as Brooke could make *sorry* happen. And she was patient.

CHAPTER 23

ELLIE

Meg stood in Ellie's office doorway, wearing a slouchy beige cardigan and looking like a guilty schoolgirl. Even her ponytail seemed to droop.

"Ellie?" Meg began. "So you know that interview with Abigail we did last Thursday?"

"What about it?" Ellie tried to read Meg's face. "Is something wrong?"

"Oh. Hang on." In one quick motion, Meg put her phone to her ear and turned away.

Ellie rolled her eyes and grabbed her coat, eager to head home. It had been a long Monday. Nothing new in her Pharminex calls, nothing new from any law firms, no government filings. Nothing from Gabe. She'd called the Medical Science Association, curious about tickets for the Vanderwald gala. Whoever they'd transferred her to had been haughty and supercilious.

"Of course," the voice gushed. "Are you interested in purchasing tickets for your entire party? It should be indicated on your invitation, of course. It's invitation only. Of course."

"Oh, of course." Ellie'd made a gagging face as

she talked, grateful that this person couldn't see her. "But I seem to have misplaced it. A whole table is—forgive me, remind me again?"

"Fifty," the man said.

Thousand, Ellie thought. "Lovely," she said. "Let me check with my husband, and we'll get back to you. I assume the tables are being snapped up."

"It's simply marvelous." The voice had apparently been reassured by Ellie's nonchalance about the price of entry. "Such a paragon. We are so thrilled Winton Vanderwald will be here, and his family too. And of course every penny goes for the Trevor scholarship, such an untimely tragedy."

"His family?" Ellie had said. "Is coming?"

"So we're told." The voice went cagey, as if divulging a secret. "It's all quite hush-hush. But I assume his family would join him. They must be so proud of him."

"Of course," was all Ellie could think of to say.

Now Meg was back at the door. She hadn't shouldered her way into Ellie's office as she usually did, but seemed to be hanging back. "So the interview with—"

"Abigail, right." Ellie reached down to grab her tote bag from under her desk. "When can we watch it?"

"Um. It was great, it really was, Ellie, and you did such a fabulous job getting her to tell her story, but—"

"Meg?" Warning bells clanged in Ellie's head again. "But what?"

"There might be a problem with it."

Ellie couldn't decide whether to feel sorry for Meg or to kill her. "Problem?"

Meg chewed at her bottom lip. "I know, I know.

And I *did* check it right after we taped. But it's like . . . gone."

"Gone." Ellie nodded, slowly, replaying how Meg had taped it. "You used two phones, didn't you? *One* of them had to work. And remember, Abigail's in silhouette, so it's only about the audio. There must be some way to get that. If you didn't delete it."

"No, truly, I didn't. And they're working on it," Meg said. "A transmission glitch in the file transfer. Something like that."

Ellie tried to understand that. "A what?"

"I'm sorry." Meg shook her head.

"Well, we'll have to do it again," Ellie said. "Tell her—"

"Yeah, well, that's the thing. I can't tell her anything." Meg pressed her lips together, then went on. "She won't answer my calls. I'm worried she's avoiding me."

Meg's phone buzzed again, and Ellie saw the woman's face brighten.

"Oh. Yay. Maybe this is her. She. Anyway. Let me go see." She clicked on the phone. "This is Meg. Yes, I'll hold." She covered the microphone. "Are you on the way home?" she whispered. "I'll let you know."

"Grocery," Ellie said, thinking out loud. "Blinker's down to her last can. I'd never hear the end of it." She dug into her pockets, relieved to find both gloves. "Good luck."

But Meg was already back on her cell, and walking away.

By the time Ellie got home, grocery bags in hand, the last of the struggling daylight was long gone, and she was as hungry as Blinker must be. When she'd first found the kitten, curled up in a tiny ball under a boxwood hedge, she had lured it out with an open can of tuna cat food. Scrawny and pitiful, her white fur spackled with sandy dust, the little cat hadn't made one sound, not one peep, just blinked at Ellie as she crept, tentative and needy, tail twitching, toward the tuna. After the puff of scraggly white had scarfed up a few bites, Ellie could hear the rumble of a contented purr, and knew it was no use resisting. She'd scooped her up, and when the kitten blinked at her again, blissed out, that was the beginning of a beautiful friendship. Now, three years later, Blinker still craved tuna, even though Ellie still hated the smell of it. But cats were easier to please than people. Cats told the truth.

She unclicked the front door and took the stairs to the third floor. The moment her foot hit the final step, Meg's door opened. Did the woman have super-hearing?

"Ellie," Meg whispered. She stepped into the hallway, Blinker in her arms.

"Why do you have the cat?" Ellie was completely confused. She looked at her own apartment door. It was ajar. "How'd—"

"I don't know," Meg said. "When I got home, two seconds ago, the door was like that. I didn't touch it. Blinker was out in the hall, wandering around, meowing. So I grabbed her and brought her inside. I knew you weren't home, and I tried to call you, but I guess the call didn't go through. Did you leave the door open?"

"I never got a—" But the phone call wasn't the point. Ellie set down the bags, then reached out, took Blinker, held her against her chest. "Why is my door open?"

"Well, like I said, I figured you left it open, but I didn't want to go in, you know? I called the—"

"We need to call the police," Ellie said.

"That's what I'm saying, I already did, in case, I mean, it's so incredibly scary, and the police are—"

Inside Meg's lemon-scented entryway, which seemed to be a mirror image of her own, the front door intercom buzzed.

"This must be them," Meg said. "Finally."

"You didn't see anyone?" Ellie kept thinking about this. Meg and her parabolic hearing. She'd heard Ellie arrive, so why not the . . . but maybe Meg hadn't been home when the intruder arrived. They must have opened the main front door too.

"Third floor," Meg said into the intercom.

Ellie ached to go into her own place but knew that was the wrong thing to do. If anyone had been there . . . or was still there . . . Her brain started a list of possibilities. And those were only the people she knew of.

Fast-moving footsteps on the stairway, and then two uniformed Boston police officers—navy twill, billed caps, squared shoulders, one with a dark chignon and one with a darker mustache, each with a hand poised over a holstered weapon—appeared in the hallway, a blue blockade.

"In there, that door," Meg said, pointing. "When I called nine-one-one I said—"

"It was like that when you got home?" The man's black plastic name tag said *Samuel Adomako*. "When was that?"

"Yes, like that, maybe five minutes ago. The cat was out in the hall. And I got the cat and went into my place." She pointed at her front door. "I listened, but I didn't hear anything. Or see anyone. Do you think anyone's still inside? I mean, my apartment was fine when I got here, all locked up. Unless you think—what if they—"

"It's *my* apartment, officers," Ellie said. "That one. With the open door."

"Could you have left it open, ma'am?" The chignon was edging toward the door. *Carolann Phillips,* her name tag read.

"No, definitely not." Ellie was certain of that.

"And I called *her* too, right away," Meg said. "I was so worried about the stuff she has inside. She just moved here and—I'm Meg. Weest. This is Ellie Berensen. It's her apartment. Are you going inside? What should we do?"

"Once inside, is there another way out?" Officer Adomako asked.

"No. Except for the fire escape," Ellie said, staring at her door. "Back door downstairs, though, yeah." The reality washed over her. Someone had been inside. Someone had been inside while she was gone, and if it was—well, she almost wished they'd taken her pitiful jewelry, or the cash she'd stashed in the bookcase. Anything to make it a run-of-the-mill burglary. Anything to make it not personal. But they'd chosen her place, not Meg's.

"Can you both wait inside your apartment, ma'am?" Adomako cocked his head toward Meg's 3-B. "I assume the super has a key?"

"Sam?" Phillips took the two steps toward Ellie's door. "We going in?"

Ellie stationed herself behind Meg's door, listening for sounds of whatever would happen. Yelling, or commotion, or an arrest. Blinker, uncharacteristically calm, purred in her arms. Meg hovered behind them.

A knock at the door made them all flinch.

"Ma'am? Ms. Berensen? It's Officer Phillips."

Ellie yanked open the door, still clutching Blinker, seeing the brown grocery bags she'd left in the hall.

The two officers stood in the hallway. Ellie's apartment door was closed.

"And?" She looked at Adomako, then Phillips, assessing their expressions. "What?"

"Nothing seems to be out of place. That we can see, at least," Adomako said. "Your TV and computer were undisturbed and your medicine cabinet appears untouched. Drawers all uniformly closed, kitchen cabinets too. Nothing seems in disarray. Window's not touched, far as we can see. No activity on the fire escape."

"Really?" Ellie put a hand on the doorjamb to steady herself. Blinker had curled against Ellie's shoulder, purring.

"Is there anyone you might suspect of breaking in?" Adomako seemed to be searching for a way to phrase his inquiry. "I don't want to put words into your mouth. But anyone who might be interested in something that's in your apartment?"

Ellie thought about what she could say as she mentally surveyed her apartment. "Well, I just moved here three-ish weeks ago." Should she bring up the Pharminex investigation? It seemed melodramatically far-fetched, and yet not.

"Before we go back in, does anyone else have a key?" Phillips asked. "You see, ma'am, the apartment door *was* open but—"

"You never gave *me* a key, Ellie," Meg interrupted. "I mean, we talked about it, Officer, exchanging keys. But we didn't do it. Ellie, you're the only one with a key to your apartment, isn't that right? Or is there someone else who goes in there sometimes?"

"The company that owns Channel Eleven owns the building," Ellie said. "They have a super. He has a key. He lives in the basement unit."

"Right. We'll talk to him." Officer Adomako flipped

open a black spiral notebook. "Though why would he leave the door open?"

"How do you know he didn't get into my apartment too?" Meg spread her arms in front of her, taking the floor. "Whoever it was? Officer?"

"And how do we know whoever it was won't come back?" Ellie tried to prevent her voice from being as shrill as Meg's. She pictured returning to her apartment, the place where someone had been without her permission. Someone she didn't know. Someone who might come back.

"Honest answer? We don't, ma'am," Adomako said. "But since nothing seems to be disturbed . . ." He left the rest of the sentence hanging in the hallway gloom.

How could they be sure nothing was taken? She would know, as soon as she checked the places the police would never know to look. Or maybe she was making too much of it.

"Ms. Berensen, again, you didn't leave the door open, did you?" Adomako pointed his notebook at her, then took it down, his face softening. "It could happen to anyone, ma'am. No harm, no foul. We're happy to help."

"Your cat always wants to get out," added helpful Meg. "Maybe you—"

Ellie lifted her chin. "I did not leave the door open."

Meg frowned, pursed her lips, as if replaying a scene in her head. "Come to think of it, I might have seen your door kind of open when I left this morning. I thought maybe you were, like, in the basement doing laundry or something."

Ellie felt three pairs of eyes on her. She heard Phillips draw in a deep breath, saw her push a blond strand of hair back into custody under her cap. Exchange glances with her partner.

"Might you have done that, ma'am?" Adomako's tone had changed, talking to her now as if she were twelve. "Maybe you were in a hurry?"

"No, Officer." She used the same tone, then regretted it. He was only being thorough. She half smiled, acknowledging her flare. "Sorry, but no."

"You've got a lot on your mind, El," Meg said. "And—"

Officer Adomako silenced Meg with a look, for which Ellie was grateful. "We can tell if things were disarranged. Drawers opened, items moved, things of that nature. There was no sign of that."

"Agreed," Phillips said.

"Just the door open." Ellie felt the chill in her own voice. The realization. "And if they could get in once, they could get in again."

Meg gasped. "You are so right, Ellie. *Sooo* right. We should change all the locks. Every single one." She grabbed a pink plastic ring of keys from the side table, jangled them like punctuation. "Oh my gosh, Ellie. It's so awful. Some stranger was in your apartment. I'd have to wash everything, absolutely everything. What if they break into mine next?"

"Officers?" Ellie felt her anger swimming to the surface. Or maybe it was fear. "Do you want me to go in? Look for myself?"

"I'll stay here." Meg shook her head, retreated into her apartment. "It's too terrifying. Too disturbing. What if there's someone hiding?"

"There's no one hiding, miss." Phillips opened the door, took a step into the corridor, then gestured Ellie to follow her. "Ms. Berensen? We'll go with you, but again, I assure you your apartment is clear."

"Really?" Ellie tried to process that.

"You'll see," Phillips said. "And Ms. Weest? I may

have a few more questions for you in a moment, so please stand by."

With one officer on either side of her, Ellie crossed the hall. Adomako put his hand on the doorknob. Turned it. Ellie's heart twisted along with it. She felt apprehensive, even with two cops beside her. *You'll see,* the officer had told her. But they couldn't have known what mattered. Or why.

Adomako went inside, and so did Ellie. The entire atmosphere, the air, the energy, felt off, disturbed, as if everything inside was the same but different.

"See?" Adomako waved a hand toward the living room. Phillips stayed in the doorway.

Ellie surveyed the place in snapshot glances. Hallway. Kitchen. Fireplace. Couch. Windows, with curtains still as she'd left them. Blinker squirmed out of her arms and skittered down the carpeted corridor.

"Your paperwork on the coffee table, see?" Adomako went on. "The coffee cup you used this morning, apparently, your yellow pad, sharpened pencils. And from the dust, not moved from their original positions. We can tell by the coffee cup mark on the glass coffee table."

Ellie stared at the coffee table, at the coffee cup, at the yellow pad and the pencils. What a reporter would use. What *she* would use. *Did* use, in fact. The cup, one from the kitchen supplies that came with her apartment, she drank from every morning. Her desk at work was stacked with yellow pads just like these. And she always wrote with the same buttercup-yellow Oriole pencils, now points-up like a graphite porcupine and stashed in her chippy old mug from college, its J-school decal long washed away.

She felt her fingers tingle, and a clench in her chest

as if a vise were closing around her lungs. "Offi—Officer? I didn't put that stuff there. I didn't."

A siren screamed by outside, the sound fading as it passed.

"You didn't?" Adomako narrowed his eyes at her. "Then who did?"

CHAPTER 24

ELLIE

"Wow, El. I mean, could you even sleep last night?"

Ellie had opened her apartment door just as Meg opened hers. Meg's voice, this time of the morning and before coffee, seemed like the universe unfairly piling on.

"I'm still freaked out over the break-in yesterday," Meg went on. "I didn't get one wink. How about you?"

Ellie stooped, perplexed, to pick up the Tuesday *Boston Globe* on the rattan welcome mat outside her door. She'd thrown on yoga pants to sneak down to the entryway, where the newspaper carrier always left it at dawn. But today her paper was already upstairs.

"Meg? Hi. Um. Do you know how this got here?" She looked at the front page as she picked it up, scanning for a possible story about the Kaitlyn Armistead crash. There'd been nothing reported since it happened a week ago. She folded the paper, stashed it under her arm. The break-in. She had slept, finally, a purring Blinker curled up beside her, but now she was worrying again. So she was up. Blinker kept sleeping. "How'd the paper guy get in?"

"Get in? Oh, no one got in." Meg's ponytail swayed, emphasized her negative response. She wore a pink terry bathrobe over leggings and a T-shirt, and her feet were bare. "*I* brought it up for you."

Meg hadn't closed her apartment door behind her, and in the distance Ellie saw a couch that looked much like hers. Yesterday she'd been too upset to notice much else but her fear. All these apartments came furnished, so maybe Meg's furniture was similar to her own.

"I'm so sorry." Meg frowned. "I didn't mean to upset you. I was trying to be nice. But, oh, you thought the burglar who got into your apartment might be coming back. Showing you he wasn't done. That he could still get in. *Yikes*. So creepy. I see what you mean. But no, no, just me."

Her bathrobe buzzed. "Oh, hang on. I'm getting a call." She slipped a cell phone from a pink terry pocket. "Can you wait a sec?"

"Sure. Go ahead," Ellie said. The break-in haunted her, truth be told. Those cops, Carolann Phillips and Sam Adomako, had promised to call her if they had any updates, though given their attitudes when they left, that seemed unlikely. A least they'd eliminated the Ellie-is-a-ditz explanation.

"If you didn't put that stuff there, someone clearly broke in," Adomako, alpha cop, had said yesterday, after Ellie had explained to him that the pads and pencils on her coffee table were not hers. "So okay, you didn't leave the door open. But—"

Like I told you, Ellie wanted to sneer at them. Instead she'd asked for permission to check her valuables. "I know you've looked," she said. "But I'll feel better when I see for myself."

She'd quickly searched the places she hoped no one had thought of, decided nothing had been touched.

Everything that could derail her was still where she'd stashed it.

When Ellie got back from her search, Phillips, clearly underling-with-attitude, had brought in a leather carryall and zipped it open.

"All good," Ellie reported.

"Like we told you." Phillips took a camera from her bag.

Adomako shot his colleague an expression that obviously meant *back off.* "Glad to hear it," he said. "We're handling this as evidence now. What do you make of it, though, Ms. Berensen?"

"It's nuts, all I can say."

"Yeah," Adomako said. "Any ideas?"

"I'm trying to think," she said. Gabe had texted her over the weekend that he was out of town for a few days. So didn't it have to be Pharminex? Maybe one of the lawyers she'd interviewed had ratted her out, and the company ordered some goon to scare her away. It was impossible, as an investigative reporter, to seal off every potential leak. Asking questions opened unpredictable doors. With unpredictable consequences.

Ellie watched as Phillips photographed and tagged each item.

"In the meantime, how about your computer?" Adomako pointed to the laptop on her kitchen table, the one she always left there, since she was the only one using the table. "Can you boot that up, see if anything's added to *that*? This is still a B and E, Ms. Berensen. Breaking and entering. Doesn't matter if nothing was taken."

"Yeah, no, Sam?" Phillips had interjected, stripping off her plastic gloves, as Ellie sat and popped her computer into life. "I'd say it's a trespass. Simple trespass. Nothing's been damaged or stolen. The lock's not broken. Impossible to gauge intent, and no explicit indication of a threat or attempt to intimidate. To charge a felony, there must be intent. So what intent is this? Leaving pencils and legal pads?"

Ellie looked up from her computer. Shimmering in front of her was the screensaver: stars twinkling in a vast dark universe, a personal reminder of her constant search for answers, of her cause and her quest.

"This isn't random." Ellie shook her head, disagreeing. "I think this is someone wanting me to understand they're aware of a story I'm working on. A company I'm investigating. Pharminex. Their *intent* is to threaten me."

It *had* to be someone from there. Warning her off the story.

"Someone's trying to tell me that my own home isn't safe," Ellie went on. "It's personal, officers. It has to be. Tell me why that isn't a threat."

Phillips collected her evidence bags, sliding each one into the leather carryall.

"Want to file a police report? We can do that, sure. But that's about it, Ms. Berensen, I'm afraid. We could possibly charge a John Doe, with trespassing, but"—Adomako shrugged—"it's a misdemeanor. If we ever catch the person, it'd be a fine."

"It's a malicious *message*. A *warning*. To *me*," Ellie insisted.

"Your colleague Ms. Weest mentioned you've been under a lot of pressure, professionally," Phillips said. "That something had gone wrong with an interview? That your boss was pushing you on a deadline?"

She had? Ellie'd frowned, wondering why Meg would say such a thing.

"Blame the victim, really? *I* left the door open? I forgot that I had stuff on the table?" Ellie looked at her computer screen as she talked, scrolled through files and emails. "Nothing in here, by the way," she said. "I mean, in addition to what there was when I left this morning."

Adomako closed his notebook and slid it back into his breast pocket, leaving the spiral top showing. Tucked his ballpoint in next to it. "Ms. Berensen? I understand it's unsatisfying. But given the parameters of the law, what do you suggest?"

"What do I . . . ?" Ellie had closed her eyes in frustration as she slowly lowered the top of her computer. She tried to control the fear in her voice. "It's a *message*. From someone at Pharminex. They don't want me sniffing around, so they're sending a message that they *know* about that, and they know where I live, and they know how to get in." She felt her fear intensify as she talked, spreading like black ink clouding clear water. "And if that's not threatening—"

"Do you have any reason to think this Pharminex is likely to do something dangerous?" Adomako interrupted, bringing out his notebook again. "Harm you? Or intimidate you? Have they contacted you? Any person in particular there?"

She put her face into her hands, trying to think. If Pharminex was warning Ellie, they knew she was on the right track. Which would—ridiculously—make this a good thing. Companies could file lawsuits for slander or false light, but only *after* an investigation was aired on TV. This might be their strategy, to try to stop her story before it aired, especially before their high-visibility Winton Vanderwald gala.

Blinker strolled into the room, aloof and tail waving, and nudged Ellie's hand with her pink nose. Ellie lifted the lump of cat onto her lap and held her like a barrier. Blinker, a silent witness, knew what had happened this morning.

"Look. We'll fingerprint, see what we get," Phillips

had said. "But you're new to this place, so a prior tenant's prints could be here. I checked with the super, and he told me the surveillance cameras were down. I'm afraid that's all we can do." The two officers moved toward her front door. "We'll be in touch. And you call us, if you hear or see or discover anything."

The cops had taken the evidence. Inside Ellie's apartment, everything looked the same. Except it wasn't. She'd have to move.

But not today. Today she was in the hallway, in her long T-shirt and yoga pants, at six thirty in the morning, on her way to retrieve a newspaper that was already at her door.

"Ellie?" Meg was tucking her cell phone back into her robe pocket. "*Hellooo*. Earth to Ellie. Where'd you go?"

"Lost in space for a second, I guess." Ellie tried to recover, get back to the moment. "Hey, Meg? Why'd you tell the cops yesterday that I was under pressure? They already suspected I was a whack. As if I'd leave my door open. Just wondering why you'd perpetuate that story."

Meg widened her eyes. "That woman came back to talk to me, yeah, we talked in the hall. But I never told her that."

Ellie made sure she had her key, then stepped away from her door. It closed, and clicked. "See? It locks automatically. I didn't leave it open. Couldn't have. And I'm not under pressure. Except about the Abigail interview you seem to have blown. But that should put *you* under pressure, Meg. Any word on that?"

"I—"

"I'd appreciate it if you didn't make me look like an idiot," Ellie couldn't resist adding.

Meg took a step closer, then another. She reached

out, almost touched Ellie on the arm. Looked square into her eyes, with such intensity that Ellie had to back a step away.

"I swear I didn't say that." Meg planted her hands on her hips, revealing the smiley Life is Good logo on her T-shirt. "I'm disappointed, and hurt, that you think so. We're a team, Ellie. And cops always do that, try to make people uncomfortable. Fight with each other. You know that."

"Maybe," Ellie had to admit.

"And I *called* the cops, right? Trying to protect you. Make sure you were safe."

"Yeah, thanks for that." Ellie felt a twinge of embarrassment that she hadn't thanked her before. "You could've ignored it."

"I'm just glad I was here." Meg's eyes got wider. Then she spread her hands, entreating. "Truce? Okay?"

"Sure," she said. "Truce."

Meg clapped her hands, soundlessly, just twice. "Great," she said. "So—you have plans for the day? What's on the Pharminex agenda for us?"

Ellie decided. Right then, she decided. "My insider interview."

"What?"

"Yup. It's time to get my source on tape. Especially before the Vanderwald thing." It happened in reporting, every time, the moment when the puzzle pieces clicked together and the curtain went up on reality. "We won't lose *this* interview, Meg. It's a sure thing. I'm arranging it today."

"*So* great." Meg clapped again. "But can't you just tell me who it is? Come on, Ellie. I'm gonna know soon, anyway. We're a team."

What harm could it do? And she'd been nasty to Meg, and that was probably unfair.

"Between us?"

"Of course!"

"Okay. She's a Pharminex employee. Access to everyone and everything." Ellie's resolve came to life. This was going to work. She'd stake her career—and her entire future—on it. She'd save so many women. And prevent so much sorrow.

"*She?* It's a woman?" Meg narrowed her eyes, nodded. "Cool. Very cool. Perfect. What's her name?"

"Her name," Ellie said, "is Nora Quinn."

CHAPTER 25

ELLIE

Saturday offices have a different feel, Ellie thought, as someone—Gabe, she figured—buzzed her through the imposing glass doors of the WorkHere shared office space. Gabe had rented a spot in this mirrored-glass downtown Boston building, he'd explained, a place for him to do his research. The reception desk sat empty, the buttons on the wide telephone console unlit and silent, a once-lavish arrangement of maroon calla lilies and yellow mums now wilting in a curved glass vase filled with murky water.

She hadn't told Gabe about the break-in. His out-of-town assignment had been extended, and she'd decided it didn't seem like a topic for a phone conversation. There was nothing he could have done but worry, or meaninglessly commiserate.

But she'd spent every night this past week sleepless, planning for her big interview with Nora Quinn. She'd also conjured grim replays of Kaitlyn Armistead's death.

She'd used her reporter status to email the state police, oh-so-casually asking about the latest in that car accident. They'd been stonewallingly unresponsive.

She'd even driven to state police headquarters to find Detective Lieutenant Rafael Monteiro, the trooper assigned to the case, but had been told he was out, and his schedule "uncertain."

"He has your number, Miss Berensen," an indifferent receptionist informed her.

At Channel 11, she'd made dozens of phone calls, to labs and lawyers and fertility experts. She'd tried to track down people who'd once worked at Pharminex, scouting LinkedIn and Facebook. Yellow highlighter in hand, she'd pored over FDA filings. She was so close. Frustratingly, agonizingly close. But with Warren breathing down her neck and the Vanderwald gala looming—close wasn't near close enough.

"You made it." Gabe, silhouetted now in front of the office windows, strode in to greet her. Like Ellie, he was dressed in Saturday clothes, jeans and a turtleneck.

At least Gabe was as eager as she was to get this story nailed down. He'd offered to meet in neutral territory, a public place like a coffee shop or restaurant, but after the break-in, Ellie needed the protection of locked doors, alarms, the reassurance of security.

Now, behind the polished expanse of the reception desk, the wide glass wall of a conference room revealed the bleak wintry landscape behind it, a dense lattice of bare branches crisscrossing the midmorning sky. They'd predicted snow again, the persistently gloomy weather making spring feel impossibly far away.

By the time she'd handed over her puffer jacket and they'd gotten coffee in plain ceramic mugs, she'd explained about Nora Quinn, how Gabe had been partly correct, how the disenchanted and disillusioned pharma rep had finally agreed to an in-depth no-holds-barred interview.

"I know what she's going to say," Ellie told Gabe. "Pharminex is fully aware Monifan can be devastatingly harmful. But because those bad outcomes are 'rare'—her word—they've made the decision to pay off the victims and keep it all quiet."

She followed him down a long hallway, galleried with gold-framed newspaper articles about Work-Here showing women with babies in cribs next to their desks. Gabe opened the door to a mid-corridor office, no name plaque on the wall.

"When did you talk to her?" Gabe gestured her inside.

"Last night, most recently." She took a seat in the corner of a cordovan leather couch.

"Did she mention being connected to the Vanderwalds?"

"Nope, she didn't. And I *did* ask her." She paused, but Gabe didn't react. "She seemed baffled by the question. Good idea, though."

Gabe walked back and forth across the tweedy carpeting, three tall strips of window behind him, as she described her discussion with Nora, the documents she could get, and the insider paperwork. No family photographs were on the desk Gabe used, she noticed. No certificates or diplomas on the walls, no degrees or honors or indications of his real name or history.

Reminded her of her own apartment.

Finally Gabe pulled up a chair beside her. Put his coffee mug on top of two out-of-date *New Yorker*s stacked on the glass coffee table next to a brass figurine of an owl. "You'll have Nora on video?"

Ellie shook her head. "Audio only. She's told me everything I need for my story and she's agreed to be your law firm's whistleblower too. She's deeply upset about Pharminex. About what they're doing to women."

"Awesome. Does she have proof? Like what?"

"Training materials, she says. She'll give them all to us, at some point. And listen to this. She says the company has prescription pads printed, already filled out for Monifan, just waiting for a doctor's signature."

"That's not illegal," Gabe said. "But it's certainly cynical."

"*And* she's getting samples. And—ta-dah—included in the training materials? Proof Pharminex instructed their sales reps to push the drug for off-label use for 'infertility mitigation.' Which is—well, not only illegal, but dangerous. And they know it."

Gabe sighed, whether in sorrow, or disgust, or skepticism. He shifted on the chair, leaning away from Ellie.

She shifted too, risking it, leaning closer to him. "And that's what our Abigail said happened to her too. The same story. That her doctor admitted Monifan sometimes made women infertile."

"Which doctor prescribed Monifan for her?"

"She won't say." Ellie flopped back against the couch's soft leather. "But I'll eventually convince her to."

"How do you know she's even telling the truth?"

"I don't," Ellie conceded. "I can only know what Abigail told me. That's why *you've* got to get the real records," she persisted. "There's no way I can obtain actual patient reports, they'd never tell *me*. Or Nora."

Gabe nodded. "True. You get your ducks in a row. We will too. Then hit them with it. Right before their precious award event. Pharminex will battle a scandal like they've never seen."

Ellie took a deep breath. The implicit threat from the break-in continued to haunt her. Reporters always dealt with angry targets, and that anger meant they were on the right track. But this was unusually personal. "Listen. Gabe. Someone broke into my apartment."

"Broke into—are you okay?" Gabe stood, then looked at the phone on his desk. "Did you call the police?"

"Meg did. It's fine. I wasn't home at the time, and they didn't take anything." She explained the whole episode in fast bullet points. "Finally, the cops just said 'be careful.' So maybe you should be careful too."

"Maybe." Gabe nodded, pacing again. "You think it was Pharminex?"

"Yeah. I guess I do."

"Because they know you're a reporter working on a story about them?"

"Yeah. I mean, why else?"

"Because they want to make you uncomfortable, and let you know they're aware of where you live?"

"Yeah. I agree."

"Uh-huh." Gabe seemed to be contemplating that. "And they're trying to scare you away?"

She nodded. "That's what they do, right?"

"And there would be no other reason Pharminex would be suspicious of you?" Gabe stopped and looked down at her.

"Not that I can think of," she said.

Ellie felt a frown gather across her forehead. People only asked questions in a tone like Gabe's if they thought they already knew the answers. And were testing to see whether the responses would be a lie.

"What are you getting at?" Every cell in her body urged her to run. She'd been right to be suspicious of him. Her instincts had screamed at her from the moment she'd glimpsed him at Spinnaker. This Gabe had another agenda. He'd been lying to her.

Pharminex had engineered Kaitlyn's car accident, she was sure of it. And now, maybe, they'd sent their handsome-but-deadly goon to eliminate her. He'd tricked her into being alone with him. In a place where no one had any idea she was. A place where the corridors were empty, the offices locked, and if she screamed and screamed, no one would even hear her. She gathered herself to run.

"Instead of interrogating me, why not simply tell me why *you* think they broke in."

"Maybe it's because Pharminex knows you're not always Ellie."

"Not always me?" She flattened a palm against her chest, protesting. "What?"

"Come on, Ellie." Gabe leaned against the edge of the desk, legs stretched out in front of him on the tweedy carpeting. "Because maybe Pharminex knows, just like I do, that sometimes you're someone else. Aren't you, *Nora*?"

BEFORE

CHAPTER 26

LACEY

The music from the church organ, Pachelbel's "Canon," of course, wafted out of the sanctuary and into the arch-ceilinged lobby where Lacey Grisham soon-to-be Vanderwald waited, by herself as she'd requested, the sweetly promising notes curling around her white satin pumps and rising to catch in her throat.

How many brides had heard this same music? Brides in white lace, like she was, and crystal tiaras like hers, counting their blessings and thanking their lucky stars and clutching somethings borrowed and blue. All she'd wanted, *all*, was a family. Predictable, comfortable, with nannies and swing sets and husbands with bulging portfolios and country club memberships and maybe even happiness.

And when they had children, soon soon soon, she'd have someone to truly love. No one could stop her from that. And when she was a mother, she'd do better, she'd *be* better, she'd shower her daughter—or son, even *better*—with affection and support and reassurance and companionship. Today was a day for vows. She made them, now, to herself.

The music changed to the lilting progression of

Mozart's D-major flute concerto, the signal that the ceremony was moments away. Tears came to her eyes with a vision of the past, then of a lush dark curtain closing off her history forever. The next step she took would be into a new life.

Lacey touched the solitary diamond around her neck, a family heirloom—not from *her* family, of course—and wished. Hard. Now that her dreams seemed to be coming true, she feared they might turn out to be her imagination. Poised to shift and change and vanish, pivot away, like everything good in her life always seemed to do.

In the moments before they walk down the aisle, Lacey had read, some women know their marriages won't last. As they take each measured and stately step toward the altar, past smiling relatives and disappointed competitors and scented grandmothers and a writhing child or two, as they smile and properly position their cascading lilies and roses waist-high, they know it's a mistake. Not Lacey. *Goodbye, mother,* she telegraphed a bitter farewell. *You cannot hurt me anymore.*

This engagement had been an education. In the past months, planning and organizing, she'd learned a new emotional ledger. Been introduced to her new power structure. The calculus of her new family. Over the pre-wedding months of luncheons and teas, shared social events and shopping trips, even in the midst of engraved-or-not invitations and passed-or-plated catering decisions, it was all about mother-in-law Brinn. Brinn, who always had her thumb on the scales. Telling Lacey what to do, making choices, designing and describing and—the balance—paying for it all. "Do call me 'Mother,'" she'd insisted.

It hadn't only been about shopping.

Brinn—who Trevor had warned her was the family's

pill-pusher-in-chief—seemed to revel in her sphere of pharmaceutical power, hinting that if Lacey's "lady system" needed a boost or a tweak, or her nerves were frazzled, or sleeplessness threatened, their family's access to doctors and medications could effortlessly provide everything she would ever need.

"It's all in the cabinet, darling. I'll show you. Or just ask me," Brinn had whispered, her breath fragrant with a lunchtime vodka-tonic. "Modern medicine is a miracle, dear. And we'll have all the Vanderwald heirs, little Trevor the fourth, maybe? And Trev's trust fund will take care of them all, and you, dear, of course."

"You are so wonderfully generous, Mother," Lacey had said. She remembered her younger self, sneaking *Southern Living* from the drugstore racks, watching how the models sat, with ankles crossed and careful posture. She'd devoured articles about proper entertaining and appropriate conversation. She'd studied the successful women as her personal mentors. Never have a photo taken while holding a cocktail. Thankyou notes must be handwritten. While her own mother edged further into her emotional netherworld, Lacey erased her, making glossy magazines her textbooks for advancement. Wasn't that what one was supposed to do? Advance? When she took the next step, into the St. Erasmus sanctuary, she'd advance. Goodbye to those years that went before. She'd won. She'd be happy.

People will believe what they want to believe. They believe what they hope is true. She could work with that.

The flute stopped, and then the church organ rumbled into life, this time with Lacey's music, the "Here comes the bride" that so many little girls long to hear. The music meant a new beginning, the acceptance of a new role. A bride, then a wife. And then, something more. A mother. Her dreams coming true. Truly true.

I do, she thought.

She turned the corner into the sanctuary, alone, as she'd requested. They'd roped garlands of eggshell-satin ribbon and strands of pearls and her favorite white gardenias on each pew. She knew tall silver candelabras, heirlooms, had been placed at the altar, and by now the bridal-white candles they held would be gently flickering.

Lacey turned the corner and saw it all come to life—candles, ribbons, relatives, future. She heard a murmur of approval as the congregants stood, then the rustle of their silk and seersucker. They came to honor *her,* the bride, the newest Vanderwald.

In the front row, the Vanderwald pew. Brinn—"Mother"—in ice-blue silk, Winton in black tie. Brooke, morose as only a sixteen-year-old girl could be, fidgeting in the simple copper silk sheath she'd finally agreed to wear. She'd refused to stand at the altar like a proper bridesmaid, and Lacey had been fine with that. No other bridesmaids either, which she'd convinced a disappointed Brinn was for the best. *"It'll keep the spotlight on Trevor and me, won't it?"* They'd giggled together, two smart women who knew what was good for them.

Her nerves dissolved, and some kind of confidence filled every cell of her body so intently, so intensely, so passionately, that she almost floated away. A soft breeze from somewhere lifted her gossamer veil, and the last rays of evening light filtered through the stained-glass windows, illuminating haloed saints and white-winged angels.

She saw Trevor, ten rows away, hair neatly trimmed and already a hint of a tan, shoulders square and bow tie perfectly horizontal. She saw his face change when he saw her, a light that came from within and not from the glow of beeswax candles. Wives and husbands were supposed to share, they *vowed* to share, for better or for worse.

Trevor was all about *for better*.

And she was about to become a new person. Leave her old life and all its baggage behind. She was about to transform, entirely, into Lacey Vanderwald.

CHAPTER 27

ELLIE

The stuffy air in the WorkHere office felt charged between them. Ellie could almost see Gabe's question hanging in the air. His discovery. And she could not deny it.

Goodbye, Nora, Ellie thought. You've been useful, but this is your final curtain.

"Right?" Gabe persisted. "Nora?"

"So what? I was undercover." Ellie came out from behind the coffee table, putting them on equal footing. She jabbed the air toward him with a forefinger. Staying on offense. "You think I was gonna blow *that*? You think Pharminex would hire a *reporter* as an employee? I had to get inside that company and the only way to do it was to be Nora. And Nora had to stay my secret. Only mine."

Her mind raced. Nora, her cover blown and her usefulness over, would have to vanish. Now she—Ellie—had to pin Gabe down about his own motives. And his identity.

"And listen, dude. Here's what's way more important. What the hell are *you* doing? Right? I was undercover for my job. But you tried to trick me. All that stuff about my imaginary green nightgown, and the mole and—" She shook her head, remembering his phone calls. "What the hell was that about? You get off on seeing if you can charm women into—"

"Hold on, Ellie."

"Hold *on*?" She ticked the names off her fingers as she recited his alter egos. "You were Gabe to me. But *Guy* to Nora. Right? *Right?* That's some juggling act, I must say. Bravo. But how was *that* supposed to work? Was it your idea? Why?"

She let herself picture that evening at Spinnaker, how she'd seen "Gabe" through the fake greenery, recognized him as Nora's "Guy," and realized she had a situation. She'd almost bolted.

But then she got curious. Decided to play it out. But he hadn't flinched when she sat down. Had not shown one glimmer of recognition.

"And—*wait*. Wait wait wait." She narrowed her eyes, baffled at her own conclusion. "You had to know the minute you offered to meet me at Spinnaker that your Guy masquerade would fall apart."

To her annoyance, Gabe laughed.

"Bingo," he said. "That's why I figured it was time for Guy to disappear. I decided you, Ellie-you, were sincere in your goal to expose Pharminex. I told you we're investigating the same thing. You think you're the only one who goes undercover to get information? I'd targeted your whole class of recruits—hung out in doctors' offices to see which sales reps might be willing to divulge secrets in return for—well, whatever I could do for them."

"But why'd you pick *me*? And hey—did you 'target' *just* me? Is there anyone else who thinks you're whoever you pretended to be? Do you have a whole cadre of women you've duped?"

Gabe put up both palms, as if fending off her attack. "No. No, honestly. I saw you—Nora—swiping through a dating app in one of the doctors' offices." He held up his cell phone. "So I knew you were looking. I, uh, followed you after you left. And lucky for me, you eventually went to Seaboard. Mentioning Shakespeare is always successful." He paused, looked at her for a moment. "Turned out, you were all I needed."

She rolled her eyes, remembering her fantasies and cursing her stupid imagination. Remembering their nights at Seaboard, their matching black turtlenecks, the truffle fries.

Did anyone ever tell the whole truth?

"You are such a jerk, Gabe. Or whoever you are."

"Come on, Ellie or Nora or whoever *you* decide to be. Surely you wouldn't condone duplicitous behavior for yourself—but not for me."

"You were pretending all that time?" she asked. "That you didn't know Nora was me?"

"Yup."

She frowned, remembering even more. "Wait. Do the police *really* think Nora had something to do with Kaitlyn's death?"

"Nope. Not that I know of, at least. I just wanted to see if that'd smoke you out."

"Jerk."

"Hey. You did the same thing to me, remember. At Spinnaker. Asked if I'd met any new 'friends.' That was pretty funny."

Ellie eyed the brass owl on the coffee table, and briefly contemplated throwing it at him.

She tried to play back all their encounters, the times she'd adjusted her blond Ellie wig, or called attention to her red Ellie glasses. The times she'd patted herself on the back for her successful disguises. How she'd thought she'd fooled everyone. Well, she had. Except for Gabe.

"I didn't fool you at all?"

"Nope." He gave half a shrug. "Women always think men don't notice them—in the *right* way, at least. I let you think I'd fallen for your masquerade. Wanted to see how far you'd push it."

Ellie weighed the owl in her hand, turned it over and over. "Is this a valuable thing? If I throw it at you, will it break?"

"Who knows? This isn't my office," he said. "I only use it when I need to. Look. I told you, Ellie, straight up, that I suspected Nora was a fraud. Remember? Fake accent, dyed hair, I said. Frankly, I thought maybe you'd own up to it then. But it was *you* who kept up the playacting. You knew Ellie's Gabe was the same person as Nora's Guy. And yet *you* said nothing. What if I had been a bad guy?"

"Exactly!" Ellie made a *duh* expression. "You might have been a spy from Pharminex. Or from somewhere else. I figured if I went along with it, I'd be more likely to find out." She pointed the owl at him. "Is your name really Gabriel Hoyt?"

He pulled a leather wallet from his jeans pocket, held up a D.C. driver's license. "Good enough for you? But I have one more question."

"Shoot." Ellie heard her phone buzzing in her purse. Someone was texting Nora, but she ignored it. There was no more Nora.

Funny how it felt, to be only one person. The actual physical release, the relief, the elimination of the Nora part of her life. No more visits to doctors' offices, with their waiting rooms full of women so needy she almost cried every time she left. Of doctors so malleable and cynical they'd believe the persuasion of salespeople for whom the sole purpose in life was to make money for the company. Not to help their patients.

No more Nora. Even if she'd been doing it for the right reasons, she'd always felt uncomfortable being Nora. Doing the wrong thing for the right reason wasn't the conscience-soother she'd hoped. She could just be Ellie now, the good one, the crusader, the one with an important cause, the powerful journalistic voice that brought this company to its knees.

"So you're dedicated to this Pharminex story, correct?" Gabe said. "Like I am? You'd do anything to reveal the false promises and deception this company has perpetuated, the profits it has made from the harm it's done."

"Yup." She put the owl down. Maybe they could still be a team.

"And you have the inside scoop for a blockbuster story. And our lawsuit."

"Yes, because I'm about to do an interview with—" Ellie stopped.

"The light dawns." Gabe exploded his fingers across his face—*voilà*, a magician illustrating a secret. "Since *you're* Nora, what's this bull about you doing an interview with her? Ellie, are you using yourself as your own source?"

CHAPTER 28

ELLIE

Ellie clicked her key and her car beeped open, but she didn't reach for her door handle. Gabe leaned against the passenger door of his Jeep, hands stuffed into his pockets. They both wore black parkas, plaid mufflers and black wool watch caps, like yuppie cat burglars. Gabe's somber expression in the WorkHere parking lot matched how her own face must look. She'd figured she could pull off the Nora deception. And she had. Until Gabe.

They stood face to face, almost toe to toe, on either side of a yellow parking space line. His battered brown Timberlands, her snow-splotched black boots.

"If only I had stayed home. Not gone to Seaboard that first night, never talked to strange men. And by *strange*, I mean you." Her words puffed into the cold. "I should know that trying to have a personal life is never a good thing."

"Well, come on, sure it is." Gabe shifted and leaned against his car, stuffing his hands into his parka pockets. "We connected, didn't we? That was real, to me at least. And we're still those people. Guy and Nora. It's just best to be honest about your identity."

"Like *you* were?"

"We all have our reasons for being who we are."

Ellie stared at her feet, past the pavement and into the future.

"What *is* identity, though, you know?" She looked up at him, shading her eyes as the sun glared on the snow, and thinking out loud. "We're all only who we say we are. Everyone's hiding something. Everyone's undercover, struggling to be who they want to be in public, only being themselves when they're alone."

Ellie thought about the puzzle pieces of her life. "Gabe? What if I stayed Nora now? No one knows but you."

"How about your researcher?"

"Meg's never met her." Ellie shook her head. "You're the only one who's ever seen me as Ellie *and* Nora."

Ellie watched three dark crows soar in the clouds above the bleak parking lot, silhouetted against a stretch of spackled mackerel sky. Then, in an instant, they simultaneously changed their minds and swooped in the opposite direction.

"I needed being Nora to get me inside. Get the proof I needed," she went on. "I just got caught too soon."

"Way it goes."

"But we have the Abigail interview, anyway." Ellie held up a gloved forefinger, reminding him. *One way or another,* she didn't say.

"Your phone is buzzing." Gabe pointed to her tote bag.

"I'll let it go to—wait." Her Pharminex ring? She looked at Gabe, perplexed. "Hang on," she told him. Then into the phone, "This is . . . Nora."

"It's Detta Fiddler, *Nora.*"

Ellie imagined the woman behind her big desk,

gardenias scenting the room. Her mind raced in the silence. Had something gone wrong? They'd bought her bogus story, even signed an agreement saying so, and she'd have bet anything Detta and Allessandra—and all they represented—were gone from her life. Until, of course, she had to approach them for reaction to her TV story. But that would be as Ellie Berensen, the reporter who would make their lives miserable.

"Hello, Detta." She repeated the woman's name for Gabe's benefit. No use hiding anything from him now, unless she had to, and this might also prove her honesty.

"I tried to text you, but you didn't reply. So, Nora? I've thought about you ever since our meeting," Detta said. "Worried how you'd relied on us for your livelihood. And realized it was only your false name that put us in an untenable position. In fact, other than your Hawkins mistake, you were good at the job. I'm sorry we had to let you go."

"You've thought about me? Good on the job?" Ellie repeated. Gabe hadn't taken his eyes off her, as riveted to this conversation as she was. "You're sorry?"

"And now, I know this seems . . . unlikely. But we need your help, Nora. As of yet, no one but the three of us—you, Allessandra and I—know the circumstances of your departure."

"And those security guards," Ellie couldn't resist adding, remembering to put a hint of a Southern accent in Nora's voice.

"They know what we tell them to know."

"And you're saying—you need my help?"

As Gabe moved closer, Ellie turned the cell phone so they both could hear. They stood, parkas touching, her hat against his in the otherwise deserted parking lot, only the slim cell phone separating them. She tucked herself into the curve of Gabe's shoulder to keep close enough. He didn't move away.

"I'm sorry, Detta," Ellie said. "The connection is iffy. Can you say that again?"

"We've heard a reporter is looking into . . . something," Detta said. "Apparently she's approaching our sales reps, so says our anonymous phone caller. She's pretending to be a patient, hanging out in doctors' offices searching for women to tell her who knows what. We need to find out if it's true. And what else she's doing. Could you come back, Nora? Be our eyes and ears? No one would notice *you* in doctors' offices. The award gala's soon, so the timing could not be worse."

A dark sedan drove by, tires slushing through the ice-melt scattered on the pavement. Ellie glanced at the person in the driver's seat but didn't have time to see if she'd recognized him. Or her. Talk about paranoia. She looked at Gabe, wondering what he thought of Detta's proposal.

Pretending to be a patient. But Ellie hadn't done that. Then she knew: *Meg.*

"I was in a lot of waiting rooms too," she said as Nora. "What does this reporter look like? What story do you think they're working on?"

Ellie's brain raced with possibilities, the unpredictability and the risks. Nora hadn't been gone from Pharminex for long. Not long enough, Ellie hoped, for any of her colleagues to notice. For all they knew, Nora might be out of town. Sick. Or on a different schedule. Nora's cleaned-out locker could be restored by the time business opened Monday.

"It's a woman, that's all we know," Detta said. "And as for what story, we have no idea. We've done nothing wrong."

Gabe pulled away from the call, rolled his eyes in derision, then pressed back into place beside her.

"Really? No idea? That seems unlikely." Ellie decided to push her. "It'd be helpful if I had some inkling of what to look for. A disgruntled employee. A whistleblower, maybe. But disgruntled about what? Whistleblowing about what?"

Detta ignored Ellie's questions. "Can you come meet with us? Maybe later today?"

"Today?"

Gabe was waving a finger at her: *no*.

"How about Monday?" she suggested. There was no way to get answers without having a meeting, but she'd need to reorganize into her Nora self. "And I need to bring someone. My . . ."

Gabe pointed to himself.

"My lawyer. I—" She could tell Gabe was calculating as fast as she was. "I want to make sure it's legal. That our confidentiality deal holds. And maybe we need another contract."

Gabe nodded in agreement as she continued to spin out the story.

"Including your acknowledging that I was—and am—using a pseudonym."

"Understood," Detta said. "Monday, my office, nine?"

"Monday, nine?" Ellie repeated. Gabe nodded *okay*. "Got it."

After she hung up, the two of them stared at the phone in Ellie's hand.

"*Whoa*. Did that just happen?" Gabe asked. "Does this make any sense whatsoever?"

Ellie stashed her phone into a pocket. "This is their total MO. Spying. P-X is all about slimy corporate tricks. Fraud, duplicity, lies," she told him, deciding not to reveal her own entrapment by Dr. Hawkins.

"And I still can't get their possible connection to Kaitlyn Armistead out of my head. But this gives us more access to the company than ever. And with two of us, we'll be . . ." She tried to choose a word. "I was going to say 'safe.' Safer, I guess. So—you're in?"

Ellie waited for his answer, realizing her new power position.

"So funny. Now I'll be undercover-undercover," she said. "I'll be investigating Pharminex with a signed contract from the company saying I can do it. That's got to be a first."

"We'll know more once we talk with them. As your lawyer, I might have to say no."

"But it's a way to reveal what they're doing! They're dangerous and destructive. Criminal. They're essentially murderers, and they know it."

"I agree. But it's risky, Ellie. The stakes are colossal."

"Listen, I'm freezing." The stakes *were* colossal, that was the point. "I can't even feel my toes. And I'm starving." She clicked open her car door. "You want to get some food? Talk about this someplace warmer?"

"Sure. But speaking of 'some place,'" Gabe said. "I'm still wondering if whoever broke into your apartment thought they were in *Nora's* place."

"I thought of that too," Ellie said. "If it was P-X who did it."

"Who else would it be? And if Nora wasn't their target, maybe they're on to *you*. As Ellie. Could your researcher—Mary?—have alerted them to you, somehow, even inadvertently, without you knowing it?"

"Meg." Ellie, scowling, kicked at one of her own tires, punctuating her anger. "You know, Meg actually *offered* to masquerade as a patient. She brought it up in the news director's office."

"Exactly as Detta Fiddler described."

"Yup. And she's incredibly pushy. Overeager. War-ren told her in no uncertain terms that pretense was forbidden."

"Would she have ignored that?"

"Who knows. She's either trying to take over my story or ruin it. She's always looking at my notes. Offering to 'organize' my files. Probably trying to steal my job."

Gabe nodded. "Possibly. Or maybe she's just on your team. Trying to help. Right? But if it's Meg going rogue, at least you know who to look for."

CHAPTER 29

ELLIE

She'd never seen Gabe in a suit before, or in his navy overcoat and polished shoes. Monday morning, eight thirty, and Ellie needed to reassure herself yet again as the shiny silver doors closed them into the Pharminex elevator. This was as undercover as it got—pretending to be someone she wasn't, but now in service of the same enemy she was working to destroy. She felt poised on the edge of a chambered nautilus shell, about to wind deeper and deeper into its dark center. She hoped she'd be able to find her way out. Now she was taking step one, and with someone she wasn't certain was a reliable guide.

"Fiddler and Lewes have never met you, right, Gabe?" She could hear the apprehension in her own voice. "They have no idea you exist. Not in any way. Tell me the truth. You can only be my lawyer if they have no idea who you are."

"Stop worrying," he said. They both moved to the back of the empty elevator, leaned against the brass rail. Both looked up, watching the green-lighted floor indicator. They were on the way to twelve, not the company's main floor reception area but the more exclusive executive suites up above. A uniformed guard, after a smile of recognition at Nora and a check of a logbook, had key-carded them access and, since they were early, told them to wait in the upstairs reception area until they were summoned. Ellie knew that this floor, higher than where she'd first met Detta and Allessandra Lewes, was off-limits to most people.

She and her sister reps had once speculated about what might be going on there. Wild parties and debauchery, Lydia Frost had suggested. "Secret experiments!" Jenn Wahl had guessed, eyes widening. Christine, always the serious one, had put a stop to it. "I've been there. It's offices. Where they don't have to deal with the piddly likes of us."

Ellie now scanned the elevator for surveillance cameras, scanned for microphones, surprised at her own unease. *Stop worrying*, Gabe had instructed her. As if.

Talk about worry. Ellie had texted Meg that she was out doing research and asked her to check in. So far, she'd heard nothing back. If Meg truly was masquerading as a patient, in direct disobedience to Warren's instructions, that'd yank the career rug out from under her.

"What if Detta looks you up, Gabe?" she persisted now. "After they meet you?"

"They'll see me listed as a lawyer," he said. "Chill, Ellie. I mean, Nora. It's only a meeting. We'll handle it."

"What if—" She looked at the indicator, five floors to go. "What if this is a trap? What if they know I'm Ellie Berensen and—"

"How would they?" He turned to her. "You're Nora Quinn. That's all you have to remember."

The elevator pinged, stopped. The polished silver door shuddered.

"Shush. Someone's getting on." Ellie pulled out her cell phone. "This is Nora," she said into the cell.

As the doors slid open, Ellie pretended to focus on her call. Gabe created his own role and stepped away from her, turning his shoulders and telegraphing to the newcomer that they were strangers.

"Nora?" A woman stepped onto the elevator, smiling in recognition. "Happy Monday. Been a while. On your way to the lockers?"

"Lydia." Ellie held up a finger, pointed to her phone. Lydia Frost from her training class. As far as Lydia—or anyone else—was concerned, there'd been no accusations, no firing, no cleaning out of Nora's locker. This was just another day at the office. As the doors slid closed, Lydia pushed 9, where the lockers were.

Ellie continued her pretend phone conversation and noticed Lydia eyeing Gabe. She was probably wondering what this handsome man was doing in the Pharminex building, and how to meet him.

She pretend hung up the phone from her pretend call. Lots of pretending going on this morning. "Sorry, Lydia. You know how it goes."

"Yeah." Lydia hitched her tote bag onto her shoulder. Gabe edged farther away. She smiled at him, engaging and almost inquisitive, but he simply acknowledged her, then seemed more interested in watching the lighted elevator numbers changing. The elevators were the office joke, notoriously slow.

"Lyd, weird question for you," Ellie said. "I was, well, approached, in a doctor's office, by a person who said they were a reporter. Wanting to know about—" She stopped, pretended to change her mind.

"Of course, I told them to call public relations, like we're supposed to. But it freaked me out." She pretended to look at Gabe, pretended to gauge his level of interest, pretended to sound cautious. "And after we talked about the, you know, the people who might also be where we are?"

"Yeah." Lydia drew out the word. "I remember the conversation with Jenn and the gang at the lockers. About the cute—"

Gabe took off his glasses and put his phone up to his ear, covering the left side of his face. As if he were trying to hide? Oh. No. *Cute doctor,* Lydia was about to say. Who, Ellie realized with a lurch of her stomach, might have been Gabe.

"Not *that* person," Ellie interrupted before Lydia could say more. "This was a *woman.* She acted like a patient. Asking questions about . . . stuff. You see anyone like that?"

Lydia frowned. "No. And I'd remember. You did the right thing, Nora, obvs. Telling her to call PR." The elevator bell pinged, the light for 9 went green, and Lydia cocked her head toward the opening door. "This is me. You getting out? No? Okay, then, keep me posted on the reporter or whoever. See ya."

Ellie sagged as the door finally closed them back in. "*You.* Dressed in that white coat. I forgot about that," she said. "What if someone recognizes you? What if Lydia—that woman was a rep named Lydia Frost—goes and rats you out?"

"Ellie." Gabe put his glasses back on. "Look. We're about to have access to everything we need to know. I'm Gabriel Hoyt, your lawyer. You're Nora Quinn. And we're about to enter the inner circle of the very company you're investigating. What's more, they *invited* us in. We got this, Ellie."

"*Nora,*" she corrected him.

"Nora," he agreed. "For now."

The elevator doors opened into the wide reception area on the twelfth floor of the Pharminex building, and then closed behind them. Ellie—Nora—saw a familiar shape ahead: ponytail, dark overcoat, fringed tote bag, canvas briefcase.

Meg.

CHAPTER 30

ELLIE

"Hide," Ellie whispered. "Right now. *Do* it." She grabbed Gabe's arm and dragged him around the corner of the hallway.

Meg. Who did not know, and could not be allowed to know, that Ellie and Nora Quinn were one and the same.

Meg's back was to Ellie and Gabe, and she stood, apparently waiting, facing a polished mahogany reception desk with a massive Pharminex logo on the wall behind it. The desk was unoccupied, and no one else was in the room. A long gray flannel couch sat empty, as did the taupe paisley side chairs across from it. A round coffee table, supported by what looked like oversized glass laboratory beakers, was positioned between them, a faceted-crystal vase of spidery white mums in the center.

Ellie yanked Gabe behind her, and it felt like the times, so long ago, when she and her brother had played hide-and-seek in the corridors and crannies of their father's office. But the stakes were much higher now.

"Stay back," Ellie ordered. "But look in the reception room. *That* is freaking Meg."

"What the hell is she doing here?" Gabe whispered.

Ellie felt his body pressed against her back, his coat against hers, his breath in her ear. The fragrance of the cold Monday morning lingered on him, a chill laced with sunshine.

"I can find out," he said, his voice low. He came out from behind Ellie, then turned to her, frowning. He put a hand on her shoulder, as if setting her in place. "You stay here. We're still early for Fiddler. Hang on."

He left her no time to protest. She plastered herself to the dark paneled wall as he walked away, hardly daring to show herself but incapable of resisting a peek. She craned her head around the corner a fraction of an inch, no more, standing on tiptoe and trying to keep her balance. Not the best outcome if she toppled over into the reception room. Gabe was already past the couch and the mums and approaching the desk. Playing visitor, she figured. So far so good.

Meg turned to him with a quick appraisal, then a slower one. The ponytail bobbed as her expression changed from cold assessment to warmer approval. Ellie rolled her eyes. The woman was so predictable. But maybe now that was a good thing.

Gabe said something, looking amiable. Meg answered, ponytail bobbing again. Gabe smiled as he responded, engaging her.

Much as Ellie tried, she couldn't hear what they were saying. Gabe gestured to the empty desk, as if questioning, and Meg laughed, though nothing Gabe could possibly have said could be that funny. Gabe looked at his watch, shaking his head with a wry expression. Meg gestured prettily and said something again. Maybe commiserating about having to wait.

Heart pounding, Ellie turned slowly and peered the other way down the corridor. All she needed was to have someone demand to know what she was doing. What could she say?

She straightened, smoothed her hair. Amused at her own confusion. She was Nora Quinn. She worked here. No need to hide. Except from Meg, of course. *That* she couldn't risk. But she felt her shoulders relax, and her face take on Nora's confidence. When she eventually entered the reception area, she'd be Nora. But Meg could not be allowed to see her as Nora. Ellie's pretense only worked when people knew her as just one person—only Gabe had seen Ellie *and* Nora. She risked another look around the corner.

Meg was lifting her briefcase, and put it on the reception desk, talking as she did. Explaining something?

It was like watching an old silent movie, but without the captioned slides to explain the action and dialogue. She trusted Gabe, though—and then she frowned. *Did* she trust him? Until recently, all he'd done was lie to her. Maybe that hadn't stopped.

Because now here he was with Meg, chatting amicably, almost as if—she paused, another disturbing possibility washing over her. Almost as if he knew her? Ellie observed them through a different filter, as the two discussed something she could not hear.

If Gabe knew Meg, what was the connection? She pulled out her cell phone: 8:37. They still had time until their appointment with Detta Fiddler. She texted Gabe's number, watched him react to his phone's vibration, watched him read the text.

WHAT UP?

Without flinching or smiling or reacting, he put the phone back into his pocket. Meg took a pen and notebook out of her tote bag, ripped out a sheet of paper, then wrote something on it, using the reception desk as a table. She folded it into thirds and handed it to Gabe. Without looking at it, he tucked it into an inside pocket of his overcoat.

They shook hands, with Meg offering the most Megian smile Ellie had ever seen. She was up to something.

Gabe gestured toward the elevator, then made a sign with his hand—the universal signal for *I'll call you*. Or—*you call me*. Inexplicably, Meg was leaving.

Which meant Ellie had to hide again. Or head down the long corridor. The nearest door was metal and labeled FIRE STAIRS. An alarm would ring if she opened it. A sign just beyond offered the ideal solution: the silhouette of a person in a skirt. She could only hope Meg wouldn't head the same way.

Ellie hurried into the ladies' room. Into a stall, closing the door, she took a seat and put her feet up against the brownish metal wall of the enclosure. She closed her eyes. Counted to thirty.

Nothing.

Texted Gabe. *All clear?*

He texted back. *She's gone. Come back. I'll explain later.*

She opened the stall door, slowly, peeking out. No one. Taking a deep breath, she checked her Nora hair in the mirror, then touched a finger to each side of her mouth, making sure her Nora lipstick was reasonably applied.

Eight fifty-five, according to her cell phone screen. Her colleagues, sister pharma reps like Lydia, were no doubt already selecting the day's samples and giveaways from their ninth-floor lockers. What was Meg doing in the key-card-access-only, rarefied atmosphere of the twelfth floor? She opened the bathroom door into the corridor.

Empty. Quiet. No one. Heart still racing—she couldn't calm it—she tried to look normal as she walked toward the reception area. The morning had already been uncertain enough without the surprise appearance of Meg.

Ellie approached the corner of the reception area. Gabe sat on one of the armchairs, swiping through his phone.

Ellie—*Nora,* she reminded herself—squared her shoulders and lifted her chin, channeling Nora's elegant posture and infinite confidence. With an unnecessary toss of her head, since no one was there but Gabe, she strode into the room, like any woman who'd just hit the ladies' and was ready for her day.

She wondered where Meg would tell her she'd been this morning.

"All set?" She asked a benign question, in case anyone was listening, though no one but Gabe was in the reception area.

He stood, then sat down again. He gestured to the chair beside him.

"I have to keep checking your hair to remember what to call you," he whispered.

"What the hell was that about? I almost had a heart attack."

Gabe pressed his lips together, staring at the vase of white mums.

"Gabe?"

"So, uh. Meg. She told me she was here to apply for a job."

"Not as someone from Channel Eleven?" Ellie watched the closed doors of the elevator as if they might open again and reveal Meg, ready to pounce on them.

"Nope. She said she'd convinced the guard to let her up here. She wanted to just drop off a résumé.

Said she thought if she could wrangle her way to the twelfth floor, they'd be impressed with her . . . *gumption*, I think, was the word she used."

"That's weak," Ellie said. "But just delusional enough to possibly be true."

"I told her I worked here and I knew Detta Fiddler, and that she wouldn't be here for a while. Then I told her my name was Will Faraday—to make it tougher to track me down—and offered to take her name and number for Detta. Which," he patted his pocket, "I now have. Though unlikely that I'll pass her message along."

Ellie tilted her head, thinking. "Will Faraday? Sure. Whatever. But if she were job hunting, wouldn't she have given you a résumé? So why would she *truly* be here?" Ellie shrugged off her coat. "Who ever knows with that woman. Anyway, drama over. And it's still only five till nine."

"Ellie?" Gabe set his phone on the table.

"What?" Ellie sat down too.

"So, your Meg . . ." Gabe put one palm on each knee, his dark shoes flat on the carpet, his shoulders hunched. He turned toward her, his head only, like an owl.

"What about her?" Ellie couldn't read his expression.

He looked at the floor, and then, as if he'd made a decision, at her. "I think she's Brooke Vanderwald."

BEFORE

CHAPTER 31

LACEY

Not ever? Not *ever*? Lacey, wrapped in a thin blue paper robe—a johnnie, they called them—her bare thighs against the clear plastic cover of the doctor's exam table, felt her eyes well with tears. She shivered in the air-conditioning and couldn't quite make her brain comprehend what this doctor was trying to explain. It was impossible that he was telling her she could never have children.

Impossible.

She erased that from her mind. Thought about other things. She focused on her wedding ring, the velvety-patinaed rose-gold band that had belonged to Trevor's paternal grandmother, Lissy. On the icy engagement diamond, a carré cut in an Edwardian setting, from Trevor's mother's mother, Grandmère. These were the objects, heritage indelibly attached, that branded Lacey as family. But no precious stones or metals could bond her to the Vanderwalds the way children would.

She saw Dr. Sheppard's mouth moving, but he could not be telling the truth, so she would not listen. She would not.

His blubbery face and his open white coat and his black stethoscope and the too-bright lights buzzing over her head, it all went blurry, and the soft yellow wallpaper with butterflies all over it, why were there butterflies? Her brain seemed to float up through the butterflies and out into the sky.

"One of the things that's difficult to predict . . ."

She heard the doctor's voice through a wash of waves or the rustle of trees, or maybe it was the sound of her heart breaking. She wanted children, Trevor wanted children, she wanted Trevor, she wanted her life, she wanted *their* life, she wanted what she'd dreamed of. What she deserved. What had been so close.

"It may be that you have an allergy which causes . . ."

And Brinn. Lacey had left her sitting in the plush white leather of one of Dr. Malcolm Sheppard's private waiting areas. Here, in his tastefully furnished office disguised as a genteel suburban home, there was no congregation of patients trying to salvage some privacy by barricading themselves with magazines. Dr. Sheppard provided separate grasscloth-papered cubicles, where worried mothers-in-waiting and their loved ones could protect their secrets from the prying and imaginative eyes of their neighbors.

"He knows best," Brinn had assured her as they'd left the car with a white-visored attendant. Apparently even the cars were given privacy. Lacey wondered what Brinn was planning now. How she would handle this diagnosis. How she would manage it.

After Lacey's first miscarriage, Brinn, consoling and reassuring, had explained it was nature's way, and Mother Nature realizing she'd made a mistake, and that Lacey and Trevor should try again. Lacey did not feel like it was a mistake, but managed not to say so. After the second miscarriage, with Lacey's eyes dark-circled and her skin ashen, Brinn had allowed a moment of worry, suggesting doctors and tests and genetic assays, all of which proved Lacey was . . . healthy, but unlucky.

"Try again," Brinn had urged, "third time's the charm." The third time, she'd offered Pharminex doctors, advice, experimental treatments.

When Lacey had repeated that conversation, Trevor had chugged the last of his National Bohemian. Natty Boh was as household here in coastal Bayellen as Schlitz had been in her childhood.

"Can't hurt." He'd tossed the bottle into their bedroom wastebasket. "And Lace? Don't try to fight Mom when it comes to 'modern medicine.' It can fix anything, she always says."

"She used those words with me too," Lacey remembered. "*Modern medicine.*"

"Got to remember why she is where she is, Lace. Pharminex."

Lacey heard the opening of the bedroom fridge, heard the hissing twist of another bottle opening.

"'Take three instead of two of whatever you need.' That's Mom. Empress of the medicine cabinet."

The doctor was still talking, but now Lacey's brain could only manage to retrieve some of the words. *Never, sometimes, always. Permanent.*

"I don't understand this," Lacey replied, honestly not knowing whether her tears were rage or sorrow or loss or an enduring bafflement that at every turn the world seemed to be conspiring against her. Was there a destiny, a set path, that some deep force chose for you at birth? No matter how determined or driven you were, no matter what road map to life you created for yourself, you could only go so far until the universe, laughing, yanked you back where you belonged.

Putting on airs, Lacey's mother would have said. Like when Lacey had appropriated the more socially acceptable last name of her mother's newest husband, Karl Grisham, instead of keeping her birth name. She'd studied in high school—yes, she had—but also made sure her advisors had given her special recommendations, a well-placed phone call or two, in exchange for other favors Lacey could bestow.

No matter how you achieved it, success was all about getting in. Lacey had deduced that early on. Finally at a prestigious-enough college, her sorority sisters had embraced Lacey's blond-by-then voluptuousness as well as the heartbreaking story of her valiant determination after her parents' tragic accident and the resulting clash of predatory lawyers. Luckily, no one asked too many questions. Lacey was in. And Trevor had clinched it.

And then, as Lacey was on the verge of getting accepted into the Vanderwald world for ever and for good, came miscarriage number three.

Two months afterward, Brinn had invited her to go shopping. But instead of taking Chestnut Street to Violetta's, Brinn had pulled up in front of this white-shuttered Bayellen home, hedges artfully trimmed and a bluestone path to a filigreed front door. A tiny engraved sign, barely noticeable by the silver doorbell, said: BY APPOINTMENT ONLY.

"What's this?" Lacey asked.

"It's my special gift for you." Brinn had raised one eyebrow, Cheshire-cat conspiratorial. "For you and Trevor."

"But—what?"

"Honey, honey, honey." Brinn brushed Lacey's hair from her forehead, sweetly maternal. "You and I? We have access. Pharminex has an entire research department constantly looking for ways to help women.

Women like you. And this is so perfect. Darling. Trust me. I promise, this will make . . ." Cat with cream. "Everything work."

And soon Lacey was perched, in blue paper, on Dr. Sheppard's vinyl examination table. That first day, he'd given her an injection. Then another.

"This will help you," he'd promised. "And come back in two weeks."

And now she was hearing this impossible thing. And all because Brinn had . . . tricked her. Lied to her. Manipulated her. Like she always always *always* did. Lacey, a fully formed college-educated intelligent human being, should have been able to make her *own* decision—but Brinn had taken over her life, like a predatory animal, a tawny lioness desperate for cubs. Or for control.

"Would you like some water, dear, while we talk?" Dr. Sheppard, apparently attempting to be paternal and comforting, seemed genuinely concerned. She'd told him her body had never been what the books called normal. But was there something truly *wrong*? She'd been embarrassed to talk to her mother about that kind of thing, and certainly couldn't bring it up to her doctor at home either. He'd known her since she was a girl, and how could she ask Doc Melander about her *periods,* for heaven's sake? She could not even say the word.

But after the wedding, she'd needed her body to work. When she found Trevor, she knew, in her soulest of souls, it all had to be perfect. For their family. It was the only way she could succeed. She knew it. To be a part of the Vanderwald family, there had to be a *family*. Wives were disposable, forgettable, replaceable. Children were blood.

Dr. Sheppard, his lumpy shape balancing on a leather swivel stool, interrupted her thoughts, looking up at her behind those old-fashioned glasses. Since she was still on the table, sitting up, her lap right at his eye level, Lacey felt like the doctor was looking straight into her naked private parts. She shifted in her paper outfit, adjusting, trying to stay decent.

"In basic terms," he was saying, "your reproductive system was not producing enough eggs—enough viable eggs. And it appeared from my initial examination and subsequent testing that you might have difficulty staying pregnant."

She winced at the word.

"So you and I, together, decided it might be prudent to try a medication that's shown some efficacy in helping women *become* pregnant, and carry to term. That's why you signed the consent form last time. As we said, though this drug, Monifan, is generally used for another purpose, there's impressive gynecological research indicating it could have the result of making your uterus more receptive to the . . ." He looked up at her, pausing.

"Ms. Vanderwald? May I call you Lacey?" He stopped, searching for words. "I know this is difficult for you, and I know you've been trying. To have a baby."

Which was completely true. She had counted and calculated and decided. She and Trevor had made it a game, an adventure, a *Fifty Shades* experiment. They'd tried positions and places, and giggled, every time, that people would assume all they thought about was sex and each other. And Lacey would throw back her head and laugh, and say *it's true, darlin' Trevor, it's true, I live for it,* and she'd hold out her arms and beg him for more when the true truth? It wasn't about pleasure at all, it was about insurance.

"But Lacey? Let me put it this way. Sadly . . ." Dr. Sheppard eyed her up and down, seemed to be considering how to finish his sentence. "In rare circumstances, because of a hormonal imbalance that's impossible to predict, this drug can have a detrimental and permanent effect on the very reproductive system we are trying to enhance."

"Permanent?" Lacey could not cry, she couldn't, even though she was watching a movie in her head of her entire future life as a black hole, an endless series of lonely, unfulfilled days, like one of those forgotten plastic bags, stuck, forever, forgotten, ignored, fluttering on a jagged tree branch. She could never have children? This was completely wrong. Completely unfair. "Isn't there anything we can do? Something I can take to reverse it? Or, I don't know." She scoured the universe for guidance. "Surgery?"

Sheppard was shaking his head. "I'm afraid not."

She put her hands over her face, wishing that when she took her hands away she'd be somewhere else entirely, with Trevor and baby Trev in Paris or on a beach maybe, but when she took her hands away to see her family, there was only potato-faced Dr. Sheppard.

"As I said when we first discussed it, it's—well," he said. "It's called 'off-label' use. Remember? You did read the consent before you signed it, didn't you? But my dear, there is always adoption, and . . ."

His voice blurred into blithering nothingness, his words absurd and meant for someone else, not Lacey, never her. *Brinn*. The woman should have left well enough alone.

Brinn had brought her here. Brinn had forced her. Forced her! And had left her no choice. Brinn had convinced her, cajoled her, reassured her, even after her first injection. *Oh, you're the luckiest! Our innovation team is certain it'll work, it's new, and fabulous, it's a miracle . . .*

Lacey felt her mind flame and burn and shrivel, shrivel like her own dead insides, and then spiral into darkness and then even darkerness.

Dr. Sheppard pushed his ugly glasses higher on his ugly nose, then stood.

"I'll give you a few moments to get dressed and then come back. We'll talk about how to make the best of it."

She sat, silent and motionless, as he closed the door behind him, leaving her in antiseptic silence. She'd been so excited that morning, she remembered, with the prospect of happiness, happiness in the form of this miraculous remedy, that's what it was, hadn't he told her that? Hadn't Brinn?

She stared at the mawkish yellow wall, at the dumb diplomas and certificates that didn't mean a damn thing, and pictured the babies who would never be, and the family that would never be, and it was not her fault. It was the medicine. It was Pharminex.

And it was Brinn. She sat up straighter, as straight as she could, feeling her spine stiffen along with her resolve.

The need for a child twisted through her brain and clutched at her heart, binding it, wrapping it, insistent, relentless, demanding.

"Make the best of it." She muttered the doctor's platitude out loud, then flinched at the bitterness in her voice. She wouldn't tell Trevor, that was for sure. He thought she was perfect, he told her so all the time, and now she wasn't.

And Brinn? *Mother,* she'd insisted Lacey call her. Disgusting.

She lifted her chin, determined. She could pretend with the best of them. She'd smile and blush and be the perfect Vanderwald wife. She'd spent her entire life acting. Acting like everything was perfect. To hold on to her new life, she had to continue acting. But on her own terms now. Not Brinn's. Not ever again.

She snapped off the belt of the paper johnnie and stood in the doctor's office, naked and shivering, and like every day of her damned life, determined. Maybe this doctor was wrong. He had to be wrong. She listened for his footsteps. Nothing. *Coward*. He would pay for this. Or better—Mother Brinn would pay. She wasn't the only one with power.

She grabbed for her ivory satin underwear, *lacy for Lacey*, Trevor had said when he presented it to her, and she had laughed, putting it on, then taking it off.

Now, dressing for her next battle, she could almost hear her real mother's fetid voice hooting at her, taunting. *We plan and God laughs, little girl*, like a curse, in that saccharine drawl. *You put on airs, but He'll bring you down to earth.*

CHAPTER 32

ELLIE

"Oh, come *on*, Gabe. Not a chance. Impossible." Ellie waved him off. Just before nine now, but the Pharminex reception area was still deserted. "If Meg Weest is Brooke Vanderwald, daughter of the Pharminex Vanderwalds, that would mean that somehow, of all the cities in all the world, in all the television stations in all the world, of all the reporters in all the world, of all the investigations in all the world—"

The center elevator doors slid open. Ellie whipped her head around to see who'd emerge. But it was empty. After a pause, the elevator seemed to sigh and the doors swished closed.

Ellie shook her head. "The idea that Brooke Vanderwald would just happen to show up and become *my* researcher when I'm looking into the company that her family owns? Impossible." She consulted her watch. "Detta's keeping us waiting, I see. Anyway, Sherlock, what're you smoking to make you think she's Brooke?"

Gabe stayed in his chair, staring at the mums.

She poked his arm with one finger. "I'm listening."

"When I last saw Brooke—"

"You've seen her?"

"Her brother, Trevor, was a classmate. No real connection, no big friendship, just the same school. He had a blowout birthday party at a country club. Years ago. And his little sister was there for it. All, you know, braces. Bad skin." He looked at her, as if remembering, "Awkward. Fifteen. Or so."

"Did you talk to her then?" Ellie asked.

"Not that I remember." Gabe shrugged. "I suppose you're right. It's unlikely. More than unlikely."

"Did Meg seem to recognize *you*?" That would be a complication.

"No reason for her to remember me. I was older, in her brother's circle. She was a teenager. In an *I hate everyone* stage. When you think you're going to be unhappy forever. You know how it was." He gave half a smile. "Did you ever look her up, in your research about the company and the family?"

"Yeah, way back," Ellie admitted. "But after you mentioned it, I checked again. And I saw an internet thing, like, yesterday, that after she got out of rehab, the fam shipped her off to Majorca or Málaga, I forget, someplace ritzy like that, spending her trust fund. Or maybe she's . . . you know. Damaged goods. From the accident. The snooty Vanderwald types could never deal with that. Or *maybe*, prodigal daughter, she'll show up at the gala. That'd be something."

Gabe stood, unbuttoned his coat, folded it over his arm. "Where's Fiddler, I wonder?"

"Are we finished talking about Meg Weest being Brooke Vanderwald? Because the real Meg, the TV researcher, seems to be on an unsanctioned mission into enemy territory, which makes me wonder if *she's* actually the enemy. What if—"

"Nora." Gabe's voice changed, now formal and warning. He tilted his head toward the back of the room, where a door had opened behind the reception desk.

Ellie blinked, trying to remember if she'd even noticed the outline of a door.

Maren, Ellie remembered. Fiddler's haughty secretary. "Maybe *she's* Brooke Vanderwald," Ellie whispered to Gabe.

"Hello, Maren," Ellie said in her normal voice. "This is my lawyer, Gabriel Hoyt. He's here to—"

"Ms. Fiddler will see you both now," Maren interrupted.

I'm Nora, Nora, Nora, Ellie kept thinking, as she assumed her Nora face and her confident Nora posture, and listened to Gabe and Detta Fiddler hash out another confidentiality agreement—her second in two weeks, this one about her new mission. How would Nora feel about this assignment? Hurt, but vindicated, Ellie decided. A battered woman who'd been apologized to and offered money to secure her allegiance.

Detta's back was to the wide window. Her view, if she ever turned to look at it, was a sliver of sky, the pointy top of the Custom House Tower, and past that, a strip of Boston Harbor, water meeting sky. Detta had barricaded herself behind her desk, her gardenias in full fragrance, white flowers without a hint of browning edges. Detta seemed to be ignoring the leather-skirted Allessandra, hovering as usual behind Detta's shoulder.

Gabe had first taken the upholstered visitor's chair to Ellie's left, but stood to accept a manila file folder Detta handed him.

"Take a look," Detta instructed. "We'll wait while you read it."

Ellie yanked her Nora-self back to this center of power, this carefully appointed room where lives were discussed like entries in a ledger. She'd been lost in angry thoughts, thoughts of retribution and revenge. Trying to understand why people made the decisions they did. For power, or money, or even because they thought it was the right thing.

"Nora?" Gabe tapped the papers in the open file folder. "This proposal indicates you'll be reassigned as a customer service slash public relations representative. No longer actively repping products but tasked with assessing consumer reaction and protecting the company's market position. You'd report to Ms. Fiddler directly. Are you amenable to this?"

"What do *you* think, Gabe?" As if she would say no. As if she would refuse this access. There was always the chance that Detta Fiddler was trying to trap her again. But it was a risk she'd take. Gabe too. *Lawyers and journalists.* Together they had the power to make things right.

"I think it's likely a waste of time. But that's not for us to assess. So. Agreed." Gabe closed the folder. "But no promises. Ms. Quinn cannot guarantee she'll discover anyone—reporter or other unwanted questioner—who's approaching your employees. It may not even be true."

"Oh, it's true," Allessandra finally contributed, narrowing her eyes as if trying to read the room. "We have—shall we say—people in certain pivotal doctors' offices and other places. We know what's going on. It's a necessary evil. A cost of doing business."

"Like your spy? Dr. Hawkins?" Ellie couldn't resist saying. "The liar who cost me my job?"

"Which means our methods work, correct?" Detta drummed her fingers on her desktop, then stopped, possibly realizing the attitude it telegraphed.

Allessandra stepped forward, taking over. "We need to ensure the safety and efficacy of our products, as well as their security. The stakes are high. It's too easy to ruin a company's reputation. Too easy for the media to spin some fake story, gossip, essentially, exploiting so-called 'victims' who certainly understood—"

Ellie caught Detta's short-lived expression of disapproval.

"What Allessandra means," Detta rolled over the end of her assistant's sentence, "is that we'd be infinitely grateful to you, Nora. We need to make clear to the board and to the stockholders—"

"And to the public," Gabe said.

"Goes without saying," Detta said.

"Does it?" Gabe asked.

"That no renegade journalist is targeting our company."

Ellie looked Detta square in the eye, knowing that Detta was seeing Nora. The woman she'd had no problem entrapping, discrediting and discarding. Detta also apparently had no hesitation about using her again if she thought it was to her advantage.

Nora would assert herself in any discussion of her future, Ellie figured. "Detta? How can I help you stop something you're not sure even exists? If I'm to be part of this search, we need to be clear about that and—"

Search. She stopped herself midsentence. "Detta? Did you have someone break into my apartment?"

"What?" Detta looked surprised, though Ellie assumed the woman had practice with artifice.

"Your apartment?" Allessandra frowned.

"Is that a no?" Gabe said. "*Someone* did."

"Did you call the police?" Detta asked. "Did the burglar take anything?"

"Was it you?" Ellie persisted. Detta had not asked whether Nora was at home or if she had been harmed.

"Let me be clear, Ms. Quinn. And to you too, Mr. Hoyt. On the record. On the *permanent* record. And immutable. We do nothing—nothing—that's in any way criminal." Detta Fiddler stood, resting her fingertips on her desk, her chair rolling out from behind her with the decisive motion. "Yes, we employ people to make sure our company is not targeted or harmed. But—" She pressed her lips together and sat back down, smoothing her black skirt underneath her. "I assure you we would never cross that line. Clear?"

How do you know if someone is lying? Listening to Detta, assessing her earnest expression and persuasive techniques, Ellie had to wonder. She herself had spent much of her career doing the same thing. And expecting people to believe her.

As Nora, she'd lied to convince this company to give her a job in the first place, lied to further her investigation, then lied her way out when she got caught. As Ellie, she'd lied to convince her news director and everyone else that she had no agenda but to be a journalist exposing a powerful and unscrupulous business. Now she was being offered an assignment where the stated point was to keep on lying. And to discover who else was doing the same thing.

When the stakes were life and death, did a few lies matter?

CHAPTER 33

ELLIE

"That was pretty surreal," Ellie said, as she and Gabe pushed through the heavy glass revolving door and out into the morning, entering the Monday gloom. A messy-bunned walk-and-talker looked up from her cell phone to glare at Ellie, who apparently had dared to step into her path. This time of morning, the tail end of rush hour, the foot traffic was only post-weekend stragglers, some hurrying against the cold, others tardy and defeated. Everyone carried coffee. "You're pretty convincing as a lawyer."

"I *am* a lawyer." Gabe nudged her with an elbow as they walked toward his car. "And you're pretty convincing as pharma Barbie."

She elbowed him back. "Not pharma Barbie, dude. No detail bag, right?" She pointed to the sleek black leather shoulder bag they'd given her, illustrating her point. "I'm now a briefcase-toting customer service slash public relations representative."

Heads down and hands stuffed in their pockets, she and Gabe battled up the wind tunnels of the skyscrapered Financial District toward the parking lot. The fragrance of surreptitious marijuana mixed with bus exhaust, and a seagull pecked the ground, stalking someone's discarded popcorn. Rickety souvenir stands competed for the sidewalk space, offering tourists counterfeit Red Sox T-shirts and *Cheers* mugs.

She was as counterfeit as those cheap trinkets, Ellie realized, as they descended into the fume-filled underground parking garage. Gabe clicked open his Jeep and opened the door for her.

"Where to now? Should you check out some doctors? You're already all Nora'd up and ready to go."

Ellie slid into her seat. Yanked on her seat belt. Closed her door.

"Gabe? What if I see Meg in some office? So much of the time I'm not at Channel Eleven. And no one there knew I was being Nora. That's part of my deal, that I can research without having to check in all the time."

Gabe pushed on the ignition. The engine rumbled to life, but he didn't shift into gear.

"But see, *that* means," Ellie raised a forefinger as punctuation, "I also don't know where Meg's been while I'm gone. I keep trying to think whether I've seen her. You'd think I'd have recognized her, no matter how she tried to disguise herself. I mean, I know her."

"Or maybe she saw you first and took off."

"Could be." Ellie thought about that. "She's aware—because we discussed it with the news director—that I've visited doctors' offices. She thinks I go as *me,* though. Ellie. Not Nora."

"But she knows Ellie-you. Think she'd recognize Nora-you?"

"Impossible to say," she admitted. "And then there'd be the question of whether she'd keep it secret. Geez. It might be easier if she were Brooke Vanderwald. Listen. Let's head to Newton. I'll explain on the way."

Gabe accelerated up the parking garage's concrete incline toward the Boston morning, the gloomy daylight ahead appearing as they drew closer to the garage exit.

March in Boston was still the depth of winter, Ellie was learning. Back home, March meant daffodils, and even the floating canopies of cherry blossoms. But the dank Boston days, she'd been warned, stretched until April. Ellie drew her coat closer, chilled not only by the weather but by the path she'd chosen. She could be warm later. Happy later. Satisfied later. At peace—later.

She sneaked a glance at Gabe as he slipped a paper ticket and then a credit card into the parking fee machine. Guy, she thought. But now officially Gabe, after he'd shown her ID in his WorkHere office. She yearned to be furious about his deception, betrayed and deceived, but that was complicated since she'd done the same thing to him. Her feelings about Guy, though—before she knew the truth— had been real. And he'd told her "Guy" had "connected" with Nora. So some things were authentic. Maybe.

"I still get confused about what to call you," she said. "Gabe or Guy. They both look the same."

"Well, yeah, the same person was never supposed to see both of us. You're the only one who did."

The bright orange-striped metal of the parking garage exit arm clanked to vertical, allowing them into the morning. A brown tourist trolley trundled in front of them, red pennants fluttering and glassine windows flapped down, its bundled-up passengers peering through the smoky plastic at Boston Common and, Ellie figured, at the gold dome of the statehouse beyond.

"But doesn't it work just fine now?" Gabe asked.

"That we're both who we really are? Most of the time, anyway."

"And it's easy for you to remember when I'm Nora." She pretended to preen, twirled an auburn curl like a cheesy TV villain. "Though, yeah, the same people were not supposed to see both her and me either. That'd never work."

Gabe pulled out into the street, the silvery morning softening the lines in his face, and pulled up to the zebra-striped crosswalk, stopping for the pedestrians who'd stepped off the curb on their way to the Common. A ballet dancer of a woman wearing a pink watch cap, pink leggings and chunky boots chatted face-to-face with a swaddled infant strapped into the Snugli across her chest, oblivious to anything but their conversation. A twentysomething in a puffy red parka and pushing a stroller grabbed the mittened hand of a waddling child in a matching coat, the child pointing to a scattering of sparrows in the snow.

A stroller. A mother. A child. So random, so unremarkable, so simple. For some. For others the image might bring pain and grief, longing and disappointment. So many women wanted that, needed that, lived for that. Motherhood was a choice, and needed to be as *fair* a choice as humanly possible. That's why Ellie—and Nora—did what they did. Risked what they risked. Ellie made a silent promise. She would not give up.

"El?"

Gabe had turned to her—who knows how long he'd been watching her? He'd called her El. "Yeah?"

"I'm still thinking about Brooke Vanderwald."

"Listen. How about I just *ask* Meg? I'm *happy* to." Ellie offered.

Gabe checked his rearview, then flicked a dismissive glance at her. "Sarcasm is unnecessary, Ellie."

"No, I'm serious," she said. "Say Brooke Vander-wald created a new persona as an annoying and incompetent TV producer wannabe. Who just happened to show up where I work, and just happened to work with me, a reporter working on an exposé about her family's company. But hey, wouldn't that make our job supereasy? She can get us all kinds of Pharminex secret papers and in-house documents. Awesome. Doing it. Wanna come with when I ask?"

"Wanna get out and walk?"

"But see what I mean? I agree, I do, it'd be great. Even amazing. But . . . so unlikely."

Gabe waved her off. "Okay. Fine. No more Meg is Brooke. Meg is Meg. But we still need—"

"A plan." Ellie mentally reviewed her past appointments, the doctors' offices, analyzing which ones seemed like possibilities. She had to start somewhere. "That's why I'm thinking Newton. There's a clinic on Route Nine there I can check out. And just so you don't get all focused on what we *say* we're doing, let me remind you what we *are* doing. We're looking for victims. For information. For documentation of the company's deception and greed. For the death sentence for P-X. And Gabe?"

"Yeah?"

"No matter what Detta and Allessandra insist, you've got to believe they'll go to any length to stop anyone from exposing them. They rehired *me*, remember? To spy? And they admitted I'm not the only spy, as poor duped Nora found out. So gotta wonder who else is on their payroll?"

Gabe steered the awkward turn onto Storrow Drive, the patchy faded grass in front of the half-domed Hatch Shell on their right, and past that, the Charles River, with the mismatched architecture of MIT looming in the distance across the white-capped water. Storrow Drive, too curvy, too narrow, and too crowded, was a traffic minefield of potholes and aggression.

"Any ideas? Damn it! Hey! Watch it!" Gabe swerved right to avoid a careening Boston cab, its rear fender dented and trunk taped closed, speeding bat-out-of-hell in front of them. "*Moron.*"

Ellie'd grabbed the door handle, eyes wide, as a scene—*from what movie?*—unspooled in an instant through her mind: a flickering half-memory of snow and squealing brakes and skidding tires and a sound that somehow made her sad.

She stared out the windshield as the cab disappeared, thought about how quickly a life can change, one stupid cabdriver or a—

"Gabe," she said, staring straight ahead. "Kaitlyn Armistead."

"The one who got killed?"

"Yeah. But Gabe? It was my fault she died."

CHAPTER 34

ELLIE

"I . . . don't feel well. I need to stop for a minute."
Ellie pointed Gabe toward the Kenmore off-ramp.
"Take that exit. Can you?" She tried to gulp away
the rise in her stomach, the sick regret that made her
dizzy and seemed to cloud her vision. She buzzed
down the Jeep's window, hoping a blast of spiky cold
air would shock her brain into clarity.

Gabe turned, then pulled into a metered parking
space on the fringe of Kenmore Square. College students jostled by each other on the sidewalk, in jeans
and brazenly coatless, lugging massive backpacks
and glued to their screens. A halfhearted snow sifted
from darkening clouds, melting as it hit the windshield.

"Are you okay? Should I take you to a—"

"I'm fine, just need a second." Ellie rested her forehead against the cold glass of the passenger window.
Closing her eyes, she tried to reimagine her visit to
Dr. McGinty's office. But she couldn't tune Gabe out,
leaving him baffled and attempting to decipher her
actions.

She took a deep breath and turned to face him,

hoping she'd settled a nonparanoid expression on her face. "Kaitlyn Armistead. I met her, the day before her accident, in the doctor's office. McGinty. I was there as Nora the sales rep, but Kaitlyn didn't know that. And I was sort of pretending with her, commiserating. Hoping she assumed I was a patient. Allowing her to think so. Encouraging it."

"Okay." Gabe turned off the ignition and shifted his body to look at her, one arm draped over the steering wheel. "As part of your TV investigation."

"Exactly." Ellie nodded. "We talked about both having red hair, and books we loved as kids, and she finally confessed her husband was pressuring her about her difficulty getting pregnant. Judging her. She was so unhappy. It was way too much information, but it's a doctor's office, so people—women—feel as if they already have common ground. Which they do. Kind of a sisterhood of confidentiality. A circle of trust."

Ellie closed her eyes again, briefly, recalling her deep and honest sympathy for the woman. "So I thought, great. I was focused on my story. Saw everything through my own filter. I felt lucky. Maybe I'd happened on a potential source. I felt brave. Like an enterprising reporter."

Gabe nodded. "You thought she might be the person you needed."

"Yeah. And she seemed eager to talk, so I tried to draw her out. I was calculating, planning my next move. I thought—*Jackpot. A victim.*"

In the side mirror, Ellie saw a blue-uniformed traffic enforcement cop strolling up the sidewalk toward them. "We're going to have to pay or move, I bet," she said. "He's a block away, but here comes the parking goon."

"We can deal with that. I have quarters. So. Kaitlyn Armistead."

"Almost everything I said to her was a lie, or using truths to tell lies. And that's bad enough. But maybe someone was watching us. Seeing me, Nora, talking with her. And . . ." She didn't want to talk about this, but needed to face it. "Like I said. The crash. It's my fault."

A staccato rap on the window. Ellie's heart lurched. A cop. Ellie was so rattled she first pushed the button to lock the door instead of the one that buzzed down the window.

"Move it, you two." An annoyed face in a blue-billed cap dared Ellie to protest. He flashed a booklet of rectangular orange tickets at them. "Once I start writing this, it's twenty-five bucks. Your call."

"Sorry, Officer," Gabe said. "She's upset, and we're—"

"Whatever." The cop cut off his excuse. "Like I said. Move it."

Gabe had already pushed the ignition and clicked on the wipers. He shifted into reverse. The cop brandished his ticket book at them as he stalked away.

"Ellie?" Gabe eased them into traffic. "Why is it your fault?"

"She *called* me." Ellie heard the sorrow in her own voice. "From her *car*. And I was on the phone with her . . . when she crashed. She needed someone to talk to, I guess, about her test results. Someone who understood. And that's what I mean. I feel terrible. I keep *thinking*—if I hadn't given her my card, she wouldn't have called. Then she wouldn't have been distracted. Then—"

"You cannot go there, Ellie," Gabe said. "No. The dominoes that fall in the world—we can never predict. That was a moment in her life, a collection of moments. Of her history. You did not make that happen." As they stopped for a light, he turned to her. Put one gloved hand on the arm of her coat, a brief touch. "Ellie? You did not cause that."

As the light changed, she tried to organize her brain, see if she could make sense out of it. But nothing made sense. It hadn't, not for years, no matter how normal she tried to be.

"Kaitlyn told me about her life." Ellie stared out the windshield, remembering. "I believed her. Every woman in that doctor's office wants kids, and every one of them is having trouble with that. Who would make up something so tragic?"

Gabe glanced at her. "You want me to answer that?"

"Okay." She acknowledged reality. "You got me."

Gabe paused at a stop sign, then continued through the intersection. "But the key is, no one could have predicted she'd call *you*—Nora—as she crashed."

"Exactly. *Exactly*." Ellie's gesture of agreement was so expansive that she whapped one hand on the closed window. "Ow. But Pharminex, you know? They're vulnerable now. If they thought Kaitlyn would call the media, as she threatened McGinty she would—maybe they decided to shut her up. And whether she was simply scared or injured or even killed by it—they knew that 'accident' would put her out of the picture. Another of their risk-benefit calculations." She nodded, thinking, imagining. "But the fact that she called *me*—that was the puzzle piece they could not have predicted."

"Could Pharminex know she called you? I mean, Nora?"

"I have no idea."

They drove past the Brookline Reservoir, its high

ridged edges providing a safe path where stalwart joggers ran their daily diameters beneath the bare branches of trees that in a few short months would be lush and green. Today's runners were ashen-faced, in soggy hooded sweatshirts, trudging through the wintry day.

Ellie worried a fingernail.

The day she'd met Kaitlyn. Ellie played back her memory video. The defeated woman in the expensive Uggs. The dreamy one with the earbuds. Cashmere shawl and dark glasses. Dr. McGinty's waiting room—beige chairs, blocky coffee tables, aging magazines, a glossy philodendron.

"For someone to see Kaitlyn and Nora-me talking, it had to be a person in that same waiting room at that same time. Or around there."

"And not your pal Meg."

"Meg? No. I'd have seen her. I have to believe that. And Meg working for Pharminex *and* Channel Eleven? Who would do that?"

Gabe burst out laughing as he navigated the hub-and-spoke intersection of Newton Center, past pizzerias and coffee shops and ice cream places. "I won't dignify that with an answer, Ellie. Or Nora. Or whoever you're being this particular moment. But for the record, that's precisely what *you're* doing, isn't it?"

"All the more reason it's absurd." Ellie leaned forward and flapped down her sun visor to adjust a contact. She peered into the tiny rectangular mirror, blinking. It still surprised her to see the glamorous auburn-haired Nora looking back. *Meg as Brooke Vanderwald.* She flapped the visor back into position, then turned to Gabe.

"What's your deal with the Vanderwalds, anyway? A couple days ago you had a theory about *Nora* being part of the family." She fluttered her eyelashes, playing coquette. "Which now, you realize, is absolutely—"

"Is that your phone buzzing?" Gabe cocked his head at the back seat. Ellie reached over and grabbed her tote bag, which now sounded like a hive of angry bees. She'd switched her cell to vibrate for the Detta meeting, then forgotten to turn the ringer back on.

She looked at the ID.

"Meg," she announced.

Gabe raised his eyebrows melodramatically. "Or . . . *whoever.*"

She ignored him. "Hi, Meg. I'm putting you on speaker."

"Where are you?" Meg's voice piped through.

"In the car. Where are *you*?"

"At the station with Warren. He's wondering when you'll be back here."

Ellie slashed a *kill-me-now* finger across her throat but made her tone cheerily acquiescent. "On the way." She had to keep the morning's assignation at P-X under the radar. And wondered how Meg had finessed her own absence. "Anything up? Whoa!"

She grabbed the door handle as Gabe swerved the Jeep into a gas station, pulled to the curb, shifted into park. Ellie, regaining her balance, held the phone up, speaker toward both of them, as if it were a third person in the front seat.

"A Pharminex employee was killed or is dead, something like that." Meg's voice came out as a whisper this time.

A siren screamed by, a police car, its blue lights cutting through the gloom. Ellie stared at the cell phone. Gabe, frowning with concern, settled his hand on Ellie's shoulder, then took it away.

"What does that even mean, Meg? Killed or

dead?" Ellie's brain raced to understand this, shuffling names and possibilities.

"I don't know the whole thing. I was in the newsroom, getting printer paper. Warren was at the assignment desk and some producer was on the phone with the police. Someone said 'Pharminex' to someone, it's breaking news, and Warren wants you back here. I'm—I don't know anything else. We're finding out."

"Do you have a name?"

"Just come back."

"When did—" Ellie persisted. But the line was already dead. She switched on the radio as Gabe eased back onto the highway.

"Let's see if there's news," she said, twisting the dial. "What if—"

"I hear you," Gabe said. "I'll get us there soon."

Ellie, impatient, turned through the static, searching for news, but now, at 11:35, there was only a blur of high-decibel sales pitches and annoying jingles, relentless guitars and endless political talk. She snapped the radio off and flopped against her seat back. Stared out the windshield.

Kaitlyn Armistead was dead. And now so was someone else. She thought of the Pharminex employees she knew. Detta and Allessandra. The chic and ambitious women she'd met in training class, Jenn and Gerri and Christine and Lydia.

The heater in Gabe's Jeep struggled to keep up with the weather, puffing heat on only one of her knees, leaving her nose freezing and her fingers almost numb. *Gabe.* She wrapped her arms across her chest. Was he another puzzle piece?

Gabe admitted he'd disguised himself as a doctor. Going undercover for some law firm, he'd said. Had *he* been there that day in McGinty's office? Out of her view, watching her talk with Kaitlyn Armistead? She would have recognized him. She pursed her lips, thinking—wouldn't she?

She closed her eyes, trying yet again to picture it.

As Ellie, she'd seen him as Gabe. As Nora, she'd seen him as Guy. *You can't fool someone you know;* she'd pronounced that edict herself.

He'd confessed he'd used a white coat as a disguise. Maybe today's tailored suit and tortoiseshell glasses—his Gabe outfit—was another disguise.

She watched him drive, his eyes focused on the road, almost obeying the speed limit, seemingly lost in his own thoughts. As he made the turn and headed back onto Beacon Street, Ellie felt a shiver. And it was from far more than the inclement weather and inadequate heater.

CHAPTER 35

ELLIE

Ellie unlatched her seat belt as Gabe eased his Jeep into a parking space in front of her apartment.

"Thanks, Gabe," she said. She'd pretend she wasn't suspicious. "I'll do a quick change back into Ellie, then head to Channel Eleven. Quite the morning."

She looked at him as she gathered her tote bag and new Pharminex briefcase. He seemed thoughtful, his eyes softening as he watched her. *Affectionate,* the word came to mind. Or maybe it was more tactics. She thought she'd been the first to lie in this relationship. But maybe *he'd* been the first. Maybe the first lie was only the beginning.

"Thanks for everything," she finally said. She was on the way to hear bad news. Someone at Pharminex was dead. "I'll let you know, soon as I can. And text me if you find out anything."

"Take care." He leaned toward her, and she felt the heat rise to her face. Was he going to kiss her? Here? Now?

He reached down beside her, picked up a glove from the floor. "You're gonna need this," he said. "Whoever you are."

It took a moment, a breath, for her heart to slow down. To make sure her voice was normal. In that one frozen second of uncertain silence, as he handed her that one leather glove, identities and motives seemed to blur into pure desire.

And then, just as quickly, it evaporated. She'd fallen for him as Guy. But Guy wasn't real. And the real guy, Gabe, might simply be as adept with his seduction skills as he was with changing identities.

"Thanks," she said. Why did she keep thanking him? She shifted into all business, grabbing her stuff and hopping out of the front seat onto the snow-dusted sidewalk, not risking any personal gestures. Any personal anything.

"I've got to become Ellie in about thirty seconds," she told him. "So, thanks. See you later." *Damn* it. She'd thanked him again. She closed the door, started to walk away. When she heard the buzz of the passenger side window, she turned back.

"Ellie? I'll take you," Gabe offered as the window opened. "You change. I'll wait."

Not a chance. "That's okay. Really. Go." She waved him away. "Go to your real job. I'll let you know." She took a step toward her apartment, then turned back. The window was still open. He was still watching her. "Gabe? Thanks for this morning. You rocked it."

"You did too. And yeah, we'll plan. Call me." The window buzzed back up, and the exhaust from the Jeep plumed as Gabe drove away. He'd not only accepted her double life, he'd actively participated in it. And that imbalance, that thumb on the scales, left her staring for a moment at the empty street.

Gabe was the only person who knew her as both Ellie and Nora. She'd ceded him that power—well, in truth, he'd taken it. Whether that would be her downfall was still to be determined.

Despite what she'd just told him, she was staying Nora.

Twenty minutes later, after a call to Uber, and then one to Warren, she stood on the sidewalk across from Pharminex and tried to formulate a plan. Her news director had zero details on the death—so she'd told Warren that instead of coming to Channel 11, she'd go straight to Pharminex. See what she could find out directly. Warren didn't need to know she was working this story undercover as Nora, but Nora gave her access. As Nora, she could find out who was dead, and why and what that meant. Then Ellie could expose it to the public.

"Brilliant," she said out loud to the gathering snow. She'd just talked to her boss dressed as Nora and pretending to be Ellie. Double duplicity. She was getting good at this.

The lunch hour foot traffic instantly tripled as the Custom Tower clock hit noon. Down the block, some Pharminex employees—who else would they be, since the company had the entire twelve stories?— were escaping into the day. If Nora spotted someone she knew, all the better. As Nora, she could ask if they'd heard anything.

She revolved into the building lobby, scouting for signs that something was amiss. She waved her ID at the rent-a-guard receptionist, ready to dive into collegial sympathy or condolences or intel, but the woman waved her through, barely looking up from her cell phone.

On to the elevator, then she headed for the ninth-floor lockers, where she would scout for people she knew. And hope none of her sales rep colleagues were aware she'd been fired and then unfired. She checked her reflection in the shiny elevator doors, remembering it was business as usual and she was Nora. She made her brain Nora's brain, made her physicality Nora's physicality. Her motives, though, were Ellie's.

She heard the murmurs as soon as she clicked her ID through the locked door into the ninth-floor corridors. Conversations, whispered and subdued.

Turned out the apex of the noise was in front of her own locker. Jenn Wahl was halfway down the carpeted corridor, still wearing her coat and outdoor boots, apparently deep in conversation with two other women in coats. Nora recognized the bespectacled brunette Gerri Munroe, and the blond-chignoned Christine O'Shea.

"Oh, Nora!" Jenn's red-rimmed eyes opened wider as she rushed at her for an embrace. "We hadn't seen you recently. We were worried that it was *you*." A smudge of Jenn's mascara darkened one of her cheeks. All three of the women's faces were pale under careful makeup.

Nora made herself look perplexed and worried. "That it was me *what*?"

"Stupid snow, I bet." Gerri, scowling, jammed her hands into her coat pockets. Her black suede boots were rimmed with road salt, and her usually artful silk muffler was twisted out of place. "Could have been any of us. It's disgusting. Probably illegal. They shouldn't make us drive in this kind of weather."

"Worried it was me that what?" Nora repeated.

"In a car accident," Jenn said. "I can't believe it."

"Believe it, honey." Christine draped one arm around Jenn's shoulders, then rested her head against her colleague's. "She's dead, Nora."

The women's inner light seemed to vanish, their features softening to sorrow and their physical presence diminished. The fluorescent lamps buzzed above them all, flickering the too-bright hallway with intermittent shadows.

"Who? *Dead?*" Nora asked, unbuttoning her coat and leaning in, a newcomer to the mourning.

"Lydia." Christine flattened a palm against the locker beside her, the one with a stiff cardboard name tag that read *L. Frost*. A tribute or a caress. "We were just all here, together. How can it be that she's gone?"

Nora gulped, trying to balance her sincere distress and sorrow with her reporter's duty to get the facts. She was used to such compartmentalization, but here she was in her role as human being, Lydia's colleague, almost a friend. She'd just seen her. In the elevator. With Gabe. Who had seen her too. And Ellie had told him her name.

She put her fingers to her lips, sincerely disturbed. "Oh, no. Do they know what happened?"

All three women shook their heads, a unison of grief and the unknown.

"The state police are doing whatever they do," Jenn said. "Reconstructing. Allessandra sent an email two seconds before you got here, but it didn't say much, except they're investigating and we're all sad."

The four women stood in the empty hallway, encased by wallpaper and overhead lighting and rows of louvered beige storage lockers, now silent and solitary in their loss.

Nora spoke first, her voice still low, not wanting to ignore their sorrow but needing information. "State police? So it happened on a highway?"

"Route Nine exit, somewhere," Jenn said.

"You got the email, Nora, right?" Gerri asked.

Nora dug out her cell. There it was.

She mentally slowed her stampeding brain. Route Nine. Could that be near where Kaitlyn had crashed?

Nora knew which state police were probably

investigating Lydia's death. The same ones who'd investigated Kaitlyn Armistead's.

"Was Lydia by herself?" she asked.

All three women looked up at her, then tilted their heads the same way, like curious parakeets. "I . . . guess so," Jenn finally said. "She was on her way to some appointment, I assume. And there's nothing in the email about anybody else."

"When did this happen? Today, right, but what time?"

"Why does that matter?" said Christine, annoyed.

"The police will find out," Gerri said at the same time, and they all nodded. "It's so sad," she added. "We were right here the other day, laughing and talking. Like we'd always be together and had all the time in the world."

"Talking about that cute doctor, right?" Jenn added, wiping a tear from under one mascaraed eye. "And, like, corporate spies."

CHAPTER 36

ELLIE

This had to be an identity-changing record. Nora became Ellie again, this time switching identities in the back seat of an Uber. The driver of the ridiculously pinewoods-scented black SUV glanced at her once in his rearview mirror, and she saw confusion cross his face as she tucked the last of her auburn hair underneath Ellie's blond-bob wig.

"I'm an actor," she explained, settling the wig into place, yanking the elastic down over her ears and finger-combing her bangs straight. "I have an audition."

"Cool," the driver said. "Are you famous? I always wanted to be an actor. When I was in college, everyone said I looked like—"

"Great." Ellie tried to give him a genuine-looking smile—she *was* an actor, after all. "I'm so sorry, though? I have to concentrate. I know you'll understand."

"Cool." The driver nodded, checking his own reflection in the rearview—black watch cap, one silver stud earring—as they stopped for a red light. "I still think it might be an awesome—"

"Yeah," Ellie said. "Don't mind me not chatting, okay? Got to focus. Get ready."

"Cool," he said.

She balanced a slim silver compact in the pouch on the back of the front seat, popped out the contacts that made her eyes forest green and deposited them in a plastic container, spilling most of the lens solution on her black coat. "Fine," she muttered. She replaced the lenses with her red-rimmed glasses, then attempted to blot off Nora's red lipstick without leaving a brown smudge around her mouth. A swipe with a spit-dampened Q-tip removed the eyeliner and the taupe eyeshadow, and she tissued off most of her face makeup, depositing the blush-covered Kleenex in her tote bag.

She had seen the driver surreptitiously eyeing her again in the rearview mirror. This round-faced twentysomething—Remmie, his picture ID on the app had disclosed—was the only one on the planet besides Blinker who'd witnessed this particular transformation. She tried to remember whether there was any way this guy could find her again, through the app or something, but that was probably over-the-top paranoid. She decided to poll him for his reaction at the next stop sign.

"So?" She leaned forward, gesturing to her face, as if to present the transformation.

"Cool," Remmie said. "You look like a different person."

"Awesome. Okay, this is it."

"Your audition is *here*?" Remmie twisted his body as he approached the front entrance of the state police headquarters, questioning her over the seat back.

"I just show up where they say, right?" She shrugged, simpatico, then jumped out and closed the door behind her.

She paused in the parking lot as the car pulled away. It had been about a week ago that the hyper-suspicious statie Lieutenant Monteiro had questioned Nora. He'd let her go, saying he'd be back in touch if there was anything more he needed. She hadn't heard from him.

The murky sun had given up on the afternoon, and charcoal skies almost matched the parking lot's asphalt. The shaded windows of the state police building made white squares in the redbrick edifice. Ellie pulled open the glass doors of the entrance, reminding herself this was *Ellie's* first time here.

The cadet at the front desk, barricaded behind thick yellowing plastic in her pale blue uniform shirt and navy pants, seemed reluctant to look up from her computer screen as Ellie approached.

The cadet finally slid open a hinged plexiglass window, which stuck halfway. She banged it with the heel of her hand. "Help you?"

The mustard-brown wall behind her was papered with thumbtacked *Wanted* posters, some more tattered than others, a few with a red *X* markered over the faces.

"Ellie Berensen." She dug into her tote bag, then held up a spiral notebook the way a cop would proffer a badge, adding a helpful smile. "From Channel Eleven?"

The cadet kept one hand on her computer mouse, her dour expression telegraphing *so what?*

Ellie read the wooden nameplate on the desk. Tried the use-the-person's-name method. "Cadet Vela? I'm here about the fatal on Route Nine."

So what? again. "You need to call media relations, ma'am."

Ellie winced. "I know," she pretended to confess, "but I was in the area, and my phone battery is dying, and since my news director is freaking out over the—"

"Stop." The cadet pointed to a narrow plastic bench along the lobby wall. "Take a seat. I'll see what I can do. No promises. And ma'am? There's a plug. Charge your phone."

"Oh, thank you so—"

The cadet slammed the sliding window. This time it worked.

Ellie sat, plugged in her phone, then stared at wet footprints crisscrossing the gritty linoleum floor. A siren wailed outside, then another. She would never hear a siren again without thinking of Kaitlyn. How she—as Nora—had tried to stop her from driving. Had tried to get to her. Had failed.

But as Ellie, she'd heard about Kaitlyn's crash from Gabe. Why would he have cared about that? Why would that have been on his radar?

Gabe couldn't have *caused* Lydia's crash, could he? He'd been with her—Nora—all morning.

Kaitlyn and Lydia. Two young women. One taking Monifan, one selling it. But what else connected them?

"Miz Burnson?"

She got to her feet, startled, and then was startled again. She tried to keep the recognition off her face. *Ellie* had never seen Detective Lieutenant Rafael Monteiro before. The spit-shined square-cornered Monteiro, whose face hitched one degree off movie star and whose pale blue shirt looked tailored to a sleek fit, was not a member of the media relations team. He was, *Nora* knew, head of accident reconstruction.

She touched her red glasses to draw attention to them and smoothed her blond hair, setting her Ellie persona in place in the trooper's mind.

"Berensen," she corrected, using a hint of a TV voice. And then asked a question she knew the answer to. "Are you media relations?"

"Media sent me," he said. He pointed to himself with the manila folder he held. "Detective Lieutenant Rafael Monteiro. Come with me, Ms. Berensen."

"Call me Ellie." She looked him square in the eye, giving him the opportunity to recognize her. But he didn't react. Not a twitch or a pause or a narrowed eye. *Some cop.*

So that bullet was dodged. She wrapped the power cord around her phone and stashed it into her tote bag as she trotted after Monteiro through a number-pad locked door and down a familiar corridor. *Not familiar,* she reminded herself.

"Have a seat," he said. She'd sat on the same beige folding chair the last time. And seen the same blank flip-over bulletin board the last time, too. But there was no last time.

Ellie radiated reporter vibes: all business, rushed, brusque. Her coat was unbuttoned, but she kept it on to indicate she didn't plan to hang around. Get in, get out, get the news story on the air.

"Lieutenant? Can you confirm the victim is Lydia Frost?" She clicked her ballpoint. Might as well try to take control of the discussion. "What's the status of your investigation?"

She knew, with a nagging subtext, that this wasn't standard operating procedure—she'd covered her share of car accidents, and no trooper had ever taken her, solo, into a private back room.

She pushed her concerns away, and looked at Monteiro, *your turn,* ready to take notes.

"What's your interest in this, Ms. Berensen?" Monteiro put his manila folder on a side table, crossed his arms. Leaned against the wall across from her. The blank bulletin board beside him was dotted with blue and red pushpins, as if someone had removed everything it displayed. "Why'd you come all the way out here instead of simply calling?"

"I'm a reporter," she said.

"For Channel Eleven."

"Yes." She nodded, all-in-a-day's-work.

Monteiro scratched his forehead—dramatically, if you asked her—then shifted position. "Ma'am? Media relations tells me he never heard of you. You have no media credentials. Hell, your station doesn't hit air for, what, weeks? So why do you care about a car accident?"

"Because it's my job to—"

"Don't bullshit me." He put up a stop-sign palm. "We called your station, asked for you, got a Meg something, a producer? She was perfectly happy to tell us you're the big-time investigative reporter."

He said *investigative* as if it meant toxic waste or swine flu.

"Well, *Lieutenant,*" she tried for the same intonation, vowing to kill Meg the first chance she got, "I'm—"

"Give me a break." Monteiro removed a red pushpin from the bulletin board, stabbed it back into place. The board, mounted on swivel hinges, creaked with the force of his motion. "No *investigative* reporter is gonna be out covering a random car accident. Correct? So, let's try again. Why do you care about this?"

"Why do *you*?" The question came out before her brain even vetted it.

"Yeah. Thing is? I don't have to answer you." Monteiro smiled, apparently happy to patronize her. "I can say 'it's under investigation.' I can say 'no comment.' I can no-comment you until you hear it in your sleep. And to remind you, I can no-comment *you* but slip the scoop to your competitors. The ones who are actually on the air. The ones who are telling me the truth."

Death was too easy a solution for Meg.

"You can't threaten—" She stood, challenging him.

"Sit down, Ms. Berensen. You have thirty seconds. After that, I'm the king of 'no comment.' Twenty-nine seconds."

Monteiro must suspect something or he wouldn't be going third degree on her. She took a deep breath, ready to—maybe—cross the line. But also—maybe—to get some answers. She would kill Meg later.

"Twenty-three."

She sat back down. "Do you remember that spin-out near Route Nine last week? In the snow? Kaitlyn Armistead?"

Monteiro nodded. "Yup."

"Was this in the same place as that?"

"Nineteen." The patronizing smile again, this time accompanied by a weary shake of the head and a dramatic glance at his elaborate runner's watch. "Eighteen. You're going to tell me things, not ask me things."

"I knew her," Ellie lied. "Kaitlyn Armistead."

Monteiro blinked, remaining silent, giving her a few more seconds to make sure this tactic would work.

"Not like a friend, but professionally," she went on, growing more confident in her explanation. "She called me, at the station, because . . ." Because why? She'd head that off before Monteiro asked. "Because we'd trolled on social media for women who'd had trouble with conception and were angry because they'd experienced side effects. So she replied. Called me. *Us*. Meg and me."

"And what did she tell you?"

"She told us about her health problems, which are

private, okay? She also wondered why we were asking about it, and we explained we were looking into
a certain pharmaceutical company and wondered
whether doctors had prescribed certain drugs for her.
And whether she might be interested in going public
with her results. It's a long story."

Monteiro nodded. "Pharminex," he said.

This was a game changer. How the hell did he
know?

"How did you hear about Lydia Frost?" Monteiro
went on.

"So you're confirming the victim was Lydia Frost?"

"If I remember correctly, and I do, you asked *me*
about Lydia Frost. You're the one who mentioned her
name."

"Come on, Lieutenant." *Really?* Ellie thought.

"Off the record?" he asked.

"Off the record *what*?"

"I know who you are, Ms. Berensen. What you're
investigating. And since you're not on the air for
weeks—correct?—we'll agree you won't use what I'm
about to show you until I say so. But now we need
your help. Okay?"

"Help with what? How did you know?" She re-
considered. "Or think you know?"

Monteiro didn't answer. He uncrossed his arms,
stood and with one motion flipped over the blank
bulletin board, revealing its other side.

CHAPTER 37

ELLIE

It was as if Monteiro's bulletin board was a map of Ellie's own brain. Of her suspicions.

Attached to the upper left corner with a blue push-pin was a rectangular snapshot of Kaitlyn Armistead. In happier days, outdoors. The photographer had captured Kaitlyn's contented expression. Auburn hair fell loose across her shoulders, complemented by a sleeveless emerald-green blouse, shadows spackled on her tanned arms. Ellie even saw that sprinkling of freckles across her nose—they'd talked about her freckles, Ellie remembered, how Kaitlyn had disliked them. Kaitlyn was looking at something in the far distance, and behind her was the edge of a tree trunk and the sun streaming through its leafy branches. A family photo, maybe, casual and carefree.

In the middle of the board was a Google map, the irregular circle of the Chestnut Hill reservoir in its center, the ribbon of Route Nine interrupted by two pushpins: one blue, one red. The blue one, the scene of Kaitlin's accident, was attached by blue thread to her photo. That fragile thread connected the vibrant life in the photo to the other pin, the place that ended it.

On the upper right corner, a photo of Lydia Frost was held in place by a red pushpin. She was ice to Kaitlyn's fire, her image professional, impeccable, not a blond hair out of place, not a blemish or a shadow on her elegantly composed face. A thin strand of gold necklace embellished the stark black of her sleek suit jacket; her shoulders were square and her lips glossed red. Her red pushpin was attached by a thread to a matching one on the map, its edge almost touching the blue one: the site of Lydia's accident.

At the lower right corner of the bulletin board was a row of green pushpins, attached to nothing. Above that, yellow ones. These unused pins sent an unnerving message. Perhaps they represented unknown victims. Or potential future ones.

"So you think they're connected," she said. "How? Why?"

"Some connections are apparent," Monteiro said. "It's simply a question of whether those connections matter."

Ellie looked closer at Lydia's picture. "That's her Pharminex photo."

"She had a company ID," Monteiro said. "How we identified her. We contacted her employer, and they provided the photo. Ms. Armistead's we obtained from her husband."

Something rattled through Ellie's consciousness. She stood, shrugged off her coat. Not taking her eyes off Kaitlyn's photo. "Did you see other photos of her?"

"I'll play," Monteiro said. "No, Ms. Berensen. James Armistead didn't give me any other family photos."

"You said 'family photos.' Does Kaitlyn have children? I mean, did she?"

"The husband said they had two. Little ones, I take

it. Like I said, I didn't see pictures, but he seemed worried about them."

"She told me she couldn't have children. That's why she had been going to the doctor." Ellie tried to untangle who'd been fooling who and about what. "She told me her husband was critical and unkind, taunting her about not being able to have kids. That's why she was so unhappy."

Monteiro's face changed, his sarcastic expression evolving into curiosity. He frowned as he picked up the manila file folder he'd brought with him. Flipped through the pages.

Had Kaitlyn lied to her about infertility? Why? Ellie lifted her chin, trying to catch a glimpse of what was inside Monteiro's folder.

"I can't show you this," Monteiro said, without looking up. "But yeah, the transcript indicates he said two kids. Be pretty interesting if that wasn't true." He closed the folder.

"Or I suppose—" Ellie pointed at the photo. "Maybe they're not her biological kids."

"I'll look into it." Monteiro clicked open a ballpoint, made a note in the file then closed it, and cocked his head at the board. "That your only reaction to this?"

"Obviously not." Ellie walked to the bulletin board, leaned forward to squint at the pins on the map. The accidents were less than a mile apart. "Do you think the same thing caused both accidents? Or wait—you didn't say 'accidents.' You said 'crashes.' Does that mean you think someone *caused* them?"

Ellie's phone buzzed with a text. Meg. "Sorry," Ellie said. "My office. Can you confirm Lydia Frost? And are you saying 'accident'? On the record?"

Monteiro looked at his watch. "It's two o'clock.

Tell them media relations will release the official info at two-fifteen. Lydia Frost, yes, still under investigation. That's it for now."

"Thanks." She texted the name to Meg, fast as she could, feeling Monteiro's eyes on her. "So?" she asked as she hit *send*. "How are they connected?"

"That's where you come in." Monteiro picked up a yellow pushpin, stabbed it into the bulletin board between the two women's photos. Then he opened his file folder and pulled out a photograph, though it seemed as if he was making sure Ellie could not see whose picture it was. He pulled out the yellow pin and attached the photo to the board between Kaitlyn and Lydia, but face down.

"Is there another victim?" Ellie asked. "Oh, no. Who?"

"We need your help, "Monteiro said. "The person in this photo isn't dead, and we know their identity. That's not why I'm asking. But there's only one person we found who connects Kaitlyn Armistead and Lydia Frost. And it seems like the people they contact, the people they create relationships with, get killed in car accidents. Suspicious ones. I don't mean to be overdramatic, but you've investigated for what, a few weeks now? So what's *your* suspicion—best guess—of who this might be?"

"Someone from Pharminex," Ellie said. Might as well put her cards on the table. Whatever game this was had turned deadly. Lydia's death made Kaitlyn's into a pattern, not a random tragedy.

"Kaitlyn told me she was deeply bitter about what happened to her because of a drug called Monifan. And told me she yelled at her doctor about it, threatened to call the media. If that's true, and Pharminex knew, and suspected she'd go public, they couldn't have been happy with that."

"Unhappy enough to keep her quiet?" Monteiro asked.

How much should she tell him? She was Ellie now, she had to remember.

"How do I know? But it's not like pharmaceutical companies never hurt their customers. Want me to start naming examples? We'll be here all day."

Monteiro nodded. "I hear you. But Lydia Frost *worked* for Pharminex."

"Exactly. And that could go either way." Ellie tilted her hand back and forth, *maybe this, maybe that.* "Maybe she was some kind of corporate spy? I know it sounds unlikely, but one conversation we had, that's all she could talk about. And I know for sure that Pharminex hires people—" She paused, deciding. "To go undercover and report the transgressions of employees. You know, like you have with internal affairs."

Monteiro put one hand over the photo, holding it in place, then pulled out the pushpin. "Ms. Berensen? Do you recognize this person?"

He flipped over the photo. Stabbed it with the yellow pin. And took his hand away.

CHAPTER 38

ELLIE

In the beat before seeing Monteiro's photograph, Ellie had a flare of an idea that the picture might be Gabriel Hoyt. Or Meg Weest.

But now Ellie was looking at a grainy surveillance photo of Nora Quinn.

Three women in a row across the board: Kaitlyn, Nora, Lydia. Two of them were dead.

"You think that woman's in danger?" Ellie asked.

"You want coffee?" Monteiro checked his watch. "We should keep talking, but let's head to the caf while we do. You can leave your belongings. It's safe here, God knows."

"Sure, but—" Ellie took a deep breath. She could use some coffee, and if Nora Quinn was in danger, she was also probably safest here at the state police headquarters.

The dim hallway, mustard-painted cinder block with a tiled drop ceiling, smelled of dust and paperwork, like stepping inside a file cabinet. Ellie imagined the people who'd walked this hall before—victims, suspects, terrified witnesses or grieving families. Everyone with a loss or a fear or a secret. Or an agenda.

The corridor was wide enough for them to walk side by side, though Monteiro took up more than half the space. Ellie had left her shoulder bag and phone behind as Monteiro suggested, but now she regretted it. Not because someone would steal her wallet, but because she felt incomplete without her phone. She tried to remember if her bag contained anything incriminating. Nothing she could do about it now.

"So?" Monteiro was saying as they walked. "Do you recognize her?"

"That's a fairly indistinct photo," said Ellie. "Surveillance, right? Was it taken . . ." She pictured it. "Here in your headquarters lobby?"

"It's distinct enough." Monteiro opened a half-windowed door to an otherwise windowless room, revealing two long tables on a utilitarian-tan linoleum floor, a television flickering silently on the wall and tall aluminum coffee urns on one of the tables. Hand-lettered signs hanging from black spigots indicated regular, decaf and hot water. A stack of upside-down paper cups and a jar of red stir sticks. A bin of pastel sweetener packets jumbled chaotically in a Tupperware. Paper napkins piled on the counter marked with familiar golden arches. Apparently someone had appropriated them from the fast food place.

"Not fancy, but coffee is coffee."

Ellie dared to draw a cup of regular, to give herself time to think as much as for the caffeine. "We staying here?" Ellie hoped not.

"Sure." Monteiro rummaged in the sweetener bin, then scraped out the chair across from her, its rubber-tipped legs stubbing across the linoleum. He sat, organizing his coffee stuff, napkin and stir stick.

On the table in front of Ellie, someone had scrawled a phone number, the ballpoint pen lines smudged but indelible. She stirred her coffee, staring at it. Trying to figure out if this trip to the café was a trap.

Monteiro had opened a yellow sweetener packet, stirred it in.

Monteiro, a trained *cop,* had seen her as Nora, and now was seeing her as Ellie. And he was giving her way more time than necessary to answer his question. Maybe giving her just enough rope. Maybe this was his style. Or maybe—and this was the fear—he'd recognized her. And was testing her.

Ellie felt herself sink into overload, trying to fight her way out of a maze with too many options and not enough answers. But she'd brought all this on herself. Too late to change it now. She took a sip of coffee, then wished she hadn't.

"Her name is Nora Quinn," Ellie said. "She works for Pharminex."

Monteiro stopped, put down a third yellow packet.

"Last I heard," Ellie said.

He took out his notepad and a Bic pen, wrote something. Looked up at Ellie. "Yeah. Let me tell you this. Off the record? I'd called Ms. Quinn after Ms. Armistead's crash. Ms. Quinn led me to believe she was a medical patient, had the same doctor as Ms. Armistead, but according to that doctor's records, she wasn't. So I had to wonder what she was doing in that office. The two women had been on the phone together at the time of the crash—what're the odds? And now Quinn's not answering her phone."

True. Just because she had seen his calls come in didn't mean she had to pick up.

"And she gave the desk officer here a fake address," Monteiro said. "But we'll find her. What does she do for Pharminex?"

When his cell phone buzzed, he snatched it up,

narrowing his eyes at the screen, then slid it into the side pocket of his uniform jacket.

"Can you hang on a second?" he asked Ellie, sounding vaguely annoyed. "I'll be right back. Get more coffee if you like. Two minutes."

Ellie watched him hurry away and longed for her own phone, worlds away in that room down the corridor. Now she was trapped in coffee hell with no method of communication. Like being in custody.

She stared at a blank wall. If she continued to pretend she'd met Nora in her Pharminex research . . . She squinted her eyes, trying to play out that story. At some point, the ruse would fall apart.

Just as it had with Gabe.

CHAPTER 39

ELLIE

Ellie tossed her half-full coffee cup into a plastic-lined bin, yanked open the café door and walked out into the hall. Imbuing her posture with confidence and conviction, she strode back up the hall toward the conference room, where her lifeline phone awaited her. She hoped.

"Screw it," she muttered under her breath. "Ridiculous for him to park me in that stupid room." She bet she'd missed calls from Warren and Meg and probably Gabe. If he called her at Channel 11, would Meg have answered too? Ratted her out? She could just hear that woman's voice—*oh, Ellie's at the state police HQ, looking into Lydia Frost's car accident*. She closed her eyes. *Meg*.

"Ms. Berensen?" Monteiro's voice came from the hallway behind her.

She turned, all smiles. "Hey. Great. I needed my phone, so I—"

"For what?" He wasn't smiling.

"To call my office." She put all the sarcasm she could into her tone without sounding hostile, and continued toward the conference room. Monteiro's footsteps behind her sped up, and in an instant he'd passed her and blocked her way, all stocky shoulders and crossed arms.

"I don't think so," he said.

"Hey!" she said, skidding to a stop. She *knew* it. He was well aware she was Nora and had lured her into this deception, testing her to see whether she'd own up to it. And now that she'd lied to a cop, every word she said would be suspect. She should have told the truth in the first place—but then again, she'd done nothing wrong. She hadn't hurt anyone. There was no harm in impersonating *yourself*.

They stood face to face in the empty corridor, fewer than two paces apart. Cop and reporter. Or cat and mouse? Maybe her conscience was in hyperdrive again.

"Are you *blocking* the way to my phone?" Ellie tried humor, holding out her arms in front of her, palms up. "Wanna handcuff me?"

Monteiro's eyebrows went up, questioning, and he gestured toward the open conference room door with his file folder. "All I mean is, we haven't decided what you're going to tell your boss. We need to clinch our deal before you go making calls."

Was it her ongoing guilt that made her second-guess everything he said? Her brain processed on two parallel tracks now, along her two different realities. She juggled, constantly, to understand the game and who was playing.

"I'd never call *anyone* without clearing it with you." Ellie went full-on cooperative—Ellie, the good reporter; Ellie, doing what the all-powerful police suggested. Monteiro needed something from her. Fine. She'd give it to him.

"Right." He drew out the word, sarcastic. "Reporters are always so accommodating. Let's move on, shall we?"

He ushered her into the room, table and chairs unoccupied, where the photo of Nora—of her—was still pinned front and center on the bulletin board. A quick assessment showed her coat and muffler and gloves still in a pile on the table, and her belongings plopped on two folding chairs just the way she'd left them. As much as she remembered. She unzipped her bag and pulled out her phone, partly just to make sure it was still there. One text buzzed to life.

From Gabe. *Where are you?*

"Don't answer that." Monteiro opened his manila folder and stood, holding it, reading something inside. He talked to her while looking at the papers. "Not until we have an agreement. Take a seat. Give me two seconds."

She sat in her metal chair again. Looked at the text again. Gabe.

Who'd pretended to be two people. Gabe and Guy. Beyond coincidental, she'd often thought, that he'd latched on to both of them. Both of *her*.

Was Gabe the Pharminex spy? And then, on a mission to infiltrate her life, he'd tried to entice her—both versions of her—with romance?

She worried her lower lip, trying to find the hole in her own story. Monteiro was focused on his paperwork. Ellie wondered if he was waiting her out, trying to make her nervous.

But Gabe was the key. Had to be. Gabe connected them all. But whose side was he on?

"Sorry for all the interruptions." Monteiro closed his file, perched again on the edge of the conference table, the pin-and-picture bulletin board to his right.

"I hadn't expected you today, so I needed to rearrange my schedule. Anyway. About Nor—"

"You were saying Nora Quinn was the only one who connected the two traffic accidents." Ellie stood, walked closer to the bulletin board, peering at Nora's surveillance photo. It was so blurry and pixelated, she decided, there was no way for him to compare it with her and make a connection. "But how do you think that person caused two separate traffic accidents?"

"Caused? Did I say 'caused'?"

She straightened. "Oh. Well, okay then. If not *caused*, then you don't suspect her of whatever it would be. Motor vehicle homicide or . . ." She shook her head. "You lost me."

"We think she could help us find out why those crashes happened."

"Crashes, not accidents."

Monteiro nodded.

"So you think they're connected."

Monertio nodded again.

"So—?" She prompted him.

"So. Here's our proposition. Since you've been in contact with Nora Quinn, we'd like you to help us find her."

Ellie felt the quicksand encircling her ankles. "But you can find her yourself. I told you she works at Pharminex."

"What's her job?"

"You'd have to ask her," Ellie said.

"Yeah. But, if *we* try to contact her, we're afraid, frankly, she might run. Apparently she has a somewhat checkered past."

Ellie started to answer, then stopped. The quicksand had reached her knees.

"And by *checkered* I mean nonexistent. I talked to

Pharminex while you were having your coffee. Her
résumé is phony. So there isn't really a Nora Quinn.
There's only someone pretending to be Nora Quinn."

"Did Pharminex know the reason? Who'd you
talk to there, anyway?" He was law enforcement, Ellie reasoned, so maybe he'd been transferred right
to the top. Nora had signed a confidentiality agreement with the company, so they weren't allowed—
whatever the parameters of *allowed* meant, she'd left
that to Gabe—to discuss their current agreement.
Or the abused-wife past that Nora had concocted
for them. "Why'd they hire her if she has a fake résumé?"

"They were somewhat . . ." Monteiro shrugged.
"Evasive. It doesn't pass the sniff test, right?" When
Ellie didn't respond, he continued, "Either their HR
department sucks . . ." He winced, as if regretting
his word choice. "Or they're hiding something. They
wouldn't give me her address without a warrant.
Which I could get, but it's an escalation I'd rather
avoid. As long as I can."

Ellie was at a loss for the proper response, but
Monteiro didn't seem to notice.

"She won't suspect you of working with us, Ms.
Berensen. She'll answer your call because you've had
a prior relationship. Do you agree to help us get to
her?"

Ellie thought of a lifeline, grabbed onto it. Nora
had disappeared once. She could do it again. Ellie
thought of treasured moments as a kid, reading under her pale blue comforter before anyone else was
awake, before the summer days and responsibilities
lured her outside and the real world took over. *I
know who I was when I got up this morning,* Alice
had told the Caterpillar in her most favorite book,
but I think I must have been changed several times

since then. I can't explain myself, I'm afraid, because I'm not myself, you see.

She'd been Nora this morning and this afternoon she was Ellie. She was in the midst of her own Alice story and she could almost see the smoke from the Caterpillar's hookah encircle Monteiro as he stood silently awaiting her reply.

"So let me get this straight," Ellie began. "You said you'd give me details on your investigation into these crashes if I helped you. And apparently 'help' means finding Nora Quinn. But what if there's someone besides Ms. Quinn who might have connected with both Kaitlyn Armistead and Pharminex? Someone else who's worth investigating?"

"Who?" Monteiro pulled out his notebook. Flipped it open.

She wasn't quite sure she should take this step. Too late now.

Gabe had told her that the police suspected *Nora* in Kaitlyn's accident. Why? To make her feel hunted or vulnerable? Or to encourage her to trust and confide in him? He'd laughed it off when she asked, but the more Ellie thought about it, the sorrier she was she'd trusted Gabe. Or whoever he really was. He'd shown her a driver's license to prove Gabriel Hoyt was his real name, and she'd accepted that as proof. Like a fake license wasn't hard to get.

"He's used several names. I know that. Although it might be perfectly benign."

"How did this 'he' know Lydia Frost?"

"Hmm." Ellie herself had told Gabe about Lydia, but she couldn't say that. "I'm not sure, but he knows about Pharminex. And he knows people there, executives." She'd introduced them too. She thought she had, at least.

Monteiro nodded. "And?"

"He's interested in Pharminex, knew Nora Quinn, and knew about Kaitlyn—in fact." Ellie sat up straighter, deciding. "He told me he'd talked to *you* about her accident. But that was before Lydia Frost's death."

"Talked to me?" Monteiro frowned. "Specifically me?"

"Though I know he didn't personally cause these accidents," she went on. "During one of them he was with me."

"What's his name? What's his stake in all this?"

"Well, that's exactly what I'm wondering too." Too late to turn back now, Ellie decided. "So here's my offer. You get those answers for me. On the down-low. Find out who he is and what he's up to. And never let him find out. You do that—and I'll contact Nora Quinn."

BEFORE

CHAPTER 40

BROOKE

"I love seagulls, don't you?" Brooke, the sun toasting her bare arms, leaned back against the once-familiar mahogany fittings of her brother's beloved old *Caduceus*. He'd taught her to sail the Caddy, as he called it, when she was maybe eight, and barely strong enough to handle the jib sheets to come about. *Put some muscle into it, Smidge,* Trevor would tease, and she'd hated "Smidge" but adored Trevor, and this time on the bay was their connection. Even now, as she was about to finish grad school, the seagulls and the early summer, the fragrance of Coppertone and Trevor's strong arm and his red life vest—like hers—transported her to times long past. His vest was unbuckled, as always, webbed straps flapping, his prowess at the helm more a life preserver than any vest could be.

"Sure, Smidge," Trev told her. He sat, one hand on the tiller and tan legs outstretched, with sunglasses glinting and a backward black-and-orange Orioles ball cap, steering them out of the yacht club and across the whitecaps of Chesapeake Bay; the shore and the beach and the pin-dot-sized sunbathers on the shore a faraway impressionist blur. "Seagulls. My fave."

They sat for a moment in silence, the fragrance of the briny water and Trevor's wheaty Natty Boh taking Brooke back seven years, to the last time she'd seen her parents and the Chesapeake and her brother, and forward, to her potential new life and career, and reminding her of what she'd given up. And gained.

"Mom and Dad are really hot to go to your graduation," Trevor said. "I wish you'd tell them you're here."

"Screw them," Brooke said. She zipped up her yellow windbreaker. Summer had come early to the Eastern Shore, but the coastal weather could be fickle. "I wanted to see you, just you, and you know, since I had the job interview, it made sense. But you promised. Just us. Not them."

"Okay, but," Trevor said, "you didn't even come for Christmas, not since you went to college, and Mom still hangs up your stocking. So, you know, she misses you. We all do. It's not the same without you, Smidge. Is there anything I can—"

"Yeah. You can forget about it, okay? It's fine. You can't choose your family, but you don't have to deal with them. It's just how it is. 'Cept for you, though, Trev. I'm sorry they put you in the middle of it."

Trevor's face darkened, its own shadow in the bright sun. "Okay, but listen, is there anything I should know? About what happened? I mean . . . if anything . . . if Dad—"

"You watch too much TV," Brooke said. "But hey, no, nothing like that. Really."

"Maybe someday you'll tell me."

"It doesn't matter, okay? Seriously. Let it go. You

mean to head out this way?" Brooke pointed toward the receding shore.

"Shit. You distracted me, Smidge. Grab that line, will you? Let's come about."

"Oh, right, *my* fault." She stood, balancing on the deck, tailing the jib and ducking under the boom as the boat tacked in the other direction. "Like the time you brought home that insane hamster from school. And blamed *me* when it got out."

"They ever find that friggin' thing?" Trevor asked.

"Shut up," she said, ten years old again. "You're a jerk."

She'd yanked her hair back in a ponytail, now flapping in the brisk wind. The sails filled, and for a moment she was one with the *Caduceus,* feeling the chop of the water and the slash of the wind and the shift of the hull as it cut through the brackish water. If they kept going, simply kept on and on in this direction, somehow, they'd hit England. She wished they could leave their lives behind, just like they'd left the shore.

But the shore—and the lives she and Trev had waiting for them—would always be there.

"It's so great, isn't it?" Trevor's chest rose and fell as the boat adjusted, turned, skimmed the water. The rush of the wake and the hiss of motion—Brooke could tell, simply by the sound of it, that Trevor had found the sweet spot in the wind, the space that would carry them as fast as the laws of aerodynamics would allow. They had no destination this afternoon, no place to go but away, only the joy of motion and the feel of freedom, unattached and unmoored, making the wind and the water their personal place in the universe. "The Caddy's such a rock star."

"You sound happy." The sky, Brooke saw, was

whitecapped with clouds, mirroring the dark water of the bay. "Married man and all, livin' the life. Here at your summer place, all bougie and settled. Getting ready to take over the company. And kids? Ever? Mom's got to be going nuts. She'll probably move in with you when the baby finally comes. Lucky you."

"Huh." Trev's eyes kept focus on the horizon. "Rather talk about you, Smidge. Seriously. Mom would be so happy if—"

"Trev? Seriously. Like I said. It's history, it's— never mind, okay?" She stood, looking out toward the mouth of the bay, widening her legs to keep her balance. "Stuff happens. I know your life is all text-book and perfect, but—whoa." She grabbed a brass railing, almost tripped over her own feet, clunky in white sneakers. "Tell a girl if you're gonna turn like that."

"Just seeing if you still have your sea legs." Trevor grinned at her as he angled the boat harder, his beer clamped between his battered boat shoes. "Let's keep going, okay? Head out? You up for it? And hey, we have food. Lacey had sandwiches made for us. In the hold, in white plastic things."

"Very cozy." Brooke edged her way toward the center of the boat, then turned, sat on the hatch cover, the white wood warm under her bare thighs. "Wait. Lacey knows I'm out with you?"

"Well, hey, yeah, I mean—what's the big? Yesterday she asked if I wanted her to get food, I said yeah, for two." He shrugged. "Imagine if I said *yeah, someone's coming out with me but I can't tell you who.* Right. All I need."

"She still as *Home and Garden* as she was?" Brooke lifted the hatch, flapped it open, latched it down. Turned backward to take the three steps into the hold. "Can't believe you guys don't have two point five children already."

Brooke ducked into the musty gloom of the hold, that fragrance, too, taking her back to summers past. It smelled of wool and wind, with a scent half of salt and half of mildew, somehow comforting instead of smothering. Some of their most perfect days had been out on the water. Separate and peaceful. Feeling as if they had some control.

"Got 'em!" Brooke yelled up into the daylight. She put one plastic-covered sandwich in each windbreaker pocket, unflapping one life jacket buckle to make room, then pulled two icy beers from the cooler and tucked the bottles under her arm. Trev had let her have beer way before she was legal, she remembered, another secret they had from their parents. Beer and sun and water made her sleepy, but it was too gorgeous a day not to indulge.

She clambered back up, pausing a moment to watch Trevor as he turned the tiller yet again, the mainsail boom swinging across the deck as he tacked a textbook ninety degrees. She heard the mainsail luff before it decided to fill with the wind, and then felt the boat catch its mark and speed ahead. Trevor, concentrating and empowered in his own world, looked like he owned the place.

Brooke wondered, looking at him, if Lacey loved this as much as he did. She couldn't imagine that woman, all manicure and eyeliner, letting nature take its course as it inevitably did out here.

"Does Lacey sail?" She set one sandwich next to Trevor, inserted his beer in a brass holder.

"She did when we first met." Trevor linked his arm over the tiller, holding it in place while he opened his sandwich. "Seemed to love it. Said so, at least. Mom even sprung for a bunch of lessons, engagement present. Since we were married, though, she's not so hot on it." He shrugged, taking a bite.

Brooke took her place again, setting her beer in the middle of a roll of gaffer's tape, their makeshift cupholders. "Tell me the scoop about Lacey and Mom. I bet they're big besties. Hey, we're getting out there, bud. You mean to?"

Trevor took another bite. "You in a rush?"

Brooke shook her head, letting go. She'd had classes, and finals and her thesis, then job interviews, and now, she realized, her life was like that ocean in front of them. Vast and full of possibilities. She only had to learn how to navigate it. She rolled her eyes at her own dumb metaphor.

"So, Mom and Lacey, I was saying." Brooke twisted the top from her Boh. Took a swallow. Beer and sailing, she thought. They ought to bottle it.

"Yeah, well." Trevor's face darkened. "There's a thing about—" He blew out a breath, didn't look at her. "You asked about kids. Yeah. I'm all about that, and Lacey wanted kids too."

"So?" Brooke grinned. "You need me to explain it to you?"

Trevor didn't laugh.

"Joke," she said.

"Yeah." Trevor took another swig of beer, tried to put the empty in the metal holder, and missed. Brooke swiped up the bottle before it rolled away across the deck. Stuck it in a mesh trash container.

"Trev?"

"Ah, not sure how much I can tell you," he said. "Kinda personal."

"Huh?"

"You'd know if you were home, Brooke."

She widened her eyes, startled that he'd called her Brooke. "What? Know?"

"Lacey's, like—well, you know Mom, right? And her miracle-of-modern-medicine stuff?"

Brooke's stomach twisted, in memory or remembrance, and her tuna sandwich suddenly seemed impossible. She wrapped it back into the plastic, stashed it in her windbreaker pocket. "All too well," she said.

"So Lacey was having—I mean *we* were having, I mean . . . trouble."

Trevor seemed to be struggling for the proper words.

"I'm so sorry," Brooke said, even though she wasn't sure about what. Were he and Lacey fighting?

"Between us? I mean, you can never tell Lacey I told you. But I can't—there's no one for me to talk to. I mean, in *our* family?" Trevor's smile was full of rue. "The vaunted Vanderwalds of the pharmaceutical behemoth? To complain about medications? That's total blasphemy. Treason. Punishable by torture and death. Don't bite the hand, right?"

The water shushed by them, the shore now diminished to a slash of fading beige and far-off green, the people and dogs dotting the sand no longer recognizable. They'd passed other sailboats, bobbing on their buoys in the harbor. Brooke loved this, the vast alone. Her college had teemed with sound and motion, and her dorm quad full of chattering students, flirting or partying or earnestly solving the problems of the universe. It was never quiet in Brooke's college world; that's what she missed about the water.

"Got that right," she said. "Medications? But sure, I four-leaf-clover-swear not to tell. Remember?"

"You can't swear on a four leaf clover." Trevor repeated his line.

"Yes, you can!" She channeled her eight-year-old self, thinking about all that had transpired since then.

"Yeah, so." Trevor's voice was back to a twenty-nine-year-old's. "Lacey said her doctor said she couldn't have kids. Something's wrong with her, um. You want details?"

"Whatever feels right." Brooke watched her brother's face darken, even in the sunshine. "It's just us out here."

"Okay, well. Let's just say we were having trouble staying pregnant. She told Mom." He lifted his sunglasses, parking them on his forehead. Squinted at her. "Can you imagine that conversation? Christ. Anyway. Mom made her go to a doctor, one of Mom's cast of characters, and told him Lacey was fine, she was perfect, all she needed was a boost of this stuff. And Lacey was up for it, she told me; what else was she supposed to do? Say no to Mom? And a doctor? To make it easier for her—for us—to . . . you know. And he gave her—well, shit. He gave her some drug, Monifan? And it went wrong, she's allergic or something, now she can't have kids. And it's a P-X drug, naturally, and they're saying this has never happened before. But—"

"That's horrible." Brooke felt the blood drain from her face. "I'm so sorry, Trev. There's nothing they can do? Surgery? Or anything else?"

"Nada." Trevor flipped his sunglasses back into place with one expert snap, as if closing off the conversation.

"I'm so sorry, Trevs," she said again. "And I guess she must be miserable, thinking about how she could have said no. Did they give her a choice?"

Trevor turned his head, his dark glasses facing out over the water, staring toward England.

"There's never a choice with Mom," Trevor said.

"She thinks she can fix anything. 'Fix' meaning make it be the way she wants it to be. And then she'll say she was only trying to help."

Brooke risked a gulp of her Boh, then another.

"How do you stand it?" she had to ask. "Being with her?"

"Her? Lacey?"

"Mom. And Dad. And that whole thing. And allergic? *Allergic?* They're saying Lacey's the only one? Really? Honestly? The *only* one?"

"Brooke? Can we not—"

"And hmm. You're about to become Prince Hotshot at P-X." She toasted him with her beer bottle. "You planning on mentioning that little glitch in their miracle drug? How will that hit Dad's precious stock price?"

"Shit, Brooke. Don't ask me that, okay?" Trevor adjusted the tiller as the boat slowed, the wind falling off as the afternoon slipped by. "Your dedicated trust fund is still intact, no matter what happens to P-X."

The old Barge Point lighthouse loomed in the distance and a pair of swooping seagulls now shepherded their journey. The shoreline behind them, Brooke saw, became a distant curve of sand and sky.

"True." Brooke remembered a fireside chat one winter evening when her father had explained the family's financial structure to an impatient teenage Brooke. She'd wondered: Why do I have to know this? She knew it was hypocritical, distancing herself from her parents but not from their money. But in her equation, it served them right. They couldn't buy her love, or her loyalty, but they owed her. Big time. And she'd use their money for good. "And yours too, I suppose. Daddy made sure of that. But listen, that drug she got—"

"Let's anchor here, right? Finish Lacey's sandwiches, talk about something else?"

Trevor lowered the anchor over the side, feeding out the rope hand over hand. The Caddy bobbed in the light chop, tugging at the set anchor like an impatient puppy. Brooke tossed a few crusty edges of her tuna baguette to the fish below, imagining the winter-chilled depths and teeming marine creatures, the rocky bottom so far beneath them. The waves, gentle, sloshed against the hull of the boat, caressing and cradling, as if the arms of the sea were rocking them into silence.

Trevor, tiller lashed with a bright orange bungee cord, leaned against the brass rail behind him, grabbed his sandwich, then propped his bare feet on the deck bench beside Brooke. She faced the opposite way, toward the shore, wishing they never had to go back.

Nine years now, since Mom had taken that decision away from Brooke, tricked her, not even offering her the respect to make her own choice. And now, it seemed, probably again insisting it was "for the best," Mom had done the same thing to Lacey. Whom Brooke never liked, sure, and who'd never given Brooke a second thought. But now, Brooke let out a sigh of conscience; maybe they were victims together.

Poor Lacey went through her mind. Back on the shore, somewhere, Lacey Vanderwald, who anyone would assume had everything she ever wanted, might be regretting and replaying and wondering, maybe, what might have happened if she'd stood up for herself, or taken action or found her voice. Brooke had to hope poor Lacey had a friend.

The combination of beer with only one bite of sandwich was making her sleepy, and peacefully so,

she had to admit, as she tucked the almost-empty bottle between her legs and yanked her visor down for
some shade. She leaned against the sun-baked wall of
the hold, watching Trev and watching the water, and
wondering what to do.

BEFORE

CHAPTER 41

LACEY

"Glasses, ice in the bucket, limes, Bombay Sapphire." Lacey pointed to each item on the marble counter of her kitchen. "Sauvignon blanc if they want, and there's the good chablis if they insist. Prosciutto, melon, Brie." She pointed again, one pale fingernail indicating a pile of white linen squares, each one monogrammed with a dark green letter V. "Napkins."

The black T-shirted cater-waiter nodded, her seen-one-seen-'em-all expression bridging boredom and disapproval. And well, yes, it was another cookie-cutter cocktail party in seaside Bayellen. Lacey felt like defending herself from the judgment of banality. It was tradition, Bay tradition, and this is what one did, and if this gothy bitch wanted innovation she should take her too-short too-dark hair and go back to SoHo or wherever. Lacey was not about innovating. She was about fitting in. Even after eight years in D.C., with summers here in Bayellen, Lacey was still not quite sure she'd passed the family hazing, the initiation rite of passage, into the Vanderwald world. The more she tried to learn the rules, the more quickly another one emerged. The impatiens, white

New Guineas, in terra-cotta on the porch, but only after Mother's Day. The mums—not russet, only yellow—presented after Labor Day. No purple anything. Even under the best of circumstances, cocktail parties like today's were always a test. Some unseen social oracle decreed Schweppes or Canada Dry, round ice cubes or square, citrus wedges or twists. And how did everyone get the message?

"I think we'll be outside," Lacey went on. French doors, glistening panes of polished glass set in pristine white wood, opened onto a carefully weathered wooden deck, its fading planked floor elegantly battered by the Chesapeake winds and washed with countless summers of rain, and then sleeting winters. A dot-com-crash victim had lived here before her and Trevor, and before that, the mistress of some iffy diplomat had used it as a rendezvous spot. Now it was Lacey and Trevor's, an anniversary gift from his parents. The nursery, an optimistic buttercup of a room, remained empty. As it would forever.

Five weeks, it had been, since Lacey had heard from the doctor. She felt physically different now, lighter, and heavier, and somehow, at only twenty-nine, old. She'd examined herself in the bathroom full-length mirror, searching for external signs of her defeat. She was a shell, maybe, like a shell someone had forgotten on the beach. One of those that once had a creature inside, but it had shriveled in the sun.

The deck looked out over the bay itself, a tapestry of whitecaps this time of day. Trevor was out there somewhere. With Brooke. Lacey had not yet decided how to deal with it.

"How many people, ma'am?" The waiter, Ava or Arva or something like that, had twisted the linen napkins into a star shape with the heel of her hand, then arranged them on a white raffia tray.

"Ten? Ish?" Lacey said. "Just small. My husband, his parents, a few others. And you can click on the music at six. It's all programmed." She pointed to a control panel installed in the Italian-tiled kitchen wall. "That button."

Lacey looked out over the water, wondering which speck in the far distance was the Caddy. And Trevor. And the sister.

"Lacey?" Brinn Vanderwald's voice, a warble of polite inquiry, as always, as if she might be intruding into a place she didn't know, asking for someone she hadn't met. Brinn had been Brenda, a doctor's receptionist, Lacey knew, before she became Brinn, and now Brinn ruled the world. Somehow she had learned the rules. And then she began to make them.

"On the deck, Mother!" Lacey tried to match the timbre of Brinn's voice; *society,* she called it in her head, even knowing that's how her own mother described it. Sometimes Lacey had a momentary glimpse of appreciation for her real mother—who on her rational days would have dismissed Brinn's rules as "toe-tapping bull crap" and wondered why Lacey didn't make some rules of her own.

Brinn appeared, hair chopped into this year's steel-blond pixie cut, round tortoiseshell sunglasses masking the wrinkles that advanced on her eyes, and this season's turquoise drop earrings complementing her pale pink tunic and black silk pants. Seeing Lacey, she burst into a trill of practiced laughter, lifted a glass of white wine. Which she must have gotten before she came out to the deck. Unless she'd driven over with it.

"Well, darling." She used one forefinger to lower her sunglasses, peered at Lacey over them. "One of us is definitely going to have to change."

Lacey looked at her own hydrangea-pink tunic, the

one she'd so carefully chosen for tonight. She leaned closer to her mother-in-law, kissed her once on each cheek, abiding by the rule that prohibited lips from touching skin. "Oh, dear," she said.

"Or we could pretend we planned it, I suppose." Brinn's voice did not sound as if she honestly thought that was a good idea. "Your chablis is not cold enough, dear."

"I'll go change. Thirty seconds," Lacey said.

"Where's our Trev?" Brinn had turned away and, taking her sunglasses off, scanned the deck, as if her son might be hiding behind the stand of forced mandevilla vines, hot-pink flowers on glossy leaves. She pivoted to peer through the sliding doors into the living room, where canvas-slip-covered couches and chairs, low-slung and voluptuous, sat empty.

"He's sailing," Lacey told her. "He'll be back soon."

Lacey took a step toward the staircase to the second-floor bedrooms. She'd imagined, over and over and over, how to deal with what haunted her, what *enraged* her, and now she felt as if this moment, this space in her life, had opened a door.

"Mother? While we have a moment before everyone gets here," she began, "I've been thinking about what happened. And I want you to know, I—I . . . don't blame it on you."

"Blame what?" Brinn had positioned herself at the bay side of the deck, her wineglass balanced on the wide railing. If it toppled, it would fall two stories, past the first-floor garage level, over a hedge of white hydrangea and onto the mermaid-blue tiles of the swimming pool below. It had happened before.

Lacey felt the warmth prickle the back of her neck again, the flush of anger and resentment. She tamped it down. Not now. *Not now.*

"What happened last month. When you took me

to the doctor." Lacey tried to modulate her voice. This was supposed to be a moment of generous loving forgiveness.

"What—"

"And I don't blame Pharminex either," Lacey continued, determined to get this accomplished. "I even accept that the doctor thought he should tell you, even though—"

"I *know* him, dear. He works for us. And you're my daughter-in-law."

Lacey pressed her lips together. Why was everything so difficult? "I know, but information like that is supposed to be confidential. Personal."

"We're family," Brinn said. "I might as well be your real mother, since yours is no longer with us, dear."

Which was the good news, Lacey supposed, embracing that perception. "Oh, Mother. And I know—I love you and Winton so much, and Trevor, and I don't want this to come between us."

Brinn crossed one linen leg over the other, revealing this year's gold-link sandals, complemented by metallic-gold polish on her toes. She took a sip of wine, then stared through her glass, as if examining the wispy sky through a filter of chablis. "What does Trevor say? How does he feel about it?"

"Trevor?" Lacey thought about what to say. Trevor? How about me? "He feels the way I do. He's devastated. Disappointed."

"Hmm." Brinn took another sip of her wine. Made a face.

"But, Mother? What I wonder about—you knew this might happen. You and your Pharminex people."

"The doctor explained that, dear, how rare it is."

"How rare, though, Mother?" Lacey took a step toward her. "Exactly?"

"You'll have to ask your father—well, Winton.

Trevor's father. But from what I know . . ." She consulted her watch, a chunky silver mesh that draped from her too-thin wrist. "Mightn't you want to go change? Is now the time for this discussion?" Her low-wattage smile telegraphed her meaning.

"Of course, I'm sorry. I only—" Then Lacey bit off the end of her own sentence, hating herself for apologizing. "I thought that since we had these few minutes alone we could talk."

"People will be here soon, dear," Brinn said.

Lacey took two more steps toward the staircase, then decided. She turned back. Brinn had already turned away, so Lacey spoke to her back. "I'd hoped there'd be one more for this evening," she said. "A special surprise guest for you. But . . ." She sighed, smoothing the linen sleeve of her now imitative pink tunic. "It was not to be."

"Who?" Brinn turned to face her, curious.

"Doesn't matter," Lacey said over her shoulder, setting the bait. She felt like counting how many seconds it would take for Brinn to demand an answer, demand it in that tone Brinn had perfected. *One. Two.*

"Lacey? Darling? Who?"

Lacey turned back, adjusting one of her own turquoise earrings, gifts from Trevor, which she would not, damn it, take off.

"Brooke," she said. "But she declined my invitations."

"Brooke? *My* Brooke?"

Lacey was gratified at the spike in Brinn's pitch, a jagged peak into the red line, an un-Brinn-like yelp, raw and unfiltered.

"She's out with Trev, in fact. Sailing. Right now." Lacey stepped closer to her mother-in-law, as if the reappearance of the child Brinn hadn't seen in seven years was as common as the Brie melting appropriately on her raffia platters. "On the Caddy. You didn't know, I completely understand. I wanted it to be a surprise for you. I shouldn't have said anything, I suppose. But you know me. I want you to be happy."

"But—"

Even under the sunglasses, Lacy saw Brinn's expression change, her entire face devolve, as the woman stood, one hand on the railing to balance herself and the other sending her wineglass down down down to clatter on the mermaid stones below.

"She can't just—Trevor never told—does anyone else—"

Lacey enjoyed it, as ungracious as it was, as unloving as it was, as inappropriate. As ugly. Now Brinn knew there was something Lacey possessed that *she* didn't. Something that with all her money and all her power and all her rules had—nevertheless—been taken from her. Brooke. And with that, a daughter's love. Lacey had no idea why Brooke had rejected her mother. She couldn't wait to find out.

The doorbell rang, one discreet *ping*.

"People are arriving." Lacey fluttered one hand to her tousled hair, its waves too long for the rules, but she didn't care about that either. Lacey could make her own rules. "And as you said, there's not enough time to talk now. I'll have someone clean up your glass."

"But—" Brinn looked everywhere but at Lacey, as if searching for her power.

"I fear we'll have to go with the matching looks, Mother, so let's make the best of it. We're all friends here, after all. And you and I are family."

BEFORE

CHAPTER 42

BROOKE

The clatter of—something—startled Brooke awake. For a confused flash of a second she recovered her bearings—the boat, the water, the waning afternoon—and Trev? Her empty beer bottle rolled across the deck, clunked against a metal fitting, and then rattled back toward her, as if it were on a mission of its own. The boat was dead in the water, otherwise, sails luffing half-heartedly, knowing they had to wait for a human hand to coax them to do their jobs.

"Trev?" she called. The Caddy's tiller was still lashed into place, same as she'd last seen it. Her heart twisted in alarm. "Trev?"

"What?" Trev's head appeared from the hold, then the rest of him and then the Caddy's red canvas spinnaker bag. He plopped the bag onto the deck, and it thunked with the weight of the heavy sail folded carefully inside.

"We're screwed." He held on to the mainmast, steadying himself. "Wind's shifted, and the spinney's our best bet for getting back. Before it's totally dark."

"Is it rigged? Set to go? Why not use the outboard?"

Brooke's brain was still adjusting from the beer and the sun, and from the inevitable lassitude that came after a day on the water.

"Rigged? As always, kiddo," Trevor said. "And the outboard's on the fritz. Pain in the butt." He unzipped the top of the spinnaker bag, dragged the front halyards from the mainmast and clicked them into place in the grommets of the sail. The spinnaker would become a billow of bright orange when the wind filled it, Brooke knew, with the giant letters *P-X* in the upper right. Her mother had insisted, years ago and over her father's impotent reluctance, that it would be good advertising. *It's not all about Pharminex, Brinn,* he'd pleaded, attempting to have a say in the matter. Mom, languidly reigning from her chaise on the yacht club's weathered wooden deck, hadn't bothered to argue. She always won.

"You okay to hoist it alone?" Brooke didn't mention all the empties she saw.

"Duh," Trev said. "Couple of Bohs, I'm sailin' fine. Sailin' just fine." He reeled in the anchor rope and stowed the prongs. Then, stumbling once, he dragged the heavy spinnaker bag toward the bow.

Brooke unlashed the tiller, stashing the bungee cord. She could take over steering, no problem, but hoisting the spinnaker could be a pain for one person, with its unwieldly pole, and the necessity to balance the folded spinney, lift and drop the jib, rebalance to place the spinnaker pole, then step back in time to let the huge front sail fill.

Brooke remembered one afternoon, so long ago, with city boy Liam—*Liam Endicott;* her brain called back the face, the fragrance, the loss. The feel of the sunscreen on his back. Liam's eyes, looking at her. Liam had been bummed the spinnaker wouldn't send them skimming at top speed across the sound. She'd tried to explain about the wind, how the spinnaker was mainly used in racing when you had to go the same direction as the wind, and not against it. He'd stopped listening, she remembered. And, after his touch, she'd stopped caring, stopped thinking about anything but him. And where was he now? Even on her most wine-sodden late nights, she hadn't succumbed to the temptation to google him. He was gone and the past was gone, and there was only now.

The Caddy lurched with a random wave. "Whale!" she yelled, before she even realized it. A family joke. Long ago, on one of her first sails, an unexpected swell had put her in mortal terror. Instead of comforting her, Brooke remembered, her father had yelled *Whale!* They'd laughed about it for years, whenever something came as a surprise. Back when they all still laughed.

"You okay?" She'd seen Trevor bobble, lose his balance again, saw the top corner of the orange and white sail flutter and catch in the wind.

"All good, little Smidge," Trev shouted. "Cope-a-freaking-cetic."

She saw him grab the mainmast, still off balance. Three beers, she'd counted. Or four?

"Whoa," he said. "Keep her steady."

Brooke planted her feet, holding the tiller with her right hand, feeling the increasingly choppy swells beneath her, an occasional spray of salty water exploding onto the deck. Perfect, she thought. It had been a long time since she'd sat at the helm, but the waves and the wind were reassuringly the same.

They were still far from shore, the telltales showing the wind from the south, Trev setting the spinney on the broad reach home. Brooke stared into the distance, wondering how far she'd come, not only today, but in the last seven years. Wishing she could see into the future. *Poor Lacey. Poor Trev.* The golden couple, on the surface, but deep down . . . disappointment and sorrow didn't care who you were.

Brooke thought it was an angry seagull at first, that harsh squawking call. She looked up, shading her eyes, expecting white wings in the cloud-streaked sky. But there were no gulls.

And then she heard the splash.

"Trev?"

She leaped to her feet, the tiller loose, grabbed her way hand over hand toward the bow. No Trevor.

No Trevor.

The spinnaker pole, loose, clanked and rattled across the deck, then rolled into the ocean, so quickly Brooke could have believed it never existed.

"Trev!" But he was not here, he wasn't, and then she saw Trev's life vest, red and taunting, and bobbing in the waves as if it hadn't a responsibility in the world.

She saw him. A cap, an orange and black Orioles cap.

"Trev!" she screamed. He was a great swimmer, a terrific swimmer, and the first rule of lifesaving was that the other person should not leap into the water too. Or they'd both drown.

Keep your eye on the person, her training reminded her. He'd gone under again, but he was there. She kept focus on the spot, backing up as she did, her eyes on the water, then by feel, grabbed the white life preserver and yanked it from its hooks. But where was Trev now, gone again, which way to throw it? And why wasn't he coming to the surface? Even after a beer, or three, he knew what to do.

The radio was inside the hold. She stood, panicked and terrified, trying to decide. Scramble belowdecks, call for help? Or wait until she saw him, then reach with the life pole and haul him in?

"TrevorTrevorTrevor!" She screamed it, like one word, and then saw the top of his head, she knew it was, come to the surface for one exquisite instant. She threw the life preserver, threw it with all her might, toward that thatch of sandy hair. Wishing, as if eternity was now and now was eternity, to see that fragment of her brother again. He was there, he'd grab the life preserver, call for help.

Radio, her brain screamed, *call for help.*

The tiller flapped now, the boat under no one's control, and it tipped, side to side, the mainsail rocking and the spinnaker a puddle of fabric on the deck, one edge of orange touching the water then slipping, like a blanket from a fidgety child, into the dark water.

The life preserver, floating helplessly, ebbed and flowed and did nothing except taunt her, and Brooke turned and ran, somehow, down into the hold and hit the mayday. They'd find them by the radio signal and GPS, she knew that, and all she had to do was hold out. All *Trevor* had to do.

Back at the deck's edge she saw him, a human bubble in the waning sun, she *did,* she *did,* it was him, it was *completely* him. "*Trevor!*" she screamed again. But the life pole would never reach, and there was nothing else she could do.

"Trevor!" she yelled. She yanked off her life vest, then stuck one arm back through its webbing so she could somehow dive and not die. But how could she find him? She had to make sure they both didn't sink into the darkness, swallowed up by the sea. "Trevor!"

Screaming would not help. There was no one to hear. She licked her lips, tasted salt. She was a good swimmer, they both were, and there was no reason Trev would not pop to the surface. She scanned the water, it was still light enough to see, and kept one arm in the life jacket, trying to remember where it was she'd seen him, but the Caddy was her only point of reference, and with no steadying hand on the tiller, it listed and lurched, a drunken sailor. The shore seemed more distant than ever, the useless sails flapping them nowhere, only the unpredictable waves and the random walk of the water deciding where the Caddy would go.

She hooked the life jacket to a metal cleat on the side of the boat, took a huge breath and dived under, somehow believing she might see him, might be able to swim to him, and bring her brother back to safety. She was trained in lifesaving. She knew her stuff. This wasn't completely crazy. It could work. It could matter. She could rescue her brother.

The cold shocked her, surrounded her, and she gasped, flailing to the surface, her body recalibrating to the traumatic change in temperature. She ordered her brain to focus, but under the water was dark as a night sky, so opaque she wondered why she hadn't remembered how dense and infinite and infinitely uncaring it could be.

Her legs turned to weights. She could feel them, and then not feel them, and her clunky sneakers were bricks impelling her down. Salt water sloshed into her face, into her eyes, and she could not tell if it was ocean or tears.

She burst through to the top, grabbed at the life vest. Missed. Grabbed again.

And there was not a trace of Trevor.

She felt the water wash over her, insistent, demanding, vast as the sky. *Get that vest,* she commanded herself, and drew a last gasp of intention from her own breaking heart.

BEFORE

CHAPTER 43

LACEY

She'd always remember this place with the fragrance of limes and salt water, Lacey thought, and the wash of sinuous jazz floating out over her back deck and off into the Chesapeake Bay.

Brinn had collapsed into her wine, now holding a new glass of white and staring off over the inky bay as her Eastern Shore friends compared golf notes and complaints about whatever they cared about, a cynical undercurrent of ego and dismissals. Lacey might as well not have been there, her existence in their lives only validated by her husband. The music filled the gaps in the languid conversation, the moments when even complaints seemed too wearisome to articulate. These people, all khaki and confidence, rattled ice in their stubby glasses and tonight, for some reason, were competing to name the emerging constellations.

"Orion," one said.

"Like hell," someone else countered.

"Lacey?" Brinn's voice cut through the murmuring rivalry. "Why is Trevor so late? He's off with her somewhere, isn't he? Has he called you? It's your party night. He should be here. But why won't Brooke come home, Lacey? What did she say to you?"

Lacey shook her head as she leaned against the deck rail, ever so sympathetic.

"What did she look like?" Brinn turned, searching Lacey's face. "I haven't laid eyes on her since she was seventeen. The day she left for college. And now she's all grown up, but I can't picture her. Can you imagine how that feels?"

Lacey could. But Brinn kept talking.

"I have no vision of *my own daughter*! I see her, now, still with all that hair, and those eyes, taking in everything. And so—so confident, I remember. Standing up for herself. We called it sullen, but now I see she was simply coming into her own. Remember her from the wedding? She had no idea how beautiful she'd become. *Is* she? Beautiful?"

Lacey shook her head. "I only spoke to her on the phone."

"How did she sound?"

"Sound?"

"Happy? Sad? Is she still angry? Did she say anything about me?"

"I'm so sorry, Mother, I really am. She sounded like a normal young woman, all I can tell you, I'm afraid. I asked her, of course, about tonight, and you, but she . . ." Lacey took a sip of her club soda, tasted the lime from the carefully cut wedge. "She declined the invitation. And then must have given the phone back to Trevor."

"And he kept it all from me," Brinn whispered. "That she was here. How long have they been in touch? And wait—that means he has her phone number. Do you have it too?"

"That's between you and your son, I'm afraid.

He'll have to choose how much to tell you. I feel so bad for you, because I know how hard you must have tried with her. If I had a daughter, I'd never let her out of my sight."

"Ms. Vanderwald?" The waiter approached, an empty tray in her hands.

"Yes?" Lacey answered first.

"Shall I bring the shrimp now? Your guests have finished the prosciutto and melon, and the Brie is pretty much gone. And we're into the fourth chablis."

"Thank you." Lacey saw her company had settled into the line of green Adirondack chairs, drinks on their armrests, watching the sky as if it were nature's own home movie. "Let me show you where the—"

"Lacey. Do you know where she's staying?" Brinn persisted, interrupting. She followed, still talking, as Lacey led the waiter toward the kitchen.

"I'll go to wherever it is," Brinn went on. "I could make it look like a coincidence. How long will she be here? Is she coming to stay with you and Trevor? I'll wait here to see her, I will, I cannot bear to . . . Lacey. Please." Brinn caught her by the arm, stopping her. Then threw back her head, closed her eyes.

Lacey looked up too, at the fickle universe. Above her the sky was scattered with nameless stars, wisps of foggy clouds cloaking them, briefly, then revealing the brightness again.

"Do you? Know?" Brinn clutched at Lacey's arm. "Lacey, you have to tell me where she is. She's my *daughter*."

"It must feel terrible, losing a child." Lacey stepped away, extricating herself. "Do you think about her some days?"

The waiter turned back to them and held up one finger, *nevermindIgotthis,* and trotted into the house, leaving the two of them outside.

"Do I think about her? *Every* day."

"Especially here, I'd imagine." Lacey noticed the array of twinkling lights out over the dark bay. Some of them were red, she half-noticed. And blue. So pretty. "All that time you missed?"

"Until you have a child, you can't know," Brinn told her. Her wineglass was empty.

Until you have a child. And that was it. That was the edge. Lacey felt her heart toppling over the deck railing, past the first-floor garage, past the hydrangeas, shattering like fragile crystal on the mermaid tiles below.

"What happened between you two?" Lacey, with no heart left, no longer tried to stop herself from asking. Brinn was the vulnerable one now, not Lacey, not anymore, and this was the perfect time to pry that mystery out of her. Lacey felt brave. Sober. Strategic.

But Brinn only closed her eyes again, drawing in a breath of the evening. "And where is Winton? I swear that man—Lacey." Brinn clipped off her own train of thought. "Does he know about our daughter? Does he know Brooke is here?"

Lacey sipped at her soda and lime, keeping her head. "He would have told you, don't you think? I mean—does he keep secrets from you?"

Brinn waved a careless arm toward the stars and the bay and the people she'd probably known since her children were babbling toddlers. She shook her head, her mind elsewhere, as if she were looking into the past.

A doorbell rang, distant and otherworldly. Not Trevor, she thought. The waiter would get it.

Brinn did not react. She had both hands on the railing, looking at the water, maybe imagining her devoted son and her brilliant daughter sailing together, as if it were back in the days when they all loved each other. Back in the days that were gone.

The doorbell rang again. Lacey frowned, wondering why the waiter didn't answer it.

"Excuse me," Lacey said. "Someone's here. Are you all right, Mother?"

She didn't wait for Brinn to answer but crossed the living room—white slipcovers not in place until after Memorial Day—and down the three tiled steps to the front door. Opened it, smiling, expecting more guests.

"Lacey Vanderwald?" A police officer. Blue uniform, pocket flaps pressed and buttons shiny. "I'm Officer Teo Lane. May I come in?"

"Is something wrong?" Lacey felt her face change. Her hands tingle. Something happened between her shoulder blades.

"May we come in, please?" Behind Lane, Lacey saw a black and white police cruiser, with the yellow emblem of Anne Arundel County. Another officer stepped into view behind him. She'd apparently been there the whole time, but Lacey had been transfixed on Teo Lane's reluctant eyes. Pooled with sorrow, and maybe fear; she could see that even a trained police officer could not hide the burden of bad news.

"I'm Sharyn Forney." The woman pointed to a black plastic name tag pinned to her uniform pocket. Her braided hair coiled like nautical ropes under her billed cap. "May we come in, Ms. Vanderwald?"

"What happened?" Lacey's feet would not move from where she stood, not toward these visitors or away from them. A list of horribles spooled out faster than she could label them. Or maybe it was nothing, someone's lost dog or Boh-happy teenagers slashing tires. "What? Is everything okay? What can I do for you? What's happened?"

"Who is it?" Brinn's footsteps behind them. "Oh. *Oh*. My husband. My husband?" Brinn clutched at Lacey's arm, her fingers wrapped around the pink silk.

Someone had turned up the music in the background, and soft jazz filtered through the living room's built-in speakers.

Lacey could feel Brinn's tension, almost hear her mind cataloging her own gruesome possibilities.

"Tell me," Brinn whispered.

Lacey felt her own knees buckle. She tucked her arm through Brinn's, balancing her, balancing herself. The brittle chess game they'd begun would be forgotten; she was sure of it. The universe was about to play. And its moves would be bigger. Whatever they were.

"Ms. Vanderwald." Officer Lane looked at Lacey, then Brinn, then dropped his eyes, either in apprehension or respect. "We need to come in."

More footsteps behind them. The waiter, Anna, that was it, flustered into the room, this time carrying a thick metal tray arrayed with glistening pink shrimp and a fluted glass bowl of red cocktail sauce. "Good evening," she said. "Oh."

Lacey recoiled at the shrimp, too fishy and too wet and the red sauce too red. She looked away, straightened her shoulders, gestured toward the living room. "In here," she told the police. "Anna, will you go to the deck and serve the shrimp? And say we'll be there momentarily."

"Ma'am?" Officer Forney looked uncomfortable.

Lacey tried to read the officer's face. It was not difficult.

"Is it my husband?" Brinn, in slow motion, lowered herself to the couch.

A new song started, incongruous in the silence, beginning the beguine.

"Is it my husband?" Lacey had to ask, she had to.

Officer Lane nodded. "I'm afraid so."

CHAPTER 44

ELLIE

"Where the hell have you been?" Gabe's voice came over her car's Bluetooth as Ellie drove out of the state police headquarters lot and onto the highway. Three in the afternoon—the traffic around Boston at its most sparse during the fifteen minutes between rush hours. The threat of snow had vanished. *If you don't like the weather in Boston, just wait and it'll change,* someone had joked to her.

Was it the same with life?

"Hey, Gabe," she answered. "I'm driving back to Boston. Warren sent me out to the state police HQ." That was semi-true, although in the interim she'd made that stop at Pharminex.

Gabe. She'd just secretly thrown him under the bus by trading her access to Nora Quinn for information on this potentially unreliable "ally." But if Gabe was a bad guy, better for Lieutenant Monteiro to find out about it than for her to discover it when it was too late.

Monteiro, her new best friend, now thought Ellie was on the hunt for Nora Quinn. If he'd known or even suspected that Ellie *was* Nora, he hadn't betrayed it for a flicker of a moment. So that assignment was not going to be tough. Ellie knew exactly where Nora Quinn was every moment of every day. She almost laughed, thinking about it.

"Did the cops confirm the victim was Lydia Frost?" Gabe asked.

Ellie stopped at the light, grateful for a moment to regroup. When she was killed, Lydia had been driving, just like Ellie was now.

"How did you know it was Lydia Frost?" Ellie hoped she'd managed to sound curious, not contentious.

"I take that as a yes," he said.

"But how did you even know of her? Did you know Lydia?"

Silence on the phone as Gabe apparently decided what to say. It was not that difficult a question.

The red line of her fuel gauge was tickling E, and she scouted for a gas station. And food. She hadn't eaten since . . . whenever it was.

"*You* told me who she was on the elevator," Gabe said. "Plus, she was on my radar. Like you were?"

"From a dating app?" Ellie asked, then instantly regretted it. The woman was dead. "Never mind. Anyway. How'd you know she was in the . . . crash?"

"It was on TV, Ellie," Gabe said. "So what's the scoop? Do the police think Lydia Frost's accident is connected with Kaitlyn Armistead's?"

"Connected?" Ellie steered her Passat into a Shell, lining the car up against the nearest vacant pump. No real food here, but she'd get pretzels and maybe a cheese stick when she paid. She tucked her phone between her cheek and the shoulder of her coat, pulled off her gloves and hopped out. She could wash the gas from her hands, but her gloves always reeked. "Why would they?"

"Because—hang on a sec. Another call's coming through."

Gabe put her on hold. She watched highway traffic ebb and flow as the gas meter clicked forward, hearing the *ding* at each dollar. Thinking about how accidents happen, and wondering how easy it would be to cause one—and get away with it.

The cars straggled by, their wheels slushing on the damp pavement, some with a caked layer of snow stubbornly clinging to their roofs. A white metal awning protected customers from the weather, but attached to that, three black cylindrical surveillance cameras pointed down at the station. From underneath, Ellie saw another one, a cylinder of white metal, attached to the roof of the auto body shop across the street. Three lenses pointed out from the storage company next door.

You couldn't do anything these days without someone taping it, she realized. Did Monteiro have video? If another car had deliberately—or even accidentally—caused Kaitlyn's and Lydia's accidents, it would be evident from the video. And, theoretically, simple for the police to track. Slap thirty seconds of that footage on tonight's eleven o'clock news, Ellie thought, and helpful citizens would be all too happy to rat out their reckless—or homicidal—acquaintances.

Or maybe they hadn't used a car as their murder weapon.

She jammed the gas pump back into the slot, her neck now permanently cricked from holding the phone in place.

"Gabe?" But there was still only the on-hold silence.

She jogged inside to pay for the gas and pretzels and a pack of peanut butter crackers and a Diet Coke, still listening for Gabe's return, and ripped open the pretzels with her teeth while carting her purchases and the phone back to her car. No Gabe.

She put her stuff on the car's roof, then her fingers on the door handle. Gabe was still MIA. She clicked off, annoyed. Why call her if he was in the middle of something?

After swiping the spilled pretzel salt from the front of her coat, she sat, organizing her stash of food and getting angrier by the minute. If there was a connection between these two women's deaths, it wouldn't necessarily be *how* they were killed. It would be why.

What the hell? A sound. A loud, wrong sound. Her car lurched forward. Her neck and back clenched with fear. A cascade of pretzels tumbled to her lap, and the crackers toppled to the floor. She flattened her hand against the window to keep her balance. *What?*

"Sorry!" a voice called out.

A silver SUV had smashed her from behind. Ellie grabbed her phone and leaped out of the car, leaving the door open, whirling to confront whoever was responsible. And to see how badly her car's rear end had been damaged.

"I'm sorry I'm sorry I'm so freaking sorry!" A spindly teenage girl, wearing a black hooded down jacket and neon-pink wool ski cap and carrying a cell phone, jogged toward Ellie, apologizing nonstop. "I'm sorry I'm sorry I'm so totally *freaking* sorry! Are you okay?"

"I'm fine," Ellie said. But her knees had gone to jelly, and she had to pause—hand over her racing heart—to get her bearings. Once she did, she examined her bumper. And the girl's. "I guess the cars are okay too."

She watched the girl stash her phone in one pocket of her jacket.

"Were you, like, texting?" Ellie asked.

"No!" The girl's face went whiter as she denied it, and Ellie realized how parents know when their kids are lying.

"Right," Ellie said, feeling like someone's mom. She took out her phone and, before the girl could protest, snapped a photo of the license plate on the front of the SUV. "The cops can trace that, you know. If you were texting or talking. And aren't you under eighteen? Don't you know that—even more than drunk driving—*texting* and driving is the biggest cause of—"

"You want my number?" The girl's dark brown eyes welled in little-girl distress, incongruous with her pseudo street attire. "My dad's gonna *kill* me."

"No one is gonna kill anyone," Ellie said, weary of death and how people threw that word around like it meant nothing. This kid had no idea, Ellie thought. Maybe it was because Ellie herself was tired and afraid and pressured, but this girl had touched her, so cocooned, protected by parents and affluence and youth, unaware of the deceit and manipulation looming at every turn. And now she, Ellie, was in the midst of it, and after Kaitlyn and Lydia and Monteiro and those bulletin board pushpins, this sweetly oblivious girl had almost pushed her over the emotional edge. "And I'm all good, so you go. Your car's fine. Drive carefully, though, okay? No texting?"

"Thank you thank you thank you." The girl walked backward, hands pressed together as if in prayer to illustrate her gratitude. Then she jumped in her luxury vehicle, backed up and pulled away without another look Ellie's way. As she turned the SUV back onto the highway, she'd already pulled out her cell phone.

Ellie stood, leaning against the side of her car, watching the girl, then watching the highway. Kaitlyn

Armistead had probably been one of those statistics; on her phone, distracted. Confiding in Nora as she died.

A trio of motorcycles roared by, one with a woman on the back, long hair flying, no helmet, as if everyone lived forever and she were immortal. The roar of their engines faded away, but not the indelible picture in Ellie's mind. A small white car. Crashed on the side of the road.

She had been on the phone listening as Kaitlyn died. *She'd* been the distraction. She'd been the *cause.* She pursed her lips and closed her eyes to squeeze the thought away. Kaitlyn had called her, and that's how the world went. But if it was an accident, why did the police have Kaitlyn's photo posted on the bulletin board?

The police had called Nora for an interview. Then they'd let her go.

And, Ellie remembered, they'd also said they were calling everyone Kaitlyn had talked to before she died. So Kaitlyn had made other calls.

"You okay, ma'am?" Ellie turned to see the crazy-haired clerk she'd paid not ten minutes earlier walking toward her, waving a colorfully tattooed bare arm. He hadn't emerged when neon-hat girl bumped her car. "You lose something?"

"I'm fine. Just planning." She took a deep breath, her knees back to normal and her brain in high gear. Who had Kaitlyn talked to? And speaking of talking—Gabe hadn't called back.

Ellie climbed into the front seat as the clerk ambled to his register. Her shoes crunched on pretzels and cracker shards, and she wished for a vacuum. She pushed her ignition and shifted into drive—then kept her foot on the brake.

Wait. She played back that last conversation with

Kaitlyn. She couldn't remember it word for word, but she was a reporter and was trained to listen. She remembered enough.

Nora knew exactly who else Kaitlyn had called. Because Kaitlyn had told her.

CHAPTER 45

ELLIE

The Holiday Hills section of Wayland, Ellie saw, must have once been a desirable subdivision. Now its narrow winding streets, with names like MayDay Drive and Independence Street, felt weary and outdated. There seemed to be no hills. Cul-de-sacs were bordered by carbon-copy ranch homes, some with shrubs encased in grungy burlap and bound with twine. Kaitlyn Armistead had lived on Valentine Way, each street-side mailbox there marked on its wooden post with a fading red heart.

At the address Google listed for James Armistead, two cars sat in the asphalt driveway, one salt-spackled black SUV and one white hatchback, the vehicles crowded close together by grimy piles of melting snow.

Not Kaitlyn's car, of course, Ellie knew. Maybe the police were holding that in evidence. Maybe this white one was a replacement. *That was fast,* went through her mind. And from the judgmental way Kaitlyn had described her husband, he might just as quickly replace his wife. Though possibly that was an unfair conclusion.

At nearly five in the afternoon, the sky had already darkened almost to night. March in Boston, Ellie learned, was a time of still-early sunsets and surprising gloom. Porch lights blinked on almost in unison, perhaps on timers. The light at the Armisteads' was still off. But James Armistead was home, Ellie knew, because she'd called his landline from a pay phone at the gas station. "Armistead," a voice had answered. "Sorry, wrong number," she'd said, using her best flustered voice, and then hung up.

Now she aimed her car parallel to the curb, nose pointed toward the cul-de-sac's exit, more out of habit than apprehension. She was a reporter, and she was reporting. She snapped a cell phone shot of the house, then one of the driveway.

Through the lens she saw a curtain flutter in the Armisteads' wide front window, then settle back into place. The porch light went on.

Elle knew she was being watched as she pocketed her phone, feeling unseen scrutiny with her every step up the segmented concrete walkway. The lawn, an expanse of ice-coated brown grass, straggled up to a stubby arborvitae hedge across the front of the gray house, the scene monochromatic in the porch light's struggling wattage.

She scanned the yard. No leftover snowmen, no bikes leaning against the house. No abandoned sleds or soggy toys. *Two kids,* Armistead had told Monteiro. But Kaitlyn had told her she'd longed for kids.

"Yes?" The man had opened the white front door before Ellie's gloved finger hit the doorbell button. Seeing Ellie, he unlocked the screen door too, leaving a sliver of exposed space between them. Jeans, plaid shirt, running shoes, Ellie cataloged. Dark hair, a bit too long for the weather-worn fortysomething face, but he wore a pleasant enough expression. This ordinary-looking suburban guy did not appear to be the ogre Kaitlyn had described. But things often looked different behind closed doors.

Ellie tried but could not see inside. Lights were on; that was all she could make out. And maybe the murmur of a television.

"Ellie Berensen from the new Channel Eleven," she began, trying to appear sympathetic and unthreatening. Her words puffed into the cold. "I wondered if you had a moment to—"

"Can't you people get your act together?" Armistead's initially placid expression warped into red-faced annoyance. "Bad enough for *one* of you—"

Ellie took a step back, confused, almost falling onto the front walk. She caught her balance, apologizing at the same time. "Oh, I am so sorry, Mr. Armistead, but no, there's no one else from—I mean, oh. Maybe someone from another station called you?"

"*Called* me? Do you think I don't know what I'm talking about?" He put his wide back against the glass of the storm door, still holding it open an inch, and called into the house, "You! Reporter! Are you the left hand? Because your right hand's just arrived. Time to tell each other what you're doing."

Ellie heard a rustle from deep inside the house, a chair scraping and footsteps.

"Ellie!"

She heard the chirpy voice before she saw its speaker edging toward the front door. She wore a black turtleneck and black pants. And a ponytail. Ellie's brain sizzled, then burned to a crisp. *Meg.*

"What are *you* doing here?" Ellie's words—maybe not completely appropriate—escaped before she could strategically filter them. She gulped, regrouping. James Armistead had fully opened the storm door now, holding it in place with one hip. He seemed to be enjoying the face-off.

Meg held a small spiral notebook in one hand, but quickly tucked it into a pants pocket. "I thought you were at the—"

She stopped, maybe in response to Ellie's frosty expression.

James Armistead scratched his head, his scorn for both of them apparent.

"Don't mind me," he said. "If you two want to argue. My wife's just dead, so I have plenty of time."

"I'm so sorry, Mr. Armistead." Ellie took two steps forward, taking a chance on being allowed inside. "And I am so sorry for your loss. May I come in? It's pretty cold out here."

She tried to look needy and unthreatening. If this guy let Meg in, he could let Ellie in.

Armistead stepped back, begrudgingly gesturing her toward the living room. The place smelled like forgotten beer. And dust.

"Thank you," she said as she followed him in, undoing her coat. She'd handle this with gentle amusement. "We're a new station, I'm sure you know, and maybe we're not quite clear on our assignment procedure." She shot a critical look Meg's way, figuring that if Armistead noticed her disapproval, he'd understand Ellie was the alpha here.

"Guess so." Armistead plopped himself in a worn black leather armchair across from a couch. Ellie surveyed its rumpled beige corduroy, lumped with throw pillows and flanked by two end tables. Squat white ceramic lamps were clicked to bright, and a long coffee table strewn with scattered newspapers. A big-screen TV, on but muted, over the fireplace. Behind a dining room, a sliding glass door to a backyard, with spotlights illuminating only murky darkness, a few frantic moths darting through the yellow beams.

Again Ellie scanned for the evidence of children—a stray Lego or escaped crayon. But she saw nothing.

"I'm not sure what Meg here was asking you . . ." Ellie sat on the couch, letting that sentence go unfinished. "But she'd inquired about your wife's terrible accident, is that right?"

Wearing a guilty-puppy expression, Meg nodded from the other end of the corduroy. "Mr. Armistead was telling me how wonderful his wife was. Since I'm new and everything, he was being extremely patient, and I'm so grateful for that."

Ellie tried to keep the skepticism from her face. Had Meg mentioned Pharminex? Without conferring with Ellie, that would be going too far. "Anything else? About anything else?"

Meg's ponytail swung back and forth as she shook her head. "No, I'd just arrived, and we were talking about the weather that day and—"

Ellie realized what had been bothering her. That night she'd moved into their apartment building, Meg had revealed that she didn't drive. How did she get here to Wayland?

"I see," Elle interrupted. "As my colleague said, Mr. Armistead, we're sorry for your loss. We know this is a difficult time. But we're working on a story about distracted driving. Right, Meg?"

Meg sat, hands clasped in her lap, silently agreeing. An obedient pupil.

"I've been researching the causes for car accidents," Ellie went on. "And I'm so sorry about asking you to talk about that now—" She drew in a breath and carted out the ridiculous platitude every reporter loathed. "I'm thinking if you could save one life with your personal call to discourage distracted driving, then Kaitlyn's death would not have been in vain."

Ellie could barely get the words out. The reporter's calculus—a victim's grief versus the public good—could never truly be reconciled. But Ellie would not have been the first journalist to lie about her motives to get a story.

Armistead fingered his hair away from his forehead, seemed to be looking over their shoulders into the backyard.

"What can I say?" He set one ankle on the opposite knee and leaned back in his chair, his hands curving over the chair's leather arms. He still wore his gold wedding band. The television spackled brief shadows across his face. "Sure. If it'll help."

This was how reporters did it, Ellie thought, one step at a time. One innocuous question leading to another, then another. By the time the subject had followed the simple questions down the path to more difficult ones, they'd forgotten they were talking to a reporter and the truth simply came out. This man had no idea Ellie had met his wife, and certainly didn't know that Ellie was trying to discover if Kaitlyn had worked for Pharminex. Or—completely the opposite—whether Kaitlyn had dropped a bombshell dime to a reporter about their dangerous product. He didn't know Ellie and Kaitlyn had shared life stories. Let alone last words.

Ellie remembered, with a shiver, those unused pushpins on Monteiro's bulletin board.

"Well, first, Mr. Armistead, can you tell us a bit about your wife?" Ellie thought of something else that might be useful. "Do you have any photos of her you could share with me? Or of your children?"

CHAPTER 46

ELLIE

"What the hell are you doing here?" Ellie had to keep her voice low as she leaned across the couch toward Meg. Armistead had gone down the hall to retrieve a photo album. Ellie was hoping there'd be clues inside—maybe something her husband didn't realize was important. If Kaitlyn had lied about her childlessness, that'd be as cynical as Nora pretending to be an abused wife. *What people did to get what they wanted*—that was a line Ellie went toe to toe with every day.

She peered down the corridor. Armistead was not in sight. "How could you just show up here without asking me, Meg? Or asking *anyone*?"

"Because—because there's hardly anything about Kaitlyn online and I wanted to find out more about her." Meg's voice was entreating, maybe defensive. "It's always better to do that in person. Anyway, we knew she'd seen Dr. McGinty, and less than 48 hours after that she crashed into a pole. I had read that one of Monifan's side effects was suicidal tendencies. So, um, I thought I'd come ask her husband if—you know—he'd noticed anything like that."

"Awesome. How were you planning on broaching that subject?"

"Well, I hadn't quite figured—"

"Listen, Meg. I know you think you're just doing your job. But don't go off on your own, okay? Without discussing it? Does Warren know?"

Ellie could see Meg deciding what to say, which revived her annoyance. Either the news director knew or he didn't.

"Um, well . . ."

"So you misled your boss. Not an astute career move." Footsteps. Ellie had about twenty seconds. She could not resist. "How'd you get here, Meg?"

Meg's eyes widened. "Get here?" She shifted, moved a plaid throw pillow out of the way, then fiddled with her black turtleneck. Which, Ellie couldn't help but notice, was much like the ones Ellie often wore.

"Is that a difficult question?"

"Uber. I have to call another one before I leave. Unless!" She reached out and touched Ellie's arm. "Now that you're here, maybe you can give me a ride back to the station."

Armistead returned empty-handed.

"I'm losing it," he said, scratching one ear. "We had a photo album but now that place on the bookshelf in Kait's study is empty." He dropped back in his chair. "Maybe she got rid of it." His earlier contentiousness fell away, and melancholy colored his face. "Don't know why she'd do that."

"Did she ever give you any indication that—" Meg began.

Ellie gave her a *shut up* look.

"Wait." Armistead stood, raising a forefinger. "Be right back."

When he left the room again, Ellie glanced at the

TV above her. An animated ice-dripping graphic announced "Weekday Winter Wonderland." And predicted another snowstorm in the works.

"Kidding me?" she muttered.

"Didn't you grow up with snow?" Meg asked.

Ellie had to smile, remembering. "No, I grew up in—" She stopped. "Never mind."

Armistead was back, carrying a sleek cordovan leather briefcase. "This is her—*was* her—briefcase. Our anniversary is soon. *Was*." He clicked open the brass latch, flopped the leather strap, yanked one side away from the other. "Maybe she was taking the album someplace. As a gift for me."

Ellie heard the bitter sorrow in his voice. But investigative reporting was about possibilities. All they needed was one clue linking Kaitlyn Armistead's death to Pharminex.

Meg scooted forward on the couch, apparently to get a better look. Ellie deliberately leaned back. Civility required the widower be allowed some privacy.

Armistead removed two black leather flats. Put them on the coffee table atop the spread of newspapers. A *Buisnessweek*.

A granola bar in a green package. Three pencils.

"No album," he said. "That's all that's in there."

"It's okay," Ellie said.

"Yeah, but where *is* it?" Armistead flipped the briefcase upside down, face reddening in anger or frustration or grief, and shook it over the coffee table, as if, impossibly, a photo album might be inside. Out tumbled a cascade of whatevers: crumpled tissues and candy wrappers, a hair clip, some bronze tubes of lipstick, a tiny flashlight. ChapSticks, notepad, Life Savers, a tube of hand lotion.

Ellie's handbag probably contained the same

ordinary detritus. "Mr. Armistead? Besides the police, has anyone else been here? Since your wife's accident?"

Armistead shook his head and frowned, plopping
back down in his leather recliner. A beer-can-size ring
stained the wide right arm.

"Sure, people have been here."

"Who?" Ellie asked. "Might they have taken the
album?"

"Why would they do that?" Armistead asked.

She paused. "Allow me a strange question, Mr.
Armistead. Did you ever have a break-in? I mean,
recently?"

"Oh," Meg said. "You mean the same way you—"
Ellie glared at her again.

"Not that I know of," he said. "Not for sure. The
front door was open the other day when I came
home from the office, but I figured it was me forgetting to lock it. I'm not myself these days."

"Did you report it?"

He shook his head. "Nothing was taken. No proof
it wasn't me."

Here was her opening.

"Kids?" she asked. "Maybe they—"

"They're with their mother," he said. "My ex. In
Albany."

So much for *that* suspicion. Kaitlyn had been telling the truth. About that.

Armistead stood, glanced toward the door. Ellie's
time was running out. The break-in thing could be a
coincidence, but what could she say to find out?

"Mr. Armistead, do you know a Lydia Frost?" Ellie
asked.

He shook his head. "No."

"Gabriel Hoyt?"

"No." His tone had hardened. He stepped toward the front door. Meg gathered her stuff, as if accepting the interview was over.

"Dettalinda Fiddler?" Ellie persisted.

"Miss . . . Berensen, is there a point? I thought you were asking about Kaitlyn's last—you damn reporters. Liars, every damn one of you. You told me you wanted me to warn people about—" His voice broke, and he pulled open the storm door, then the front door, revealing the empty stoop and the night beyond.

Why did those names seem to create such a dramatic reaction? If her possibly impetuous questions sent him directly to the telephone, ratting her out to—someone—she might be in trouble. She scrambled to explain. "Sir? Those people are connected to a company that—"

"You *people*." He cut her off. "Never should have let you start. My wife is *dead*."

He stood and looked away, a silent statue, waiting for them to leave.

CHAPTER 47

ELLIE

Feeling almost propelled by the force of the slamming door, Ellie hurried down the front walk, defeated, Meg close behind. The night felt heavy with cold, dense with the sharp fragrant fog of impending snow. Had they learned anything?

She clicked open the door of her car, and watched Meg picking her way over the bumpy space between the sidewalk and the passenger side. *Got here by Uber, huh?* Made sense, Ellie supposed.

Meg opened her door, tossed her tote bag onto the floor and plopped onto the passenger seat. "Go," she said.

"What?"

Meg yanked on her seat belt. "Really. Ellie. Go!"

Ellie looked back to Armistead's front door. "Is he coming out with a gun or something?"

"El—" Meg jabbed one forefinger at the windshield. "Let's leave. Hurry. I'll explain in a minute. Trust me on this."

The lights from inside the Armistead house hadn't changed, and Ellie couldn't see anyone at the window.

She imagined James Armistead already on the phone. She wondered who he would call.

"El-*lie*." Meg's eyes were wide, pleading.

Ellie hit the ignition, shifted into reverse, and pulled onto Valentine Way.

Meg yanked her tote bag onto her lap and started pawing through it.

"What're you looking for?" Ellie glanced at her, curious. Meg seemed spooked, almost frantic to depart.

"You know when he dumped out Kaitlyn's briefcase?" Meg's attention was still on the bag, both hands inside it.

"Yeah."

"And a couple of things fell on the floor?"

"Yeah. Purse junk."

"Pencils," Meg said. "*Specific* pencils and a specific sticky pad. I picked them up real fast and stashed them in my bag."

Ellie pulled onto the main street, out of the Holiday Hills subdivision. The road expanded to a crowded four-lane highway, with cars honking, swerving, jockeying for position and skating through yellow lights, everyone in a hurry to get where they were going before the snow started. "What's a *specific* pencil?" she asked.

"Look." Meg held two yellow pencils, points up, her fingers curled around the eraser ends.

"Meg. I'm trying to drive. What pencils?"

Meg turned the pencils sideways, briefly held them in Ellie's line of vision. "Pharminex pencils."

"Pharmin—*what*?" Like any good reporter, Ellie's mind raced to come up with explanations other than the ones they were hoping for. "Kaitlyn had them? She could have gotten them at Dr. McGinty's office."

"You've seen these?"

THE FIRST TO LIE

Nora has, Ellie wanted to say. She'd distributed them every day. "Yeah," she said. "Around."

Meg thrust a pad of off-white stickies directly into Ellie's line of sight. "I took these too."

Ellie recognized it instantly. A preprinted prescription pad for Monifan.

"That was in her briefcase?" She moved the pad so she could see the road again. The predicted snow had started in earnest, a thick-flaked promise of more to come. She turned on the wipers, wishing she were home.

"Yup." She heard Meg flipping the edges of the pad, making a soft riffle. "Do you think Pharminex had something to do with Kaitlyn's death?"

Ellie punched the heater to high, and someone behind them honked, though the light was still red. The windshield wipers clacked and swiped, back and forth, fighting a persistent but losing battle with the increasing snow.

"She had Pharminex things. Monifan things," Meg went on. "See? *Connection.*"

"You took them, though. You can't steal stuff."

"I thought you'd be happy. Because now we know—"

"We *don't,* though, do we?" Ellie tried not to be angry as she edged into traffic. "Let's say they turn out to matter. We're going to tell Warren and the police how we got them? That you *took* them? What if Armistead says they weren't in her briefcase? There's no way for us to prove they were. It's called chain of custody. Now it's broken."

"What should I have done?" Meg asked.

"Left everything where it was."

"But—"

"Or you could have simply shown them to me, right?"

"Guess so, but then we wouldn't *have* them. You and your *rules*."

"Rules are how we get this story on the air. Without getting sued."

"Never gonna happen." Meg sounded like a petulant teenager. "Stupid."

In silence, Ellie navigated the cloverleaf entrance onto the Mass Pike back to Boston, feeling a brooding sulk emanating from her passenger. Ellie caught a glimpse of her, her chin buried in the puff of her jacket, eyes downcast. No question the woman should not have stolen from Armistead's home.

But why would Kaitlyn have prescription forms?

She heard Meg pawing in her purse again. *Kidding me?* What else had she swiped?

Meg had pulled out a plastic container, dumped three caplets into her hand and palmed them into her mouth. Chewed, puffing out a blast of peppermint. "Look. I get why you're—whatever. I'm new, and I didn't have the guts to tell you about my potential job at Channel Eleven that night we first met. You must have been so mad when you saw me in Warren's office." She reached over, touched Ellie on the arm. "Guess I've been trying to make up for that since then. With, you know, cookies and cat toys. And now with a prescription pad and pencils."

"*Specific* pencils," Ellie teased, trying to be empathetic. "Okay. But . . ." How should she handle this? "We have to assume, or hope, that Armistead is not going to call me or you or Warren and complain about stolen pencils and a pad. Maybe he won't notice." She shook her head. "Maybe."

"Maybe they fell out of the briefcase and *into* my bag. And we didn't realize it."

"Let's hope we don't have to go with that explanation," Ellie said.

They approached the Seaport District exit, and Ellie steered into the proper lane. A ridge of white snow lined the top of the green highway sign, and the lighted crawl spelled out DANGEROUS WEATHER CONDITIONS. SPEED REDUCED. WATCH FOR SNOWPLOWS.

"I'm *so* sorry," Meg said. "I was only trying to—"

"Listen, it's late," Ellie interrupted. "The driving is horrible. I don't have to go back to the station. Do you?"

"No. I—"

"Want to come over?" She should give the woman a chance. Be a good colleague. "Maybe have a glass of wine. Brainstorm the story."

"Sure." Meg had turned in her seat, seat belt straining as she faced Ellie. "But it's my turn. Wine at my place instead? I have cookies."

"Sure," Ellie said. "Wine and cookies. Basic food groups. I'll dump my stuff, feed Blinker and then come right over. What fun."

CHAPTER 48

ELLIE

From her parking spot half a block away, Ellie recognized his shape. Gabe stood on the top step of the
front stoop of her apartment building. The porch
light revealed his black jacket and black watch cap
were dotted with snowflakes. His hands were stuffed
into his pockets.

She and Meg approached, tramping through the
snowy slush on the sidewalk. At least Gabe knew all
about her relationship with Meg, so that made this
easier.

No. No, it didn't. Ellie almost stopped in her
tracks. Meg had talked to Gabe at the Pharminex reception area this morning and he'd told her his name
was Will Faraday. Meg was now seeing Pharminex
employee Will Faraday on her stoop.

"Hey," Ellie said, raising her hand in greeting as
they approached. She'd leave his name out of it for
now. "What's up? This is my colleague Meg Weest.
Meg, this is—"

"Will Faraday?"

Ellie wished she could read Meg's mind as well as
she could read the surprise on her face, even in the

gloom of this March evening. Plus, what *was* Gabe doing here? Not smart of him to show up unannounced. And somewhat disconcerting.

Who'd make the next move in this game without rules? She would.

"Such a surprise, *Will*," she said. "Why're you standing on my doorstep? Did I forget we had an appointment? And hey, Will, you know Meg? How?"

"Ellie?" Meg's white wool cap was drawn low over her forehead, her ponytail peeking out the back. Her eyelashes were flecked with white and her eyes seemed wary. "Um, Will works for Pharminex. I met him because—" She winced. "You're gonna kill me," she said. "I went to Pharminex to apply for a job."

Ellie burst out laughing, figuring that was the most destabilizing thing she could do. "Kill you? That's close to the truth, Meg." She dropped her shoulders, as if in defeat. "We're not supposed to be deceptive, Will," she pretended to explain. "Or omit the fact that we're journalists."

"Whoa." Gabe—Will—pretended to be surprised. Then concerned. "A journalist? You told me you wanted a job. Are you allowed to lie? Ellie, did you know about this?"

A car sluiced through the icy street behind them, the snow falling in earnest, drifting through the streetlight beams as the early evening darkened into night. A blue glow flickered in some of the apartment windows of the brownstones lining the street; in others, orange shapes revealed who had working fireplaces. Normal people were making dinner now, correcting homework, watching TV, Netflix and chilling.

Ellie's toes were growing colder by the second. She picked up on Gabe's reaction and improvised her next lines, hoping he would understand their roles.

"Of course not, Will. And I am so sorry. I'm just hearing about it now."

She turned to Meg. "Listen. We'll deal with your deception at some point, but here's the deal. You can't *ever* tell anyone you saw Will here. Ever. Will's a good guy. Trying to help. But if anyone discovered what he was really doing—giving me—well, *us*—guidance, he'd lose his livelihood at Pharminex. And he's got a wife and kids at home. Right, Will?"

"Right. Three. Going on four."

Meg looked back and forth between the two of them, as if trying to gauge the weight of her predicament. "Sure. Of course. And I'm really sorry. We only just met in the reception area and—"

"Anyone else cold? And getting colder?" Ellie gestured toward the entryway. "I've got to feed my poor starving cat. And Will, Meg and I have plans. So I don't have much time."

"I love cats," he said.

"Perfect," Ellie said. "You come meet Blinker while Meg hides all the stuff she doesn't want me to see."

"There's nothing—"

"Kidding!" Ellie pulled open the outer front door, and the three of them crowded into the tiny vestibule, where a scatter of mail was strewn on a marble ledge under a line of locked metal mailboxes. Gabe's tortoiseshell glasses fogged up, and so did Ellie's red ones. Simultaneously they each took them off, inspected them and, laughing, put them back on.

"Hey! Why don't you come too, Will?" Meg looked at him, then Ellie, for approval. "So we can make sure we're on the same page? Wine and cookies. Ten minutes-ish?"

"Ah . . ." Ellie began. This seemed unnecessarily complicated. Gabe was here for some reason, and it wasn't cookies.

"Sure," he said.

"Ten minutes," Ellie said. By the time the elevators deposited them on three, the building's blasting
steam heat had them all unzipping their coats and un-
wrapping scarves.

"Ten minutes," Meg called out, as she opened her
door, and disappeared behind 3-B.

As soon as she and Gabe got inside, Ellie turned
to face him. "Well, that was a moment. What the—?"

"How was I supposed to know you two were coming here together?" he asked. Blinker, in high affection mode, was already curling around his legs. The
cat purred so enthusiastically that Ellie was almost
embarrassed.

"Hey, wait," she said. "You told me you were allergic to cats."

"*Guy* is allergic," he said. "He was trying to make
sure you didn't invite him over."

Ellie waved him off. "Stop. No more Guy. So—
okay. Why're you here?"

"Really, ah, nothing." Gabe looked sheepish and
had stooped down to pet the cat. Talked at Blinker
instead of to Ellie. "Just wondered, ah, if you might
want to grab a bite. Talk about our project."

She toed off her heavy boots and switched them
for the flats she'd left by the door, then took off her
coat and tossed it onto the couch. He was asking
her out? What kind of ploy was this? "Another first
date?"

"Huh?" Gabe shrugged off his jacket, folded it
over his arm.

"We've gone out as Nora and Guy. But never as
Ellie and Gabe. So—yeah. Sure." She had to smile,
despite her nagging uncertainty about him. "Maybe
that's a plan. But now we're doomed to go to Meg's.
Some date. Give me a second to feed the cat."

She headed for the kitchen and opened the swivel cabinet where she kept the cat food. Blinker scampered after her the moment the door squeaked open. "Don't come in here, Gabe. Cat food smells hideous."

"Where've you been today, anyway?" Gabe called out.

"So yeah, pretty interesting." She couldn't say—*yeah, the state police asked me to find Nora Quinn for them, which I agreed to do if they'd find out who you really are.* She'd stick to safer ground. The truth but not the whole truth. "We went to Kaitlyn Armistead's house—well, *I* did, at any rate," she called across the room to him. "And guess who—she lives in 3-B—was already there? Much to my surprise."

She twisted open the flat can with a handheld opener, lifted the lid and wrinkled her nose, Blinker mewing insistently at her feet. "This is gross, Blink," she said. "You cats are nuts."

"What?"

"Nothing, talking to the cat." She spooned out the lamb and rice, rinsed the can, tossed it into recycling. Refilled the water dish. Blinker was already off, reveling in food world.

"We met James Armistead, who didn't appear to be the nasty, wife-shaming bad guy Kaitlyn described."

"Described to *Nora*, you mean." Gabe still stood just inside her front door. "But you went there as Ellie."

"Well, yeah, luckily." Ellie washed her hands, then joined Gabe by the door, tossing a crumpled paper towel in a wastebasket on the way. "When I saw him, listened to him, I kept thinking of how Nora was the last person his wife had ever talked to. How that conversation might have caused her death. What if he'd known Nora was me? That I pretty much killed his wife?"

She heard the stress in her own voice, surprised by the sound of it. "I'm sorry. It's just—"

Gabe grabbed Ellie with both hands, one resting on each of her shoulders, not a caress, not a threat, just enough to get her attention.

"Look," he said, his face close to hers. "Like I said in the car. You have to stop thinking this. You did *not* have anything to do with her death. It's terrible, I can only imagine, to have been through that. But it's not cause and effect. Something else, even some*one* else, caused her death. Or nothing did, it was an accident. But not you."

Ellie didn't move away from him. The air in the room felt cold and still, the rising wind now rattling the windowpanes in the wall behind them. No matter what Gabe said, or how often, nothing could erase her guilt. But she could use that guilt, that *responsibility,* as fuel to work even harder. Pharminex had killed Kaitlyn Armistead—whether on a snowy highway, or by giving her a dangerous drug, or by breaking her heart.

She lifted her chin to look up at him, his eyes sincere under those glasses. Then she turned, ending the moment. If this man turned out to be a con artist, compassion was probably part of his repertoire.

"Thanks," she said, moving away from him and back to business. She zipped open her tote bag, looking for her cell phone. "I was hoping Armistead would reveal something about Kaitlyn. But he didn't."

She tapped through her phone, pulled up a photo and turned the screen so he could see it. "This is where she lived, the front of their house. And look, do you think he got a new car? The white one. Because she had a white car, but this can't be that one."

A sound from the kitchen. Something falling or crashing. "Now what? Blink!" She handed Gabe the phone and raced into the kitchen, where the cat had jumped onto the counter and into the stainless steel sink, knocking the can opener to the floor and into her water dish. Blink, head tilted at a ridiculous angle, was trying to lap water dripping from the faucet.

Ellie righted everything, wiped up the spilled water, glared at the cat, then looked at her watch as she came back into the living room.

"Cat disaster," she explained as Gabe handed back her phone. "And Meg awaits. At least there'll be wine."

Gabe was shoving one arm into the sleeve of his coat. "I think I'll pass," he said, shrugging into the other sleeve.

"Chicken," she said.

"No, really, you two have work business, and I was only thinking that we . . ."

Ellie waited, curious. What did he want from her? This morning at Pharminex, they'd been co-conspirators, partners in their mutual goal of bringing down the pharmaceutical giant, Ellie using journalism and Gabe using the law. But though she was clear about what she herself was doing, all Gabe had seemingly done so far was hang around *her*.

"How's your lawsuit going, by the way?" she asked.

"It's going, thanks," he said. "I only do the legwork, right? Work the leads they give me."

"Had they given you leads about *me*?" She tried to keep her tone neutral, *just curious, no big deal*.

"You called *us*, remember? So, no, they didn't say anything about you. But Pharminex needs taking down. You're not the only one who knows that."

Three raps on the front door, then three more. "Hey, you two in there! You forget about me?"

Ellie winced at Meg's voice, and Gabe stepped aside as she went to the door.

"Cat situation, sorry," Ellie explained as she opened the door. "Now I'm on the way. But Will has to leave. Family thing."

Meg made a pouty-ingenue face. "We'll miss you, Will," she said. "Give your wife and kids my best."

CHAPTER 49

ELLIE

It was disconcerting for Ellie to sit in a clone of her own living room. Even the furniture in Meg's mirrored her own, Channel 11 apparently having bought it in bulk for its temporary employee housing. Ellie kept having flashes that she was home.

Meg sat across from Ellie on the familiar tweedy couch. "So Will's, like, what?" Meg asked. "Bringing you, like, documents or paperwork? What kind of stuff is he telling you? And why's he doing this?"

Ellie took a sip of her wine. Weirder and weirder—it was the same brand of malbec that Ellie had in her kitchen wine rack. When had Meg been in Ellie's kitchen? It was creepy to think such minor details had been noticed, registered, remembered. An array of chocolate chip cookies, brown-edged and fragrant on a fluted pink ceramic plate, sat on a coffee table just like Ellie's.

"Will and I just met. I'll let you know if he tells me anything or hands over something useful, but so far . . ." Ellie shrugged. "You know, we're just feeling each other out."

"Ooh," Meg said. One eyebrow went up. "That sounds interesting."

"Puh-*leeze*." Ellie took another sip. "Don't even go there."

"Okay, okay, kidding." Meg saluted Ellie with her still-full glass. "But you mentioned a boyfriend that first night I was here," she said. "Where is he? I never see—I mean, I haven't heard you talk about him since."

"Well, it's personal, not work stuff." Ellie knew she should never have alluded to a boyfriend that first night—so funny to remember that throwaway line during what she'd thought was a throwaway encounter. Now she changed the subject.

"How are you liking Channel Eleven?"

"Are you still mad about Abigail?" Meg chose her own subject. Selected a cookie, broke off one edge, nibbled at it.

Okay, let's go there, Ellie thought. "So you think the interview is truly gone?" She sighed, bereft. "I mean, she was the narrative we needed. Her passion, and the harm she's suffered."

Every time it hit her, every time Ellie remembered what she was doing and why, it seemed all the more necessary. When she saw a baby in a stroller, or an ad for diapers or some ancestry-finder company. When families died out, it was like a species going extinct.

"It's so awful," Ellie went on. "Listen, Meg. If you can't recover the audio, maybe you—we—could interview her again?" She took a bigger sip of wine now, thinking about Abigail. And how for some things, there could be no do-overs. What was done was done. "What she told us can help other people. Help us stop Pharminex."

Meg adjusted her legs under her. "Yeah, I've told her that."

"So she *has* answered the phone? That's good news."

Meg looked skeptical. "Maybe. But she's suspicious. Hurt. Thinks no one tells the truth. She believes the drugs she was given killed an actual *person,* you know? Not simply her chance at having children. She feels Pharminex killed her children, her potential children. And then they get to say 'oh, that happens sometimes. Sorry. Mistake.'" Meg shook her head, downed her wine. Paused for a beat.

"I told her I have a brother—had one, at least," Meg went on. "He got killed. Abigail says it's like someone murdered a *potential* brother, you know? I'm not saying it as articulately as she did, as passionately, but in her heart, she feels they took away her family, that's what—what she's trying to convey." She puffed out a breath. "You're right. It's incredibly awful."

Both women stared in silence at the redbrick fireplace that didn't work, just like in Ellie's apartment. Meg's hearth was decorated with a basket of silver-sprayed pine cones and two battery-powered ivory candles, now glowing robotically.

"I'm sorry about your brother," Ellie said. "That must have been devastating."

"It was." Meg looked pensive, as if remembering times gone by. "D'you have any siblings?"

Yeah, well, Ellie thought. I'm not going to talk about that. It was a long time ago, now. But time is endless when you miss someone.

"Can we not talk about it?" The too-harsh dismissal came out of her mouth before Ellie could filter her tone.

"Sure. You seem unhappy, though, El. Are you sure you don't want to talk? It's just us. Off the record. I don't want to push, but it always helps me to talk about what happened. Gets it out there. Like saying to the universe—I accept it."

"We shouldn't have to accept grief when it's *imposed* on us." Ellie tried to change the conversation's direction, like turning a massive ocean liner in a vast dark sea. "That's why we're doing this story. To prevent grief like that. Sorry if I sound like a TV promo, but that's why we need Abigail. We have to convince her to let us interview her again. Plus, Will is secretly trying to get us a Pharminex insider to go on camera—"

"Really?" Meg clapped her hands in approval.

"Trying." This sounded so plausible, Ellie almost believed it herself. But "Will" had told Meg he worked for Pharminex, so she had to stick to that story. "Will admits it—they tell women that bad reactions are rare, and they consider that statement sufficient warning. It's like those side effects they rattle off in commercials. No one even listens to that stuff, let alone thinks they really happen. Will's as angry about it as I am. As we are."

"Ellie. I have an idea." Meg's eyes brightened as she spoke. "Does he know that woman you've been talking to? Nora Quinn?"

"I'll ask him," Ellie said, trying not to laugh at the crashing dominoes. She'd set them up, after all.

"Maybe *she'll* talk to him. Whatever happened to her?"

Ellie shrugged. "We'll get Will to find out. Or come up with someone else."

"It's disgusting, El. It truly is." Meg put her wineglass back on the coffee table with such force that it almost tipped over. She rescued it, barely in time.

"How can they work there, those people? Messing with lives?" Meg went on. "Rolling the dice? Except the company never loses. The patients do. And

their children, who will never exist. They should
know how it feels, that's what I think. More than just
statistics on a ledger. And as a journalist, don't you
want to do everything you can to ruin them? And everyone connected with them?"

"I'm doing my job." Ellie wondered where this fe-
rocity came from. Maybe the wine had hit Meg too.
"'As a journalist,' as you say, that's not how I see
it. My job is to discover the truth and let that lead
where it may."

"But don't you think Pharminex is responsible?
And everyone who's connected with them? They're
all complicit. They're murderers. Wouldn't you say
that? Who knows how far they'll go to cover up,
right?"

Ellie assessed her colleague's narrowed eyes, the
challenge in her tone. Wine or not, this wasn't a casual conversation. Not even between working journalists.

"How'd you wind up here, Meg?" Ellie shifted
on the couch, assessing the hostility she heard. No
matter how small the world of investigative reporting, as Gabe kept pointing out, Ellie couldn't shake
how unlikely it was that someone as seemingly im-
passioned as Meg would present herself just in time
to help Ellie's research into Pharminex. Might she
work for P-X? Be one of their paid informants? That
specter had never quite faded from Ellie's consciousness. Now, motivated by proximity and malbec, she
thought—why not just ask her?

"Do you work for Pharminex?"

"What?" Meg put a hand to her throat.

Either she's a terrific actor or authentically surprised, Ellie thought.

"Are you kidding me, Ellie? Where'd that come
from?"

Or protesting too much. "Or are you involved with Pharminex people in any way? Know them, connected with them?"

"What? *Our* investigation is the most important thing in the universe to me. What have I ever done to make you suspect—?" She stood, tears welling in her eyes, staring down at Ellie. "You never liked, me, okay? I know that. Let's get that on the table. Yes, I lied to you, kind of, sort of, that first night. I *already* apologized for that. But you've never ever given me a chance. Never. You were pissed that I went to Kaitlyn Armistead's house. If you'd have been supportive, a teammate, you'd have applauded my enterprise. I mean, *you* showed up there, right? So how bad of an idea could it be? Right?"

"Well—" Ellie looked up at her, feeling almost trapped in the corner of the couch.

"No. Let me finish. For once. Without you rolling your eyes at me." Meg whirled, ponytail swinging, paced to the edge of the living room. Then turned back, holding her hands out in frustrated surrender.

"And yeah, okay. I took those damn pencils from his floor, and the pad, right? That was awesome, an awesome find, and you should have—"

Ellie was not going to be tantrumed into giving that a pass. Stealing was stealing. "You *can't*—"

"See? This is exactly what I'm saying. If you liked me, you wouldn't make a freaking federal case out of pencils. So now I'm the one who's the bad guy? *I'm* a freaking *spy*?"

"Meg, come on." Ellie stood now too, arms out, smoothing the space in front of her, not quite sure how this evening had spun so emotionally out of control. "It's been a long day for both of us, and stressful. With Lydia Frost, and then James Armistead. But this is what I do. Ask questions, worry, investigate. I don't know you, and here you are, supposedly an instantly devoted ally and—"

"Supposedly?" Meg clamped a fist on each hip. "Let me get this straight. I should have been, what— *un*helpful? Unsupportive? Unenthusiastic?" She nodded, sagely, as if she'd discovered the answer to a difficult puzzle. "Oh, I get it, I get it. You want the spotlight for you. For you! Not me. And crap, I happened to screw up, I know, and lost Abigail. But you never made a mistake? A wrong choice? You were never a beginner?"

"Sit down, okay?" Ellie patted the cushion beside her. "Let's talk about this. Okay?"

Meg plopped back onto her couch, crossed her arms over her navy sweater.

Maybe pouting, maybe assessing, Ellie thought. Maybe embarrassed. Maybe acting.

"I didn't mean to freak," Meg finally said. "Sorry. It's just because you brought up my brother."

CHAPTER 50

ELLIE

Ellie took another sip of wine to mask her confusion. Ellie had not brought up Meg's brother. Meg had done that herself. But now that the woman seemed to be retreating from the precipice of battle, Ellie let that go.

"I'm so sorry, Meg. Is this something you want to talk about? Or—not?" Ellie somehow felt as if she should comfort the woman, but where was the line? Especially since Meg appeared to have a volatile side. Or at least a vulnerable one. An arm's length separated them on the couch, but their emotional distance was measured in miles. "I'm here, either way."

"We were best pals." Meg picked at her sweater, gathering tiny fuzz balls. "Yes, he was older, so he was cooler, and pretended not to pay attention to me. Especially around his, like, college buddies."

Where had Ellie just heard something exactly like that? Right. From Gabe.

"But even then, I knew he'd stand up for me if I needed him to, no matter what. He loved sports and sailing and my parents—well, they doted on him. He could do no wrong. I was always the little afterthought to them, with my bad skin and all that teenage angst. They always seemed a bit surprised I was even born. Or maybe disappointed."

Ellie blinked at her, smoothing a row of silky fringe on a striped throw pillow, just like the one on her own couch.

Meg took a deep breath, let it out. The living room was so still Ellie heard the soft sound of her sigh expelled into the dimming light, saw the fake flickering candles in the fireplace, the random glare of passing headlights catching the edges of the half-curtained windows.

"I knew he loved me and that when we were grown-ups—sorry, that's how I thought of it back then—we'd be friends, and our families would spend summers together at the shore, just like ours always had."

"What shore?" Ellie asked, almost afraid to hear the answer.

Meg waved a hand. "Doesn't matter, wherever. Anyway, he met someone in college, and they were madly in love. I mean, he couldn't see anyone else but her. She was all flossy and golden . . ." Meg spiraled her finger in the air. "Fancy. Everything I wasn't. Looking back on it now, I was so—so envious of her. She had everything. I had nothing. And then they decided to get married."

Meg dropped her head into her hands, and Ellie watched her back rise and fall. When she looked up again, she was smiling.

"Am I not the goofiest?" Meg's rueful laughter barely made it the length of the couch. "Give me one glass of wine and I'm off down memory lane. Whew. Sorry. You're going to think I'm a complete basket case, Ellie, and I am so—" She grimaced, looked at

Ellie from under her lashes. "Embarrassed. What happened in the past is long gone. I'm fine now."

"No worries." Ellie yearned to look at her watch, longing to get out of this mirror-image apartment and away from this woman who'd just related a deeply unsettling story. Almost exactly what Gabe had described when he'd thought she was—

"Question for you." Ellie tried to behave as if Meg's outburst had never happened. "Did you ever meet the Vanderwalds? Or know them?"

"Who?"

Ellie frowned, surprised. "You know, the—"

"Oh, the *Vanderwald* Vanderwalds, who own Pharminex?"

Ellie nodded, risking another sip of wine.

"I know them from our story, sure." Meg furrowed her forehead. "And the gala. How come?"

"Brooke Vanderwald, the daughter? Had an older brother," Ellie said. "From what I've seen in my research, they had the same kind of relationship you describe. He died too. He's the one they're having the event to honor, right? Your story is . . . an odd coincidence."

"I suppose so," Meg said. "But kinda textbook, I guess: gawky younger sister, cool older brother gets married and leaves her behind." Ellie saw the shadow fall over Meg's face. "I never even got to say goodbye."

"Brooke was an awkward teenager too," Ellie had to go on. "And younger than her brother. And the brother married his beautiful college sweetheart. According to Google. And then he died."

"Huh," Meg said.

This silence was impossibly thick, Meg's distress almost visible between them.

"We have to go to that Vanderwald event," Meg finally said. "I can't get it out of my head. How they're showering affection on that family. Those people who've ruined so many lives. Hideous. We *can* go, right?"

"Maybe," Ellie said.

"We're TV!" Meg put her arms out, entreating. "We can get in, somehow, we have to! It's our *story*!"

It was all Ellie could do not to leap up and run. Meg had flared, in an instant, from her remembered grief to this . . . insistence. She checked her watch. "It's almost eight. We're both exhausted. And now the wine. I should go. We can rethink tomorrow. Okay?"

Meg's posture deflated, and she put her hands to her cheeks. "Whoo. I am *so* sorry. Went a little overboard there, right? You are so patient to put up with me. Sometimes I . . ." She smiled at Ellie, almost wistful. "I had hoped we'd be friends, somehow. Now I've blown it. Yelling at you, so unprofessional. Then my brother. Then the gala thing. You're gonna tell Warren I'm a nut."

"We all have bad days." Ellie shifted on the couch and put down her wineglass, signaling her exit.

"No, no, stay." Meg stood, walked toward the kitchen. "I'll get more wine, and maybe cheese. We need sustenance."

Ellie heard the refrigerator door opening, wondering if what was inside was a duplicate of her own food.

"We were supposed to talk about the Pharminex story." Meg's voice sounded muffled; maybe her head was in the fridge.

"I'm pretty talked out," Ellie called after her. "Tomorrow?"

"How did you get onto the Pharminex story, anyway?" Meg went on as if Ellie hadn't answered.

Ellie could hear her puttering in the kitchen, drawers opening and closing, cabinets too. "You never talk about that."

Ellie pretended to think. She got up from the couch, feeling trapped, and regretting her misguided idea for them to bond. So much for being the good guy.

Her phone buzzed across the coffee table, its black plastic cover whirring against the familiar polished wood. *Gabe.* Maybe she could use this as an excuse to leave?

"Hello?" She kept her voice low. "I'm still—"

"Yeah, listen." Gabe's tone was all business, edgy and somber. "I'm at the front door. Buzz me in."

Ellie stood, confused and concerned. "Sure. But what's up?"

"Can you just let me in? It's freezing."

"I'm still at Meg's," she whispered. Ellie couldn't risk using the word *trapped.*

"Let me in. I'll be Will."

"Will's back," Ellie called out to Meg. "I'll go let him in."

"Goody," Meg's voice carried from the kitchen. "I'll get more cheese and stuff. We'll have a party." She appeared in the arched entryway to the kitchen, cheese knife in hand, leaning against the jamb. "I guess that's pretty terrible," she said. "I mean, Lydia Frost is dead, and Kaitlyn." She winced. "I'm a total jerk tonight."

Gabe was stomping his feet on the front stoop when Ellie opened the door. Outside, snow swirled, and the street had filled with cars, many already covered in a layer of white. Leading Gabe inside, Ellie headed for the stairs instead of the elevator to give them more time.

"What's so important?" she asked, as they tramped their way up. "You okay?"

"It's about Lydia Frost." Gabe stopped on the first landing, unzipped his coat and unwrapped his plaid muffler. Stuffed his gloves into pockets. A scatter of white snowflakes melted into his hair. "And Kaitlyn Armistead. The police think their tires were . . . *compromised* was the word they used."

Ellie put a hand on a wooden newel post, her legs momentarily unreliable. "How? By who?"

"No idea," he said. "So they tell me."

"They who?"

"My employer knows guys."

"Did his guys say how it was done?"

"There were stabs in the sidewalls of both cars. The leaks from that would be slow but inexorable."

Ellie considered this, pictured it. "And that'd be enough to cause a crash?"

"Might've been. If road conditions were bad, maybe. They—you know how those accident reconstruction people are."

"Reconstruction," Ellie said. Monteiro, she thought. That's who his boss talked to?

"Point is—" Gabe began.

"Point *is*," Ellie interrupted, "I'm no expert, but how could someone rely on such a thing to kill someone?"

She plopped down on one of the steps, her flats on the landing's hardwood floor, elbows on her knees, chin in her hands. Picturing it again, putting herself in the driver's seat.

"Someone knew those cars," Gabe said. "Targeted them. And vandalized them, without getting caught. No matter what the outcome, that's . . ." He paused, leaning against the stairway wall, apparently to let her imagine the possibilities. "Your Passat is out there on the street, isn't it? I drove by it myself."

"Do you think it was Pharminex?"

"That's all I can think of." Gabe's eyes narrowed. "And, theoretically, if they decided to get rid of Kaitlyn for some reason, or even just scare her . . ." He pressed his lips together for a second. "It's so *out* there, Ellie. Lydia too? But, okay, say this wild theory is true. Pharminex is—" He shrugged. "I can't even finish such a sentence. But you've got to be the reporter they're searching for. So . . ."

Ellie stared at the carpet. Envisioned people with knives, or whatever implement, how easy it would be—wouldn't it?—to weaponize a tire. "Gabe? Shouldn't you be careful too? You're helping a law firm *sue* them. That case could ruin them."

Being two people was twice as confusing as being one, and Gabe was the only person who knew both Ellie and Nora. She had to trust someone besides herself.

"Ellie, I'm not worried about me. I'm worried about you. That's why I'm here. I think you should be careful."

"Me, Ellie? Or me, Nora?" Ellie grabbed the wooden bannister, hauled herself to her feet.

"Not sure what world you're living in, Ellie," Gabe said, "but whatever happens to Nora happens to you. And vice versa."

BEFORE

CHAPTER 51

LACEY

They probably thought she couldn't hear them whispering, the ruthless sleek women in their funeral-black sheaths and their careful hats sitting in the church pew behind her for Trevor's memorial service. But she could. Every word. She wouldn't say their phony-solicitous *poor-Lacey* sympathy was entertaining, but it reassured her in a way she hadn't predicted.

She touched the puff of black netting that fell artfully from her own black hat, a widow's veil designed to allow privacy in her grief but that now also allowed her to watch the sideshow of mourners in this perfect little seaside church, and listen to their not quite muffled discussions of her travails and sorrow.

Poor thing. Poor Lacey.

"They'd only been married eight years." That was Claire Demarchi, who, Trevor's mother once confided, had staked her claim on him since they crewed as junior sailors together at the Bayellen Yacht Club's summer sailing camp. She probably thought she'd dodged a bullet now, with poor Trevor dying so young. Sailing, of all things. He'd always been such an expert sailor.

Brooke, the doctors were saying, still had no memory of it.

"And didn't they want children?" She recognized India Nee's breathy whisper. Claire never went anywhere without India, her tennis partner, bridge partner and, according to double-entendre country club whispers, quite a bit more.

"So sad." Claire's perfume wafted over the pew, mixing with the pale lavender lilacs and white peonies Brinn Vanderwald had ordered for the service.

Lacey hadn't seen her mother-in-law since they'd arrived at St. Erasmus an hour earlier. Stoic Brinn wore her grief as a mask of brittle emotion—her eyes red-rimmed, lips pale, hair slicked back, taut as the thin line of her mouth. She spent her days now at Maryland Rehab, sitting by her precious daughter's bedside, waiting for her to recover.

Why hadn't Brooke saved her brother? Lacey had said the words out loud, one wine-sodden night on her deck, the words she knew everyone was thinking. Or maybe Trevor had died trying to save her, Lacey had continued, watching Brinn's face crumble. *Maybe your son died to save his little sister. Who may now never recover. It's awful, isn't it? So awful? So awful to lose a child? Maybe both your children?*

Trevor had vanished. After days of imagining "miracles" and tear-drenched reunions, there'd been another visit from shore patrol. The *Caduceus,* apparently swamped, was "unsalvageable" and "unrecoverable," they reported.

Soon after, the search ended. "We've done all we can," a somber lieutenant had told her. "Now we wait."

Lacey had watched the whole thing on the news, over and over, and described in numbing detail. She'd unwittingly observed it in real life too, the same night it happened. Helicopter rescue beacons—those had to be the lights she'd seen from the deck, the moment her husband was drowning, somewhere in that inky darkness, and she'd been viewing it as if it were entertainment. The red lights of the arriving onshore ambulances, and blue of the police cars and then the white glare of the TV spotlights. The news showed what Lacey hadn't been able to see from her deck: Brooke in the netted basket, winched aboard the hovering copter, a limp and sodden marionette fished from the murky bay below.

"Brooke Vanderwald had the presence of mind to hit the *Mayday* on the boat's radio," one coast guard officer told a reporter that night, his rescuer's face wind-chapped and solemn in the TV crew's harsh lighting. "Could be she went in to save him, or maybe the wave took her overboard too."

The reporter's voice had haunted Lacey, the woman's dark hair flying wild in a blustery wind as she closed her story. "Officials say they'll have to wait to hear what Brooke Vanderwald remembers when—and if—she recovers."

"She's all we have now," Brinn had sobbed later, in the bleak empty hours after midnight as they hovered in the stale-green emergency room corridor of Anne Arundel Hospital. Lacey, who was right there in the hallway at the time—right there!—felt her existence begin to blur around the edges, as if she were being erased. She drew her black shawl around her shoulders, her eyes stinging and red-rimmed, her grief over Trevor unabashed and relentless.

"She'll get better," Lacey promised. "And of course we hope there's nothing that's—do we know how long she went without oxygen?"

The look on Brinn's face. "I'm so sorry, darling,

of course she'll recover, fully recover. I'm just so devastated. They might still find Trevor. He might be fine. He might be on the shore somewhere. Hurt, and dying and waiting to be found. They have to find him!"

A high-pitched alarm bell *beep-beep-beeped* through the antiseptic corridor, and Lacey gasped, as if the noise came from inside her brain. A white-uniformed nurse rushed by, ignoring them. The hospital alarm stopped.

Lacey had plopped onto a hard plastic chair in the waiting room corridor. "I know they're looking, but I can't stand it. I should be out there. Helping. What if he's somewhere, hurt and waiting?" She felt her face dampen with tears. "I don't even know who I am anymore. Oh, Brinn, we've both lost . . . all we have. All."

Winton Trevor Vanderwald III had not been hurt and waiting, officials had decided after a few days.

"I'm afraid we're suspending the rescue operation," Officer Something had told them. "We are now calling it a recovery, not a rescue. Only wind and tide can provide a time frame."

The officer had been the one to catch Lacey when her legs finally gave out. Brinn, without a hint of irony, had offered pills, yellow ones and white ones, and Lacey had taken them. She always did what Brinn said. Even still.

Now an unseen church organ began to play, velvet with funereal sorrow, and Lacey recognized "Nearer My God to Thee," like they played on the *Titanic,* and whose idea was *that*? She bit the inside of her cheek, hard, because she had to concentrate on *something,* and she had to get through this memorial service. Thank goodness for her veil. Maybe she could wear it forever. She'd taken an extra yellow pill. Because what more could hurt her now?

"We're so sorry, darling."

Lacey peered through the mesh of her veil at whoever it was—she'd seen these people, at the club, or on her deck, maybe guessing at constellations and drinking her gin. *Were* they sorry? Was anyone honestly anything?

"Give our best to Win, could you? Tell him we understand why he can't be here."

"Of course," she lied. She watched the couple, all linen and pale silk, slide into a polished oak pew. To them it was Winton Vanderwald who mattered, the man whose son had vanished, had probably died. *She* didn't matter, not at all. Not Lacey, his wife, who'd now not only lost her children but her husband, and if she wasn't careful, she'd be alone, alone, alone.

Winton Vanderwald would not join the mourners for his only son. Trevor's father had "not been able to cope with it," so went the proffered explanation of his absence. For Winton, Lacey imagined—hoped for—endless bourbon and endless regret. According to the buzz Lacey overheard, his "indisposition" was being viewed almost reverentially, as if the bond between father and son was too tender and private to put on display.

Poor Brinn. Poor Winton. Their only son had been taken from them. And their daughter, who'd finally come home—bottom line, the moment they'd longed for and now look what had happened—was still in the hospital, tranquilized and uncertain. Lacey, cloaked in black and with only a hint of makeup, had gone to see her, as one did.

The sixteen-year-old girl who had been her reluctant bridesmaid now rested, Ophelia-like, on the starched sheets of the Vanderwald wing of Maryland

Rehab. Brooke, sedated and closed-eyed, hadn't seen Lacey of course, and Lacey felt as if she were at some sort of viewing of a body in limbo, a face bereft of cognition, a mind deciding whether to return. How much would Brooke remember? Doctors said the prognosis was good, and all they could do was "let nature take her course."

Lacey had a moment, an unworthy flash of schadenfreude, that all the Pharminex horses and all its men could not put their Brooke together again. Only nature could do that.

The sanctuary whispering had started again.

"They'd tried and tried to have children, hadn't they? So incredibly well off, everything anyone could ever want, and yet . . . She's only, what, twenty-eight?" India's inquiry could not hide her subtext. People relish disaster when it happens to those they envy. Some sort of proof that money can't buy happiness.

Of course it can, Lacey yearned to correct them. She leaned back, the better to hear, not wanting to miss a syllable. She was hooked on this dissection of her life, on their envy and spite.

"It's all they talked about. All Brinn talked about too. They didn't adopt. I'd always wondered about that, but," Claire paused, "one cannot ask."

"Shhh." India hushed her BFF.

Lacey heard more footsteps entering the sanctuary, the same one where they'd been married eight years before. More ironic symmetry. And the voices of the mourners, their *gone-too-soon*s and *such-a-shame*s and *he-was-so-young*s seemed far more prevalent than the *poor-Lacey*s.

She dabbed a lace handkerchief at her lips.

She and Trevor had moved away from Maryland, and her difficult pregnancies had often prevented her from returning to the Vanderwald home for holidays and special occasions. She got the feeling that they hadn't missed her, the one who'd married their dear son in such a celebration of love and family, only to disappoint them again and again with possibilities that turned out to be false alarms. Failures.

Then they'd returned to Maryland, where she could no longer hide what her body was doing. Then Brinn—*I'm-here-to-help-you Brinn*—took over. Brinn had *been* a mother. She *knew* how it felt. It felt a way Lacey *had to* experience. Then Brinn took that away.

It's rare. She kept hearing that doctor's voice. Remembering how it felt in that blue paper johnnie, hearing her future laid out in platitudes and actuarial tables. *Who cares how rare it is when it's you?*

A photo of Trevor, windblown and smiling, ocean in the background and that orange spinnaker with the damn Pharminex logo—branded even in death—billowing out behind him, had been placed on a silver easel at the front of the church. There was no casket, because there was no body. Lacey tried not to think about that. Would they find him someday? A beachcomber, a sunbather, a child? She'd had a moment, a yellow-pill moment, when she'd imagined him having concocted some grand escape plan, conniving to free himself of his Pharminex responsibilities. To free himself from *Lacey*, no matter what the cost. Imagined that he was somewhere, selecting a new life, same as she had.

But that was the pills, and this church was real, and Trevor was never coming back.

Now Lacey Grisham Vanderwald had to figure out what to do next.

Her life depended on it.

CHAPTER 52

ELLIE

Ellie stood inside her apartment building's chilly entryway, holding her second coffee of the morning in a paper cup, waiting for a five-star Uber driver named Xavier to arrive in his white Prius to take her to Channel 11. She knew it was silly, probably paranoid and possibly embarrassing. But as Ellie tapped her cell phone to call the ride share service, she figured it was better to be safe than sorry. Especially if it turned out *sorry* meant she wouldn't be alive to discuss her choice. Four minutes until arrival, the app promised. Last night's snow had settled into this blustery Tuesday, leaving an icy coating on everything. Easier, she'd rationalized, to call a ride than to clean off her car.

You should be careful. Will—Gabe—had told her that again last night as she'd walked him to the front door two glasses of wine later. As the two had lingered on the front stoop, she'd given him a quick rundown of her perplexing evening—Meg's you-never-liked-me outburst, and the disconcerting confession about her brother.

"Just like you said after you saw her at Pharminex.

Kind of the same memory you had." Ellie had worried that Meg might be eavesdropping, and tried to gauge Gabe's reaction through the gloomy darkness. "Even to the bad skin, and the angst and the brother."

Gabe had listened, eyes locked on hers. Seemed to be searching her face. "What do you make of that, El?" he'd asked.

Meg had appeared then, breathless, carrying a plate covered with shiny aluminum foil. "Cookies to take! For the kids!" She'd thrust the plate between them. "So glad you're still here."

Will—Gabe—had sneaked Ellie a look; then, carrying the plate, he'd turned back onto the streetlighted sidewalk. She'd watched him, Meg by her side, until he vanished into the night.

What did she make of Meg's story? Gabe had asked. Good question, Ellie thought now. She stared out the foyer's leaded front window into the dour morning, imagining tires and skids on highways. If anything happened to her, at least Lieutenant Monteiro was aware she was looking into Pharminex. Later today, she'd call him and ask for updates. See if he thought she should watch her back. Or her tires.

Two minutes, the ride share app said.

Plenty of time. She tossed her empty cup in the entryway wastebasket, yanked open the building's front door and picked her way down not yet shoveled front steps. She wasn't the first to leave today, she could tell from the footprints, but she couldn't tell if any were Meg's.

Once on the sidewalk, a fierce gust of wind hit Ellie so hard she felt her eyes tingle.

At least she didn't have to feel guilty for not warning Meg about the sabotaged tires. Meg didn't have tires.

Her moon boots padded silently on the layer of snow. No one else on the street this morning, and even the scraggly, bare-branched municipal trees, their surfaces embellished with white, seemed to shrink into themselves with the cold. Everything seemed airbrushed, hard edges removed, wrapped with a layer of cotton. Her own car was parked halfway down the block, one in a row of identical white lumps.

A pinged alert on Ellie's phone signaled Xavier's arrival time had "adjusted," giving her three more minutes. She stopped a few feet before approaching her car, scanned the sidewalk and the street for footprints to see if someone might have tampered with it recently. If it had happened last night, their prints in the snow would be long gone. As the three of them had chatted at Meg's, it had snowed intermittently. Will had finally pretended he'd gotten a call from his wife. "Gotta shovel," he'd lied.

The snow fell in earnest as Ellie tried to fall asleep, staring out her window and wondering about her goals and her future, Blinker curled up beside her.

No footprints. She used a gloved finger to examine the left front tire, smoothing away the icy white on the sidewall and wondering if she'd even recognize if anything were amiss.

Ellie stood, fingers frozen inside her gloves, face raw, tears welling from the wind or fear. Her quest to protect women from a predatory and greedy company had led to this bleak and lonely morning searching for imaginary vandalism—

"Ellie? What're you doing?"

Meg stood on the sidewalk, a black tote bag slung over one shoulder of her black parka.

Ellie straightened, brushed the snow from her

gloves. Her guilt returned, full force. Meg might not have tires, but if Ellie was in danger, Meg was too.

"Is something wrong with your tire?" Meg persisted.

"Meg? Remember that lawyer who called me the other day? When you answered the phone?" Ellie hopped back onto the sidewalk as a cab sloshed by, spattering slush in its wake. She began with a lie. "He called me late last night."

And then, the truth. She bullet-pointed the whole thing for Meg: the police, the sidewalls, the slow leaks.

"You think it's Pharminex?" Meg looked around, apartment to apartment, as if to check whether anyone was watching them. "And *that's* why you're looking at your tires?"

"Yeah," Ellie admitted. "Not that I'd know what to look for. And yeah, I called a ride share to get to Channel Eleven. This is freaking me out, Meg."

"Don't blame you, sister." Meg pulled out her cell from her parka pocket, yanked off a glove, tapped the screen. "I called a ride share too. It's on the way. You could cancel yours, if you want? And come with me?"

Ellie sat behind the driver of the black hybrid SUV, Meg in the back seat beside her. Nora's undercover work for Pharminex would have to wait. She needed to be Ellie today.

She'd accumulated enough research to make a powerful paperwork case against the company, but that wasn't enough for a television story. Without Nora Quinn as her whistleblower, Ellie had slammed into an obstacle. Then Meg's incompetence had provided another obstacle by losing the interview with

Abigail. Ellie needed one or the other: Nora or Abigail. Since Gabe knew of her ruse, Nora was no longer an option.

"Traffic," the driver grumbled as he pulled toward Columbus Avenue. "Tunnel is closed. For the snow."

"Of course." Meg scowled, defeated. "Hey, before I forget. Have you talked to Nora Quinn? She's okay, isn't she? I mean, if she was talking to you, maybe she's in Pharminex's sights. Should we warn *her*?"

"Good idea." Ellie fidgeted with her seat belt. She hated sitting behind the driver; she couldn't see out. Now he seemed to be taking a shortcut.

"I could find her," Meg offered. "Want me to snoop around?"

"No, thanks." *All* Ellie needed. "I'll contact her."

The Uber made a turn she wouldn't have made. But she'd only been in Boston two months, so what did she know?

"Ellie? Can I ask you a weird thing?" Meg had turned in her seat and looked at Ellie, concerned. "What if Will was sent to trap you? Trap *us*? He knows where we live. And you had that break-in. Pharminex is on to you, Ellie. They're on to *us*, and we ought to tell this guy"—she pointed at the driver—"to take us right to the cops. Tell the police everything."

"The police know," Ellie said. Meg might be smarter than Ellie thought. She wasn't sure of Will—Gabe—herself. "I've talked to them. They're on it."

"Why didn't you tell me that?" Meg's voice went up, taut and demanding. "Don't you think I have a right to know?"

Ellie saw the driver check them out in the rearview. Poor guy must hear all kinds of bizarre discussions.

"I'll tell you when we get to the station, okay?" Ellie cocked her head toward the driver, trying to signal the need for privacy.

"Got it," Meg said. "Oh. Is that you or me?"

"Is what you or me?"

"It's me." Meg pulled out her phone. "Text," she said.

Ellie hadn't heard anything, but maybe Meg had the sound off. Then her own phone vibrated. She grabbed it from her bag. *Gabe.* She had to signal Meg was there. "Hey. Hi, *Will.*"

"Can she hear you?"

Ellie glanced across the seat. Meg seemed deep into her texting.

"I'm fine," Ellie said, trying to sound as if she were answering a different question. "And probably not. I'm in an Uber with Meg. We're on the way to the station. How are *you*?"

"Listen," he said. "Does the name Mary Grace Thibodeaux sound familiar?"

Ellie's heart twisted in her chest. "Who's that?"

"You sure she can't hear?"

Ellie glanced across the seat. "Will says thanks for last night."

Meg put up an acknowledging hand. "Uh huh, no prob." Her eyes stayed trained on her texting.

"Go ahead," Ellie said.

"Remember you showed me the photos of the Armisteads' house? There were cars in the driveway, and I ran the plates. My employer has guys, like I said. And so—no Mary Grace Thibodeaux?"

Meg was leaning over the back seat talking to the driver, pointing out the windshield. Ellie rolled her eyes. She had known the guy was going the wrong way. Maybe Meg had been checking her GPS. Thank goodness.

"Who's that?" Ellie said again.

"Mary Grace Thibodeaux is the owner of that white car."

The blood drained from Ellie's face. "The—"

"Ellie. Listen. Mary Grace has a nickname. Lacey. Does the name Lacey Thibodeaux mean anything to you? Or Lacey Grisham? Sometimes she used that name."

"Used?" Ellie latched on to the word. "Is she dead?

Out the window, Ellie saw they were on the Expressway. A white jet flew low across the overcast sky, descending on its flight path across Boston Harbor to Logan Airport. They passed a massive white-bladed windmill on the right, and on the left, a huge rainbow-painted gas tank. They were going the wrong way. Seriously the wrong way. She'd intervene in a minute.

"Call me," Gabe said. "When you're alone."

"But why are you telling me this? What's this— *person*—got to do with—"

"Ellie? Was there *anyone* else at Armistead's when you were there? Any sign of another woman?"

"No," she said. "Didn't seem like it. You think, um, that person is somehow significant?"

"Just call me," he said.

And the line went dead.

Meg yanked out one earbud. "What'd he say?"

"Oh," Ellie searched for an answer. "You know, thanks for last night, all that. Loved your cookies. No biggie."

Ellie looked out the window again. The highway exit they'd just passed was marked *Braintree, Quincy, South Shore*. This was wrong.

"This guy is going the wrong way," she said.

"Nope. He's not." Meg's perky smile surprised her. "Guess who was just texting me?"

"Who?"

"Abigail," Meg said. "And our happily flexible Uber driver is not going the wrong way. He's headed to her house. She's half an hour away. And yay, me. I've convinced her to talk."

CHAPTER 53

ELLIE

She'd lied to Gabe. Of course she knew of Mary Alice Thibodeaux aka Lacey Thibodeaux Grisham and, later, Lacey Vanderwald. Looking for someone who might give her what she needed, Ellie had researched all the Vanderwalds. Lacey had seemed like a dead end, a Vanderwald wannabe who'd faded from public attention after her husband died.

As their SUV wove through the rush-hour traffic, Ellie rested her forehead on the car window. The traffic toward the city was at a standstill, as usual on a Tuesday morning, and was now doubly congested because of the snow. They passed a massive motorized billboard, electronically flipping from an ad for the Encore casino, all fireworks and roulette and cleavage, to a mother-and-child Pharminex ad—WOMEN'S WELLNESS IS WHO WE ARE—to a promo for the new Channel 11. ON THE AIR SOON, the billboard promised, and then the news anchor team's permanently smiling faces rotated away, back to the casino.

Lacey Thibodeaux was a Vanderwald by marriage, Ellie knew. She'd seen photos of her on Google. There were surprisingly few for someone who, according to a local paper's wedding announcement, had been fully embraced as part of the "new generation of Vanderwalds." Had she missed some recent ones?

She pulled out her phone, typed the name into Google Images.

The photos appeared, one by one, exactly as Ellie remembered. In the first, Lacey's face was glamorously obscured by a swoop of gossamer bridal veil. A tiny rectangular photo of Lacey in a lineup of other Tri-Delts in her college yearbook (and now online all these years later) showed a plump-faced wide-eyed Southern belle with cranberry lip gloss, a tumble of auburn curls and aggressive eyelashes. At her husband's memorial service, Lacey's face had been protected by black netting. Ellie zoomed in on the picture. Under the hat, Lacey's auburn hair had been lightened to what looked like strawberry blond.

Had Gabe seen these same photos? Because of the car registration, clearly Gabe suspected Kaitlyn Armistead was Lacey Vanderwald. Ellie closed her eyes, merging faces in her mind, trying to see if that could possibly be true. She'd talked to Kaitlyn, one-on-one, without a shred of suspicion that she was someone whose photo she had previously studied online. But she was the right age. Ellie shrugged, as if she were speaking out loud. Maybe five years older than Ellie herself. But unlike the current situation in her own double life, most people were who they said they were. Too bad the Armistead photo album was missing.

She stared at the pictures, keeping the screen tilted away from the still-texting Meg.

Why would Lacey Vanderwald be in Boston? For the Vanderwald gala, Ellie assumed, now just twenty-four hours away. But why would she have visited James Armistead? Ellie tried to weave a story in her head, to see if she could come up with a reason. Lacey might have been dispatched by the Vander-walds to Armistead to apologize. Or maybe offer a financial settlement? She wrinkled her nose. Neither of those seemed likely.

She looked out her window, lost in thought, as the highway out of Boston changed from garish bill-boards and cinder-block industrial to frost-capped wetlands, an occasional shorebird swooping through the concrete-colored sky, the thick stands of trees, branches bare, many of them snapped and broken, victims of the past winter's storms. Journalists were storytellers, tellers of *true* stories, but how to logi-cally explain Lacey Thibodeaux being at Kaitlyn Ar-mistead's home? As Ellie had said to Gabe, it was all about which speculation became the truth.

The car chunked over a pothole. Ellie glanced at Meg. She was oblivious, deep into her phone.

So. Say grieving and beautiful young widow Lacey Vanderwald was still connected to the Vanderwald family. Maybe they'd marshaled her sorority-sister sweetness and powers of persuasion to convince victims—victims as damaged and broken as those roadside trees—to settle their damage claims. Maybe Lacey, protecting her inheritance, had helped to bro-ker those settled lawsuits Ellie was trying to uncover.

Could it be? Maybe Lacey had signed onto the Vanderwald greed and avarice when she'd said "I do," joining the Pharminex mind-set as well as the Vanderwald family. Lacey and her husband never had children. Ironic, when Lacey's new family was sup-posedly the pharmacological bestower of mother-hood to needy women everywhere.

Ellie widened her eyes. Wrote the story another way.

What if Lacey Vanderwald had gone to James

Armistead's not as an emissary of the Vanderwalds but as their enemy? To try to convince him to join a crusade against the company?

Ellie shook her head, dismissing that. Too complicated. Risky.

What if Kaitlyn Armistead herself was Lacey Vanderwald? Maybe she had tried to start a new life as someone else, only to have her past catch up with her. If so, had her husband, James, known that?

And if that was true, Lacey Vanderwald was now dead. Just like her Vanderwald husband. Leaving Brooke, the daughter, as the only remaining Vanderwald heir.

But Ellie—Nora—had *seen* Kaitlyn. Close up. Talked to her. She closed her eyes, trying to imagine, in retrospect, if there was any resemblance. Context distorted everything.

Or maybe . . .

"Ellie, yoo hoo," Meg said. "Are you taking a nap? Want to brainstorm questions for Abigail? We're almost there."

"Meg?" Ellie asked. "What's Abigail's last name? Her real last name?"

The SUV veered off onto an exit, taking the curve so hard Ellie had to hang onto the strap to prevent herself from falling onto Meg.

Meg chewed at a pink-painted fingernail. Shook her head. "I can't tell you."

"Why not?"

"She's—her—um. Her family is—inflexible, I guess you could say. She doesn't want them to know what happened to her. If you meet her and if she wants to, she'll tell you."

"If?"

"She's skittish. She's damaged enough, you know? It's difficult for her to keep it all together. She still feels that loss every day. She says." Meg smoothed back her ponytail, keeping her hair away from her face. Not one bit of gray, Ellie saw. The woman had to be, what, pushing forty? Under her wig, the roots of Ellie's own auburn hair were threatening to add salt to the cayenne.

"She *might* even want to stay back in her room while she and I record. And you stay in a different room." Meg scrunched up her face, as if she hadn't wanted to reveal that yet. "If she does, no big deal. We do it the same way as before, you on speaker and me shooting the video on my cell."

"Oh, come on." Ellie tried to swallow her frustration. "If she'll talk to you and trusts you, she's got to trust me. What's the difference?"

"She feels like she knows me," Meg said. "The whole thing is fragile. And she's afraid of Pharminex too. That they could ruin her life. Or, you know, kill her, like maybe they did Kaitlyn and Lydia."

"What? How would she even know about those people? Meg? Did you tell her?"

"Of course not," Meg said. "And I didn't say she did. Know. I'm just saying—she *would* be afraid of that."

Ellie pressed her lips together, quieting her brain as the SUV stopped for a light. There were homes, now, lining the streets—wood and siding triple-deckers, painted a half-hearted spectrum of white to gray, all with front stoops and unstained wooden balconies, some with snow-laden planters hanging forlornly from hooks. A rickety convenience store took up the corner lot, its lopsided windows plastered with off-kilter lottery signs and beer ads. Ellie didn't know, really, what Pharminex would or wouldn't do. Proof of that: her car, still parked on her own street.

"We need this interview, right?" Meg persisted.

"The gala is tomorrow. *Tomorrow!* Maybe we can get her interview on the air. Like a tease of what's to come. We're five minutes away. Come *on,* Ellie. You can't back out now. This is our big chance."

CHAPTER 54

ELLIE

Ellie watched the SUV drive away up Fogarty Street, leaving her standing with Meg on the front stoop of number 348. The triple-decker was a fading carbon copy of its neighbor, with weary lace curtains in some of its shutterless windows. Scraggly thick shrubs divided the lots, an almost successful attempt at privacy. The downside of ride shares, she thought as she surveyed the unfamiliar neighborhood, was that she and Meg couldn't depart here until another one was summoned and arrived. Seemed efficient in the downtown bustle of Boston, but not so much in whatever town this was—Braintree, Ellie gathered from the signs. She'd never been here before.

Meg was heading up a half-shoveled front walk, just enough snow pushed aside for a single-file approach or departure. A row of saucered terra-cotta pots, each one coned with snow, lined the shoveled half.

"Think we'll be okay getting back?" Ellie asked.

"Oh, sure." Meg turned to her as she walked. "I asked the driver. You saw me talking to him, right? I had to change our destination. Like I said. Yay."

"Okay." Ellie faced a panel of black-buttoned doorbells, its upper left screw missing, with mottled paper squares hand-numbered 1, 2 and 3. No names. "Which bell is it?"

"No bell." Meg lifted one of the terra-cotta pots, then set it back into place. "Damn."

"What?"

Ellie scouted up the street, then down, fearing Neighborhood Watch, or maybe nosy residents who'd be wondering what two women were doing messing with the flowerpots in someone else's yard. But not a curtain fluttered. And driveways were empty of cars, each one with a dark asphalt rectangle showing where the vehicle had protected it from the snow.

"We got here faster than I thought," said Meg. "She's not home yet. She said she'd leave a key."

Ellie frowned, confused.

"Hang on, though." Meg used a forefinger to count the pots, then pivoted, looked toward the street, counted again. "Three from the *street*, maybe she meant."

She picked up another pot and held up a key from underneath it, triumphant.

Two minutes and a single-bulbed stairway later, they were inside the third-floor apartment, a pristine rectangle, living room–dining room–kitchen all in one, and a white-walled corridor where Ellie saw three closed doors. Two bedrooms, she guessed, and a bathroom. The place smelled like lemon furniture spray and something pungently clean, maybe bleach. In the front windows, pulled-down blinds backed the drawn lace curtains. A center light in the ceiling, frosted white glass with a gold knob in the middle, had been left on. The room had an edgy chill, as if someone was scrimping on the heat bill.

"She just texted," Meg announced. "She's on the

way. She's nervous. We can use the dining room
chairs to set up—in front of the windows? You might
have to stay in here while we do the interview in
the bedroom. Aren't you so happy this all worked?
Won't *Warren* be so happy?"

Meg planted her hands on her hips, assessing, then
unbuttoned her coat.

"Okay, you sit," she instructed Ellie, "and I'll go
down the hall and check, make sure it'll work. I know
the place from when I was here before. All good?"

"Not much of a choice," Ellie muttered as Meg
trotted down the hallway. Ellie undid her coat. Deposited her tote bag. Checked her watch: 10:45. Sat
in the middle of the two-cushioned beige canvas
couch, annoyed. Things were not always easy, she reassured herself. It'd be worth it. She needed this. Her
phone buzzed.

Text message. From Gabe.

Call Monteiro.

Now? W/M at interview, she texted back. Hoping
he'd understand her "with Meg" shorthand.

Do it.

"You okay in there?" Ellie called out.

"All good!"

She scrolled through her phone to find Monteiro's
number. She poised her thumbs over the text box. Did
Monteiro know Gabe had told her to call? Was she
responding to his request for her to contact him? Or
was Gabe giving her info on the down-low, letting
her know something was up? *This is Ellie,* she finally
typed.

Three dots instantly appeared.

Lacey Vanderwald? The name appeared on her
screen. As if Monteiro had typed out Ellie's own
thoughts.

?? she texted back.

You know her?

Of her. That was true enough.

Seen her? Recently?

Don't think so. You?

She is now wanted for murder. Monteiro's texted words were chillingly formal. *Let me know if you see her. Instantly. BTW: Your lawyer buddy checks out.*

Gabe was not "her" lawyer, and not her "buddy," but good to know that Monteiro deemed him a reliable guy. But that was not the key now.

Murder of who? she typed.

"Ellie!" Meg called from down the hall. "She's on the way. Just texted me."

The three dots on Ellie's cell phone had vanished. Monteiro had stopped typing.

Ellie stared at the screen. Would she recognize Lacey Vanderwald if she saw her? She'd seen wedding photos from, what, fifteen years ago now? And the veiled memorial service photo after that. But that woman had never been on her radar, a widow who'd faded from significance after her ticket to power drowned in Chesapeake Bay. And now Lieutenant Monteiro seemed to believe she was a murderer. *Murder of who?*

"She wants you to go get coffee or something." Meg was walking toward her, holding her phone. "She says go to Wally's down the block. That little store. We'll text you when she's ready."

"Kidding me?"

"You want this or not?" Meg held up her phone as if Abigail were inside. "She's jittery as hell. Now that you're here, she won't come in. She doesn't want to meet you until she's sure."

"Why?"

Meg lowered the phone. "I can only speculate, and

it doesn't matter because she's not gonna change her mind. Her way or the highway. So to speak. Sorry."

Ellie put her coat on again, trying to think. What if Abigail was Lacey Vanderwald, murder suspect? Ellie couldn't leave her alone with Meg. If Ellie followed Abigail's orders, it was Meg's safety she'd be risking. In fact, maybe they should both get the hell out of here.

She shook her head, deciding.

"Why are you shaking your head? Go." Meg lifted one of the front window blinds, peered out for a beat. "If she sees you—"

"Okay." Ellie pretended to agree. "Wally's. The store on the corner."

"She wants coffee, black. But we'll call or text you. In about fifteen. When she's here. And I'll leave the door open so you can get back in."

"Sure." Ellie picked up her bag and her phone. "All good."

CHAPTER 55

ELLIE

With a solid five minutes to spare, Ellie deposited the three black coffees—which she'd purchased in record time at Wally's—on a patch of bare ground behind a thick boxwood hedge. Hiding behind a stand of shrubbery was not how she'd planned to spend the morning, but Abigail would not appear and go inside until Ellie left, and Ellie would not leave Meg alone with her. The chances of her being Lacey Vanderwald were remote, she knew, but the way to resolve such a question was for Ellie to see the mysterious Abigail in person. Would she recognize her? Only one way to find out.

If she *was* Lacey—and hadn't Meg revealed inadvertent hints about that? That Abigail was nervous, hated Pharminex, didn't want her "inflexible" family to know what had happened to her. That seemed important. Ellie should call the cops. Call Monteiro.

But he'd stopped texting. Something was going on, and this was not the time to interrupt him. She had no answers for Monteiro, only more questions.

She kept her gloved hand on the phone in her pocket, set to vibrate when Meg signaled Abigail's arrival. As soon as Abigail headed up the front walk-way, Ellie planned to get inside. *Would* she recognize Lacey Vanderwald?

This entire Abigail-as-Lacey scenario was so unlikely that Ellie was almost embarrassed at herself. But not enough to abandon Meg. *Murder of who?*

Still no cars on the street. No movement in any yard. Ellie's freezing ears would never be the same. Should she tell Gabe where she was? *Yes, sure, probably, definitely*—all the answers skated though her mind.

Her phone buzzed with a message. What? No one had gone inside the house.

She pulled it from her pocket, baffled. Gabe. *Checking in. He tell you?*

Yeah. What was the most important question if she had to hang up? *Who is the murder victim?* she typed.

Husband. Trevor Vanderwald.

That took a second to comprehend. One gasping life-changing second. A snowplow rattled by. Ellie barely registered it.

Not a sailing accident? Ellie almost couldn't get her thumbs to work. She edged back into the bushes, twigs scraping soft complaining whispers against her coat and catching in her hair. *Many years ago?*

Cold case but parents never gave up. She left town. But new info, Monteiro says: She might be in Boston.

Photo?

Three dots. Was he consulting someone? Her time was ticking away. Any minute now, she'd have to end the conversation.

Gabe? We at 348 Fogarty. Braintree. Soon talk w/victim "Abigail." ???? She LV? About to see her. Need current LV photo.

Coming.

The dots disappeared. He'd gone silent. Did Gabe mean he was coming here? Or that the photo was coming? Ellie pushed deeper into the boxwood branches, and a clump of snow dropped onto her head. She swiped it off, freezing and frustrated, as if nature herself had joined the conspiracy to make everything impossible. Talk about impossible. The police thought Lacey Vanderwald had killed her husband, Trevor. That it wasn't an accident.

She took a deep breath, the cold air shocking her lungs. Tried to steady herself. She could not think about what might have happened to Trevor Vanderwald.

Meg should have texted by now. Meg, inside with the person police think killed him.

Staring at the lifeless screen, Ellie looked into the past and into the future. Lacey Vanderwald hadn't been on that boat when he died, so said the news stories, so how could a sailing accident be murder?

Now, just in time for the Vanderwald gala and the ceremony honoring the Vanderwalds' son Trevor, Lacey Vanderwald was in Boston. And her white car had been parked at James Armistead's house.

She left town, Gabe had texted.

Her phone vibrated. Meg. *You at Wally's? Come back.*

There was not a chance in hell anyone had passed Ellie on the way inside. No cars, white hatchback or any others, had passed by or parked. No pedestrians had been on the sidewalks.

She yanked open the triple-decker's front door.

Ran up the three flights, fast as she could.

She put her hand on the apartment's metal doorknob. Pulled. Locked. Knocked. Had Abigail—or Lacey—locked it to keep her out? Ellie knocked again, impatient and worrying, in case they hadn't heard her.

"Hey, El." Meg opened the door while she was still knocking, and stayed in the threshold of the apartment, not letting Ellie by. "That was fast. We're pretty much set. Abigail says thank you."

Ellie frowned. No one had come in. She put on an embarrassed expression. "Yeah, I'll confess, okay? I didn't get the coffee and just walked around." She pretended to wince. "That store was kind of skeevy. So I was out front the whole time. How'd she get in?"

Meg stepped aside from the door, gesturing Ellie inside. "*Duh*, back door?" she said. "She lives here and parks in back. I was just about to text."

"Silly me," Ellie said. Maybe, late in the interview, she'd risk it. Ask Abigail: *Does the name Trevor Vanderwald sound familiar?* But that might put them—Meg and Ellie—in more danger. "Okay. Call me when it's ready. Just make sure we get it on video."

"Hey—are you ever gonna let me forget that? I'm *sorry*. Okay? Can we just—"

"When this works, all will be forgiven." Ellie tried to behave as if this were just an interview. Plus, being alone in the living room would let her see if Gabe had sent a photo of Lacey. The glitch—she wouldn't be able to access it on her phone after the taping began. "Is she okay?"

"Well, she wanted coffee . . ." Meg left that hanging for a second. "Kidding. She's fine. I think the coffee was an excuse to give her time to get inside. This is about to work, sister. She says she has all kinds of Pharminex stuff. Inside documents. Slam-dunkers. So she says. And perfect, right? The day before the big gala."

"What does Abigail look like?" Ellie kept it casual.

"Why?"

"Just trying to picture her," Ellie said. "You know, so I can be interviewing a real person."

Meg glanced toward the hallway. Seemed to make a decision. "After the interview, maybe? Let's see how it goes. I'll call you in three minutes when we check the final setup."

"Tell her . . ." Ellie tried to think. Was it safe or sensible to let Meg be alone with Abigail? Ninety-nine percent yes. Plus, they both knew Ellie would be in the next room. "Tell her she's incredibly important," Ellie finally said. "Tell her women all over the world will be grateful to her. Look up to her."

"Okay. She'll love that. I guess." Meg looked concerned. Kept turning toward the bedrooms.

"Tell her that if we can put her interview on TV, it will ruin Pharminex."

"You think that's *true*?" Meg's voice dropped lower.

"Definitely," Ellie said. "And tell her we'll introduce her to lawyers who can make her millions in damages for what she has suffered."

"Millions?" Meg's eyes widened.

"Yup. Tell her all she has to do is help us with the story."

CHAPTER 56

ELLIE

The three minutes Meg had estimated she'd need to do the final arrangements ticked away, with Ellie hearing voices from down the hall, then a door closing, more voices but unintelligibly muffled. As soon as Meg called and the interview began, Ellie would not be able to receive text photos. Ellie stared at her cell phone screen, willing a photo to appear.

With about a minute to go, because the universe loved suspense, the text popped up. *Gabe*. Thank goodness.

All LV photos old, he texted. Her shoulders dropped. *This one? This?* The screen showed the same photos she'd seen on Google: the wedding shot, gorgeous cascading hair and eyelashes. Another, at the funeral: no ears showed, no eyebrows. Anyway, every facial characteristic was easy to change these days, especially if you had money like Lacey Vanderwald did.

Seen those pix, Ellie texted back. *Abigail here now. W/Meg.*

Age same? Anything same?

Haven't seen her yet. Long story.

Three dots.

Long shot, Gabe finally typed. *LMK asap.*

For once Ellie hoped she was completely and ridiculously wrong.

Lacey Vanderwald. Wanted for murdering her husband. Might be in the next room with the exceptionally naive Meg. About to reveal inside information in an attempt to take down the family company she hated. Or something.

Was it ethical to get information from a murder suspect? She was only a suspect, Ellie reminded herself—innocent until proven guilty. Ellie's reporter imagination offered another possibility. Could the nefarious Pharminex be setting Lacey up?

Maybe they had found out she was talking to Channel 11. To stop her, they'd somehow uncovered—or fabricated—new evidence that implicated her in murder. After all, Ellie told herself, you don't have to kill someone in a car accident to get rid of them. If you're rich and powerful enough, you can let the justice system take care of that. Even if your scheme falls apart, the danger was mitigated. And the target destroyed. *Oh, sorry, mistake.* But too late.

Ellie heard a hallway door open.

"Ready?" Meg yelled.

"Ready." Ellie adjusted her place on the couch, set up her phone. No matter who this woman turned out to be, if she could deliver the goods on Pharminex, they could work out the details later. Ellie would discuss the interview openly with the news director, and Warren would likely bring in the station's lawyer. All fine. Ellie just needed this story.

"I'm sitting on the bed," Meg began the interview, her voice buzzy through the phone's speaker. "Abigail's across from me on a dining room chair. She's in front of the window, with the light coming in behind her through the white slatted blinds. The stripes look kind of cool. She's just head and shoulders, wearing sunglasses to change the shape of her face, and a baseball cap so you can't see the outline of her hair. You okay with that?"

As the interview progressed, Abigail related the same heartbreaking story she'd told before, speaking even more passionately and articulately. She seemed more at ease on this second recitation, emotionally describing the devastating results of the medicine she'd been given.

"I lost everything," she whispered. "My body, my soul, my health, my future. My children. My happiness."

Ellie could hear her crying and, cynically, had a reporter's moment of wishing her tears would be visible on the tape. In silhouette, they wouldn't. Still, her voice, thin but determined, came out like an indictment—of her doctor, of Monifan, of Pharminex and the entire medical system that had lied and cheated her out of a future.

"Having children was all I ever wanted. And Pharminex took that dream away from me, took them from me. *They killed them.*"

Ellie heard sniffing, and the unmistakable sound of tissues puffing from a cardboard box. "I'm crying too," Meg said. "Can we wait a moment?"

"I'm here, whenever you're ready," Ellie whispered. This story was heart-wrenching and powerful, and the reason she became a reporter. In her mind and in her heart, Ellie felt the enormity of this woman's tragedy. No matter who she was.

"Okay." Meg's voice. "She's fine now."

"Abigail?" Ellie said. "You're incredibly brave. I thank you for this."

Abigail's voice did not waver. "I'll tell you whatever I can."

"Did you ever sue the company?" Ellie asked.

A sigh came over the speakers, and then what sounded like a laugh. "I mentioned it," Abigail said. "I suppose, you might say, I threatened it. Those people came at me like a ton of bricks. Terrified me. Said their lawyers would ruin me. That's the word they used. *Ruin*." Another soft laugh. "As if I weren't already ruined."

"Ruin?" Ellie repeated. "Forgive me for this question, but do you think Pharminex would try to protect itself that aggressively?"

"They kill people every day. With their drugs. It's all for profit."

"I understand." Ellie tried to tread lightly. There was no simple way to broach her suspicions about what had happened to Kaitlyn and Lydia. Besides, how would Abigail know? But maybe she did.

Ellie heard muffled conversation, as if Meg had asked the woman something.

"Sorry, I didn't get that," Ellie said.

"Abigail says she doesn't know Kaitlyn Armistead," Meg said. "Or Nora Quinn or Lydia Frost."

Ellie's jaw dropped. It was super-aggressive of Meg to ask on her own. But too late now.

"Thank you, Meg." Now Ellie was dying to ask— what was your car doing at Kaitlyn's house, then? If you don't know her? She opened her mouth to go for it, then heard the sound. Someone knocking at the apartment door.

"You expecting someone else?" Ellie said into the phone. "Someone's knocking."

Ellie stood, slowly, not sure what to do.

Meg appeared in the hallway. "I told Abigail we were done. Did you lock the entryway door after you came back in?"

"Ah, no," Ellie admitted. "I guess I—I guess I thought it would lock itself."

Another knock.

"Meg? What does Abigail say? This is her apartment, after all. Maybe it's the mailman. UPS. Amazon. A neighbor with a cat."

Meg strode toward the door. "Who is it?" she called.

CHAPTER 57

ELLIE

"It's Will." His voice came through the wooden door. "The front door was propped open, so I just came on up. May I come in?"

Ellie had never been so happy to hear someone's voice. Monteiro had given him the all-clear. So, all good. She checked that the Abigail interview had properly recorded. Clicked out of the app so her phone would work again.

"Hang on!" Meg called out. "I'm just changing clothes. I spilled coffee all over myself."

Ellie turned to her, baffled. "Changing *clothes*?" she whispered.

"He's a Pharminex em*ploy*ee." Meg's eyes got bigger. She whispered, too. "How the hell did he know we were here?"

"I told him."

"You told—" Meg raised her eyes to the ceiling, folded her hands as if in prayer. "Look, Ellie." Meg took a step closer to her. "Abigail *knows* Will. She says Will Faraday is a Pharminex hired gun. He's trapping you. *Using* you."

Ellie stared at her, trying to take in all she was saying. Especially in light of Monteiro's verdict about Gabe's trustworthiness. "Abigail told you that?"

Meg nodded, eyes wide.

"Did you *tell* her about Will?"

"Of course not!" Meg whispered. "*She* brought it up. She knows what he's doing. Somehow."

"Abigail knows *Will*," Ellie confirmed. "From *Pharminex*."

Meg nodded again, then held up a forefinger and mouthed the word: *Wait*.

"Can you come back in ten, Will?" Meg called. "Go get coffee down the street. I'll be decent again by the time you get back."

"Okay." Will's voice sounded uncertain, and Ellie didn't blame him. "See you in ten."

"Meg—" Ellie began.

"Will befriended *Kaitlyn,* did he ever tell you that? *And* Lydia Frost. They were, like, an item. I have to get Abigail out of here before he returns," Meg went on, glancing toward the back room. "If he sees her . . ." She pressed her lips together. "That'd be horrible."

"Yeah. Wow." Ellie heard a *ping*. Picked up her phone. She glanced at the text on the screen. From Warren. Read it again. Grabbed her coat and began to ease toward the apartment door. "Wow. Abigail knows about Will. Amazing."

"I *know*. I need to warn her to be careful when she leaves." Meg looked as if she was about to burst into tears. "She's probably trying to hear us now, poor thing."

"Listen. Here's an idea. I'll run after Will and pretend I don't know any of this, okay? Like I'm still all on his side. I'll take him for coffee, saying I need to tell him something. And then you set up your phone to record in the living room. Hide it somewhere. And *then* you sneak Abigail out of here. Does she have a car? A phone?"

"Sure. And then—"

"And then, when Will and I come back," Ellie interrupted her, "you and I can get him to . . . I don't know. Implicate himself. We can do it. That in itself will nail Pharminex. Pharminex is the bad guy, right? And he's their *spy*. You are so smart."

"So terrifying, Ellie. He probably killed Kaitlyn and Lydia—for Pharminex! We could be next."

Ellie put a hand on the doorknob. "You are *so* right. I'd better go. If this works, you'll get so much credit. You found Abigail. And arranged that pivotal interview. And now we have to get Will back here and trap him. You could even be the one to do it. I'll follow your lead."

"Great." Meg nodded. "I'll think of something. And can you confirm my spilled coffee story? That was all I could think of, I was so terrified."

"Sure. Ten minutes? Is that enough time to get her safe and set up the secret taping?"

"Of course." Meg was already tapping on her phone. "Be careful."

"You too." Ellie opened the door, stepped into the hall.

She did not have to run after "Will." He was on the landing below, looking up at her. She took the stairs down, two at a time, as quickly as she could, one hand on the railing and the other holding her cell.

"Oh my god, Gabe," she said. She showed him the screen. "Look at the message I got from Warren, my news director. Just read it."

She watched him take it in. Try to digest its meaning.

Her heart pounded, and Ellie tried to control her breathing. "James Armistead phoned Warren, wondering why Channel Eleven employee Meg Weest left a car in his driveway yesterday. Warren called the police, and they came and took it."

"Wait—her *car*? Meg's car? But, El, it's Lacey's car."

"Gabe, listen. Meg might have been in the car, but *Meg doesn't drive*. So who was driving?"

"Abigail? Could *she* be Lacey?"

"Come *on*," Ellie said, grabbing his arm. "Let's get out of here. We've gotta get to the back, to the parking lot, see what happens. See Abigail when she comes out."

She half dragged him down the rest of the stairs, talking at him over her shoulder. "We can hide in the bushes. Come *on*."

She cut across the scraggly snow-dappled front lawn, beckoning him to follow. "Over here. Where we can see the back."

They huddled in their dense boxwood refuge, shoulders touching, their eyes trained on the back parking lot of Abigail's apartment. Three cars. No people.

The winter sun was high in the sky, noon, but its cloud-muffled heat didn't reach the ground. Two adults hiding behind an evergreen hedge was not the cleverest tradecraft, but it was their only option. When Abigail came out, they'd duck. Abigail. Who Meg had told Ellie was terrified of Will. But Abigail could *not* have known Will—because he did not exist.

Gabe and Ellie knew Will was a fiction. But Meg believed he was real. Only Meg.

Meg was lying.

Why?

She stared at the grim apartment, thought about who was inside. Thought about Meg's passion for the story, her arrival in Boston, her disturbing behavior. Her dead brother. Her intense and continuing interest in the upcoming gala. Her insistence that Abigail knew Will.

"Gabe," Ellie whispered. She clamped her hand on his arm.

"What? Do you see Abigail?"

"It's Meg," she said. "Meg wasn't *using* Lacey's car."

"Of course she was, Armistead said she was."

"No, we just assumed that. But Gabe?" Ellie said. "I think Meg was driving it. That car was *Meg's*. *And* Lacey's. Because Meg Weest is Lacey Vanderwald."

CHAPTER 58

ELLIE

The words caught in Ellie's throat as she said them, realized what they meant. Meg was Lacey Vanderwald. Wanted for murdering her husband. Gabe and Ellie stood, surrounded by branches and the dark cold of the afternoon and the dawning understanding of Meg's dark charade. *Murder, Trevor, murder. Not a sailing accident. Not an accident at all.*

The words throbbed in her head, pounded through her heart. She could almost hear them. *Not an accident.* Ellie's balance gave way as she stood in the cold, and somehow the sky began to spin.

Gabe grabbed her, catching her, held her up. "Ellie?"

"I'm okay, I'm okay," she lied. But she couldn't lose it, not now, not when they were about to—*not an accident.* A wave of power overcame her, determination.

She pulled her phone from her coat pocket and yanked off one glove with her teeth, tucking it under her arm. "I'm texting Monteiro. Telling him Meg is Lacey. Lacey is Meg. Holy crap. Watch the back door. Watch the front. Watch everything."

"I am. But Ellie? What's Lacey Vanderwald doing at Channel Eleven? Helping you bring down Pharminex? Why would she do that? She's a Vanderwald, it could only hurt her."

"I know, I don't know." Ellie tried to text and talk at the same time. "I mean—how do I know? Maybe there's some financial thing that protects her, maybe she's not liable, maybe she doesn't care, who knows."

"But she's in there with a Pharminex victim," Gabe said. "We should go in. We have to go in because . . ."

Ellie looked up from texting. "Okay, done. Monteiro knows."

She hit *send*, relieved to put her glove back on. She kept her voice low. Kept her eyes on the triple-decker. Tried to keep her head straight. "*Meg*. I still can't believe it. I mean, Lacey Vanderwald is in that building right now."

Ellie's phone pinged. She read the message out loud. "Monteiro. Sending guys. There's a warrant for her. They'll arrest her, and—"

"They'll never get here in time, Ellie, she'll bolt. I have to go in. What if Abigail's in danger? If Lacey killed Trevor—"

Ellie's heart twisted; she could not hear that again, *killed*, not one more time. She had to think about *now*, what to do right now.

"It's got to be both of us," Ellie said. "That's what she's expecting, that I bring you back, and we trap you with our clever secret taping. But we're not supposed to go in until she signals that Abigail is gone."

"But no one's come out, front or back." Gabe shook his head. "Maybe that was Meg's way to get rid of us, then she'll run. If that's true, there'll be no one inside when we go in. No one alive, at least. Let's do it. *Now*."

Gabe grabbed her hand, pushing the branches away, pulling her toward the house. They headed across the snow-tipped grass. Ellie looked up at the third-floor windows as they arrived. Paused. Not a flutter of the blinds, still down.

"Okay, *Will.* You ready to confess you're a Pharminex goon?"

But Gabe had already yanked open the front door, taking the steps to the third floor two at a time. Ellie dashed after him, grabbing the bannister to pull herself up, his black parka and jeans racing ahead of her. *Lacey frigging Vanderwald.* Ellie searched her imagination, trying to fit Lacey's face—as she'd seen it—into Meg's.

They arrived, both panting, on the third floor, the mud-brown carpet soggy under her sodden boots, the overhead light struggling to cut the gloom. Ellie tried to quiet her breath, thinking about what was ahead, and what was behind. About Trevor Vanderwald, his body never found, languishing forever in the depths of Chesapeake Bay. *Not an accident, not an accident.* But she could not think about that. They paused, listening, but there was no sound from apartment 3, only the rumbly hum of a heater, somewhere, fighting the outdoor bluster. No word from Monteiro, no sounds of sirens, nothing to do but go in.

"Knock?" Gabe whispered. "Or go?"

"She said she'd leave it open." Ellie put her hand on the knob. "It should be me she sees first, okay? So it seems according to plan."

"Hope we're not too late."

Ellie turned the knob. It gave with a soft metallic click. She swung it open. "Meg?" she called. But the apartment was silent. "Abigail?"

She looked at Gabe, eyes wide: *Where are they?*

Gabe looked back. *Don't know.*

"Meg?" She took a step into the living room, scanning, Gabe behind her. Front window, empty couch, bookshelves. Kitchen. Windows to the parking lot. Hallway. Two doors open. One door closed. She cocked her head, pointed down the hall. "Meg?" She tried again. "Abigail?"

Nothing.

"Could Meg have gotten Abigail out of here without us seeing her?" Ellie tried to picture it. "I guess she could have gone out the back the minute we hit the front, before we could watch. Cutting it close, though."

Gabe nodded. "Yeah."

"Meg too, though? They *both* left? Meg?" She called again. The place had the feel of empty, not a creak or a footstep. "Let's go in. What if someone's hurt?"

Gabe took another step into the silent apartment, left the door open behind him. "If Meg or Lacey or whoever she is has harmed Abigail—"

Ellie had just thought of it another way. "Or *Abigail* harmed *Meg*."

She took a step down the hall, then another, her body taut with apprehension. What if *Abigail* had *lured* Meg and Ellie here? Maybe Abigail had contacted Meg after seeing her social media search for victims. Targeted her, somehow knowing she was Lacey Vanderwald? Ellie had always thought that connection had happened too easily. Maybe this Abigail had set them both up.

They took the final steps toward the closed bedroom door. Ellie realized she was holding her breath. She felt Gabe's presence close behind her. The door was within reach.

But no. *Meg* was the first to lie. Because there was

no real Will Faraday. Meg had insisted she knew the inside scoop about him. But in fact, Will only existed in Meg's imagination. Meg's true identity had been exposed by a person who did not exist.

But no matter who was really who—where were they?

Gabe took a step past her, reached toward the doorknob.

"Gabe, wait." She grabbed his arm, stopping him. "Meg insisted that Abigail knew you."

"Knew *me*?"

She tried to read his face. "Yeah, you. 'Will' you. The made-up you. From Pharminex. Why would Abigail say that? And if Lacey is Meg, who is Abigail?"

"That's what we've gotta find out. Ready?"

She put her hand on the bedroom doorknob. Turned it. And pulled open the door.

Bed. Nightstand. Lamp. Dresser. Window. Closet, open and empty, except for a few metal hangers tangled together at one end.

Ellie took it all in. Looked again and again, as if someone would somehow appear.

"Stating the obvious." Gabe's voice was not quite back to normal. "They're gone. And no one's dead."

"That we know of," Ellie said.

She stood in the silence. Stared at the bedroom window. At the window where there were no blinds, closed or open, but only white lace curtains. *White slatted blinds,* Meg—she still had to think of her as Meg—had said. Describing how "cool" the stripes looked behind the silhouetted Abigail. But there were no blinds. Meg had lied again.

"Shit," Ellie said. "She tricked us."

It took only seconds to open the other bedroom door—a white-painted office, bare desk chair and throw rug. Empty. They yanked open the next door—a yellow tiled bathroom. Translucent yellow shower curtain. Empty.

"I'm an idiot." Ellie planted her hands on her hips, now standing in the center of the living room, taunted by the emptiness around them. "They must have gotten out the back as we were going out the front. And one of those cars in the back was hers, Meg's, I have to still call her. And that's how she was getting everywhere—Miss 'Oh I don't drive and I take Ubers.' Bullshit." Ellie remembered, calculating. "Lacey Vanderwald could probably afford to rent a million apartments and a million cars. Her bank account must be bottomless. This is where she hides her other life."

"Didn't you notice she was gone all the time?" Gabe asked. "From the station? Or your apartment building?"

"Yeah, but no biggie," Ellie said. "She has other assignments at the station. And if you remember, I was more interested in juggling my own—"

"Double life." Gabe finished her sentence. "Yeah." Ellie's phone pinged with a message.

"Monteiro," Ellie said. "He's on the Mass Pike."

"But she's gone!" Gabe said. "Tell him—"

"I know, doing it." *She's gone!* Ellie typed back.

Got it. Going to apt. Monteiro's words came back. *You OK?*

OK.

"He's headed to her apartment—my apartment. He'll get there before we can."

"Do you think Meg took Abigail with her? Lacey, I mean." Gabe frowned, as if trying to game out a scenario. "Like she abducted her, or lured her, or—"

"Gabe," Ellie interrupted. "Here's the thing. I read somewhere that Lacey Vanderwald is a Monifan victim. It wasn't . . . confirmed. But there was some chatter online that she'd been harmed by Monifan. Just like Abigail was. Supposedly."

"Supposedly? You don't think Abigail is a real victim?"

Ellie played back everything she knew. Everything Meg had said. Why she'd never let Ellie see Abigail, be in the same room with her. Why Abigail appeared at the perfect time. And vanished at the perfect time. And then came back. At the perfect time.

"No," Ellie said. "I don't. I don't think Abigail is a real victim."

"You don't? But Meg *interviewed* Abigail. They were both here."

"Were they? Did she?"

"Of course they were here. Meg—or Lacey— interviewed her. In there." Gabe gestured toward the bedroom. "It's recorded!"

"*Something's* recorded. *Someone* told a victim's story." Ellie saw the puzzle pieces fit together. Understood the picture they made. "But I think Meg and Abigail—Lacey—are one and the same person."

CHAPTER 59

ELLIE

Ellie's phone pinged again. Monteiro. "Monteiro says she's not at the apartment," she told Gabe. "Super let them up. They're getting a search warrant now, staying there till it comes through." She typed in her response.

Meg=Lacey?

Looking.

Now what? Ellie typed back. She said it out loud as she thumbed in the letters. *Gabe here with me.*

She almost felt the message fly through cyberspace. But there was no answer. No three dots.

"No Abigail." Gabe seemed to consider that. "If you're right, and maybe you are, do we need to warn Monteiro? We should head to your place, anyway. There's no reason to stay here. It's empty."

"Gabe? Yeah, there is." Ellie thought about reasons someone would want a second apartment. A secret apartment. "Because like you said. It's empty."

Ellie turned, scanned the living room, the bookshelves, the cushioned couch, the cheap travel posters hanging on the walls—Rome, Paris, London. "There's no 'Abigail's apartment.' Because if I'm right—and I think I am—there's no Abigail. Meg's using this as a hiding place. And who knows what she might keep here. You're a lawyer. It's not illegal or anything for me—us—to check things out. Right?"

Gabe pulled out two couch cushions as he answered. "Nope," he said, peering behind them. He puffed them, one at a time, as if feeling for something hidden inside, them put them back. "We were invited in. We're nosy. Rude. Impolite." He slid a hand into the opening behind the cushions, pulled out a quarter. Put it on the coffee table. "But we're not criminals." He unzipped his parka. "Her office?"

"Bedroom." Ellie dumped her coat on the couch and brushed past him, on a mission. If Lacey was on the run, there was no way for them to find her. But if she'd left something incriminating behind, they could probably find that. "Wait. Kitchen. I'll do it. You keep looking in here."

Gabe stooped, looking under a flowered club chair as Ellie headed to the kitchen.

She opened the white-painted cabinets, one by one, running her hands under the empty shelves and behind the doors. Under the sink, nothing. Where pots and pans might be stored—nothing. She yanked open the narrow clattering drawers. Two forks, two knives, a corkscrew, ice pick, a few mismatched spoons. Could Meg have used the corkscrew to stab the tires? Ellie reached out to examine it for rubber. Stopped herself. Plus, no one would be dumb enough to keep such a suspicious item.

"Anything?" she called out.

"Lint," Gabe called back. "I'm going into her office." She heard him trot down the hall. Inside the white fridge, Ellie saw only a deflating plastic bottle of water and a twist-tied package of English muffins. Freezer? She yanked at the door, letting out a puff of cold. The freezer, domed with opaque frost, sat empty. Frost, Ellie thought. Poor Lydia.

"Nothing, nothing," Ellie muttered as she hustled down the hall to the office, where Gabe was taking out the desk drawer. "Kitchen is nothing," she told him. "Bedroom."

"Where was she, all these years? Lacey, I mean." Gabe peered under the wooden desk, patted his hand along the frame. Wiped it on his jeans.

Ellie shook her head. "There's not much online. No one seemed to care. The Vanderwalds—well, to them, who was she but their son's wife? Without him, she was nobody. And after he—Trevor—" She stopped midsentence, picturing it, the sailboat, the bay where Trevor Vanderwald had died, fallen off the boat putting up a spinnaker, an accident, everyone had said so, every article and report she'd seen online. The photo of Trevor Vanderwald she'd seen, the one they'd put on display at his memorial service, with that orange spinnaker billowing behind him, his grin, his eyes gazing somewhere out to sea. "He was a champion sailor, did you know that?" Ellie asked.

"I read that, yeah." Gabe flipped a spindly desk chair upside down, looked underneath. "But what *happened* to Lacey? Nothing in here, that I can find anyway."

They paused in the open bedroom doorway. "She probably took her big bucks and set off to snare another rich husband. But she's here now. If you were Lacey Vanderwald, where would you hide something? Bedroom?"

"Under the bed?" Ellie stepped into the room, determined, and lifted the fringe of the thick white bedspread, then crouched to peer underneath. She reached out an arm and patted the thin blue pile of the carpet. Nothing. She aimed her cell phone screen at the lattice of wooden slats that held the mattress. Nothing.

She heard the closet door open. She backed away from under the bed, brushed off her pants legs as she stood, then yanked open each of the three dresser drawers. Empty, aside from a vague floral scent. "Gabe? Anything?"

She checked her phone as she took the few steps to the open closet. Nothing from Monteiro. Had he found anything in Meg's apartment? What would that even be? She had a fleeting thought of Blinker, alone and clueless. He'd be fine.

"Nothing," Gabe said.

"And *that's* the proof, right?" Ellie said. "There's nothing because this whole place, it's not 'Abigail's apartment.' It's phony. Phony as Meg is." Her phone pinged. Monteiro. "*M-I-A,* Monteiro says."

"Damn it. Where'd she go?"

"She's Lacey Vanderwald," Ellie said. "A scheming widow with a bottomless bank account. She could be anywhere. Question is, what's she scheming *about*?"

"We just got in." Monteiro, stationed in front of Meg's—Lacey's?—apartment, had greeted them on the landing, the door of 3-B open behind him. After finding nothing in "Abigail's" place, Ellie and Gabe had messaged Monteiro, and he'd summoned them back to Ellie's. Gabe had insisted on staying with her. *We're in this together now,* he'd said. Ellie hoped that was a good thing. Whatever "this" meant.

Through Meg's open door, Ellie saw what she figured were camera flashes, had a sense of white-clothed people moving through the place. She heard a low mutter of quiet almost-conversation, the mono-syllabic back-and-forth of a search. *Yes, no, over here.*

"Super opened the door, Ms. Berensen. After the warrant." Monteiro, wearing a thin black quilted vest over a tweed jacket and with sleek sunglasses propped on his head, held a silver cell phone in one hand and a folded piece of paper in the other. "If you don't mind waiting out here a bit, Ms. Berensen? We'll need to check your place too."

"For what?" Ellie had a flashback of hiding-Nora PTSD. But that charade was over. Her Nora clothes were integrated into her regular wardrobe, her blond-bob Ellie wigs necessary for the on-camera needs as a television journalist. "I mean, sure. You think she's inside?"

Ellie heard Blinker meow, inquisitive, from inside her apartment. The cat had probably heard Ellie's voice and decided it was mealtime. She remembered the crocheted dead bird toy Meg had left. Her scrutiny of Ellie's comings and goings. Remembered the non-break-in. Meg's clingy prying. Her confession about her "brother." And the fancy blonde he'd married. The sailing accident.

"I'm—" Gabe began.

"Oh. This is Gabe Hoyt," Ellie said. Then winced. Then hoped her expression hadn't revealed her discomfort. She'd asked Monteiro to check Gabe out. And he'd given Gabe the all clear. Was this the first time they'd met? They were sure acting like it. Plus, *she'd* promised to connect Monteiro with Nora Quinn. She worried again, remembering that he'd never followed up. Which made this face-to-face either embarrassing or perplexing or reassuring. She'd let Monteiro make the first move. At least she was still Ellie Berensen to him. "This is Detective Lieutenant Monteiro. State Police."

Monteiro raised an eyebrow, acknowledging. "So, Ms. Berensen. Besides in your place, which seems improbable, any idea where Lacey Vanderwald might be? We've got someone at your TV station checking with management about how she happened to show up while you were investigating her dead husband's family—any idea about that? And to let those people know to contact us—confidentially—if she shows up there. We figure that's also unlikely. We told your news director you were okay, by the way."

Ellie figured Warren was the least of her worries. "So you do think she's Lacey Vanderwald?"

"Yup."

"Why?" Ellie and Gabe said the word at the same time.

"It's *her* white car." Monteiro had leaned against the hallway wall, crossed his black-booted ankles. "Right age, right everything. She looks different from the photos we've collected, but you know, women and money. Hard to tell from exteriors. Give 'em a new hairstyle and a new nose, maybe some glasses— you know."

Ellie fought the urge to adjust her bangs. "Might she be at James Armistead's? Did he have anything to do with her past?" Ellie remembered the "specific" pencil and P-X pad that came out of Kaitlyn's briefcase.

"Swears he has no idea who she is. Thought she was 'some damn reporter.' His words. Even wanted to know whether he could keep her car. We're taking prints from it now. And from inside the apartment." He cocked his head toward the open doorway. "I'm hoping it'll be easy to confirm her identity. Homeland Security says she's got Global Entry, so that puts her prints on file. She can't leave the country again. Not easily. You're the one who's closest to her, that we know of, at least. Any thoughts? Ideas? Suggestions?"

Ellie draped her coat over the newel post of the apartment stairway. A ray of afternoon sun, carrying motes of glittering dust, beamed through the four-paned landing window. It seemed like an eternity since this morning and Meg's sudden switch of directions to the Uber driver—though it was possible it wasn't sudden. Maybe Meg had wanted to get Ellie to that Braintree apartment. A place where no one would know to look for her. What had been Meg's— she still thought of her as Meg—what had been her true goal? If there was no real Abigail, that meant only the two of them had been there.

"You think she killed Trevor Vanderwald?" Ellie had to ask. "I thought it was an accident."

"Why are you investigating now?" Gabe unzipped his parka and hung it over Ellie's coat on the newel post. "After all these years?"

Monteiro scratched his cheek, turned to look inside Meg's apartment, seemed to be considering.

"It's been almost seven years, in fact," Monteiro said. "Since Trevor Vanderwald's death. The big gala, the family thing, is in his honor. I'm sure you know about that."

"Tomorrow," Ellie said.

"Tomorrow," Gabe said at the same time.

"After seven years, the family knew, would come the legal declaration of death. Since there was no . . ." Monteiro paused, seemed to be choosing his words. "Since no body was recovered, the legal procedures for that declaration had to proceed. They gathered all the paperwork, medical records, all that."

"Which meant Lacey would get all the money from her husband's estate fund, I'm guessing," Gabe said, nodding. "Once her husband was officially

declared—well, wait. That doesn't make sense. She'd
have more money if he was alive. So why—"

"Rafe? Lieutenant?" A lanky woman wearing
white paper coveralls stepped into the doorway,
holding an ice pick and a corkscrew in her lavender-
gloved hands. "Marking these? FYI."

"Can't hurt," Monteiro said. "Thanks, Lisa."

"Ice pick?" Ellie had one too, in her apartment,
courtesy of the furnishings Channel 11 provided.
"Corkscrew? You think *she* caused those accidents?
Crashes? Kaitlyn Armistead and Lydia Frost?"

"Off the record?"

"Sure," Ellie said.

"Yes. We do."

It all came back, washed over her yet again, how
she'd heard—as Nora—the gaspingly unmistakable
sound of Kaitlyn Armistead's last moments on earth,
the fear and the metal and how Ellie had been unable to save her. And Lydia, her colleague, and almost
friend, who'd worried about corporate spies and
someone watching her.

"A Pharminex patient." Ellie touched one forefinger
to the other, counting off. "A Pharminex employee.
And—her husband? About to be a Pharminex big
shot. But how did you connect that to Meg?"

"She'd Bluetoothed her phone to her car," Monteiro said. "I suppose we can tell you that. Did you
know your car's computer saves all your searches?
Like it does on your desktop. Once we took her car
from Armistead's, we downloaded that thing and—
well, there it was. Gotta love technology. How to
disable a tire. A roster of Pharminex salespeople.
Several searches for Lydia Frost. And one for
Kaitlyn Armistead. Not sure how she knew that
name—but we'll wait for her to tell us. Once we
find her."

"The car's computer saves it? Like a search history?"

"Yup. GPS destinations too." Monteiro seemed almost proud. "Don't tell the bad guys, okay?"

"Sir?" The white-coveralled investigator was back. She leaned close to Monteiro.

Ellie watched the lieutenant's face change. Change again.

"Can you come with us? Both of you?" Monteiro made his request in a way that did not sound as if there was a choice. "Trooper Quinlivan wants to show you something. Let me know if you're aware of it. Don't touch anything. Ready? Show us, Lisa." The four trooped into Meg's apartment. Quinlivan led them toward a door along the hall. The second bedroom. In Ellie's apartment, she'd made it her office.

They stood in the open doorway, Monteiro and Quinlivan behind, Ellie and Gabe in front.

"What?" Ellie tried to comprehend. "But she doesn't . . ."

"A crib?" Gabe said. "But there's no—"

"You've never seen this before?" Monteiro's gesture encompassed the room. A white wooden crib with a mobile of crocheted birds, each with cross-stitched eyes, barely swaying above it. A shelf of plushy stuffed animals, bears and unicorns. Puffy white letters attached to the wall, spelling out *LOVE*. A box of disposable diapers. A music box, open, with the figure of a smiling snowman. The room smelled of pink baby lotion.

"What's—?" There couldn't possibly be a baby. Ellie knew, in one racing moment of analysis, there was simply no way that could be.

Quinlivan pointed. "Inside the crib."

Ellie felt the blood drain from her face. She'd never

heard a baby. There was a baby? Did Meg have a baby? Had she adopted a baby? Taken a baby?

Monteiro took a step forward, paused, then motioned to Ellie. "If you will, please," he said.

Ellie moved closer to the crib, fearing . . . fearing everything. What had Meg done?

And there on the blue-striped flannel sheet of the crib, swaddled in a fuzzy blue blanket, was a baby doll, timeworn and translucent-skinned, pink cheeks faded, but ice-blue eyes open and staring at the ceiling.

The four stood for a moment in silence.

"A doll," Ellie said.

"A doll?" Gabe echoed.

"You don't know about this, I take it?" Monteiro said.

"No." Ellie shook her head. "She's . . . taking care of a doll?"

"Seems to be," Monteiro said.

"Lieutenant?" Ellie had to ask. She closed her eyes for a moment, blocking out the doll, blocking out the grotesque reality that Meg had given a doll its own room.

"You don't think she's hiding in my apartment, do you? I had a break-in last week, nothing was taken— long story—but we never figured out how whoever it was got in. Maybe it was Meg. Lacey. And she got in the same way this time. Maybe she's there now."

CHAPTER 60

ELLIE

"You want me to open the door?" Ellie dug into her tote bag for her keys. "She can't be in here, though. It'd be too risky. She knows you all are looking for her, she—"

"Let's not assume what anyone would do or know, Ms. Berensen." Monteiro pulled lavender plastic gloves from his vest pocket, snapped them over his hands. "Mr. Hoyt, you stay here. We don't need to worry about Ms. Berensen's prints." He pointed a purple finger at Ellie. "Okay. Go ahead. Open the door. But I'll go in first."

With a click and a thunk, the deadbolt lock turned with Ellie's key, and Monteiro entered. Gabe grabbed the white blur that was Blinker, who had apparently been poised to escape again. Standing on her own threshold, Ellie tried to sense the presence of anyone who shouldn't be there. She still half believed in Abigail—maybe she *did* exist.

"Stay here," Monteiro ordered. Then he headed down the hall. Ellie turned to see Gabe in the hallway, Blinker still in his arms. Behind them, the sun had dimmed the hallway into gloomy shadow, as if

Boston were trying to cling to the last of winter. Meg's apartment door was still open, lights on, their glow highlighting the intensity of the ongoing search.

Blinker had burrowed herself into Gabe's navy-blue sweater. "You two okay?" Ellie reached out. "I'll take her."

"We're fine," Gabe said.

Ellie saw Monteiro open her bedroom door and go inside, heard the closet open. The bathroom door was already open, but she heard a swish as Monteiro yanked aside the shower curtain. "Kitchen," he said, as he crossed past her. "Stay there."

Ellie heard cabinets opening, then drawers, then the fridge and the freezer, the way she and Gabe had done, to no avail, in the Braintree apartment. In a beat, Monteiro was back. "We're clear. No place for a person to hide in here, Ms. Berensen," he said.

"Ellie," she said, "is fine."

"Sure." Monteiro paused. "Can you come with me a moment, though?" He led her back to the kitchen, where he pulled open a narrow white drawer next to the sink. The frame rattled as the drawer rolled out. "You'd told me earlier your apartments came furnished, everything exactly the same."

"Seem to be," Ellie said. "Same furniture, dishes, silverware. Same towels, even, I saw when I was at Meg's."

Monteiro nodded. "Ice pick? Corkscrew?"

"In that drawer." Ellie frowned, analyzing where this might be going. "The ice pick? I've never used it, but yeah, one's in there. And the corkscrew." She gave half a smile. "Yeah. That I use."

"Can you show me?" He pointed to the drawer.

Ellie took a step toward it, baffled. Looked in the drawer. Blinked at it. Then again. "Not there," she said. "But—"

Ellie kept staring at the empty slots where the corkscrew and ice pick had always been.

"You know, Lieutenant? There was an ice pick and a corkscrew at her other—at the Braintree place. They all look alike, though."

"Yeah." Monteiro pulled out his cell, snapped a few photos of the open drawer. "Maybe she took yours. She's been in here, I assume. Maybe she was planning to blame you. Frame you. After—whatever she had in store for you in Braintree, I'm wondering if she wasn't planning on letting you leave there alive, Ms. Berensen."

"Me?" Ellie sank onto one of the kitchen chairs. "Why?"

"At this point we can only speculate. She's a murder suspect, after all. Maybe she'd set it up so it would look like—in the aftermath—that you were full of remorse for what you did to your archrival Lydia Frost. And also what you did to the crusading victim Ms. Armistead, who was about to call in a squad of reporters to ruin the company you worked for."

"Remorse? For what *I* did?" Ellie pushed up her red glasses, as if trying to see through Monteiro's seemingly casual statement. "Wait. The company *I* work for? But—"

Footsteps behind her. Gabe, still holding Blinker.

"I told him, El, who you sometimes were," he said. "Nora Quinn."

"You *told*—when?" She'd asked Monteiro to check Gabe out, and Monteiro had confirmed Gabe was a good guy. Maybe that's when they'd talked about her. She wondered what else they'd discussed.

"He'd already figured that out, though," Gabe went on. "He's a cop, Ellie. Plus, even though your

Nora look is convincing, it's hard to fool someone who's seen both her and Ellie. As you always say."

"No big deal." Monteiro leaned against the kitchen counter. "I'm all about undercover. I get it. You just undercovered yourself into a corner, and I let you stay there. Question is—was Lacey Vanderwald targeting you as investigative reporter Ellie Berensen, the pit bull who was trying to ruin her family's company? Or as the duplicitous insider Nora Quinn? Or for some other reason?"

"Like I told her," Gabe said to Monteiro. Blinker twisted out of his arms, scampered away. "What happens to one of them happens to the other."

"Yeah, well. Maryland cops think Lacey Vanderwald killed her own husband, so neither of you is safe. That's why we need to find her."

Ellie studied the pale blue and white swirls on her kitchen tabletop, *like waves,* she thought, and traced them with a finger, wondering about the world and how she got to be where she was, and why people did what they did. She remembered the pictures she'd seen of Trevor Vanderwald's memorial service, the image of that one oversize photo of the lost young heir to fortune and family, his golden sunlit face looking ahead into a life full of promise, and a future that ceased to exist. Ellie's imagination conjured impenetrable waters and bone-numbing cold, and a mind's frantic searching, grasping hope, and then some final understanding of ultimate and unrelenting darkness. Were his final seconds a surprise? A terror? A relief? She felt a hand on her shoulder, Gabe's, and she turned to him, tears in her eyes.

"It's okay," he said. "I'll stay with you. Here, or at my place or wherever. If you think that's safe, Lieutenant."

"I'll assign a trooper if you like, Ellie." Monteiro's face had softened.

Ellie felt as if she herself were drowning, drowning in dread and worry and uncertainty. But there was more to find out. And fear would only drag her down.

"Lieutenant?" Ellie began. "You never said why you—I mean, the Maryland police—decided she was a suspect in Trevor Vanderwald's murder. You started to say they'd pulled the paperwork for the formal declaration."

Monteiro nodded, checked the screen of his cell phone. "The reason. Well." He sighed, as if gathering his thoughts. "Trevor Vanderwald wasn't the only person on his sailboat that day. There was a sister."

CHAPTER 61

ELLIE

"So strange to see you as Nora again, and in that getup." Gabe extended his hand to help her out of the back seat of the cab. A pair of massive spotlights crisscrossed in front of the New Science Auditorium, a broad red carpet spread across the sidewalk and up the steps to the front door of the white-columned building. A soft snow, glittering through the lights and sprinkling on the fur-coated and coiffed attendees, brought umbrella-carrying aides scurrying to usher the arrivals inside. "But you look incredible, if I may be so bold."

"Ellie had nothing to wear to the Vanderwald gala," she said. "Luckily Nora had her black velvet. And an appropriate evening bag."

She tucked her arm through the crook of Gabe's elbow as they headed for whatever would unfold tonight. He'd bought a tux for the wedding of a college pal a few years ago, he'd explained, but then decided not to go. His pricey ticket for tonight came courtesy of the law firm working the Pharminex investigation, Gabe had told her. *Billable expenses*, he'd said.

Especially after the files Monteiro had shown them yesterday.

The lieutenant had leaned against the counter in Ellie's kitchen, then tapped on his cell. Once, twice, then again. "On the sailboat with him," Monteiro had continued. "His sister."

Ellie had pivoted her chair to face him. "What about the sister?"

Gabe stood behind her. Blinker padded to the kitchen entrance, tail in the air, then hopped onto Ellie's lap.

Monteiro cleared his throat. "I'm not supposed to show you this," he said. "And you need to promise me this will not go any farther than this room."

"Sure," Gabe said.

Ellie had taken a beat to agree, apprehensive of what was to come, and suspicious of the drama and secrecy. But she needed to know. "Sure," she said.

Monteiro raised his phone. "Remember I told you about the formal declaration of death," he said. "The paperwork."

Ellie nodded.

"The sister—Brooke Vanderwald—was on that boat. The *Caduceus,* it was called. The boat sank, was never salvaged. They only found a spinnaker pole and a life jacket. Trevor Vanderwald's body was never recovered. A terrible accident, the public was told. Vanderwald had apparently slipped trying to set up the spinnaker—from all accounts a risky move under the best of circumstances, and especially so because he'd been drinking. He went overboard. That was it."

Ellie narrowed her eyes, thinking. "How'd they know that? About the spinnaker?"

"The sister," Monteiro said. "Brooke. She was in bad shape. That was pretty much all she could remember, Maryland police told me. The spinnaker, and lunch, and beer. Is there a beer called Natty Boh?"

"Yeah," Gabe said.

"So—the paperwork, you were saying."

Monteiro handed Ellie his cell phone. "This is the tox screen for Brooke Vanderwald. Standard procedure, part of Maryland Medical Center's customary blood tests done after an accident. Look at line . . . think it's number eight."

She used her thumb and forefinger to make the picture bigger. "'Zolpidem tartrate,'" Ellie read out loud from what appeared to be a black-and-white photo of a medical report. She looked at Monteiro, then at Gabe, then at the phone screen again. "Ambien. *Ambien?* In Brooke?"

"Yeah. Guess you learned Ambien's chemical name at your undercover job." Monteiro reached out, took his phone. "But back then, Brooke's mother apparently went nuts over this result. Maryland police told me she kept saying her daughter never took drugs. Of any kind, not even over the counter. The mother was . . ." He shook his head. "Upset. It wasn't clear, Maryland says. But according to her mother, this Brooke had something against medicine. Never took anything, her mother insisted. Made a big deal about it. Funny, since she'd be an heir to the Pharminex fortune, but whatever. The fact that she had this in her system was—"

"Suspicious," Gabe said.

"Suspicious. And Brooke managed to tell Maryland—the investigators at the time—that they'd both had tuna sandwiches. Sandwiches Lacey Vanderwald had made. Lacey insisted she hadn't. Problem was, apparently Brooke was in and out of lucidity. The next day, she couldn't remember anything about it. Head injuries, the doctors said. Lack of oxygen. Unpredictable. Lucky she lived, apparently."

"They think Lacey Vanderwald tried to drug her husband? And Brooke? Kill them? Both?" Ellie tried to picture this, how that would work. And why.

"They do. And the mother, Brinn, was all about arresting Lacey right then, charging her with murder. But—"

"How would they prove it?" Gabe interrupted. "There was no evidence. No evidence of anything. Except Ambien in Brooke's blood, which could have come from anywhere. Plus . . ."

Ellie turned to him, watched him think. Blinker jumped to the floor.

"Plus," Gabe said again, "Trevor wasn't dead. He wasn't dead. He was only missing. So, technically, there was no murder."

Monteiro nodded. "Exactly. Tough case, when there's no body. Lacey Vanderwald—the grieving widow—would probably walk."

"And the family would be humiliated," Ellie said. "Scandal and drugs and murder."

"So they let it go," Monteiro said. "They had to. And they let Lacey fade from their lives. But now, seven years later—"

"Oh." Ellie felt her eyes widen. "He'll be officially dead."

"And there's no statute of limitations on murder," Gabe said.

"Does she know?" Ellie asked. "Does Lacey know she's wanted?"

"Good question," Monteiro had replied. "But whatever it takes—the family is demanding justice."

Justice, Ellie thought now, as she and Gabe passed through the stand of spindly metal detectors outside the ballroom. A white banner, edged in orange, fluttered from the ceiling, proclaiming THE TREVOR VANDERWALD MEMORIAL FUND. Through three sets of open double doors, Ellie saw a vast room sparkling with strands of pin-dot white lights, festooned like loops of glistening pearls across the ceiling.

Black-jacketed assistants spirited away their winter coats, and as she and Gabe entered the ballroom, they were surrounded by sequins and brocade, by the pop of champagne bottles and the classical undercurrent of Mozart, melodic strings a politely festive soundtrack—to a celebration, but also to a remembrance of a son who had died too soon. Ellie calculated the money in the room. Every guest meant thousands of dollars for the Trevor Vanderwald fund. But how much of that came from the cynical targeting of vulnerable women?

"I hate how much money this is," Ellie whispered. "Pharminex, foisting their medications on women who will never be happy again, and now . . . they're reveling in it. Glorifying it." She sighed, battling emotional overload.

"It's to honor their son, though, Ellie," Gabe reminded her. "This must be difficult for them. D'you think Brooke will be here? That's what fascinates me, too. Even though she's not front and center in the family, she apparently loved her brother, and this is all for him."

"Difficult? For Pharminex?" Ellie frowned. The music changed to Cole Porter, seductive and mellow, and the hum of conversation grew louder. "Reap what you sow. Wait till your lawsuit's filed. Wait till my story gets on TV. Then these people will understand what 'difficult' means. I'm so disappointed it couldn't air before tonight—but Warren said it wasn't ready. And I'd rather be ready than wrong. Plus, now they'll have further to fall."

A smiling server in a black turtleneck offered champagne flutes, delicate stems balanced on a lace-covered silver platter.

"No, thanks," Ellie said. Disgusting, she thought. Somewhere in this building, Brinn and Winton Vander-wald were probably holding court. She imagined a private suite where the senior Vanderwalds, stoic but magnanimous, were receiving sympathy and con-gratulations. For what? Ellie wondered. For having a murdered son and a wayward daughter? She scanned the room again, looking for Lacey, looking for Meg. Would she appear in Meg's ponytail? Or maybe as the Lacey in the internet photos, elegant and glamorous. Neither would recognize Nora Quinn.

"Duck paté?" A server proffered a glossy black tray. "Ahi tuna?"

Ellie shook her head, her stomach churning, and the server glided back into the crowd.

Across the room, a single microphone on a three-legged metal stand had been placed on the center of a raised stage, ocean-blue velvet curtains hiding the area behind it.

"Look. Over there." Gabe cocked his head toward the front of the room. "Detta."

Detta Fiddler, in long-sleeved black and holding a champagne flute, stood among a covey of attendees. Allessandra Lewes, in taupe sequins, hovered by her side. Would Christine O'Shea be here, and Jen Wahl and Gerri Munroe, smiling and congenial? Their lives had changed because of Pharminex. Lydia Frost, their colleague, would never taste champagne again.

But it was Meg who Ellie needed to find. Meg—Lacey—would not recognize her. Meg had never met

Nora. Would Meg be here? Maybe to stake her claim on the family? To prove she was part of it?

"If she doesn't know she's wanted for murder," Ellie had told Monteiro yesterday, "she might just show up."

"We're relying on that," Monteiro had replied. "We'll have people there. They'll find you, if need be."

"You see any cops?" Ellie noticed Gabe was now checking the room too. He'd accepted the champagne, but his glass was still full.

"Not that I can—"

With a flourish, the music stopped. The unexpected silence softened the conversation; talk lowered to whispers. Ellie saw Detta Fiddler climb three stairs to the left of the stage and disappear behind the soft folds of the deep blue curtain.

"Let's get closer." Ellie took Gabe's arm and inched them toward the front. "Detta just went backstage. And I saw the curtains move, like more people are back there too. I think it's about to start. Excuse me." She drew him around a clump of sleek-coiffed gowned women and uncomfortable-looking men in dinner jackets. A brief squeal of feedback had some of the women clamping their hands over diamond-ornamented ears. "Sorry," Ellie said, and she kept moving toward the stage. "Coming through."

They found a spot by the steps. She saw Allessandra Lewes glance her way, but her gaze swept past Ellie—Nora—without acknowledgment. Nora had been invited, of course, so she was not a surprise.

Ellie stood on her toes, trying to look over the crowd for Meg, but all she saw were the guests closest to her. She took a step up onto the first of the stage stairs to get a better view. And then the second step. The draped white lights were supposed to transform the room into festive elegance, but all they did now was block Ellie's view.

"What're you doing up there?" Gabe asked.

"I need to see." She squinted, shaded her eyes. "I'm looking for Lacey."

"Right," Gabe said. "Just hope she's not looking for you."

CHAPTER 62

ELLIE

"Go!"

Ellie heard the voice from backstage give the signal, and then felt the rumble of the wooden step beneath her as some mechanism, inch by inch, drew open the heavy blue stage curtains. The pearls of light across the ballroom dimmed, leaving only a soft glow, as if even they were waiting for what was to come. The audience, quieted, had all eyes focused forward, but as the curtains swished into place on either side, like the motion of deep blue waves, center stage remained dark.

Ellie took a deep breath in that moment of hushed silence, wondering what was to come, and how she'd gotten here, dressed to celebrate but with a darkened heart. Somehow this night seemed a grotesque celebration of death—the death of family, and families, and of futures longed for and then destroyed. She thought of her notes about the Pharminex story, about these people and their duplicity, printed out in careful files on her desk. Warren had dubbed them almost ready to reveal but tantalizingly, frustratingly, not solid enough to make public. As a journalist, she had a responsibility. But as a person, as a woman, her heart was breaking. Again.

A change in the energy brought her back to the present. The lights on the stage came up, gradually from darkness to promise to illumination, and as they brightened to full, the string quartet began again. In one note, then two, Ellie recognized "The Sailor's Hymn": "*Eternal Father, strong to save, whose arm doth bind the restless wave . . .*" And there on the stage, alone and bathed in a wash of white spotlights, that oversize photo of Trevor Vanderwald, forever young, eyes forever on the water, that Pharminex spinnaker behind him, smiling into the sun-filled future that would never arrive.

Ellie clutched the stair rail. The music, sweet and simple, continued. "*Oh, hear us when we cry to Thee, for those in peril on the sea!*" Ellie realized she had mouthed the words as the mournful hymn ended.

Footsteps above her. Detta Fiddler swept to the microphone, and the room dimmed again, with a single spotlight giving her a halo. All heads were upturned to watch her, Ellie saw, from Nora's colleagues in the front row to the august guests who'd paid so much to be included.

"Ladies and gentlemen." Detta's familiar voice, tinged with formal solemnity, was the only sound in the silent room. "We are honored you are here on this important and vital occasion. We know you feel the loss of Trevor Vanderwald as much today as we all did seven years ago, but tonight we are here not only to remember and honor him, but to look ahead. And without further ado, I give you . . ."

Ellie's heart stopped, and she felt Gabe move closer to her. He put one hand over hers, just a brief touch, and she searched his face in the steely light.

"Brinn and Winton Vanderwald."

Detta moved out of sight, and the applause from the audience exploded into a jangle of bracelets and murmurs of approval as the couple, hand in hand, arrived at the microphone stand. Winton Vanderwald, sixty-three, Ellie had calculated, proud-shouldered and elegant in black tie and gray temples. And Brinn Vanderwald, hair swept back in a chignon like Ellie's own and a slash of red lipstick. Demure in a long-sleeved ivory gown, opulent with a single square-cut diamond hanging from a gold chain around her neck.

As the applause quieted, the couple turned toward the portrait of their son. Ellie saw Winton steady his wife with a flat palm against the small of her back, saw Brinn move closer to him. They had been affected by the loss, Ellie had to acknowledge. And if it really had been murder, she wondered, what must they be thinking now? Would they even mention their daughter? She was as missing from their lives as Trevor was, it seemed. And for all they knew, she might be dead too.

Ellie glanced at Gabe, but his eyes were on the stage.

Winton turned back to the microphone, his wife by his side. He shaded his eyes with one hand. "I can't see you out there." He leaned forward, scanned the crowd, affable and cordial. "Can we kill that spotlight on us? Or swivel it the other way? Because the spotlight should be on *you,* on all of *you,* for what you've done, for how much you've helped us memorialize"—his voice seemed to catch—"our son, Trevor."

The lights brightened, but barely a notch, keeping the audience in an artificial twilight.

"And we are so grateful," Brinn began. She put a hand to her chest, covering the diamond for a beat.

"Even in our continuing grief, for knowing Trevor's memory will live on, and his—"

Ellie thought Brinn might have been choked by emotion, as her husband seemed to be, but then saw the look on Brinn's face. Perplexed, confused, bewildered. Ellie felt, even as she turned, a shift in the atmosphere. Looking out over the audience, she heard sounds like—cell phone pings. And then, *ping. Ping. Ping. Ping.* Then one by one, faces in black tie and gowns and glitter were brightened by the glow of individual devices.

Faces no longer looking at Brinn. No longer looking at Winton. But faces, artificially green and blue, studying tiny screens.

The rear doors of the ballroom clanged open, and Ellie saw three men in black suits rushing out, gowned women trailing behind them, the exit doors clanging again as they slammed shut.

"Ellie," Gabe whispered. And when she looked, his cell phone too glowed like it bore a secret.

"His memory will live on," Brinn continued, her voice now wavering, "and we know you'll . . . we know you'll . . ."

The exit doors clanged again, and again, as other couples left the auditorium. The murmur of the audience had grown to an insistent hum, and the *ping*s did not stop.

Ellie longed to read the phone, but couldn't take her eyes off Brinn Vanderwald, who'd turned to her husband, raw panic on her face.

"Your story," Gabe whispered, moving up to the step behind her. "It's posted. Breaking news. Alerts are pinging all over social media."

"What? *My* story?" Ellie grabbed the phone, scanned the words. "BREAKING NEWS. PHARMINEX DEADLY COVER-UP," the headline screamed. "PHARM

CO HIDING DANGEROUS DRUG." *Monifan*. Ellie saw the word over and over as she scanned. *Infertility, nondisclosure, incapable, women, danger. Liability, lawsuits, fraud, deception, highest levels.* "How the hell—?"

"Ladies and gentlemen?" Winton Vanderwald stepped back to the microphone, put himself almost in front of his wife. "We cannot help but wonder—"

Ellie felt the mechanism rumble under her feet again, and the navy velvet curtains began to close, slowly, slowly. She saw the crowd, almost as one entity with one intent, turn its back to the stage and flood toward the back doors. She saw Detta Fiddler, her own phone aglow, dash onto the stage and hurry the couple off. Now only the gradually closing curtains separated Ellie from the Vanderwalds. One step, and she'd be up there with them.

CHAPTER 63

ELLIE

The sound came from backstage, a wail or cry like *no* or *what* or simply alarm or fear or surprise, and Ellie could not bear it. She heard Gabe step up behind her, felt his hand trying to hold her back, but she twisted away, up the last step and behind the blue curtain.

Winton Vanderwald was being hustled though a door offstage by someone in a dark suit. That door stayed open, but behind it, Ellie saw only light. Brinn, face white and drawn, just that slash of red lipstick, stood listening as Detta Fiddler whispered in her ear, holding up a cell phone so Brinn could see, scrolling, while Brinn seemed to be trying to comprehend.

"But no," she said, her hand to her chest. "That cannot be!"

Detta whispered again.

"No!" Brinn's eyes went wild, and she grabbed the phone herself, scrolling through the screens. "No. I won't allow it, it's—it's—"

Ellie stood, almost an arm's length from the woman, watching this drama unfold, concealing herself in the folds of the velvet curtain. No one noticed her, so focused were they on what had turned a celebration into a calamity. Brinn looked smaller than Ellie had imagined; maybe her sorrow had physically diminished her, made her no longer the powerfully vital woman Ellie knew she once had been. The delicate bones of her shoulders showed through the sheer fabric of her dress, her tiny wrists were diamond-encircled but fragile, and her veined hands, fingernails bright crimson, held the cell phone that Ellie now understood contained the end of life as Brinn knew it.

But how did the story get there? Who had—

"Good evening, Brinn." A figure stood, silhouetted, in the backstage door. Then walked toward Brinn Vanderwald and Detta Fiddler.

Ellie saw who it was and eased farther into the curtains.

Meg, or not-Meg, but appearing as someone else entirely: glamorous in movie star makeup, her hair tumbling voluptuously down her shoulders, her pocketed black sheath dress chic and severe, both wrists jangling with bangle bracelets, her elegant pumps glittering bronze.

What would Brinn call her?

"It's been a long time, Lacey," Brinn finally said.

Lacey.

"I see you've read my big news story," Lacey said, as she stepped closer.

"Your . . ." Ellie saw Brinn's chin rise, her gaze assess this newcomer.

Ellie knew Brinn thought this woman had killed her son. But did Lacey know that? Ellie could almost hear Brinn's mind calculating, deciding how to handle this reunion.

Detta stepped between them, but Brinn waved her away. "Will you go get my husband, please?" Her voice was a whisper in the darkened wing of the stage.

Ellie didn't dare move from her hiding place as Detta left the two of them—mother-in-law and widow—face-to-face.

Brinn, smiling, stepped forward and linked her arm through Lacey's, held on to her as if she needed support.

"Lacey, darling, we're so pleased to see you after all this time," Brinn said. "We did hope you'd join us this evening—it's all for your poor Trevor, after all. And especially now, with whatever annoying unpleasantness has occurred. Winton will have his people take care of it, as always, so come with me, dear. We'll find Win, together, just like old times, and then we'll want to hear all about what you've been doing."

Go, Brinn, Ellie thought. Had to hand it to her. She'd essentially taken the woman into custody. All Ellie had to do was get Gabe and call for the cops Monteiro had assured her were there. But to do that, she'd have to reveal herself. And Brinn seemed to be managing this.

"What I've been doing? Mother? *Darling?*" Lacey seemed to draw Brinn even closer, and Ellie saw the older woman wince, just a flash, just for an instant. "What I've been *doing,* since you ask, is writing that little story that seems to have all your devoted friends in such disapproval that they've turned their backs on you. Walked out of your life. How does that feel, Mother? And how does it feel, knowing your precious Pharminex is about to—how shall we put it? *Drown?* In its own immoral, vile—"

"*You* wrote this story?"

Ellie's eyes went wide.

"But you know?" Lacey went on. "All I wanted, all I ever wanted, was children. A child. To have a family. To have someone love me. And you took that from me! You took me to that damn doctor, and you didn't warn me, and you took my children, and my life, and my future and my happiness and now—"

"Lacey, darling, I never meant to hurt you. You must know that. Sometimes it happens, sometimes it—"

Brinn, Ellie saw, was trying to pull away from Lacey, but Lacey was not letting go.

Ellie saw Lacey reach into her dress pocket and pull out a—

"No!" Ellie almost didn't think, leaped forward, before even the entire weapon was out of Lacey's pocket, but Lacey had twisted and stabbed the ice pick into Brinn, once, just once, as Ellie screamed for help and yanked Lacey away. Ellie grabbed at her, twisting and grabbing and wrenching the ice pick out of her hand. The thing flew into the dark recesses behind them. Ellie ducked and spun as Lacey fought back, screaming at her, clawing at her, but Ellie had to stop her, *stop* her, and Brinn, with a choking gasp, fell to the wooden floor, a bloom of bright red creeping across her ivory silk.

"No!" Ellie's cry did not sound like her own voice and she knew she was bleeding too, but then Gabe was behind her, grabbing her, and two people in black were clamping onto a shrieking Lacey, dragging her toward the door. *Monteiro?* Ellie registered, before her knees crumbled.

"I called nine-one-one, everyone's on the way, and ambulances." Gabe clutched her close, keeping her upright against him. "Hey. You're bleeding."

"It's fine, I think," she said. "Just my arm. But . . ."

She looked down at Brinn, face now ashen, the pool of red on her chest spreading from her dress to the dusty floor.

The light in Brinn's eyes faded, then brightened, as she searched Ellie's face. Her lips moved silently. Then, as Ellie watched, Brinn seemed to draw on some inner strength, and she tried again.

"Brooke?" she said. A quiet smile changed her face, briefly, to relief. And then to peaceful certainty. "My Brooke."

CHAPTER 64

BROOKE

More footsteps, and commotion, clattering toward the three of them backstage—Brinn, as pale as her ivory dress, thin-lidded eyes closing, fluttering, opening again. Brooke and Gabe, kneeling on the dusty floor, side by side in black velvet dress and black tuxedo. An upstage door banged open, lights flicked on, spotlights snapped to bright, one after another. Brooke looked up to see that portrait of Trevor, still smiling, still carefree, still gone.

"I need that," she told Gabe, and grabbed the white handkerchief from his jacket pocket. She held it, with both hands, over the wound in her mother's chest. "Mother?" Brooke said. "Hang on. I'm here."

"Brooke?" Brinn whispered. "Your father? Does he—has he—?"

"He's fine. You'll be okay, Mother," she lied. "You'll be fine." She looked at Gabe, still beside her. "Right?"

Gabe shook his head, almost imperceptibly. "Brooke," he said.

"Right. I'm Brooke. Ellie is Brooke. Now you know." Brooke focused on the increasingly crimson handkerchief instead of on him. "Crazy, huh? You've been theorizing almost every woman we met was Brooke. Everyone but me. But I *had* to hide who I was, can you understand? I had to take this company down. But I couldn't—not as Brooke."

"Yeah," he said. "But I mean, what *you* don't know is that I—"

"My family, my mother—back when I was a teenager—there's no way to explain it," Brooke interrupted. She didn't care what he said. Or thought. And she couldn't cry, she couldn't, not now. Whatever was happening with her mother was out of her control, and it felt like the past had come back, and instead of as the solution she hoped for, as disaster. Brooke—Ellie—Brooke—had vowed to make things right. To stop more people from being manipulated and harmed and deceived by the Vanderwald power. Harmed like the Vanderwalds had harmed her, their own daughter.

And the child teenaged Brooke had been forced to destroy.

And, as Trevor himself had told Brooke that day on the *Caduceus,* the Vanderwalds had also deceived Lacey. Whose mind had snapped as a result.

That doll in Lacey's crib.

Both women, Brooke and Lacey, had vowed revenge, Brooke realized. Each in her own way.

Now it had come to this again, mother and daughter and power and life and death.

"It's a long story, Gabe," Brooke said. "Too long for now."

"I know all about it," Gabe said. "You—"

Brinn stirred. A feather-light motion, and her eyes turned clear and determined.

"Mother?" Even saying the word felt distant, of another time.

"We were only doing what we thought was right

for you, Brookie," her mother whispered. "Back then. I'm so sorry. We wanted you to be happy."

"I understand," Brooke lied again.

Footsteps from all sides now, clattering up the stage stairway where Ellie had watched the ceremony, pounding through the open back door, running across the stage itself, uniformed police and white-jacketed EMTs, turtlenecked security guards and a woman in dazzling gold sequins.

"I'm a doctor," she yelled. "Let me through."

"Oh, thank you, *thank* you." Brooke kept the pressure in place, knowing that was her mother's only hope. "She—"

"Got it." Bejeweled hands replaced Brooke's on her mother's chest as the sequined doctor took charge. Bustling EMTs unlatched orange suitcases of equipment and oxygen and blood pressure cuffs, and one of the medics gently, firmly, moved her and Gabe out of the way.

"Where will you take her?" Brooke asked.

"Mass General," the doctor called over her shoulder.

In the recessed velvet of the stage curtains, Brooke felt the tears stream down her face—she could not stop them—whether from loss or joy or confusion or relief or an overwhelming wave of change and uncertainty. Of being who she was, finally. Brooke.

Her wash of tears was making this feel like a dream, otherworldly and diffuse, but it wasn't a dream. The EMTs clanked open a folding metal stretcher, and as Brooke heard a soft count of three, they lifted her mother onto it, wheeling her away, the gold sequins hurrying behind.

Lieutenant Monteiro. It took her a beat to realize who had approached from the shadows, nearly unrecognizable in bow tie and dinner jacket.

"You have her?" Brooke asked. "Meg? Lacey? She didn't get away. Tell me she didn't."

"That's why I'm here, *Nora*," Monteiro said. "I need Ellie now, though, to—"

"Where's my—where's Winton Vanderwald? He needs to know where his wife—"

"Her mother recognized her, Lieutenant," Gabe said.

"Did she recognize *you*?" Monteiro asked.

"She who?" Brooke looked at Monteiro, then Gabe, then Monteiro again. "Recognize who?"

CHAPTER 65

Monteiro's phone buzzed. He put it to his ear. "Yup. Got 'em both," he said into the phone. Then he turned to Gabe and Brooke. "You have two minutes. Then I'll need you both in the back. Deal? 'Cause then I've gotta get her out of here."

Brooke watched Monteiro start to stride away, phone clamped to his ear.

"Wait! Lacey, you mean?" she asked him. "Or my mother? Recognize who?"

"Two minutes," Monteiro called over his shoulder. "I mean it."

"Who recognize who?" Brooke, bewildered, brushed the dust from her velvet knees and sleeves. This dress will never be the same, she thought, and then almost cried again at her own ridiculousness. The dress was not what she was grieving.

"You, Brooke," Gabe said. "Recognize me. It's me, Brooke. Liam. Liam Endicott."

"Liam?" She frowned, her brain suddenly cotton and glue and impossibility.

He put both hands on her shoulders, looked her in the eyes, and in them she saw the sapphire sky and the seagulls, and maybe even smelled the sweetly summery fragrance of the ocean.

"I love you more than the stars and the sky, Brooke. Remember?"

"Liam?" Even saying his name, a name she hadn't allowed herself to say out loud for so long, it all rushed back over her, consumed her, how much she had adored him, and her loss, and her mother's betrayal, and the hopelessness of youth and love. This Liam—*Liam*—she almost saw him now, behind the no-longer teenaged face, the no-longer-bleached no-longer-shaggy hair, the tortoiseshell glasses and the confidence. His voice was lower now, and thick with emotion.

"Your mother finally told me what 'happened.' What she'd done. I was there, in your rehab. After the sailing . . . accident. She may have felt guilty about what she'd done to you. She may have had her guard down, seeing you like that. But I told her I'd never stopped wondering about you. I was such a jerk. I am so sorry, Brooke. Back then my parents demanded I never contact you again. They told me they *knew* you hated me. That I needed to go to college. That this whole mess could ruin our lives. *Would* ruin them. And when I realized they were full of shit, it was too late."

And in the musty gloom of the now-silent stage, Brooke saw tears in his eyes too, tears of maybe regret and guilt and something left behind. She opened her mouth to say something, but now her brain was going too fast to create any words.

"Brooke? I lost a child too," he went on. "I know it's not the same, but—"

She looked at the floor then, afraid to meet his eyes. It wasn't the same, not at all. But she'd never considered what he'd lost too. Still, she'd thought of him every day. Even chosen her name for him—Liam Endicott. *L. E.* Ellie.

"So funny that we took the same tack for our lives. Justice. Retribution. Bringing down—well, not just Pharminex, in my job, but any pharmaceutical company that uses drugs as power. One that takes people's money and then destroys their lives. Like they did to you. And to me."

"And to Lacey. And Trevor," Brooke said. "And all those people we'll never know."

"And when I finally found you—I mean, it was more like you found *me*. You'd called my law firm, researching, so of course we looked you up. I recognized you instantly, even under that blond wig. And your Nora 'disguise'—well, that's just grown-up Brooke with a lot of makeup. But I needed to tell you I did the wrong thing. I needed to tell you I made the wrong choice."

Brooke tried to battle back through the past. At least he'd *had* a choice. She felt angry, and bitter, and hurt and thrilled, and how could that be?

"You're an idiot!" She felt like punching him, or falling into his arms. "Why didn't you just *tell* me? Why did you pretend to be someone else? Guy, or whoever? And Gabe? And why did you keep telling me about every damn one else you supposedly thought might be Brooke?"

"So you wouldn't realize I knew it was you! Brooke, we were kids back then. And after all those years I just show up? What if you actually *did* hate me? Wouldn't see me? Wouldn't listen to me? Or didn't even remember me? I wanted to prove to you that I—that I cared about what happened to you. To us." He let out a long breath. "I wanted to take responsibility. To prove to you that there was still good in the world. That even in grief, there's love."

"I lost that, long ago," Brooke said. "The belief in love. And good."

"Can you forgive me?" Liam asked.

"Now!" Monteiro shouted from the open stage door. "Time's up!"

"Then, let her talk, okay?" Monteiro was walking Brooke toward the rear of the stage, giving her quiet instructions along the way. They approached a wooden door, with a hand-lettered sign tacked to it that said: MAKEUP—CAST ONLY.

"It'll take me two seconds," Brooke said as they went inside. "If you think this'll work."

"It'll work," Monteiro said. "That's why I asked you to bring it. Just in case."

Brooke pulled her Ellie-wig and glasses from her evening bag. "Luckily I'll never have to wear this thing again," she said, shaking the wig out.

"I've parked her in the other dressing room," Monteiro went on, as Brooke changed to Ellie. "She's handcuffed, there's a trooper—you remember Lisa Quinlivan—babysitting her. I told Lacey we've gotta clear the scene and wait for a cruiser. But I'm betting she'll say something to you. She won't be able to resist. Okay?" He reached for the doorknob of a weathered wooden door. "Okay? *I* can't ask her questions, but you can."

"She ask for a lawyer?" Gabe said.

"Not yet, " Monteiro told him. "And if she talks to Brooke—I mean, Ellie—how can I stop that?"

Gabe opened his mouth as if to protest. Then closed it.

"Ready?" Monteiro asked.

They went to the door of the adjacent dressing room and Monteiro opened it, a mirror image of where Brooke had just changed. Lacey, still in her black dress but now with her hands cuffed behind her, sat on a tufted stool in front of a lighted makeup mirror, a rectangle of light bulbs like a picture frame around her. She tried to stand as the three of them entered, but the serious-faced Lisa Quinlivan, now wearing a taupe dress, black pumps and a gold shield hanging like a necklace, put one hand on Lacey's shoulder and pushed her back down. Brooke felt Monteiro behind her, blocking the open door.

"How'd you like the Pharminex story?" Lacey, with russet lipstick smeared and hair in chaotic disarray, was as congenial as if they were back in the newsroom. "Pretty fabulous, right? And perfect timing? Totally what we were going for. Have their world come crashing down. Humiliating them. Ruining them. But only *I* had the guts to make it happen."

Brooke had to stay calm. Not push it. Use Ellie's reporter skills to get Meg—Lacey—to talk. "You took my files."

"Well, more precisely, *our* files." Lacey tilted her head, correcting her. "We worked together. Supposedly. Except you were so concerned with the damned rules, all your ridiculous *ethics,* that the story was never going to see the light of day. You, so endlessly *superior,* and Warren, and all those lawyers, and—" She stopped. Pointed her chin at Gabe. "What's Will Faraday doing here? Doesn't he work for—"

"Good question, Lacey. I'll tell you if you tell me something." Brooke could feel Monteiro hovering. She only had a few more minutes. "How'd you know about Lydia Frost? And Kaitlyn Armistead?"

"From your notes. Right on your desk. That was no biggie. You had it all written down in your files, good little reporter that you are. But I could see that the story was doomed, so I decided to—"

"Decided to what?" Brooke stopped herself from pouncing, stayed chill. Spoke quietly. "What, exactly?"

"Oh, no. That I can't divulge. Not with *them* here." Lacey fluttered her eyelashes, one of which had come unglued. "But it sure made you wonder, right? And with the additional evidence of those pencils and prescription pad, and then Lydia's insider position, you would have *cleverly* connected her and Kaitlyn, and *wham*, nailed that company for murder. If only you'd been smarter. And hurried the hell up."

"You can't just *kill*—"

"Really? Can't I? Pharminex does, right? Every damn day they kill people. So hey, this is not *my* fault. It's theirs. The way I see it? Kaitlyn and Lydia were simply two more Pharminex victims. And a means to an end."

"I think we're fine here." Monteiro had eased in beside Brooke. "Say goodbye, Lacey. You're done."

"*Brooke.*" Lacey's eyes seemed to fill with tears.

"You knew I was Brooke?" She glared at Lacey, then turned to Monteiro, accusing. "Did you tell her?" Then Liam. "Or you?"

"Please. Give me some credit." Lacey fidgeted on the unsteady stool, trying to stand. Trooper Quinlivan stepped closer. Lacey twisted away.

"You think I showed up in Boston by chance?" she asked Brooke. "I tracked you from the moment you left Maryland. From your dinky little reporter jobs to here in Boston. I planned to just befriend you, so simple, poor abandoned ditzy me just waited in the hallway for you to come home. Pretending to talk to 'Jimmy.'" She rolled her eyes. "You fell for the whole thing. But I'd already seen those job listings at the new station, and . . ." She shrugged prettily, full ingenue. "I managed to get hired. It's perfectly perfect, isn't it? We got to work together to get what we always wanted. And how much did you love it when I told you your *own* story that night in my apartment—but made it be about *me*? You didn't even notice. Pitiful."

"You killed my brother." Brooke had to say it to her face. Make sure she understood how much Brooke knew. "You tried to kill *me* too."

"Oh, please. Brooke. Gimme a break. Your *brother* let his mother destroy our lives—and even then, he said nothing, did *nothing*, simply went back to work for those people. For money. For power. He got exactly what he deserved. And as for you? Well, I wanted your dear parents to know what it was like to lose a child. Or two. They did it to me, right? So I did it to them. Fair's fair."

"*Fair?*" Brooke felt her eyes widen, wondering about fair.

"We got this, Brooke," Montero whispered. "Good job."

In two steps, Monteiro had crossed to the handcuffed Lacey, nodded at Quinlivan, and each took their suspect by one elbow and brought her to her feet. Lacey planted herself in place, chin in the air, and looked square at Brooke. Tears were now rolling down her cheeks.

"Brooke, Brooke, don't forget! We're still *sisters*. You and me. Now and forever, I'm a *Vanderwald*. Just like you. We're *family*."

Brooke felt Liam's hand on her shoulder but she stepped away. Stepped into the pool of overhead light in front of Lacey Vanderwald. Stared her down.

"You're not *family*, Lacey," Brooke said. "Not for now. And not ever."

EPILOGUE

An aerial loop of squawking seagulls seemed to be calling attention to them, Brooke thought, as she sat side by side with Liam on the bright green bench in the daffodil garden behind the curved glass and redbrick edifice of Boston's federal courthouse. She felt Liam's arm drape across her shoulders, saw the water in the vast harbor in front of them glassy and mesmerizing in the sparkling noontime sun.

Spring had finally arrived, and the April daffodils held their heads proudly, showing off for the lawyers and judges and reporters and victims who had come here today. Those who'd stood in line to get courtroom seats for the arraignment; to hear in person the breaking news they'd read this morning, bullet-pointed, in *The Boston Globe* online edition: *U.S. Attorney announces whirlwind grand jury indictments of Pharminex. Feds charge crimes of off-label promotion and failure to disclose safety data. Government files multibillion-dollar civil lawsuit charging kickbacks to doctors and lying about the effects of Monifan.*

Brooke had devoured the fast-breaking story,

though now, as a Vanderwald herself, she could no longer report it. Detta Fiddler turned state's evidence. Dr. Douglas Hawkins—who had agreed to trap Nora—was a key witness. Christine, Jenn and Gerri were subpoenaed. Wall Street was predicting Winton Vanderwald himself—with his wife's life now hanging in the balance—would see his fortune and reputation vanish.

"They'll wind up paying billons," Brooke said. "Pharminex is doomed. And they deserve it. I still think they should have been charged with murder, the murder of all the lives they ruined with the lies they told."

"Honey, they—"

"I know, I know." Brooke stood and turned to face him. Tilted her head side to side, as if parroting a line: "'They helped a lot of people.'" She went back to her own voice. "Sure. But they also lied, and manipulated, and it was all for money. Now they'll have to admit they knew they were misleading patients, and they knew their 'miracle drug' could harm women, and that they tried to cover it up. Can you believe Meg—Lacey—swiped my story? I worked so hard on that."

"But you couldn't have done it anyway, Brooke. Once it was known who you are. But it's strange, isn't it? In the end Lacey did at least one good thing. She made this all public."

"Yeah." Brooke had to admit the irony. "And I— kind of—feel sorry for her. All she asked for, in her jail cell? All she wanted? Was that doll. The one we saw in her apartment. 'Her baby,' she called it. I can't even . . . that's just so heartbreaking. Lacey even admitted it—the loss of her ability to have children finally shattered everything inside her. And then she was so enraged at Trevor for siding with the company instead of grieving with her that she drugged him. Killed him."

"And you too, don't forget," Liam said. "She tried to kill you too. Twice."

"I know. Yeah. I do. She even admitted she'd done it to Trev before. Given him that stuff, hoped he'd be driving or something."

Brooke stared at the daffodils, missing her brother. She'd never let go of it, the idea that she might have saved him that day on the *Caduceus*. But she hadn't, no one could have, and it was over, and that was how life—and death—sometimes unfolded.

"But her scheme finally worked when he tried to raise the spinnaker. And at that moment, she had what she wanted." Brooke sighed, plopped back down on the bench. "They'd just argue he was drunk, though, and I'd have to admit . . . maybe he was."

"But even if they can't prove she killed Trevor, she'll be charged for Lydia and Kaitlyn," Liam said. "She'll plead guilty, I predict. Make a deal."

"Can you believe Lacey wanted me to believe Pharminex was responsible? Make it look like they were retaliating? She even pretended she'd found Pharminex pencils and a prescription pad in Kaitlyn's briefcase, when she herself swiped them from doctors' offices."

"Cops think she was going to kill you too, in that Braintree apartment. She knew you were Brooke. And she might have succeeded. Until she slipped, and made up that one last story about Will Faraday's motives. Will, who never existed."

"Talk about never existed. Lieutenant Monteiro *knew* you were Liam? He told me he checked you out. You, *Gabe*. He said you were a good guy."

"True. But he never specifically said I was Gabriel Hoyt."

Brooke sighed. "I guess not."

"Plus, he was right. I *am* a good guy. And so are you," he said. "Now I'll proceed with our cases, and you'll administer the Trevor Vanderwald scholarship fund. All that money they raised—you can use it to help Pharminex victims. That's kind of justice, isn't it?"

Brooke didn't answer. What was justice? When people simply did the best they could do. And she'd tried.

"Walk with me." She stood and took his hand, and they wound down the ivy-lined sidewalk and then along a rocky path to the harbor shore. A thick length of mold-slick rope looped between cast-iron stanchions, keeping children and adventuresome adults from getting too close to the water. A seagull landed, two posts away, then blinked at them and tilted its gray-white head.

"Go away, bird," Liam told it. "Our Brooke is not fond of seagulls."

"It's okay." Brooke tucked her arm though Liam's. "He is where he's supposed to be."

"Like we are," Liam said.

Brooke looked out over the vast harbor, the watery sunlight dappling its surface, but hiding depths and dangers in the fathoms beneath. "You said it yourself," she remembered. "We all have our reasons for being who we are."

"And?"

"And for now, I choose to be me." She turned to him, searched his face. "And if you'll be you? And there'll be no more lies? Then we'll see what happens."

ACKNOWLEDGMENTS

Unending gratitude to:

Krisitin Sevick, my brilliant, hilarious, and gracious editor. This book was the result of a true brainstorming, and you have the majority of the brain.

The remarkable team at Forge Books: the oh-so-wise Fritz Foy, the incomparable Linda Quinton, the indefatigable team of Alexis Saarela and Libby Collins, and copy editor Karen Richardson all saved me from career-ending errors. And thank you, Jamie Stafford-Hill. I can't stop applauding this astonishing cover! Patrick Canfield, Jacey Mitziga, and Linda Kaplan, you're the best. Brian Heller, you're my hero. And my dearest darling powerhouse Laura Pennock. Eileen Lawrence, Lucille Rettino, and Sarah Reidy—you are life-changing. What a terrifically wise and unfailingly supportive team. I am so thrilled to be a part of it.

Lisa Gallagher, my stellar and incredible agent. You changed my life and continue to do so every day. I am so honored to work with you.

Dana Isaacson, you are such a rock star. Your editing skill—and care and commitment and friendship and generosity—shines on every page.

The artistry and savvy of Madeira James, Mary-Liz Murray, Nina Zagorscak, Charlie Anctil, Mary Zanor, Jane Ubell-Meyer, Elisa Fershtadt, Andrea

Peskind Katz, Judith D. Collins, Betsy Maxwell, and Club Red. You are all so fabulous.

Sue Grafton, always. Mary Higgins Clark, ditto. Mary Kubica, Lynne Constantine, Angie Kim, Samantha Bailey, Lisa Unger, Erin Mitchell, Barbara Peters, Joanne Sinchuk, Kym Havens, and Robin Agnew.

My incredible blog sisters at Jungle Red Writers: Julia Spencer-Fleming, Hallie Ephron, Roberta Isleib/ Lucy Burdette, Jenn McKinlay, Deborah Crombie, and Rhys Bowen. And my Career Authors posse: Paula Munier, Dana Isaacson, Jessica Strawser, and Brian Andrews. Brian—I am so lucky you know all about sailing! Whew. Thank you.

My dear friends Mary Schwager, Laura DiSilverio, Elisabeth Elo, Shannon Kirk, Len Rosen, and Paula Munier. And my treasured sister Nancy Landman.

The pharmaceutical company insiders who revealed so much—as long as I promised never to say who they are.

Jonathan is my darling husband, of course. Thank you for all the carry-out dinners, your infinite patience, and your unending wisdom.

Do you see your name in this book? Some very generous souls allowed their names to be used in return for an auction donation to charity. To retain the magic, I will let you find yourselves.

Sharp-eyed readers will notice I have tweaked Massachusetts geography a bit. It's only to protect the innocent. And I adore it when people read the acknowlededements.

Keep in touch, okay?

www.hankphillippiryan.com
www.junglereadwriters.com
www.careerauthors.com

Read on for a preview of

HER PERFECT LIFE

Hank Phillippi Ryan

Available in Fall 2021
from Tom Doherty Associates

A FORGE HARDCOVER

PROLOGUE

They say you can't choose your family, but if you could, I would still have chosen Cassie.

She was my big sister, and everything she did was perfect. Her perfect dark hair, which curled or didn't depending on what Cassie wanted. She had perfect friends, and perfect dates, and whispered phone calls, and boys came to pick her up in their cars. She got to wear lipstick. Once when I sneaked hers and tried it, she caught me. She didn't even laugh. Or yell. Or tell on me.

But when Cassie went away to college that year, something changed. She came home for winter break, but she stayed in her room. My mother and I couldn't figure out what she was doing. Cassie would come out only to make cups of coffee, then stare out the window at our snow-dappled backyard, at the pond where she'd tried to teach me to ice-skate, and at the big sycamore tree where we once found a huge hornets' nest that fell in a summer wind. I'd picked it up, and wanted to save it for show-and-tell, but Cassie screamed and told me it was full of bugs. She grabbed it from me, and one stung her. She didn't even cry.

We had a dog, too, a dear and dopey rescue named Pooch. Cassie never liked the name, but our dad did. And then Dad died, and Cassie never wanted to change Pooch's name again.

When she left for college, Mumma kept her room

just the way it was, with all her stuffed animals and souvenirs and photographs, and didn't let me move out of my little bedroom into her bigger one. Cassie was always the favorite, and I always thought of it as her right.

That first college winter vacation, my mother found a notebook, one of those black ones with white dots on the cover. She opened it to the first page. I saw her face change. Without a word, Mumma turned the notebook to show me. Cassie had drawn a calendar, with carefully ruled pencil lines spaced equally apart. November. Then December. She'd crossed off the days, each one, with an X in black marker.

"Poor Cassie," Mumma said to me. I remember how soft her voice was, carrying an undercurrent of worry or sorrow. "I wonder what day she's waiting for. This is not the work of a happy person."

"I know," I'd agreed, nodding sagely, though at age seven, I didn't really know. And it was almost as if Mumma wasn't talking to me, but just to herself. I do remember how I felt then, even remember my eyes widening in fear of things, dark things or scary things, under the bed or in the closet—things that kids' imaginations, if they're lucky, conjure as murky vanishing faraway nothings. Things that come in the night. Visitors. My mother's worry was contagious, too, a chronic disease I have yet to conquer. "Mumma? What do you think is wrong with Cassie?"

And then Cassie was gone.

The police said they looked and looked for her, even said they'd tried to make sense of the calendar she'd left behind. My mother got sicker and sicker waiting for her.

Years later, I went off to college myself. By then, Pooch had died.

Mumma eventually died, too, never knowing.

And then there was only me.

What happened to Cassie? I imagined her dead, of course. I'd imagined her kidnapped, imprisoned, hidden, brainwashed, indentured, enslaved, made into a princess, transported by aliens to their faraway planet. I saw her in grocery stores, on book covers, in the backgrounds of movies, a lifted shoulder or sunlight on a cheekbone, that little dance she did when she was happy. Once I saw the back of her head three rows in front of me on a plane from Boston to New Orleans and leaped out of my seat with the seat belt sign still on, but it wasn't her dark hair and not her thin shoulders, not her quizzical smile after my lame *Oh, I thought I knew you* excuse.

We were too far apart in age, I guess, to have that sister connection some people talk about, the sense of knowing where the other is, or when they're upset. Sure, she was my only big sister. But she was already wrapped up in her own concerns, and I was a goofy little kid, and my sibling worship didn't have the time to evolve into mystical bonding. Was she still alive?

I still have a picture of her and Pooch, the one Dad took with his camera that wasn't a phone. The almost-sepia rectangle of daughter and dog is faded now, and cracking, with old-fashioned wavy oncewhite edges. The original one is in my apartment, and the copy thumbtacked to the bulletin board over my desk at Channel 6.

At some point you have to stop looking, I told myself. But still. If she did something truly bad, how much did I want to know? How would that knowledge change my life? My career? Maybe it's better for me to pretend she never existed.

But I know she did exist.

Sometimes it feels like she still comes to me in my dreams, this time asking me to find her. So I couldn't help but imagine that; approaching her, confronting her, gently, gingerly, or standing in her line of sight to see if there was a glimmer.

Would I even recognize my big sister after all this time? I was seven when she vanished, and Cassie was eighteen, so . . . maybe.

Maybe not.

Or maybe she'll recognize me. She'll find *me*.

CHAPTER 1

LILY

Standing center stage at the spotlighted podium, a newly won Emmy in hand and a glitteringly bejeweled audience applauding her, Lily knew she was being ridiculous. But she examined each face, quickly as she could, from the big shots in the front row to the smaller-market wannabes in the back of the Boston Convention Center auditorium to the randoms scurrying the periphery—the latecomers, the technicians, the bustling event staff and black-uniformed security. Was that one Cassie? Was *that* one?

It was absurd. Foolish. Delusional. There was no way Cassie would be in this audience, but that would not stop Lily from looking, scanning, wondering. Not just tonight, but everywhere she went. Her brain had developed its own facial recognition software, grown adept at comparing and analyzing. And always rejecting. *So far.*

But tonight it wasn't only Cassie she was looking for. And that made Lily's scrutiny all the more intense.

The applause quieted, most upturned faces now expectant. Lily saw a few glance at their watches.

Ten fifteen on a Saturday night. Losers yearned to go home.

"I'm so thrilled to accept this on behalf of all the Lily Atwood team . . ." She knew that sounded glib, but rules allowed only one recipient at the podium, necessary to prevent rambling wine-fueled acceptance speeches. "We all work so hard, and let me especially thank my darling producer, Greer Whitfield, without whom—stand up, Greer!"

She pointed to a front table, saw her gesture magnified, becoming gigantic on the huge TV monitors flanking her, the white sequins of her body-hugging gown shimmering. Greer stood for a fraction of a second, and Lily could see her colleague's discomfort at being the center of attention even for that long. Lily blew her a sincere kiss, then went on.

"And thank you to all who have contributed to our success—including my confidential sources." She winked and got a murmur of laughter in return. "This is a shared honor." She heard the wrap-it-up music, spoke more quickly. "It's an inspiration, and a promise to continue to protect the public from . . ."

She finished her speech, did one last crowd check as her colleagues applauded again, then accepted the arm of the tuxedoed host who escorted her backstage to the professional makeup person they'd hired to make sure the winners looked even more perfect in their triumphant photos.

The makeup artist in her white apron—*Too young, not Cassie*—and hairstylist in a black smock—*Too old, not Cassie*—and the officious pompadoured photographer with his too-tight black shirt and too-tight black jeans. *Not Cassie.*

"Congratulations," the photographer said. He eyed her up and down. "I'm Trent. I'll make you look more gorgeous than you already do. Big, *big* fan."

Lily smiled, accustomed—and inured—to the scrutiny. Leering men, brash and brazenly familiar, were part of her life. She'd dealt with it too long to be unnerved by it, most of it at least, and the ones who pushed too hard got pushed right back.

As long as none of the ugliness touched Rowen.

Rowen was safe, Lily knew, safe with nanny Petra, probably deep into one of Rowe's beloved spy-kid novels. Since Rowe had started on chapter books, she'd insisted she wanted to be a spy, "Just like you, Mumma." No matter how often Lily explained investigative journalism, Rowe, with the stubborn wisdom of a seven-year-old, would have none of it. Lily's cell phone was set to vibrate at a call from Petra, and Petra had learned to be just as vigilant as Lily. Not on the lookout for Cassie, of course, but for the unknown.

Fame, Lily knew, had two conflicting sides. The glory. And the danger. The power. And the spotlight. The raging relentless spotlight.

"Smile, Lily." The photographer—Trent—had used her first name as if they were the best of pals. Familiarity was permanently attached to fame. The smiles of recognition. Selfies-on-demand with people in grocery stores and on the T, people at airports and the dry cleaners. Lily's face was in their living rooms and bedrooms and on their cell phones via streaming video. They saw her, close up and constantly. No wonder they felt like they knew her. But Lily, on the opposite side of the TV camera, could never see whose eyes were on her. What strangers heard her every word.

"Lily? Hon? Turn your body this way now." Trent demonstrated, angling his own shoulders, tilting his chin, eyes looking up from under his lashes as if Lily didn't know exactly how to arrange her face for its best angle. A black-shirted assistant adjusted a battery of lights on metal stands, fumbling with clanking flaps that softened the high-wattage bulbs.

"Give us that famous Lily smile," Trent ordered. "*Love* the camera."

As his flashbulbs popped and bloomed, Lily heard more applause from inside the auditorium, other winners and more losers. Was her source here? Somewhere? Tonight, Cassie wasn't the only person she was looking for. Lily was also searching for *him*. Her new and unerringly knowledgeable source. The one who had, in just the past few weeks, given her a couple of amazing stories. Lily couldn't help but wonder if he—or she?—would be here tonight. To share Lily's success? Or maybe, although disturbing to consider, with some other agenda. A motive.

Lily had to laugh at herself. That worry—her chronic assessing worry—helped make her a good reporter. If whatever she feared didn't happen, all the better. If it did, she'd be prepared.

Trent fussed with his lights, instructed his assistant, demonstrated yet another pose. One particular security guard wearing a black cap and starched black shirt seemed to eye her with more than ordinary curiosity. Was *he* the source? A vested waiter, carrying a tray of empty wineglasses. Why had he stopped to adjust the linen-covered high-top table directly across from her? *Everything isn't about me,* she reminded herself. But it was difficult to ignore the spotlight when it followed you everywhere.

"Two more, Lily," Trent announced. He'd tilted his head the other direction now, motioning her to copy him. She remembered the first time she'd heard her source's voice. To this day, she and Greer debated whether the caller was really a man.

But he'd told them to call him Mr. Smith. And the caller's tips had turned out to be true.

The stories were nothing Lily and Greer couldn't have found on their own if they'd thought to look. But they were dead-on accurate. Lily and Greer had begun to trust him. To look forward to his calls.

Last week, he'd blown the whistle on the local health inspector's school cafeteria reports. Dozens of them, he'd revealed, were signed and dated the same day.

"It's impossible," Mr. Smith had whispered. "How can they properly do all those inspections in one day? I fear they are faking them. And it is putting kids at risk."

Lily, imagining her own first-grader Rowen with food poisoning or salmonella or some hideous virus, had tracked down the documents. Mr. Smith was correct. The health inspector—facing Lily and her photographer's video camera and barricaded behind his institutional wooden desk—had denied, made excuses, stalled, misdirected, and then outright lied.

"We have no evidence of foodborne illness," the man said.

That's when Lily knew she had the goods. "Have you ever *looked* for evidence?" she asked.

"That's absurd. Of course we've looked."

"I see. Then let me put it another way." Lily had pulled the stack of questionable reports from the manila files she held on her lap. "How do you ex-plain this, then? You did *all* these inspections the same day?"

She'd placed the incriminating paperwork on the desk in front of the inspector, at which point he stood, yanked off his lapel microphone, and ordered her out of the room. They'd caught it all on camera.

The inspector's wife—enraged—had called Lily after the damning story aired. And her husband fired. "How could you do this to him?" the woman demanded.

"I didn't do it to him," Lily had gently reminded her. "He did it to himself."

Now she looked again at her newest Emmy. People had gone to prison as a result of the story the shiny statue honored. Lily's victories, in the strange calculus of television news, were someone else's disasters.

"Got it, Lily," Trent said as a final flash came from his camera. "You're—"

A burst of applause came from the auditorium as the double doors clanked open. Three tuxedoed men, arms draped across each other's shoulders, barreled out, hooting self-congratulations and brandishing their trophies.

"Take our photo!" one demanded. "Move it, Lil! Our turn!"

"Thanks, Ms. Atwood," Trent's pink-haired assistant whispered as Lily stepped away from the backdrop. *Too young, not Cassie,* Lily's brain registered as the young woman went on. "You're so awesome. I wish I could be just like you."

Lily's cell phone, tucked into the black satin evening bag hanging on a thin chain over her shoulder, vibrated against her thigh.

She grabbed it, clicked it. "Thank you so much," she said to the assistant, but her mind was racing. Petra was only supposed to text if something—

It wasn't Petra. *Sender unknown.*

Congratulations, the text read. *The white sequins are perfect.*

Lily gasped. Her eyes darted to the left, to the right, to closing doors and winding corridors, to the marble-floored lobby milling with celebrants clinking glasses and laughing and posing for selfies. He—or she?—was here. Had to be. No other way for him to know about her dress.

Who is this? she typed back. *Where are you?*

You know who it is. The words appeared, dramatic in their time delay. She could almost hear his—her?—voice saying them.

Lily began to type, but the next words came up before she could send.

I'll call you Monday. The words seemed to glow, and the hubbub around Lily faded into the background as another message appeared. *And I'll give you the best story ever.*

CHAPTER 2

GREER

Did I want to be Lily Atwood? Well, sure, I suppose. But a whole lot would have to change for that to happen. Like everything. Right now I was too mismatched, too awkward-faced, too curly-haired, too exactly not what a TV star looked like. So I learned to be the smart one. Greer Whitfield, the smart one.

I'd watched Lily, same as everyone else, as she accepted her Emmy—ours, really—in front of the worshipping crowd in the convention center. She'd thanked me, extravagantly and elegantly, with a toss of her Lily hair and a sincere smile on her Armani lips and those white sequins glittering her personal starlight. I'd stood, briefly, as she'd ordered me to, the audience murmuring their approval. They weren't approving me, though, but Lily's effortless generosity, her understanding of team spirit, their longing to be just like her. Approval is such a sister to envy.

Lily's now-empty chair was next to me at the banquet table Channel 6 purchased, the white damask tablecloth littered with shards of baguette crusts and the purple blotch of someone's spilled cabernet, but Lily's napkin was folded artfully by her empty dessert plate, not even a lipstick smudge on her white china coffee cup. I worry that I sound envious when I describe this, but I'm not. It's not me who creates the food chain, it's the rest of the world. I was smart enough to know how that works. And where my place is.

But being the smart one can take you a long way in television. The smart one is not your rival, the smart one is not your adversary or challenger. The smart one, if they're smart *enough,* is the team player who'll make you more famous, be the brains and the messenger and the organizer. And have the confidence—or pragmatism—to let you take the compliments and applause. Or, on the days things don't go your way, the blame. It was fine for me to take the blame; blame rolled off me like whatever cliché you choose. And I honestly didn't care, that's another critical element. I was the one you're not *supposed* to like. The tough one, the rule-enforcer, the keeper of deadlines. The protector of Lily's flame. Her fame.

Other women in the Emmy audience—the ones not captivated by Lily—sneaked a moment to check their own reflections in fancy compacts, comparing the lift of their eyebrows to Lily's carefully natural ones, the color of Lily's lipstick to their own, wishing their hair were better or different or more like Lily's; wondering how long their faces would last and how Lily, at only thirty-three, an age she'll reveal instantly if asked, can look so young and so chic and so wise at the same time. *So Lily,* as I have actually heard people say. Now they've clicked their compacts shut, given themselves a personal score that only counts in the mathematics of fame.

I was seriously not jealous of her, that's what people didn't understand. I honestly admired her. I wanted her to succeed. If she succeeds, I succeed, and the station succeeds, and everyone is happy. Especially me, since as long as she has a job, I have a job. Television only works if the hierarchy is respected, each person does their designated job to the best of their ability and understands no matter what, it's the "talent" who gets the credit.

Lily was the definition of talent. And it's not that she doesn't work hard, and it's not that she isn't sincere, and she's definitely not a diva.

Just ask her, ha ha.

No, truly, she's terrific.

She's so super-terrific that last year she turned down a New York network job—a job they'd offered us as a team—so she could stay in Boston and not have to make her daughter, Rowen, change schools. "I'm so sorry," she'd told me, tears in her eyes.

"Forget it," I'd assured her. And it was true, I was perfectly fine staying here. It was just me, no family, no life. No pets, because how could you be fair to an animal when work is 24-7? The way I looked at it, and really there's no other way to look at it, I was married to television. I didn't need to be a bigger fish in a bigger pond. I didn't need friends.

In the tumult of the and-the-winner-is applause, Lily had urged me to join her onstage, even though she knew it was against the rules, because Lily doesn't care about rules. Plus she knew I'd refuse, as I have for the past almost-two years we've worked together and the past two times she's—*we've*—won Emmys. We're a good team, she's told me, Lily-and-Greer, and she's right. She has the fame, and all that comes with it. I don't need that. I have other skills.